When Lightning Strikes Twice

That smile obliterated the little that was left of her equilibrium. He kept his arm locked firmly around her, gently, slowly kneading the hollow of her waist, and the thought of stopping him never crossed Rachel's mind. His fingers were long, and he stretched them so the tips reached the curve of her hip, the soft swell of her stomach, and it felt so good. So very, very good.

Rachel felt something that had been dormant within her all her life stirring, blossoming, unleashing tendrils of heat that streaked through her. She could almost feel her common sense abandon her as if melted by the fiery, deliciously erotic sensations surging through her.

She had never felt this way before, and she didn't know how to fight against it. She didn't even know if she wanted to.

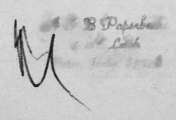

Other Contemporary Romances by
Barbara Boswell
from Avon Books

WINNING WAYS

BARBARA BOSWELL

When Lightning Strikes Twice

AVON BOOKS ◣ NEW YORK

This is a work of fiction. Names, characters, places, and incidents either are the product of the author's imagination or are used fictitiously. Any resemblance to actual events, locales, organizations, or persons, living or dead, is entirely coincidental and beyond the intent of either the author or the publisher.

AVON BOOKS
A division of
The Hearst Corporation
1350 Avenue of the Americas
New York, New York, 10019

Copyright © 1997 by Barbara Boswell
Published by arrangement with the author
Visit our website at http://www.AvonBooks.com
Library of Congress Catalog Card Number: 97-93787
ISBN: 0-380-72744-7

First Avon Books Printing: December 1997

AVON TRADEMARK REG. U.S. PAT. OFF. AND IN OTHER COUNTRIES, MARCA REGISTRADA, HECHO EN U.S.A.

Printed in the U. S. A.

WCD 10 9 8 7 6 5 4 3 2 1

1

"Rachel, the Tildens are here," Katie Sheely whispered. She'd sidled stealthily into Rachel's office and touched her shoulder.

The interruption caught Rachel Saxon, a junior partner in the family firm, completely unaware. She jerked, accidentally hitting the escape key on her keyboard.

The file she'd been working on disappeared from the screen. All gone in a microsecond. Rachel stared at the blank screen in grim disbelief.

"Sorry. I didn't mean to startle you," Katie murmured.

Rachel suppressed a sigh. She'd definitely been startled, whatever Katie's intention. She leaned back in her chair and met the younger woman's eyes. Nineteen-year-old Katie, the receptionist at Saxon Associates, seldom left her desk, which she had customized into her own little world with photos of family, friends and pets, easy access to favorite internet sites, makeup and nail polish, piles of catalogs and CD-ROMs. Coming into Rachel's office *in person* to announce the presence of anyone was a first.

But even Katie knew that the Tildens were Saxon Associates' wealthiest longtime clients. Rachel interpreted Katie's unexpected presence as a warning. An urgent one.

"They don't have an appointment with anyone 'cause I checked," Katie continued. "But six of them barged in, and they don't look very happy. I tried to stall them with some magazines while I—"

"Young lady, we didn't come here to read outdated copies of *Time!*" A booming Tilden voice sounded in the hallway. "We must see Eve immediately."

Rachel jumped to her feet and hurried to the door to see Townsend Tilden Junior striding toward the spacious corner office of Eve Saxon, senior partner, who also happened to be Rachel's mentor, role model, and aunt.

"She isn't in today, Mr. Tilden." Rachel hurried to intercept him. "I'm her niece Rachel. I'm an attorney here, too."

She always introduced herself to Townsend Tilden Junior because he never remembered her. Not because his memory was failing—at sixty-five, the scion of the prominent and influential Tilden clan was as sharp as ever. But he never bothered learning the names of any underlings anywhere. He considered them mere lackeys, not worth his valuable time. Town Junior dealt strictly with the top management.

"May I help you, sir?" Rachel asked. Even to herself, she sounded a lot like an obsequious lackey.

She saw Katie grin broadly.

"Get Eve here right away!" demanded Town Junior. "We have a serious crisis on our hands, and we need to address it immediately."

Five more Tildens of varying ages lined up behind Town Junior in the narrow corridor. Their expressions ranged from somber to furious.

"She's in court in Philadelphia today," Rachel explained, knowing how well that would go over.

Not well at all. The Tildens turned their collective glares on her. "Perhaps I could be of some assistance?" she tried again. She assumed they wouldn't take her up on her offer, not the Tildens who did not deal with junior nobodies.

Rachel waited expectantly for them to stage an immediate, disdainful walkout. Instead they stayed put, all six of them.

"There's another will!" blurted Marguerite Tilden Lloyd, a fiftyish woman, who Rachel knew had gone to an all-girls prep school in New England with Aunt Eve years ago. "That little floozy claims it was drawn up within the past year, and she's taken it to Quinton Cormack." She pronounced "floozy" and "Quinton Cormack" with identical inflections of disgust, as if merely saying the words was an offense to her tongue.

"Another will," Rachel repeated breathlessly. She felt a sinking sensation. "The little floozy" could only be one person, Misty Czenko Tilden, the twenty-five-year-old widow of the late Townsend Tilden Senior, who had died suddenly, though not altogether unexpectedly, last week at the age of ninety-three.

"And she's taken this—uh—new will to Quinton Cormack?" Rachel was dismayed but tried not to show it. His name rattled ominously in her head.

Quinton Cormack? Oh no, not him! Anybody but him! Every nerve in her body went on full-scale alert.

She shouldn't be so surprised by the news, she admonished herself. What other lawyer would the treacherous Misty hook up with, especially if she wanted legal representation here in Lakeview? None other than that conniving, manipulative shark Quinton Cormack, of course. He'd arrived in Lakeview a little over a year ago—descended like a toxic cloud was more apt, to Rachel's way of thinking—to help his unfortunate attorney father Frank Cormack with his hapless law practice.

Rachel tensed, as thoughts of the humiliating Pedersen Car Shoppe case inevitably sprang to mind. Before Quinton's arrival in town, Frank Cormack's legal practice had been nothing but a joking afterthought. Currently retitled Cormack and Son, it was pure trouble. Particularly for Saxon Associates. And now, it seemed, for the Tildens as well.

"Quinton Cormack has a copy of another will," she murmured, feeling her initial ripple of anxiety swell to a full-fledged torrent. Calling Aunt Eve out of court would definitely be an overreaction, but she was beginning to consider it.

"That's what we just told you!" a thirtysomething Tilden

offspring snapped at Rachel. "Is it really necessary to re-
peat everything back to us? What are you—a parrot?"

Katie tittered. When seven pairs of disapproving eyes
focused on her, it seemed to dawn on her that no humor
had been intended. "Uh, gotta get back to my desk," she
called over her shoulder, making a fast getaway.

The Tildens returned their attention to Rachel. "This is
an emergency situation, young lady," Town Junior roared.
"Call Eve out of court if you have to. *Nothing* is more
important than this."

She was caught between the proverbial rock and a hard
place, Rachel acknowledged glumly. She tried a diversion-
ary tactic. "Do you know what the provisions are in this
alleged will that Misty is flaunting?"

Her ploy worked. All the Tildens began to talk at once.
Apparently they couldn't pass up a chance to blast the former nude lap dancer whom the late Mr. Tilden had brought
into their family fold three lamentable years ago. There
were no further demands to summon Eve Saxon from court.
The Tildens crowded into Rachel's office, regaling her with
Misty's latest perfidy—her possession of the newest, most
up-to-date last will and testament of her late husband
Townsend Tilden Senior.

Naturally, it left his entire estate to her, his devoted
grieving widow.

"I have a strong hunch that the Tildens' attorneys will
try to get you to agree to an out-of-court settlement, Misty.
That means you would give them some portion of your
husband's estate in return for their not contesting the will
in court."

Quinton Cormack handed the platinum-haired young
woman a Double Derby. Misty had a taste for difficult-to-
mix drinks, and the skills he'd acquired during his years
tending bar had proven invaluable in overcoming her aversion to lawyers. She trusted a lawyer who knew the fine
points of icemanship and whether to shake or stir.

The two of them were in the office/den located in the

basement of Quint's house. Both found it preferable to the depressingly dilapidated official Cormack and Son legal quarters right next to the High Speed Line, located in the only undesirable business zone in Lakeview. At least his home office didn't shake like an earthquake every time a train to or from Philadelphia went by.

"What you have to decide is whether or not you want to agree to a settlement or go ahead with a court fight," Quint added, coming to sit beside Misty on the thickly cushioned gray-blue sectional sofa.

It was shaped like a very long L and lined two of the wood-paneled walls. He knew Misty didn't like to drink alone, so he sipped from a bottle of dark Canadian ale.

"Why do I have to decide anything at all?" Misty pouted. "The will says what it says. Townie wanted me to have everything. Why should I have to give *them* a dime? How come we have to go to court in the first place?"

Quint took a long swallow of his ale. Was this the hundredth—or hundred and fiftieth—time Misty had asked these same questions, to which he would again give the same replies?

"Misty, I drew up that will at your husband's direction four months ago, and Mr. Tilden and I both knew at the time that the family would contest it. It was inevitable. Our choices are either to fight them in court or offer to pay them off."

"I don't know why they have to be so greedy! They already got their trust funds and their big salaries from Tilden Industries, so they're all richer than God anyway. They don't need another cent from Townie!" Misty raged, jumping to her feet to pace the rectangular area within the L.

She downed the remains of the Double Derby in two gulps. "How come they won't let me have what Townie wanted me to have? They have so much, and I never had nothin' till Town. What if they—"

"Town made sure that you'll be well taken care of for the rest of your life, Misty," Quint interrupted. "You'll never be poor again."

He winced at the sheer melodrama of the remark. It sounded like he'd lifted it from a scene in *Gone With the Wind,* one of Scarlett O'Hara's fervent pledges to herself. He'd recently rewatched portions of the old classic on video, so maybe he had.

Fortunately, it was just what Misty needed to hear. She calmed down and dropped back down on another section of the sofa. "Do you mind if I smoke?" She was already fumbling in her chic Ferragamo purse for a pack of cigarettes.

Quint shrugged his indifference. He was willing to tolerate his clients' vices—and most of his clients had many. He didn't require a pedigree before he accepted a case, unlike the wellborn attorneys at the lofty firm of Saxon Associates.

Quint's brown eyes gleamed. Since his arrival in Lakeview, New Jersey, fourteen months ago, cases for Cormack and Son had been increasing exponentially. The highly respectable, well-established firm of Saxon Associates definitely was feeling his presence.

He could only imagine how very much the Anointed Attorneys there must hate his legal competence and success, which increasingly brought new clients to his door. Recently, he'd been retained by the kind of clients who would've automatically bypassed Cormack in favor of Saxon Associates. The glorious Pedersen Car Shoppe case had been the turning point, and the upcoming Battle of the Tilden Will would boost—

"You want one, Quint?" Misty's voice jarred him from the midst of his very pleasant reverie. She held out the cigarettes. "I noticed you starin' at the pack."

She had obviously mistaken his glow of legal triumph for a nicotine fit. Well, he'd had his share of those, too.

"No thanks. I gave them up when my kid came to live with me," he added by way of an explanation. "It was hell."

"Giving up smoking or having your kid come to live with you?" Misty was curious.

"Well, at the beginning—both. But it's working out well. I haven't taken a puff in fourteen months and Brady is doing fine."

"Brady is your little boy's name? I saw his picture in your crummy office down by the tracks. How old is he, about two?"

"Two years and two months," confirmed Quint, a little surprised by her accurate guess. The photo on his desk in the office had been taken the week of Brady's second birthday.

"I used to do a lot of baby-sitting." She inhaled on her cigarette, long and deep. "I like kids, but I won't be having any of my own."

"Don't rule that out. You're a very young widow, Misty. And a beautiful one." He didn't bother to add the obvious, that Town Senior's will made her certifiably rich, always a potent lure. "You'll marry again and—"

"I mean I *can't* have kids. I got some kind of infection, and it wasn't treated for years. The doctor said I'm sterile now." She lit another cigarette from the half-smoked one. "I did more than dancin' in those places on Admiral Wilson Boulevard, y'know. And even worse stuff before I ended up there."

Quint said nothing. He knew that Misty considered her nude lap-dancing stint at Fantasy's Gentlemen's Lounge on Camden's seedy Admiral Wilson Boulevard to be the most respectable aspect of her past. Also the luckiest, as it had led to her meeting one of Fantasy's regular customers Townsend Tilden Senior—whom she had subsequently married three years ago.

"Where's your kid's mother?" Misty broke the brief silence. "I know she's not here in Jersey with you."

"True. She's not in the picture at all." Quint's voice was clipped, discouraging further questions.

Misty asked anyway. "Well, is she like, dead or something?"

"Like, or something." Quint's lips curved into a cynical smile. "Sharolyn gave me permanent full custody of Brady shortly before his first birthday. Her new boyfriend is a freelance travel guide who likes to travel light. He goes all over the world and wanted Sharolyn to come along, but a baby was an inconvenience. The last I heard they were in Bulgaria, scouting out possible tourist packages.''

"The bitch!" Misty was indignant. "What kind of mother is that?"

"I have this noble spiel where I say that a woman has as much right to seek her bliss as a man and that a child's father is equally responsible for raising him. Want to hear more?"

"No, it's crap, and we both know it. Nothing's worse than a rotten mother, I know that for sure. My mother dumped me, too, except I ended up a ward of the state of New Jersey." Misty sighed. "It sucked."

"But now you're Mrs. Townsend Tilden Senior. I'll bet your long-gone mother would be thrilled to renew your acquaintance."

"And then some," Misty agreed. "But she'll never get the chance. If that whore would ever try to come back and claim me as her long-lost little girl, I'd blow her off the way the Tildens tried to blow me off for the past three years."

"Well, they failed to get rid of you, didn't they? You're still here, and they're also going to fail to get anything from Town's will unless you choose to give it to them, Misty."

"To avoid a court fight," Misty said slowly.

Hallelujah! She's got it! Quint felt as proud as a math teacher whose slowest student had finally managed to grasp the gist of subtraction. "That's right, Misty. The decision is yours to make. And even if you choose to settle with the Tildens out of court, you will still be a very rich lady."

"Woman," corrected Misty. "I don't want to be no tight-assed lady." She stood up. "Okay, what would you do, Quint?"

"Are you asking me to advise you as your lawyer? Or just making idle conversation?"

"Geez, you're so—so—"

"Precise?" Quint laid his hand lightly on her back as he walked her to the door. "One of the tools of the trade. Of course, I can also obfuscate with the best of them."

"That sounds like something they do in the private booths at the Club Exotica Erotica." Misty angled closer to him. "I used to work there, too."

"Obfuscate means to confuse, to make obscure. Another talent you want your attorney to have."

She was pressing her ample breast against his arm and her hip brushed his. A few years ago he might've gone for it, Quint acknowledged a little ruefully. His reckless, live-for-the-moment younger self never let anything like boundaries or restraint or scruples stand in his way.

"I bet you have all kinds of talents, Quint," Misty purred.

He bet she had all kinds of talents, too. Too bad he wasn't going to sample any of them. He suppressed a sigh. Sometimes being a responsible, dependable adult was a real pain. But the Cormacks badly needed one, and he'd taken on the position. A hot fling with the sensually talented, former nude lap dancer who was now his wealthiest client was off-limits for Quinton Cormack, Brady's father. Pathetic Frank Cormack's son. Austin and Dustin Cormack's big half brother. Or was he their half big brother?

Whatever, he was now the Cormack patriarch-by-default. He gave his head a slight shake and a self-deprecating smile quirked his lips. He had morphed into a chronic, play-by-the-rules type, the kind of guy he used to mock. The kind he'd once sworn never to be.

If his friends from the good old days could see him now, they wouldn't believe it. On the other hand, if his mother could see him now, she would be truly thrilled.

The orchid stretch limousine was parked alongside the curb in front of his house, the uniformed driver awaiting Mrs. Tilden Senior. Quint chuckled at the sight. "That custom paint job must've sent the rest of the Tildens into orbit."

"Townie thought it was pretty." Misty slid him a sly

glance. "And you're right. Those stuffy, stuck-up creeps went ape-shit when they saw it." She ran her fingertips along the curve of Quint's jawline.

"Let me know what you decide, Misty." He took her hand and held it between both of his. He hoped she would interpret it as a paternal gesture, not a repelling one. And definitely not a come-on.

But Misty's attention was focused elsewhere, not on him at all. "I don't want to give *them* anything." Her eyes narrowed to slits. "Why should I? They treated me like I was lower than garbage from day one. Can we really win this, Quint?" She lost some of her bravado. "What if they take us to court and we lose?"

"We won't," Quint said firmly. "I guarantee that the will will stand up in court. I ought to know; I drew it up anticipating a court fight, remember?"

"Of course, you'll charge me a ton of money for going to court." Misty smiled, batting her thickly mascaraed lashes at him.

"Absolutely. I have a child to support, remember? Not to mention—oh, never mind, I'll spare you the tale of the convoluted Cormack family ties. So your final decision is not to settle?"

"That's it," Misty said grandly.

Quint nodded his approval. "Why settle when we hold the winning hand?"

He saw no need to mention to Misty how much he relished the prospect of taking another swipe at Saxon Associates—and winning again! Just the thought of besting Rachel Saxon and her aunt Eve and cousin Wade warmed him.

An image of Rachel Saxon flashed before his mind's eye. He couldn't seem to visualize Aunt Eve or Cousin Wade very well but Rachel appeared in clear detail.

She was the epitome of class, illuminating intelligence and good taste and impeccable manners like an aura. She was also a bona fide knockout, though he doubted she would appreciate hearing herself described in such plebeian terms. Especially by a prole like him!

He'd heard others proclaim her resemblance to "a young Jacqueline Onassis," and Rachel's high cheekbones, wide-set eyes, and full generous mouth did lend credence to the comparison. But Rachel's uptight, icy demeanor and I'll-strike-you-dead-if-you-come-near-me-stare made the late Jackie O seem like a warmly accessible, down-home country girl.

Quint remembered some of his meetings with various Saxons during the twists and turns of the Pedersen case. Eve was always pleasant and professional, Wade possessed a disarming mellow charm, but Rachel . . .

Quint actually smiled at the memory. Rachel didn't waste a second being pleasant or charming; she treated him like the upstart marauder she considered him to be. Those hazel eyes of hers blazed with unconcealed fury as she glowered at him, and when he came within a foot of her, she stiffened and stepped back as if to avoid contamination.

For some reason, her wholehearted scorn amused him. It was so pure, so elemental and intense, one had to admire her for it. Of course, it probably didn't hurt that her looks progressed from beautiful to spectacular when angry, making it a pleasure just to watch her. He'd spent a good deal of time gazing at her during those meetings . . .

"Got it, Quint?" Misty's voice suddenly resounded in his ears. "No settlement. I'm keeping it all, just like Townie wanted me to."

"When I'm contacted by Saxon Associates on behalf of the Tildens, I'll tell them we'll see them in court," Quint said, grinning in anticipation.

"Daddy!" A blond toddler in baggy swim trunks printed with ducks came running around the side of the house toward Quint. He was followed by a petite red-haired girl in a bright blue bikini.

"That's Brady and his nanny," Quint explained, stooping down to wait for Brady to run into his arms.

"Must be convenient having a cute young nanny living with you," Misty said cattily.

"It's convenient but not the way you mean. Sarah is one of the Sheelys. See that kid over there with the lawn mower?" He pointed to the bare-chested young man starting up the mower. "He's Shawn, another Sheely. Does yard work for a lot of people in town. Sort of a one-man business."

"The Sheelys?" Misty's brow furrowed in concentration. "Is that the family with the zillion kids? The one that always wins the prize for the biggest family in Lakeview at the Fourth of July Festival?"

"The Sheelys have ten kids, a few short of a zillion, but they still have a virtual lock on winning that particular prize." Quint glanced up at her. "Town Senior always underwrote the costs of Lakeview's Fourth of July Festival. Do you think you'll keep up the tradition, Misty?"

"Maybe. Or maybe Town Junior and the rest of the Tildens can cough up the cash for it. I've never been much for festivals, especially in a place where people look at me like I'm as gross as a used cat box." Misty's eyes returned to Sarah Sheely and Brady, and her expression grew even more bitter. "So are you sleeping with your kid's nanny, Quint?"

"God, no!" He laughed out loud. "Sarah is twenty-one years old and engaged to a kid her own age. She would die of shock and horror if you were ever to insinuate that there is anything between her and an old guy like me. To her, being thirty-five is having one foot in the grave."

Misty snickered. "Imagine what she'd think of me and Townie!"

"Daddy!" Brady arrived and Quint scooped him up.

"Hey, sport. Were you swimming?"

"Swim!" Brady repeated enthusiastically.

"Hi!" Sarah Sheely joined them, her smile including Misty. "I put out Brady's little pool in the backyard. He's been going wild with the hose. Look at me, I'm drenched!"

"Swim, Daddy!" Brady demanded.

"I may as well. You're getting me as wet as you are."
Quint set the soaked, wriggling child on his feet and turned
back to Misty. "I'm sure the Tildens set a speed record
racing to their lawyers when they got our message about
Town Senior's updated will. I expect to be hearing from
Saxon Associates very shortly. I'll keep you posted."

"Okay." Misty permitted the chauffeur to settle her into
the luxurious backseat.

"Wow! A purple limo!" exclaimed Sarah, and they
watched it move slowly down the tree-lined street. "Is that
hideous or what?"

"I suppose you prefer the traditional black? You have
no imagination, Sarah," Quint drawled. Brady was already
running toward the back of the house to his pool, and the
two adults followed, picking up their pace to match his.

"Matt and me want a white limo for our wedding,"
Sarah said. "You can get a six- or eight- or ten-passenger
one and we've been pricing them but we still haven't decided on the size yet. I guess it'll depend on the size of the
wedding party and we haven't decided on that yet either.
If I have all my brothers and sisters in it, it'll be huge
enough, but Matt and I both want some of our best friends
to be bridesmaids and groomsmen, too."

Quint's eyes had a tendency to glaze over when Sarah
started talking about her wedding plans, which was scheduled for next May, a year away. He knew he would be
hearing a lot more about it and ought to work on perfecting
a feigned expression of interest.

"So that was ancient Mr. Tilden's slutty wife, huh?"
Sarah asked, dropping the wedding talk much sooner than
he'd expected. "Yikes! What a vision!"

"Sarah, please. Misty is a client," he scolded with mock
severity. "Her checks for legal services rendered pay a lot
of bills, and included among them is your salary. Now re-
peat after me—she is the lovely and charming widow of
the late Mr. Tilden Senior."

"Dana told me about some of the outfits the lovely and
charming widow's worn to your office," Sarah chattered

on, undaunted. "But this was my very first Misty sighting. A forty-six double-D cup for sure. Poured into a skintight black crushed velvet jumpsuit and the spikiest heels I've ever seen. Color me amazed. Just think, Brady and me are wearing bathing suits today and she's running around in crushed velvet!"

"Maybe she's a stickler for fashion etiquette and doesn't don her summer wardrobe till after Memorial Day," Quint replied dryly. "That would give her another week."

"But it's eighty degrees today! Of course, her jumpsuit was unbuttoned almost the whole way to her navel. I guess that's one way to keep cool. Dana says all Misty's clothes look like they're right out of a Hookers 'R' Us catalog."

Quint arched his brows. "Tell your sister to stop gossiping about the clients or I'll have a talk with her myself."

Twenty-six-year-old Dana Sheely was the paralegal he'd hired when he had arrived in Lakeview to take over the faltering—no, in truth it was almost moribund—law practice his father had begun ten years earlier. Quint couldn't remember if he'd hired Dana first and she had recommended her sister Sarah as a nanny or if he had hired Sarah first and she'd suggested her sister Dana as a paralegal.

Both sisters had offered their brother Shawn—whose place in the Sheely birth order fell somewhere between them—for whatever yard work needed to be done. Quint knew that another Sheely sister—the one Sarah referred to as "the family flake"—was currently working as a receptionist at Saxon Associates. Quint enjoyed a silent chuckle every time he thought of the Saxons hiring the lone Sheely airhead.

Sarah climbed into the small pool and sat down beside Brady, handing him a plastic cup. He filled it with water, then poured the contents over Sarah's head. She laughed good-naturedly and did the same to him. Brady squealed with delight.

"Hair wash!" he exclaimed.

"That's right, Brady, it's like when we wash your hair," Sarah agreed. "Brady is cool," she observed fondly. "He never screams during a shampoo like some kids.''

Quint felt a bittersweet warmth stealing through him. Sarah was very good with Brady. From the moment she'd moved in she had become an invaluable member of their household, but next May she might be gone. She and her husband-to-be weren't sure of their plans, but they hoped to move to Florida after their wedding. Quint desperately hoped they wouldn't.

Still, having Sarah around was a stopgap measure and he knew it. She was a terrific nanny, but she was very young and full of plans for her own life. He wanted his son to have a mother complete with powerful maternal instincts and drives, a woman willing to commit herself to the unending, day-in-and-day-out constancy of raising a child. Instead, poor little Brady had Sharolyn, who acted as a mother only when it suited her own agenda.

Quint watched Brady line up his fleet of toy ducks, naming the color of each when Sarah asked him. He was a bright little boy, learning new things every day. And though he seemed to have made a good adjustment this past year, Quint wondered. Brady had spent the first year of his life with his mother, the second year with his father and Sarah. Moved from California to New Jersey.

Sometimes the enormous changes still boggled Quint's mind. What did little Brady make of it all?

Brady deserved a mother like Quint'd had, a strong, loving, fiercely dedicated woman who willingly accepted the sacrifices and inconveniences of child rearing, who'd taken them on with humor and grace. Sharolyn certainly didn't fit the bill; Sarah Sheely would fill that role for her own children.

Of course, providing a permanent live-in mother for Brady would mean marriage, a fact that never failed to send a dark chill through him. The Cormack marital track record wasn't very good; in fact, it was abysmal. His father had been married four times. Quint and Sharolyn's unwanted quickie marriage of necessity had barely lasted till the end

of her pregnancy. No, maintaining a successful marriage
was not a talent that ran in his gene pool.

"Duck, Daddy. Blue duck." Brady held it up for Quint
to see.

"Blue duck," he repeated. "Show me the red one,
Brady."

Brady chose the correct duck, garnering much praise.

"Y'know, the Saxons are going to freak out when they
hear about an updated will," Sarah said conversationally,
as Brady began to throw the ducks out of the pool, one by
one. "They're real thick with the Tildens. Wade gets sick
of it. He told Dana that sometimes he feels like a—"

"Wade Saxon?" Quint's ears perked. "He talks to
Dana?"

"Sure. They're practically best friends." Sarah grinned.
"What a waste, huh? Wade's so cool. And smart and rich,
not to mention a definite hunk. But Dana's dating some
nerdy actuary and Wade is—well, I don't know who his
girlfriend is this month, but he's sure to be dating somebody. He always is."

"Did Wade ever say anything to Dana about the Pedersen Car Shoppe case?" Quint cut in, not at all interested
in either Wade or Dana's personal lives. But the idea of
having access to the inner workings of Saxon Associates
made him feel like a bloodhound must when getting that
first whiff of a scent on the trail.

"Oh man, did he ever!" exclaimed Sarah. "Dana said
the Saxons were obsessed with that case! They couldn't
believe they'd lost. And to *you!*"

"Ouch, I think."

"I mean, the Saxons always win. Or they always used
to. Your dad wasn't exactly much competition," Sarah said
frankly. "Then you came and things changed. We're sure
the only reason they hired Katie to work at their snobby
firm is because Dana works for you."

"They're hoping some of the magic will rub off, huh?"
Quint drawled. "Does Dana ever mention Rachel Saxon?"

He sounded casually offhand. Well, why shouldn't he?

He was merely on a fishing expedition here, looking for some extraneous facts that might prove useful in future litigation. Because if the Tildens reacted as expected, it wouldn't be long before he was again sparring with Saxon Associates. With Rachel Saxon. A distinctly pleasurable tingle of heat radiated through him.

"Rachel is Wade's cousin," said Sarah. "She kinda drives him nuts."

"Ah."

"Wade is calm and laid-back and Rachel is—how does Dana put it?—wound really tight. Really, *really* tight. She, like, lives for her work—probably because there isn't anything else in her life."

"Nothing else? She's a very attractive woman, surely there is a man who—"

"A man for the Freezer Queen?" Sarah giggled. "Wade told Dana that Rachel could end global warming all by herself, just send her out on a few dates."

"She's cold, huh?"

"The word is Lady Antarctica never melts."

"Though many have tried to defrost her?" Quint no longer sounded casual. He waited for more details with an eagerness he rarely felt for anything anymore. Not even Misty Tilden's multimillion-dollar inheritance had fired his enthusiasm like imagining . . .

What exactly was he imagining?

Another one of those images of Rachel that he'd unwittingly stored in his mind played before him. Rachel standing rigidly in court wearing a custom-tailored, impeccably neat pale gray suit, her hair as dark, thick and rich as sable, cut in a precisely perfect bob that swung just below her chin without a strand ever out of order. He'd watched her, fascinated, during the entire Pedersen trial, waiting for her clothing to show a single wrinkle, or maybe for her hair to be rustled, even slightly, by the annoying air vents in the ceiling that blew everybody else's hair, including his own.

But it had never happened. Her clothing stayed impeccable, and her beautiful hair was impervious to the air vents. She remained as pristine and perfect as a porcelain doll secured behind a glass dome. Clearly, being wrinkled and mussed was not a condition achievable to Rachel Saxon.

Intimidating fastidiousness. Iciness beyond the essence of the human condition. Sarah had called her Lady Antarctica. It was obvious, Rachel was a textbook case of untouchable frigidity. From the looks and the sounds of it, she could qualify as the poster girl for the Sexual Repression Foundation, should one exist.

Quint felt his breathing quicken and his loins begin to grow heavy. He had no difficulty identifying his symptoms of sexual arousal, but the cause floored him. *The idea of sexual repression was turning him on?*

He hadn't expected it to come to this, but maybe he shouldn't be surprised. The last time he'd had sex had been during his short miserable marriage to Sharolyn and it had been duty sex, lousy for both Sharolyn and himself. Perhaps to punish himself—getting Sharolyn pregnant on their third date had been an epic blunder—he'd cut himself off. No sex, not even a single meaningless one-night stand.

Maybe his body was now experiencing the consequences of acting against nature. Simply discussing a sexually repressed woman who hated his guts was arousing him. He was becoming unhinged, a victim of self-induced celibate lunacy.

"Wade says no sane man is brave enough to take on Rachel, let alone get lucky with her," Sarah prattled on cheerfully.

Quint felt as if he were strangling. He cleared his throat. "Is—Is that so?"

"You have a really weird look on your face, Quint." Sarah was staring at him. Her eyes widened. "Omigod, you're not thinking of trying to nail Rachel Saxon, are you?"

He quickly attempted to rearrange his features into an impassive mask. "Of course not. I'm—uh—merely trying to plot strategy in the Tilden case."

"'Cause Rachel is really pretty." Sarah continued to study him curiously. "But you won't get anywhere with her, Quint. Wade told Dana that more guys have struck out with Rachel than have been up to bat in the history of baseball."

"Definitely some hyperbole there, but I get the point. Thanks for your advice, Sarah," Quint gritted through his teeth.

Lectured by a twenty-one-year-old nanny. He was truly humbled.

2

Rachel's hands trembled. Her insides felt as if they'd been twisted into knots. Her face was flushed, her breathing rapid and shallow.

"Hey, cuz, are my eyes deceiving me?" Wade Saxon appeared in the doorway of her office and leaned against the frame. "You actually look ready to blow your cool. Seems we're on the verge of an historic occasion here."

"Have you seen what arrived via messenger this morning?" Rachel asked tightly, ignoring his cousinly humor. Wade took nothing seriously. Unlike her.

"Okay, I'll bite. What arrived via messenger this morning?" Wade ambled into her office.

"This!" Rachel shoved a manila envelope into his hands.

"And I was hoping for a candygram." Wade feigned disappointment. "Or maybe a bundt cake."

Rachel resisted the urge to start throwing things. It wasn't Wade she was angry with, though his diffident air and lack of competitive zeal tended to irritate her even at the best of times. Which this morning definitely wasn't.

"I suggest you read it." Her suggestion sounded more like a command, but Rachel didn't care. She wanted Saxon support, Saxon unity—Saxon outrage! And since Aunt Eve was out of the office this morning, the support, unity, and outrage would have to be supplied by Wade.

Surely not even he could remain immune to this deliberate insult from that unmitigated master of legal gall, Quinton Cormack.

Wade removed a document from the envelope. "The Last Will and Testament of Townsend Tilden Senior. It's dated four months ago." He glanced at the neon green Post-it note stuck to the top page. **For your reading enjoyment** was handwritten in broad bold strokes and signed, **Q. Cormack**.

"Uh-oh!" Wade grimaced wryly. "We've been Cormacked."

Since the Pedersen defeat, Wade had developed the annoying habit of using Cormack's name as a verb. Loosely translated, to be Cormacked meant to be unsuspectingly kicked in the head and left reeling. A rather effective description of the way she was feeling at this moment.

"For your reading enjoyment!" Rachel fumed. "Cormack is mocking us, Wade. He—He's laughing in our faces!"

"Wonder why he sent the will to you instead of Aunt Eve?" Wade studied the envelope, which was addressed to Rachel Saxon and marked personal. "An egalitarian touch, maybe? Q. Cormack is letting us know that unlike the Tildens he doesn't mind dealing with lowly junior partners?"

"He sent it to me to remind me of the Pedersen case—and how I lost it to him. He is implying that the same thing is going to happen with this phony new will scheme he's conjured up with that—that tramp!"

Wade's lips quirked. "May I assume that tramp you're referring to would be the young Widow Tilden?"

"Don't you dare try and make a joke of this, Wade! It isn't funny. Take a look at the signature page. Look who he has down as witnesses!"

Wade flipped to the final page containing the signatures of those persons who had officially witnessed the signing of the will. The witnesses who would testify under oath in court, when asked, as to the mental state of Town Senior at the time of the signing.

His eyes widened. "Reverend Andrews of the Lakeview

Presbyterian Church, Rabbi Newman of Temple Sinai, Cherry Hill, and Father Cleary of St. Philomena's, Lakeview. Hmm, pretty impeccable list, Rachel. Imagine this crew taking the stand in court. Who would want to try and impeach any one of them? Ingenious.''

"Ingenious? Ha! Don't you see, Wade? It's all a scam. The entire thing is just a Quinton Cormack con job. Those three witnesses—"

"Do you think Cormack was going for some sort of Three Wise Men symbolism, or is this trio a nod to political correctness?''

"Wade, stop kidding around! Those so-called witnesses didn't witness a thing, none of them signed that will! But Quinton Cormack is hoping we'll believe they did.''

"Uh, I'm not exactly following you here, Rachel.''

"Quinton Cormack thinks I'm stupid and naive.'' Rachel seethed. "Oh, I know exactly what he's doing, Wade. This faux list of witnesses is a despicable ploy by that snake. It's his less-than-subtle way of telling me that he thinks I'm an incompetent idiot!''

"Cormack is really psyching you out,'' Wade said thoughtfully.

"No, he isn't! He might try, but he'll never succeed!''

"I'd say he's already halfway there if he has you believing that Town Tilden's will is a little memento betweeen you two. And if you really believe he forged the signatures of a minister, a rabbi, and a priest, Cormack has you right where he wants you, Rach.''

"I shouldn't have expected you to understand!''

"Rachel, Cormack realizes how much you personalized the Pedersen case and he's working that. Meanwhile, you're not only leaping at the bait, you've already gulped it whole.''

"Stop using overextended fishing metaphors! They're clichéd and irrelevant.''

"I should stick to those really original reptile metaphors, like snake?'' Wade grinned. "Or is that a phallic one? Because from where I stand, Q.C.'s effect on you has nothing to do with either fishing or reptiles and everything to do with—''

"Can't you ever be serious?'' To her consternation Rachel felt a hot flush sweep through her. Which stoked her anger even higher. She was *not* in the mood for Wade's jokey innuendos. "And—And I did not personalize the Pedersen Case! True, I wasn't happy about the outcome . . .''

Rachel felt a peculiar stabbing sensation rip through her as she remembered the expression on Quinton Cormack's face when the Pedersen verdict had been rendered. His victory, her loss. She could remember every detail of the little encounter that had followed.

Quinton Cormack had turned to look at her, his smile cocky, his brown eyes shining with triumph. He'd arched his brows in that maddeningly mocking way of his when she had glared back at him. And then he'd approached her to stand right in front of her, so close . . . *too close!*

He'd laughed when she had refused to shake his hand, which he had proffered as the others in the courtroom began to file out. "Give it up, Counselor,'' he'd leaned down to murmur against her ear.

Even now, she could conjure up the sensory images of that moment. His warm breath rustling her hair, the scent of his aftershave, a tangy masculine aroma she couldn't identify but couldn't forget, his solid muscular frame that made her feel—small and helpless.

Just thinking the words made her blush. Never had she expected to experience such a disconcerting sensation. She'd reached her five-foot-eight at the age of thirteen and learned to use her imposing height to intimidate her adolescent male peers, most of whom took years longer to achieve their full adult stature. By then, Rachel's daunting body language skills were formidable enough to unnerve even gigantic athlete types because she had also developed verbal skills that could annihilate any male ego with just a few well-chosen words.

The pattern seemed to be set in cement—men were attracted to her beauty but couldn't cope with her outspoken, edgy personality. The men she dated seemed to expect what she considered an alarming degree of simpering and pandering from a woman and when she refused to accommodate, potential partners fled.

At the age of twenty-eight, she'd had but one significant relationship, and disappointingly, it wasn't all that significant. On her twenty-fifth birthday, she had decided she'd better experience sex at least once; after all, her younger sister Laurel—who was *five years younger!*—had recently given birth to a baby girl.

Rachel had allowed Donald Allard, whom she'd been dating for months, to take her to bed—where she had experienced sex once and decided she hadn't been missing a thing. Just as she'd always suspected, the whole thing was highly overrated. She'd stopped seeing Don and resumed dating others, who stopped seeing her when she didn't simper or pander or sleep with them.

Rachel told herself she didn't care, she wouldn't sacrifice who she was for any male. She dedicated herself to her career, patterning herself after her aunt Eve. After all, it was Eve Saxon who'd joined the family firm in Lakeview and continued its success while brothers Hobart—Wade's father—and Whitman—Rachel's dad—chose other careers in nearby Philadelphia.

But somehow Quinton Cormack was oblivious to Rachel's forbidding demeanor, or worse, he was fully aware of it and found it funny. Because the smile on his face had been devilish that day in the courtroom when he'd *taken* her hand—after she'd refused his taunting handshake!—into his.

"Not going to offer me congratulations on a well-fought victory?" His voice echoed in her head.

Rachel felt the warmth of his big hand engulf hers, felt his thumb glide lightly over her palm. Her heart slammed against her ribs and she stood stock still, her gaze compulsively drawn to his. She had to tilt her neck to look into his eyes because at six-foot-four, he towered over her despite her courtroom pumps with their chunky two-and-a-half-inch heels.

Rachel gulped, then and now. She couldn't remember the last time she'd looked up to any man, but there she was, looking up into Quinton Cormack's intense brown eyes while he held her hand.

He was so tall, so strong and he exuded a masculine virility that had a potent and totally uncharacteristic effect on her. She still squirmed when she remembered how completely immobilized she'd been as she'd gazed into his dark eyes. Like a mouse under a cobra's stare.

She'd also remained mute. A first for her. She'd never been unable to come up with just that right phrase necessary to level her opponent.

"You won't say it? You're not going to say anything at all, are you? Well, then I won't offer you better luck next time, Rachel," Quint had said softly, releasing her hand.

Hearing him say her name left her as breathless as a sucker punch. It wasn't until later, when she'd replayed the scene in her mind for the fiftieth time that the note of mockery in his voice finally registered with her. *"Then I won't offer you better luck next time, Rachel."* He'd been needling her. Ridiculing her! And she had stood there passively and taken it!

Rachel burned. No wonder he thought she was an insipid twit, she'd certainly acted like one that day in the courtroom. And she had given him no further opportunities to change his mind about her. Since the disastrous Pedersen verdict, she had taken great care to keep her distance from Quinton Cormack.

If she saw him walking her way on the street, she assiduously turned in the other direction. If they accidentally turned up in the same place, like the courthouse or supermarket or a shop in town, she avoided eye contact and made a quick getaway. Her natural vigilance kept her safely away from the man she'd come to regard as her nemesis.

He seemed bent on proving it, too. Quint Cormack hadn't messengered this ridiculous faux will to Aunt Eve or Wade, he had marked it personal and sent it to her. Obviously, he saw her as the weak link in Saxon Associates. The acknowledgment stung, but Rachel forced herself to face it.

"I didn't personalize the Pedersen case," Rachel insisted once more, but her words rang hollow, even to herself.

"Okay, if you say so. But Cormack's decided to personalize this case, Rach." Wade pointed to the word *personal* on the manila envelope, his expression wry. "He's just made his first move."

"Yes." Was it possible to implode from pent-up anger? If so, Rachel feared she was dangerously near that point. She had to do something, to take action, to get out of here!

"I'll be back." She stalked from her office, nearly knocking over Katie Sheely, who was entering it.

"Kind of reminds you of Schwarzenegger in that *Terminator* flick." Wade smiled at the younger girl. "Or maybe a disgruntled postal worker looking for revenge is even closer to the mark, huh?"

"What's up with her, anyway?" Katie asked, peering into the narrow carpeted corridor. Rachel had already disappeared from view.

"I'm going to take a wild guess that she's on her way over to the offices of Cormack and Son to lodge a protest— or maybe even wreak some havoc. A very unRachel-like action, but her response to Quinton Cormack is also very unRachel-like."

"She looked awful mad." Katie nervously sucked in her cheeks. "What you said about postal workers. . . . Maybe I should call Dana over there and warn her?"

Wade chuckled. "Maybe you should. Advise the staff to take cover. After all, Rachel's broomstick makes great time. She ought to be arriving there real soon."

Despite her anxiety, Katie giggled.

Dana Sheely met Rachel at the door of the Cormack and Son law office and ushered her into the dingy reception room, which was about the size of the utility closet at the Saxon Associates suite of offices. There was barely enough space for the receptionist's desk tucked into the corner and the four uninviting folding chairs that lined the walls. The receptionist, a plump, grandmotherly-looking woman, glanced up from the magazine she was reading.

It was as though Dana and the receptionist both had been expecting her, Rachel decided, glancing from one woman to the other. But how was that possible?

"I want to see Quinton Cormack immediately," she decreed, fully expecting to be refused entry. She wouldn't take no for an answer, of course, she would burst into that manipulative, insulting weasel's office and then—

"Come right this way, please," Dana said agreeably, smiling at her.

Rachel stared at her. Had Quinton Cormack guessed that bogus will would send her runing over here? Her cheeks pinked. How humiliating to be that predictable!

"Your cousin said you were on your way over," Dana told her.

"Wade called you?" Rachel frowned. He'd guessed where she was going and called his pal Dana to alert her? His actions struck Rachel as treasonous. She'd been counting on the element of surprise.

As for the rest of her strategy . . . Rachel swallowed. It suddenly occurred to her that she had no strategy whatsoever. She had acted impulsively, which was most unlike her. Yet clearly, she had been embarrassingly obvious because Wade had known exactly where she was going.

And took no time informing his dear friend Dana Sheely.

Rachel slid a covert glance at the paralegal. Dana had the red hair, blue eyes, and fair skin that characterized all the Sheelys but the throw of the genetic dice had given her finer, more delicate features than her brothers and sisters, making her pretty rather than merely cute.

According to Wade, Dana was smart, too, an ace paralegal who would've made a talented lawyer had she gone to college and law school. Instead she had taken paralegal training following her high-school graduation and landed a job in a Philadelphia law firm, where she'd worked until Quinton Cormack hired her last year.

Wade had wanted Saxon Associates to hire Dana, Rachel recalled, but Aunt Eve had vetoed the idea, claiming their firm didn't need a paralegal's services. Saxon Associates' mistake, according to everybody, not only Wade. Dana Sheely had proven herself invaluable to Cormack and Son, her expertise in bread-and-butter legal cases freeing Quinton to pursue more difficult, lucrative ones. *Like the Pedersen and Tilden cases!*

Perhaps acknowledging her lapse, Aunt Eve had agreed to Wade's suggestion to hire young Katie Sheely when the Saxons' longtime receptionist Mavis Curran retired six months ago. Rachel still missed the extremely reliable, efficient Mavis. Katie was personable enough but could be extremely scatterbrained, a truth not even disputed by Wade, a longtime Sheely loyalist.

"Quint, Rachel Saxon is here," Dana said, opening a nicked, scratched door without a name on it.

"Miss Saxon, come in." Quint, seated behind an atrocious metal desk that looked like a government-issue reject, stood up.

He was wearing a dark blue suit and he looked both professional and respectable, like he belonged in a law firm with plush Oriental rugs and antique mahogany desks and a distinguished client list instead of this seedy place. Rachel's heart seemed to come to a complete stop, then start again at a frantic rate.

"Can we get—" Quint began.

"You can get a grip on reality," Rachel cut in. Since she was without a game plan and forced to wing it, she might as well immediately go on the offensive, which would stick him with the less desirable position of defense. "Before things escalate beyond your control."

"Get a grip on reality," Quint repeated lazily. "Are you suggesting that I'm delusional?" He did not seem at all disturbed by the charge.

"Either delusional or criminal. You're one or the other

if you think you'll get away with this latest hoax.''

"I sense a veiled threat, Miss Saxon. Or is it panic? Maybe both, hmm? Well, go on, I'm curious. What brings you down to the wrong side of the tracks this morning?''

"As if you didn't know.'' Rachel folded her arms in front of her chest and subjected him to a severely disapproving glare. She waited for him to acknowledge the bogus will he'd messengered to her this morning. *Marked personal!*

"I don't know.'' Quint shrugged. "I'm afraid you'll have to enlighten me. Why did you race over here in a panic to make accusations and threats? If you'll give me a few clues, I'll try to guess if you want me to. I'm fairly skilled at deducing—''

"Let's not go through with the rest of this charade,'' Rachel cut in tightly.

She was dismayed but hoped it didn't show. Quint's counterstrategy had turned the tables on her, putting her on the defensive, making her look impulsive and somewhat hysterical. She could only be thankful they weren't in a courtroom with a judge and jury observing this unfortunate turn of events.

Rachel heaved an impatient sigh. "You know very well I'm talking about that absurd version of Town Tilden's supposedly newly discovered will. The one that you and Misty Czenko have dreamed up in hopes of getting my clients to agree to an out-of-court settlement.''

"Since Town Tilden Junior is very much alive, I assume you're referring to the will of the late Town Senior. And to my client, Misty Czenko *Tilden.*'' Quint arched his brows in that sardonic way of his, which had its usual effect on Rachel.

It made her want to choke him.

"You know I am. And stop trying to stall with a deluge of trivial details.''

"I was being accurate, Miss Saxon, not trivial. It's very important to have each and every fact validated.'' His placating smile didn't cancel the sting of his words. "You see,

accuracy and specificity can mean the difference in the verdict of a case.''

Rachel wildly resented being addressed like a dim-witted
first-year law student at a third-rate law school, and his
blatant reference to the Pedersen case made her burn even
hotter.

''I'd've thought we would schedule an appointment to
discuss the Tilden will, but hey, I've got some time this
morning, so we can talk now.'' Quint seemed the soul of
congeniality, but Rachel wasn't fooled. The man was as
congenial as a rattler whose rock had been overturned.
''I'm willing to be spontaneous, just like you are.''

''I am not spontaneous!'' No one had ever accused her
of that! *''I'd've thought we would schedule an appointment
to discuss the will.''* Of course that was the usual protocol.
To have Quinton Cormack, of all people, point out her unorthodox behavior was mortifying.

''You could've fooled me.'' He had a definite gift for
subtext, managing to sound both scornful and sincere at the
same time. Irritated, Rachel wondered how he did it and
wished that she could, too.

''Dana, would you mind getting us some coffee?'' Quint
turned to his paralegal.

Rachel whirled around, suddenly remembering Dana's
presence. Since entering this office, she had been aware of
no one but Quinton Cormack. It was as if the two of them
were alone in some peculiar universe.

''And tell Helen to hold my calls during Miss Saxon's
visit.''

Rachel was unnerved. She was always so acutely attuned
to everything going on around her. Her hypervigilance was
practically a family legend. How could she have completely
forgotten Dana Sheely's very existence when the younger
woman had been standing only a foot away from her? ''I—
I don't want any coffee.''

''Hmm, you're right,'' Quint eyed Rachel assessingly.
''The last thing you need is more caffeine. You're so wired
right now you'll probably short-circuit after a couple sips

of coffee. And we don't want you bouncing off the walls. This isn't a rubber room, after all.''

Rachel bristled and tried to think of an appropriately insulting rubber-room retort. None came to mind, which only rattled her more. She knew what he was doing. Keeping her on the defensive, enhancing his position with a personal attack. She should ignore it, she knew that too. Yet here she was, doing exactly what he'd set her up to do, taking issue with his insulting allegation. His ridiculous allegation.

"I am NOT wired , Mr. Cormack."

"I beg to differ." Quint's grin of satisfaction only underscored her mistake.

Rachel balled her fingers into fists and breathed deeply. It was definitely time to regroup. "Let me explain my position in the simplest terms, which even *you* can understand. I don't want any coffee because I didn't come here to socialize. I do not want this visit to bear even the slightest trappings of a social call."

"And drinking coffee would elevate your visit from a business meeting to a social call? Hmm, that's interesting. Maybe you could fill me in on proper Lakeview etiquette, Miss Saxon. I've only lived here a little over a year and I'm not completely familiar with all the local nuances. What exactly constitutes a social call in this town? Give me the specifics."

Quint moved from behind his desk to walk toward her, his pace unhurried. "Is a social call something like a *date?*" He exaggerated the inflection, his expression one of mock comic horror.

Once again, the object of his derision was her, Rachel noted darkly. Perhaps deservedly so? She was aware she must seem psychotically uptight, and he had no qualms calling her on it. She winced.

Dana looked amused. "I'll run up the street to Starbucks and bring you a large Kona, Quint. You want it black, right?" He nodded, and she headed to the door. "Be right back."

"Remember not to bring anything for Miss Saxon, Dana.

Not because she's as wired as the Tasmanian Devil on speed, but because—''

"We wouldn't want anyone to think this was a date." Dana rolled her eyes. "Got it." She left the office amidst Quint's laughter.

Rachel knew she should do the same. Laugh. Act blasé. Ignore the fury roiling through her. Wade was right; Quinton Cormack was trying to psych her out, and she shouldn't let him. Determinedly, she attempted a blithe smile.

"Are you in pain?" Quint stepped directly in front of her. "Your face looks ready to crack."

Rachel's false smile was instantly erased and she glowered balefully at him. "Being forced to deal with you is painful, all right."

"Because I whipped your pretty little butt in the Pedersen case?" There was laughter in his eyes. "Are you still holding a grudge against me for that?"

He smiled at her, a genuine smile, not one of those infuriating smirks that made her want to smack him. Rachel's breath caught. He was incredibly appealing when he smiled like that, his face alight with humor.

Involuntarily, she found herself studying his face. He had interesting, strong features. A sharp blade of a nose, a well-shaped mouth, a dimple in his left cheek that she'd never actually noticed until today. Until right now. It also occurred to her that he was what her mother and sister would call "good-looking." In fact, on second glance they would probably upgrade that description to "very good-looking."

Her heart gave a peculiar little flutter. Disconcerted, Rachel sought an explanation. It certainly could not be attraction! She had proven her immunity to "good-looking" men for years by repeatedly rejecting each one that her mother and sister attempted to set her up with. In her experience, handsome men were fully aware of their appeal, trading shamelessly upon appearance and the predictable effect upon the opposite sex.

"Just because John Pedersen is the owner and boss of the Pedersen Car Shoppe doesn't mean he can bully his employees," Quint said softly, his legalese totally at odds with the warmth in his gaze. "Bullying by an employer is as taboo as sexual harassment. In fact, the highest incidence of workers' compensation lawsuits currently under litigation include stress, embarrassment, and humiliation in the workplace."

"And—And sharpie that you are, you managed to convince the jury that John Pedersen caused William Dumond stress, embarrassment, and humiliation at the Car Shoppe." Rachel scowled at the very idea.

"Because I had a truckload of evidence to prove it. Your case was a dog, Rachel. It was unwinnable. Your side's big mistake was in not convincing Pedersen to settle."

Was he trying to console her? By excusing her performance in the case while enhancing his? Rachel was outraged. And more than a little bewildered. "Pedersen's case was winnable. Don't flatter yourself, my aunt Eve would've won it. I—I lost because I . . . because you . . ."

Words failed her. She'd spent hours obsessing over the details of the case yet now, given the chance for a rebuttal, her mind seemed to have crashed like an on-line service on overload.

Her gaze flew to his dark brown eyes and expressive black brows. In her worst dreams, she saw him directing contemptuous glances at her client during the Pedersen trial. Rachel was convinced those potent eyes and arched brows of his had been invaluable visual aids for his verbal arguments, winning a unanimous jury verdict along with a sizable cash compensatory award for his client.

"Aunty Eve isn't Super Lawyer. I guarantee she would've lost that case, too," Quint said firmly. "Anyway, it's all in the past now. What do you say to wiping the slate clean and starting over?" He smiled *that* smile, the one that was practically a force of nature.

Part of her wanted to smile back at him. It would be so easy . . . A reaction to his own particular, disturbing magic? Rachel's mouth was actually tilting upward at the corners when her steely control reasserted itself, reminding her exactly who she was dealing with.

Quinton Cormack, the enemy. The man was a slick, smooth operator, out to bilk the Tildens, *Saxon Associates' most important clients,* out of God-only-knows-how-much. His power couldn't be dismissed, not after the way he'd prevailed over the Pedersens.

Well, she was not about to fall under his spell! The break in her guard was only momentary. Rachel stiffened and did not smile.

At that precise moment, she realized that he was standing far too close to her, just as he had in the courtroom that fateful day. His proximity violated the rules of personal space governing social acquaintances and business colleagues. He had thrust himself into the special zone designated for intimate family or friends.

Not Rachel's intimate family and friends, of course. All who knew her well, knew to maintain a certain physical distance from her. She was not the touchy-feely type. If someone mistakenly came too close, she subtly backed away, creating the needed distance herself.

She backed away now, but her movements were certainly not subtle. Her anger abated somewhat, displaced by the almost-overwhelming urge to turn and run. Only her fierce Saxon pride prevented her from indulging *that* catastrophic whim! She could imagine the gales of laughter her hasty retreat from him would evoke, were she foolish enough to make one. And she'd had more than enough of him laughing at her.

Rachel squared her shoulders, determined to put this smug, overconfident clod firmly in his place.

"I know what you're doing." She adopted her stentorian courtroom tone, and her voice boomed throughout the small office.

"Do you?" He stared down at her. "Then maybe you could fill me in because I sure as hell don't."

And now he was playing the part of befuddled male, needful of a wise woman's guidance. Oh, he was a crafty one! Rachel met his eyes. An almost-tangible current siz-zled between them. "This game of yours isn't working, Mister Cormack."

"No? Well, since I'm clueless as to what game, it's a good thing you're here for a play-by-play analysis, isn't it?"

"I refuse to indulge in games of one-upsmanship with you. Out of the courtroom, of course." Rachel took a giant step backward. He was still too close for comfort, and she was excruciatingly aware of his size and strength.

"Is that what we're doing?" He took a step toward her, closing the distance, and they went through the paces again. Her retreat, his advance—until she had backed herself against the door. He stopped when she did, inches away from her.

"You're deliberately trying to physically intimidate me— and it's not working!" She was aware that she was obfus-cating, a useful courtroom tactic, but not too convincing right here and now. His tactics were working all too well. She'd literally backed away from him, her breathing quick-ening, visible symptoms of a successful physical intimida-tion.

"It's not working at all," she added, striving for total denial.

"Just to set the record straight, I'm not trying to physi-cally intimidate you. Which means I'm glad you aren't— physically intimidated by me, that is."

His voice sounded oddly thick, a husky rasp. Rachel raised her eyes to his.

She could feel the heat emanating from his body and a bolt of undeniable sexual electricity rocked her. *Why did he have to be so masculine, so virile?* And why was she acutely, and uncharacteristically, susceptible—to him, of all men?

A strange combination of confusion and fury tornadoed within her. She alternately felt like laughing and cursing. In her entire twenty-eight years, she'd never met anyone who affected her like Quinton Cormack. Everything he did or said got under her skin and provoked an overreaction.

In fact, he could do nothing and still evoke a response from her, Rachel admitted grimly to herself: Simply being in his presence unsettled her like nothing else ever had. . . .

And then, shockingly, alarmingly, the floor began to shake and the framed pictures and diplomas on the walls rattled as the entire office seemed to go into motion.

Startled, Rachel pitched forward. She heard a great roaring sound and immediately remembered watching CNN's earthquake coverage and the survivors who always mentioned a terrible, roaring-engine sound that accompanied those great jolts in the fault lines.

Now, the unthinkable had happened—an earthquake had hit New Jersey. If she survived, she herself might be one of those shaken victims talking to eager on-site reporters.

Automatically, she reached for the nearest, strongest, and most stable object to hold onto. That happened to be Quinton Cormack. Her fingers grasped the lapels of his gray suit jacket and she felt his arms come around her. He held her firmly, anchoring her against him. For a moment, she leaned into his solid frame, her eyes squeezed shut, feeling the strength and power of his arms encircling her.

"Relax." His lips were somewhere around the vicinity of the top of her head. "It's just the ten-eighteen commuter train into Philadelphia."

Rachel opened her eyes. The sound was already receding into the distance and the building had stopped shaking. It wasn't an earthquake, only the High Speed Line. Still too unnerved to feel the acute embarrassment that would surely follow, she lifted her head to see Quint gazing down at her. She felt a hot melting sensation deep inside her.

"Does that happen often?" Her voice was soft and slightly breathless. "It felt like we were being launched into space from a rocket pad. How do you stand it?"

"You get used to it. The trains run to and from the city twice an hour." He dropped his arms that were holding her tightly against him, but not before running his hands over the curves of her hips, turning the release into an intimate and possessive caress.

Rachel quickly stepped aside, but Quint was already moving away from her. She watched him stride to the window and stop in front of it to stare out, his back to her. Compulsively, her gaze swept the long, strong length of him, lingering on the nape of his neck, where his thick dark hair was cut bristly short. She studied the width of his shoulders, his broad strong back, abruptly averting her eyes from a downward perusal.

Her nerves were tingling, her pulses were in overdrive, and her knees felt weak. She walked shakily to the nearest chair and sank down into it. *She had been in his arms!* And she was still reeling from the forceful sexual tension that had vibrated between them.

Silence fell, so heavy and charged that Rachel knew she had to break it. Otherwise, she would sit here and obsess about the feel of his hard body next to hers, about the unfamiliar but thrilling sensations his nearness had evoked within her. She felt dizzy and defenseless and more off-balance than she'd ever been in her entire well-ordered, controlled life.

"I—I guess I didn't realize how close to the High Speed Line this office actually is," she mumbled.

Inwardly, she groaned at the remark, which was nothing short of inane. This was a well-paid, functioning attorney? She cringed, waiting for Quint to annihilate her with a choice bit of sarcasm. Ruefully, Rachel decided she deserved it.

Instead, he seized upon her feeble comment and picked up the conversational ball, his tone—grateful?

"Yeah, we're really close to the High Speed Line down here. Any closer, and we'd be on the track itself. My father boasted to me about the low rent he paid for his office space, and when I saw the place, I guessed why. Then the train went by and I *knew* why."

"Maybe the landlord should pay *you*." Rachel attempted

a little joke, but glancing around, she wondered if it wasn't a statement of truth.

The office was singularly unattractive, with peeling dull gray paint on the walls, ugly institutional furniture, and aging linoleum floors. Every frame hung on the walls was crooked, adding a peculiar lopsided feel. And to top it all off, this eyesore came equipped with sound effects. Twice an hour it sounded as if a runaway train was crashing through the office.

"There's no getting around the fact that this place is a dump," Quint said bluntly.

"I—didn't say that."

"Because you were being polite. Thank you."

Clearly, she wasn't the only one being polite. Rachel fiddled with the leather strap of her watchband, carefully keeping her eyes averted from him though she was achingly aware of his exact location in the office.

They were both being so cordial, it would've been funny under any other circumstances. But neither one was laughing.

She willed her breathing to return to a normal rhythm but didn't have much luck. If someone were to enter the office and see her gulping for air, it might be assumed that she'd been running laps around the building. Surely, nobody would ever guess that Quint Cormack had held her in his arms, that she'd felt his body crucially hardening against her while she grew moist and soft, as though anticipating . . .

The sound of a double beep made her jump in her chair. Quint snatched up the receiver of his telephone. "Helen, I told you to hold my calls," he snapped.

Rachel noted with a certain satisfaction that Quint's usual laconic air was missing, replaced by a noticeable tension bordering on—uptight? Fascinated, she stared at him. Was it her imagination or had a flush of color stained his neck?

Quint looked up and saw her watching him. As her gaze became more intent, he suffered an abrupt loss of coordi-

nation, fumbling and accidentally pressing the button for
his speaker phone.

Helen's voice was broadcasted into the office.

"I know what you said." Helen was not at all apologetic
for her intrusion. "But this is one call you're going to want
to take, Quint. It's Sarah Sheely on line one. She's calling
to tell you that your father's house is on fire."

3

"What?" Quint's voice was loud and sharp as a shotgun blast.

Rachel jumped to her feet. Her entire body was trembling but she instinctively moved toward Quint.

"Hi, Quint." A young woman's voice sounded over the speakerphone. "Your father's house is on fire and I'm—"

"Sarah, where's Brady?" Quint cut in. "Is he all right?"

"Don't worry, Brady's here with me. Say 'hi' to Daddy, Brady."

"Hi, Daddy!" A baby voice boomed throughout the office.

Rachel grasped the edge of the desk and stared at Quint, wide-eyed. He had a child? Quinton Cormack was a father? Certainly, she had never asked about his marital status—as if she cared!—yet she'd known early on that he was a bachelor. The existence of his child came as a distinct shock.

"See, Quint, Brady's fine," Sarah's voice came over the line once again. "We're at the neighbors across the street from your dad's house. That's where Carla called me from, and I drove right over."

"Why did Carla call you?" Quint demanded. "Wouldn't calling the fire department be a more logical choice?"

"She was trying to reach you. Maybe she thought you were home instead of the office, I don't know. Carla's scared out of her mind, Quint, she's not thinking too straight. The neighbors called the fire department and the truck's here now. The police too. Quint, you'd better get over here.''

Sarah paused to audibly inhale. ''Nobody knows where Dustin is. Somebody said he was seen running back inside the house yelling he was going to get their dog.''

''And he hasn't been seen since? My God, Dustin is trapped inside?''

Quint's voice echoed through Rachel's head. She didn't know who he was talking about, but the implications of anyone being trapped in a burning building were horrifying.

''What was the kid doing at home at this hour? It's a Thursday, why in hell wasn't that child at school? I know he's not sick, I just saw him yesterday,'' Quint thundered in a raw furious voice that was light-years away from his effective, controlled courtroom tone of oh-so-righteous anger. ''God almighty, Sarah, why didn't someone grab him before he went into that house?''

''I don't know!'' Sarah shouted back. ''Just get here, Quint. Carla's running around screaming and everybody's starting to go crazy.'' A loud baby wail nearly drowned out her voice. ''See what I mean? Even Brady's getting scared.''

''I'll be right there,'' Quint promised, and raced from his office.

Automatically, Rachel followed him, so close on his heels that when he stopped suddenly in the reception area she crashed into him, colliding full force with his broad back. Reeling from impact, gulping for breath, she swayed backward.

''Dammit, I don't have my car!'' Quint seemed unaware that he'd dealt Rachel a body blow equal to an offensive lineman's sack of a quarterback. He was talking aloud to himself, oblivious to everything around him. ''That damned recall—I finally took the car in to the dealership, today of all days, and now I'm stuck without—''

''Wish I could help, but my husband dropped me off on his way to the warehouse, as usual,'' Helen lamented. ''Dana doesn't have her car today either—one of her brothers borrowed it. You know how those Sheelys are always juggling rides. Should I call you a taxi, Quint?''

''I have my car,'' Rachel heard herself say.

For a moment, she wondered if her forceful collision with Quint had left her delirious. Was that really her offering to help her avowed enemy? Then she thought of the fierce panic in his voice, the fear she'd seen in his dark brown eyes when he'd heard that the child named Dustin had run inside the burning house. She was acting on a natural humanitarian impulse, she assured herself.

''Thanks.'' Quint breathed a genuine sigh of relief. ''Give me the keys.''

Rachel's humanitarian impulse faltered a bit. ''I'll drive you where you want to go, but I can't give you my car. I— uh—need it later, for an appointment.''

Which wasn't entirely true. She had no appointment scheduled later but she wasn't about to be left stranded without her car. Especially not in this place where carlessness seemed to be the order of the day.

''Right, come on.'' Quint grasped her arm and half dragged her from the office.

They saw Dana Sheely across the street, standing on the corner waiting for the light to change, a cardboard carton of coffee cups in her hands.

''Dana, hold down the fort, okay?'' Quint shouted to her. ''Helen will explain everything.'' He turned to Rachel. ''Where's your car?''

''There.'' Rachel pointed to her dream car, a royal blue BMW convertible that she would be making car payments on for many more years. But it didn't matter; she'd wanted a convertible her entire life and had fallen in love with the car at first sight two years ago. At the Pedersen Car Shoppe.

And now she was offering to give Quinton Cormack a lift in it. Maybe she'd been concussed by that body slam back in his office and her thought processes were off-kilter, but suddenly there seemed to be something cyclically cosmic going on. She stared at him, her hazel eyes huge.

"Ever put the top down?" Quint tapped the roof of the car, which was securely in place.

"Of course. Often. What's the point of having a convertible if the top is always up?"

"This isn't what I'd expected you to drive," he muttered, climbing into the passenger side as she slid behind the wheel. "I'd've bet my house that your car would be something big, black and sturdy, something solid and traditional. Conservative."

"Sounds like a hearse." Rachel turned the key and the engine purred to life. "It's enlightening to know that even in the midst of—of acute anxiety you still have the presence of mind to insult me."

"I wasn't insulting you, Rachel."

The sound of her name on his lips made her shiver. Desperately, she tried to tamp down the sensation. "You'll have to direct me to your father's house," she said, hoping she sounded businesslike, maybe even severe.

"It's not far from here. Take a left at the next light."

She quickly became aware that the directions were leading toward Lakeview's only marginal residential neighborhood, consisting of several crowded streets of small wooden houses on undersized lots. The neighborhood directly bordered the less desirable zip code of Oak Shade, and the aging houses in varying states of disrepair and untended yards were far more typical of Oak Shade than tony Lakeview.

Rachel knew the neighborhood was referred to as "Lakeshade", and the appellation was not meant to be flattering. It wasn't a surprise to learn that Frank Cormack, that inept and unlucky lawyer, lived there with his much younger wife Carla.

Whose house was currently on fire.

"Who is Dustin?" she asked suddenly, her voice breaking the silence.

"Frank and Carla's kid. He turned seven last month." Quint's voice was taut. "He's a first-grader and a smart little boy. He'd do even better in school if his mother ever gets it through her head to send him every day, instead of letting him decide when he feels like going.''

Rachel shot him a sidelong glance. He was sitting rigidly in the seat beside her, his jacket laid across his lap in deference to the heat of the day, although he was already visibly perspiring. His eyes were riveted straight ahead, his hands balled into fists. He was virtually a body-language textbook case of nervous tension. A pang of something that felt very much like sympathy streaked through her.

"So he is your half-brother,'' she stated the obvious, for she felt the need to say something. Anything. Quint's tension was contagious; she felt it seeping into her every pore. "Do—Frank and Carla have other children?''

"Another boy, Austin, who's nine. Take a right here.''

Rachel did as bidden. "I—I sort of know Carla. That is, I know who she is. I went to high school with her. She was Carla Polk back then.'' She couldn't seem to stop talking, but even realizing that didn't shut her up. "Carla was in the class two years ahead of me.''

"I bet you two were never friends, probably not even nodding acquaintances. Not Carla from Oak Shade and Princess Rachel. I'm surprised you even went to the public school. I'd pegged you as an alum from an exclusive prep school.''

His tone was unmistakably insulting, but Rachel decided not to take offense. That flash of sheer terror he'd displayed in his office upon learning little Dustin's whereabouts—or nonwhereabouts—opened her compassionate vein, allowing her to give him a lot of extra leeway in word and deed. Who could fight with a man who feared his baby brother might be burning to death?

"My cousin Wade went to Lakeview Academy, but my sister and I were students at good old Lakeview Public High. It has an excellent reputation,'' she replied mildly. "And just for the record, my family isn't actually rich. There is no big Saxon extended family fortune. Wade's parents are both bankers and are well-off, but my father is a sociology professor at Carbury College, right outside

Philadelphia, and we always lived on his salary. He received only a very small inheritance from Grandfather, as did Wade's father.''

"So Aunty Eve is the one with the big bucks, huh? The Porsche, the jewelry, the Italian leather attaché case, the designer clothes. I'll be tactful and not mention her Park Avenue plastic surgery which must've cost as much as—"

"Aunt Eve hasn't had plastic surgery!" Rachel exclaimed. "She wouldn't! She believes in natural, graceful aging.''

"And I'm Santa Claus. Come on, Rachel. The rest of you Saxons might be regular folks struggling to make ends meet, but Eve Saxon is *actually rich*.''

He was mocking her family a bit too gleefully, even using her own words to do it. Rachel stiffened.

"My aunt Eve has been very successful, professionally and financially. She followed my grandfather into the family law firm and his will heavily favored her because of her career decision," she added defensively.

"Bet the rest of the clan loved that." Quint was sardonic. "Too bad I wasn't in town then. You could've hired me to contest the will. You Saxons are into that, aren't you? You get off on contesting wills.''

"There was never a thought to contesting Grandfather's will. Everyone was familiar with the terms beforehand," Rachel stated succinctly. "Contrary to your low opinion of the Saxons, we're not a greedy, money-hungry tribe.''

"So you're saying you aren't like your eminent clients, the Tildens, huh?" Quint gave a decidedly nasty laugh. "Because they are greedy and money-hungry, and they do get off on contesting wills, especially a certain one about to be probated.''

Rachel's lips tightened. "I don't want to talk about the Tildens right now.''

"No, you'd rather talk about how different you are from Carla. How you aren't filthy rich but you are genteel and classy while Carla is the stereotypical fast girl from the trashy neighborhood who was stupid enough to get mixed up with a loser old enough to be her father. Who, unfortunately, happens to be my father.''

Rachel slammed on the brakes at the stop sign. If Quint hadn't been buckled in, he would've been propelled through the windshield. A rather satisfying image. Right now she'd like to see him propelled into orbit.

''I never said anything of the sort about Carla,'' she gritted through her teeth. ''*You* said it all.''

''I merely stated what you were thinking, sweetie. It was written all over your face.''

She drove through the intersection, then deliberately jammed on the brakes again, for the sheer pleasure of watching the shoulder strap nearly hang him. She saw him cast a glance at her, saw him open his mouth as if to speak. But he said nothing.

That was fine because she had plenty to say. Rachel felt a surge of adrenaline pumping through her. ''I'm going to take issue with that last statement of yours, Counselor. First and foremost, don't ever call me 'sweetie' again. Second, despite your alleged talent for *reading faces,* I was not thinking about Carla at all. I was thinking what an insufferable, ungrateful jerk you are.'' The words flowed easily; she felt charged and inspired, as if presenting the winning final summation to a jury.

''Given the circumstances, I've been trying to be patient, but you don't deserve any special consideration. You aren't worried about your poor little brother, you're too busy taking verbal potshots at me and my family. Well, I don't want to hear another word out of you, the sound of your voice makes me sick! Don't speak to me again.''

He immediately proceeded to disregard her order. ''If I don't speak to you, how am I supposed to direct you to—''

''I'll manage to find the place. It shouldn't be hard—it's on fire!''

Rachel drove down the street with no further directions from him. She didn't need any. The noise of chaos and smell of burning matter filled the air, and she unerringly followed. Around the corner, flames were shooting out of a small brick house while firemen held hoses directing steady streams of water onto the blaze. The street was blocked by a hook and ladder truck, an ambulance, and two police cars. A crowd of people, growing larger by the minute, watched the fire as if fixated by the sight.

Quint's stomach clenched. He couldn't stand to look, couldn't stand to think that little Dustin might be inside that blazing house. He stole a quick glance at Rachel, who was clutching the steering wheel, looking grim. He couldn't stand to think of the way he'd behaved toward her, either.

She had called him an insufferable, ungrateful jerk, and he agreed that she was right on the mark. He'd deliberately been rude to her. It wasn't fair, it wasn't right, and she didn't deserve it.

He wasn't proud of himself, though he could offer grounds. Guilty by reason of insanity. Because from the fateful moment back in his office when he'd taken one step too close to her and felt the potent wallop of her allure, his head had been spinning, his body possessed by a wild desire that obliterated all rational thought. And didn't the absence of all rational thought constitute insanity in its purest form?

Rachel seemed to think he knew exactly what he was doing, that he had plotted his every move like the game plan from a football team's playoff strategy book. That was good for a laugh, but he knew the joke was on him.

He could only be thankful she was unaware that he'd been operating on pure animal instinct, no doubt passed along in his genes from some prehistoric ancestor, perhaps some hominid species. *Homo erectus* came to mind. Quint nearly groaned aloud at his woefully lame reference.

And even now, under these most difficult circumstances, hard as he tried to block the sensory images, they remained vivid. It was as if he and Rachel were still back in his office. He could still smell the enticing aroma of her perfume in his nostrils, he could feel the heat emanating from her where she stood just crucial inches away from him.

When the train had come roaring down the tracks, momentarily scaring her out of her wits, he'd been permitted to experience the tangible, physical pleasure of her body pressed into his. She had reflexively reached for him and clung, seeking protection, and he'd felt the irresistible warmth of her, felt her soft curves molded against him.

He'd seized the opportunity to hold her, relished it. His sex had swelled impossibly fast to iron-hard thickness, and he had pressed himself against her belly like a pathetically overeager teenager with his first erection.

His instantaneous sexual response to her forced Quint to face facts. To face the unwelcome, intolerable realization of just how much he had been wanting to be close to Rachel Saxon, to touch her, to hold her.

Since his very first sight of her!

The revelation was humbling, it was horrifying. He wanted her madly, and she hated his guts.

Lucky for him, his instincts for self-preservation were first-rate, enabling him to summon his considerable willpower and walk away from her. It hadn't been easy; he'd been dangerously close to giving into the sensual fire raging within him. Before moving away from her, he had foolishly given in to that vestige of primitive impulse and run his hands over her hips in what was definitely a sexually possessive caress.

Lord, he had wanted to do so much more. . . .

But already, the images were forming in his head, of Rachel and himself back in his office while the train rumbled past. He imagined yanking her classy little brown skirt up to her waist. Smoothing his palms over her spectacular long, shapely legs. Slipping his hand between them to feel the revealing wetness of her panties. And then pulling them off before finally, blissfully thrusting into her soft, moist warmth. Of course, she would be ready for him, she wanted him as much as he wanted her. He had seen that hot dreamy look of passion in her eyes when she'd gazed up at him.

Lady Antarctica? Freezer Queen? If the image of a sexually repressed Rachel had aroused him, the reality of a passionate, hungry Rachel drove him wild.

But then, as now, reality intruded most harshly. He knew a wallbanger in his office with Rachel Saxon was so out of the question that he had no choice but to get away from her fast, before he dared to try it. He'd dashed to the window to stare out, studying the drab view of the tracks with fierce concentration, as if bent on counting each railroad tie, vaguely aware they'd had some sort of conversation though he couldn't remember a thing either of them had said.

That phone call from Sarah had sent him from sensual disorientation into a panicked frenzy. His dad's and Carla's house was burning down? His kid brother was inside?

And his car was unavailable to take him to the scene. The world seemed to be unraveling until Rachel had offered him a ride.

From that moment he had been downright rotten to her, spoiling for a fight, determined to fend off any attempt at niceness on her part because God help him, he still wanted her. Badly. That raging hard-on of his had hardly subsided. His jacket was draped over his lap to conceal the evidence of his erection; he was sweating, but his heat was sexual and had nothing to do with the warm temperature outside.

It was outrageous, it was shameful, and he knew it. Despite the latest calamity befalling the Cormacks at this very moment, he was hard and hot and hungry for Rachel Saxon. He deeply, furiously resented her power over him.

Knowing that she was making a genuine effort to be understanding and patient with him only made things worse. He couldn't have her, and she was making him want her even more. He needed Rachel to be cold and cranky, not likable. Acting in sheer self-defense, he'd made her act like the bitch he needed her to be. *He'd had to!*

As usual, he was very good at getting the results he wanted. Rachel had turned back into a sharp-tongued shrew, actually forbidding him to speak to her. Mission accomplished.

"Hey, lady, you can't drive down here!" A young policeman approached Rachel's window, looking frazzled and impatient. "In case you haven't noticed, there's a fire."

"Yes, Officer," she replied politely. "I'm dropping off Mr. Cormack. He's a family member who is—"

"Cormack?" The officer peered further into the car and saw Quint. "Thank God you're here!" He sagged against the door, as if he needed support to stay on his feet. "We can't find one of the kids and Carla is out of control. Way beyond our control. I know this sounds nuts, but she's commandeered the ambulance. She won't let anyone in, the paramedics are totally pissed, and who can blame them? Do you think you can calm her down?"

"I can try," Quint said grimly.

"I'll park your car for you, miss," the policeman said to Rachel, this time addressing her with an almost-ingratiating courtliness. "You go with him to the paramedics down there at the ambulance. They need help real bad."

Immediately, Rachel got out of the car and turned it over to the policeman. She automatically hurried after Quint.

"They're already on a first-name basis with Carla, not a good sign," he muttered, racing toward the vehicle with its red lights flaring.

"She commandeered the ambulance?" Rachel was still pondering that. "How? I mean, why?"

"How and why are questions that Carla and Dad seldom have answers for."

In her brown stacked heel pumps, Rachel found it difficult to match his pace and fell slightly behind him. She was beginning to have second thoughts about her impromptu presence here—and third thoughts as well. The young policeman had gallantly absconded with her car, she didn't know the Cormacks, and Quint certainly did not want her around. Officially, they weren't even speaking to each other though they'd just exchanged a few words.

"Careful, she's armed," a paramedic hollered to Quint as he drew near to the ambulance.

Rachel arrived moments later. "Carla has a gun?"

She stared at Quint, aghast. What a nightmare this must be for him, and it only seemed to be getting worse! She immediately forgave him for using her and the other Saxons for verbal target practice on the drive over here. So what if he'd taken out his anger, fear, and frustration on the nearest person available? Who happened to be her!

She was sometimes guilty of doing the same thing, Rachel admitted to herself. If asked honestly to describe her own behavior in a crisis, sweetness, patience, and forbearance would not be the first characteristics to leap to mind.

"No, there's no gun," the paramedic replied tersely to her query. "But she's got a loaded syringe in each hand. We tried to give her some sedatives, and she wrestled them away from us. She's locked herself inside and is threatening to stick anybody who comes near her." The paramedic wiped his brow. "She won't let us into our own ambulance and God only knows what she's doing in there. She won't talk to anybody, she just keeps screaming."

The uniformed emergency personnel milled about , looking worried and uncertain. Yet another round of screams came from within the ambulance.

"Somebody do something!" implored a nurse.

Quint began to bang on the back door of the ambulance with his fists. "Carla, open up. Do you hear me? Open this door and put down those damn syringes. Now, Carla!"

The screaming stopped. The sudden cessation of noise was almost disorienting.

And then: "Is Frank with you, Quint?" a female voice shrieked from within. "I called the office earlier and Helen said he wasn't there. But he was supposed to be; he left for work this morning." The voice grew higher with hysteria. "Where is he, Quint? Where's Frank? I was doing the wash when I smelled smoke. Oh God, Quint, they said Dustin is inside the house!"

"Carla, open the door," Quint's voice lowered, his tone soft and coaxing. "I know how scared you are, honey. We need to talk. Come on, Carla, let me in."

The back door swung open and a weeping brunette flung

herself into Quint's arms. "Oh, Quint! What am I going to do? My baby, we have to find my baby!" Carla flung her needle-weapons to the ground and nestled closer to Quint.

The EMTs scrambled to pick up the syringes before climbing into the ambulance and reclaiming it.

Rachel watched Carla Polk Cormack, curvy and voluptuous in snug jeans shorts and halter top, hanging on to Quint; she watched him enfold the woman firmly in his embrace. An unfamiliar yet thoroughly sickening sensation hit her squarely in her middle.

"Is that the husband?" someone standing nearby asked Rachel.

She supposed she must appear to be some sort of authority-figure-in-the-know, her conservative brown suit, cream silk blouse, and sensible shoes setting her apart from the other onlookers, who were dressed in shorts, tank tops, and sandals.

Well, she did have some information to impart.

"He is her stepson," Rachel said coolly.

She didn't add that Carla was five years younger than Quint, and that the two of them seemed to share a very close bond. She didn't have to. Wasn't a picture worth a thousand words? Certainly the image of Carla clinging to Quint while he physically comforted her spoke volumes.

Those spectators dedicated to watching the fire remained oblivious to everything else, but the newly revealed information about the couple spread quickly through the restless group who'd gathered to observe the ambulance takeover.

Rachel left as the snickering and innuendos began, but she overheard some remarks as she made her way through the crowd.

"Stepson, huh?"

"She's sure not like the wicked stepmother from out of them fairy tales."

"Maybe she is a wicked stepmother. But I mean wicked in a whole different way, if you get my drift."

Everybody got it.

Rachel searched the street, hoping for a glimpse of her

car or the policeman who had parked it. *She had to get out of here!*

"Omigod, I know you! You're Rachel Saxon."

Rachel turned to see a Sheely approaching her. She didn't know which, but it was definitely one of the red-haired Sheely sisters. The girl was carrying a wriggling, disgruntled blond toddler in a bright blue sunsuit.

"I'm Sarah Sheely. I met you at your cousin Wade's apartment last summer, but you probably don't remember. Your cousin is good friends with my brother Tim and sister Dana," Sarah continued to list her reasons for addressing Rachel, while the child she held made a concentrated effort to escape from her grasp. "And—um—my sister Katie works at your law firm," she added nervously.

Rachel felt like a dragon lady. Was she really so unapproachable that one needed credentials to speak to her? "Hello, Sarah." She tried to sound friendly, not forbidding as she stared at the little boy struggling in the young woman's arms. "Is—that Quinton Cormack's child?"

"Yeah, this is Brady, and he shouldn't be here," Sarah replied frankly. "A fire is no place for a two-year-old but I had to bring him along because I couldn't leave him alone and the neighbors said I *had* to come over here and try to calm Carla down. She was going beserk in their living room."

"Having seen her at the ambulance, I understand their desperation," Rachel murmured.

"I have to talk to Quint. I've been trying to, but he's totally busy with Carla," Sarah complained. "I couldn't even get near him. Some nurse just pushed me out of the way."

"The emergency rescue team would fend off anyone who tried to take Quint away from Carla at this point. She might regroup and hold their ambulance hostage again."

Rachel heard the note of sarcasm in her voice and was instantly ashamed of herself. Carla's son was in danger and she'd sounded . . . *jealous* was the word that instantly sprang to mind, but Rachel rejected it, appalled. She was not jealous of Quint's attentions to his terrified young step-mother!

Purposefully, she started the thought all over again. Carla's son was in danger, and that ambulance crack she'd made had sounded . . . less than sympathetic.

"I feel very sorry for Carla," Rachel recited dutifully.

"Well, things are about to go from bad to even worse for the Cormacks unless I get Quint to either take Brady or stop Austin." Sarah looked morose.

"Brady down. Brady go! Go down now!" Brady demanded, bucking and rearing and nearly unbalancing the petite Sarah.

"Stop it, Brady! Bad boy!" his nanny scolded.

The child began to howl, keeping his arms and legs in constant motion, even more desperate to be free.

Sarah appeared ready to cry, too. Still clutching the vigorously protesting Brady, she turned tear-filled eyes to Rachel. "What am I going to do? I saw Austin headed down the street with his BB gun and I know he's going to shoot out the windows in that vacant house at the end of the block, but I can't drag Brady down there 'cause I'll need both my hands to—"

"Austin is Carla's older child," Rachel recalled, trying to make some sense of Sarah's desperate monologue. "And he has a BB gun? Which he uses to—er—shoot things?"

The girl nodded, sniffling. "Quint talked to Austin about not, well, vandalizing property after the cops caught him shooting out streetlights, but now Austin's real upset, and who can blame him? I mean, his brother and his dog are in his house that's on fire and—"

"Could you get the BB gun away from Austin, Sarah?" Rachel cut straight to the point. "Before anything happens?"

"Sure. I have four brothers, plus I've been baby-sitting for half of Lakeview since I turned twelve. I know exactly how to handle Austin Cormack." Sarah's confidence was unshakeable.

"Then why don't I take Brady while you—uh—disarm

Austin,'' Rachel suggested quickly. "I agree that having the police catch him shooting out windows would be more than this family can cope with right now.'' She looked at the small, wailing, flailing figure of Brady Cormack. "Do you think he'll let me hold him?'' she asked uncertainly.

"He'll have to!'' Sarah dumped the toddler into Rachel's arms. "I'll go after Austin. Thanks, Rachel.'' She took off down the street.

Brady stopped crying the moment he landed in Rachel's arms. The two of them eyed each other tentatively.

"Hi,'' he said, his lower lip quivering.

Rachel melted. He was only a baby! And she liked children; her little niece was one of her very favorite people. "Hi, Brady,'' she said softly. "Do you want down? Do you want to walk?''

While that had definitely been his goal when restrained by Sarah, now Brady appeared to be reconsidering. He remained still as his little hand touched Rachel's cheek, then he curled his fingers around the small gold stud she wore in her ear.

"Earring,'' said Rachel.

"Ear-ring,'' Brady repeated. "Lunch?'' he added hopefully.

"You want to eat an earring for lunch?'' Rachel launched into the type of nonsense game she played with her small niece. "I think I want a hamburger and french fries and a soda for lunch.''

Brady laughed appreciatively, catching the humor. Quick as lightning, he closed his teeth around Rachel's earring. "Eat ear-ring for lunch.'' He licked her ear like a puppy.

"I bet that tastes yucky,'' Rachel said jovially, not minding the baby drool on her ear and neck.

"Yucky!'' Brady sang out. He bounced up and down in her arms, beaming from ear to ear.

Rachel smiled, too. He really was an adorable child, as cute as her little niece, which was very cute indeed. He had thick blond hair, dark brown eyes, and a deep dimple in his left cheek. Rosy cheeks and tiny white teeth and a darling smile. She felt ridiculously happy to be holding him and hoped that Sarah took her time confiscating Austin Cormack's weapon.

"Do you want down?" she repeated the offer, remembering his earlier determined efforts to achieve freedom. "Do you want to walk?"

"No!" Brady settled himself more comfortably against her. "Carry me," he ordered grandly.

"Yes sir. Whatever you say, sir." She grinned at his two-year-old confidence. He'd expressed his wish and expected it to be fulfilled. And she was touched by the trust implicit in his toddler command. That she would take care of him. That he was safe with her.

She would, and he was.

Rachel carried Brady up the street, winding her way through the spectators, talking to him about the things around them. The trees, the flowers. A baby in a stroller. A cat sitting in the front window of a house. She was careful not to mention the fire or anything to do with it.

And then they came upon her car, parked along the curb just a few yards away. "That's my car," she told him, pointing at it.

The window was rolled down and she could see her keys dangling in the ignition. It wasn't until then that it occurred to her how completely shaken the young policeman had been by Carla Cormack's ambulance antics. One of Lakeview PD's own officers had unwittingly extended an invitation to a potential car thief by leaving her car unlocked with the key handily available. Rachel imagined how ridiculous that particular stolen car report would read and murmured a silent thanks there was none to file.

Explaining her own willingness to simply hand over her car while she traipsed after Quinton Cormack wouldn't have been easy either. She pictured Aunt Eve's bemused expression and Wade's droll one as she attempted to justify her uncharacteristic impulsivity to them. Thank heavens, no explanations or justifications were necessary to anyone!

Except herself, perhaps? Rachel blocked that thought.

"Blue car," Brady said knowingly, as they reached her car.

"That's right, Brady. My car is blue." Rachel was impressed. He was only two and he already knew his colors? Her niece was three and still struggled with them.

"Ride in blue car?" Brady suggested.

Rachel stared at the grim scene down the street, which would probably become far worse. Sarah was right, a fire was no place for a two-year-old. Little Brady didn't belong here, where he might see or hear something horrible that could traumatize him for life.

"I don't have a car seat for you but I could buckle you up in the back." She wasn't sure if she was talking to Brady or speaking her thoughts aloud. "That would be safe if we drove someplace close for lunch, wouldn't it?"

"Lunch!" exclaimed Brady, his face wreathed in ecstasty.

She couldn't disappoint him now! Rachel glanced at her watch. It was past noon and the child was hungry. There really could be no harm in taking him to lunch.

"Okay, Brady, let's have lunch."

4

"Hey, Sheely, it's Thursday. You know what that means, Happy Hour at Riggin's, two beers for the price of one. Meet you there at five-thirty?" Wade Saxon phoned to extend his usual weekly invitation to Dana Sheely.

"I can't meet you there, Saxon." Dana glanced at her watch. It was four-fifteen, rather early for Wade to be calling. Over an hour's notice? He seldom made plans this far in advance. "Sorry."

"So am I." Wade heaved a resigned sigh. "Which one of your sibling pests borrowed your car this time?"

"Brendan, and he's not a pest. He has football practice after school and a new girlfriend who needs a ride home from cheerleading practice." Dana smiled. "A guy *has* to have wheels, y'know."

"A direct quote from Brendan, no doubt, that weasely little moocher. Okay, I'll pick you up at five-fifteen, Sheely." He sounded vaguely martyred.

"And I didn't even have to ask." Dana chuckled. "You're a real pal, Sax."

"Don't I know it. Be on time, Sheely. I don't want to hang around that hellhole you call an office. It's like being trapped in an erupting volcano every time a train goes by."

"Why not try to see things from a different angle, Saxon? Every time a train goes by I pretend I'm on a thrill ride at Disney World. People pay those big park entrance fees to experience what I can enjoy for free, twice an hour.''

"There's that scary Sheely optimism rearing its nasty head again.'' Wade groaned. "Try to keep it in check, huh, Sheel? See you later.''

He hung up before Dana could reply.

At five-thirty-five, they walked into Riggin's, a popular sports bar in nearby Cherry Hill. The place was quiet and uncrowded as Dana followed Wade to their usual corner table. It offered the best view of a gigantic TV screen that was currently broadcasting a baseball game. Since the Phillies weren't playing, Dana had no interest in watching.

A waitress immediately came to the table, and Wade waved away her offer of a menu and placed their order. The Happy Hour special, two beers for the price of one, and an order of Nachos Grande. Wade always paid for the first round, Dana paid for the next, and they split the cost of the nachos. Had the Phillies been playing, they might stay longer and divide the tab as need be. Thursday Happys at Riggin's had become something of a ritual.

Dana slipped off her tan suit jacket and adjusted the cuffs of her pale blue blouse. She lifted her eyes to find Wade watching her instead of the TV screen, unusual behavior for him. Wade was an avid baseball fan; he didn't limit his interest in the sport strictly to the home team, as she did.

She arched a questioning auburn brow. "Something wrong?''

"Was that John Pedersen I saw leaving your office building when I arrived to pick you up?'' he asked, far too casually.

She knew him too well to be fooled by his display of faux indifference. And she knew him too well to lie to him. "Yes. Mr. Pedersen had an appointment with me about restructuring their company pension plan.''

"John Pedersen had an appointment with *you*?'' Wade's hazel eyes widened, and he made no attempt to hide his incredulity.

"I was assigned to the pension department when I

worked in Philadelphia, remember? It used to be my area of expertise." Dana gave a weak smile. "Not anymore, though. Thank heavens Quint gives me all kinds of other cases to handle. Makes my job much more interesting since the ins and outs of pensions can be—well, dull."

She shifted in her chair. The intensity of Wade's gaze was making her uncomfortable. This was not a subject she'd wanted to discuss with him. Given their positions in rival law firms, she probably *shouldn't* be discussing it with him. But stonewalling him felt all wrong.

"I've had several meetings with Pedersen, and we're on the verge of finalizing their new plan," she admitted.

"Congratulations, I think." Wade drummed his fingers on the table. "Interesting that Pedersen would seek you out. Not that I doubt your talent, but you aren't even a lawyer. If Pedersen was so keen on a new pension plan, Aunt Eve could've handled it. She has a respectable track record in almost every area of law."

"Oh, yes, your aunt Eve is respected by everybody," Dana was quick to agree. "I think she's terrific."

"Everybody thinks she's terrific. So why did Pedersen call Cormack's firm instead of Saxon Associates, who've always represented him and the Car Shoppe?"

"Because I'm a pension-paralegal-*wunderkind?*" Her smile invited him to share the joke on herself. When he didn't, she sighed. "Look, Saxon, there is no big conspiracy. All I did was talk pension plans with Mr. Pedersen."

"Which you didn't see fit to mention to me."

"No, I didn't see fit to mention it to you." She frowned at the accusation in his tone. "Don't try to send me on a guilt trip over this, Saxon. I won't go," she warned.

"Have no fear, Sheely. Guilt trips are journeys I do not take or send others on."

Wade was pleased that he sounded unconcerned, for he certainly wasn't. To his consternation, he found himself more disturbed by her loyal silence to her employer than Pedersen's possible defection from the Saxons' firm to the Cormacks.

"But you can hardly blame me for wanting to know more. For instance, did Pedersen talk to Quint, too? About things other than this new pension plan?" Wade feigned a nonchalant smile.

So did Dana. "I believe I heard them discussing the Eagles' quarterback controversy."

"You're cute when you're being evasive, Sheely. You know I mean *legal* things." He managed to sound downright jovial, which he was also far from feeling. Wade leaned forward, his eyes holding hers. "Is Pedersen planning to dump our firm and go with Cormack because Quint won the lawsuit against the Car Shoppe? Kind of a 'if-they-beat-me-they-must-be-great' mentality at work?"

"I honestly don't know." Dana broke their gaze, feeling guilty in spite of her vow not to. She wasn't buying his air of insouciance. Any lawyer with half a brain would be bothered by the possibility of an important client taking his business elsewhere, and Wade Saxon had a very sharp mind.

Though he rarely used it to full advantage, she mused. Wade had it all—looks, brains, charm, and money—but he was a classic underachiever. Things had always come so easily to him that he'd never developed either the will or the skill to apply himself wholeheartedly to anything. Unlike herself, who doggedly used both to succeed.

"How about taking an educated guess, Sheely? C'mon, spill. Is Pedersen going to bolt?"

The waitress arrived with their beers. Grateful for the interruption, Dana took several big gulps.

But the reprieve was only temporary.

"You're guzzling your beer, Sheely. A radical departure, since you're an expert in the art of nursing a drink," Wade said wryly. "And you keep dodging my questions. Makes me think that something really is up with Pedersen. Wait'll Rachel hears that." He wrapped his hands around his frosted beer mug, but left it in place on the table. "It won't be a pretty scene. She'll probably call for Cormack's head on a spike."

Dana shuddered and took another long swallow of beer. "Gee, I'm hungry. I hope those nachos get here soon."

"Real subtle change of subject, Sheely."

"It's the best I could do right now. No, wait, here's something better." She brightened a little. "Speaking of your cousin Rachel, you'll never guess who she spent the afternoon with."

"You're probably right, Sheely. I'll never guess who Rachel spent the afternoon with." To Dana's relief, he allowed her diversion to proceed. "I only know she left the office this morning and never returned."

"My sister Sarah called around one with the news that Rachel was baby-sitting Brady, Quint's baby boy. Rachel told Sarah she'd be glad to keep Brady for the rest of the day so Sarah took the afternoon off. She and Matt planned to drive down to the shore."

"I'm not even going to ask how Rachel ended up with Cormack's kid," Wade replied, deadpan.

Dana was all ready to tell him. "It's a long, convoluted story, involving a fire, a BB gun, and little Dustin Cormack and his dog being unaccounted for. He was thought to be inside the burning building, but was found eating cookies at an elderly widow's house down the street. Turns out the kindly old lady is hard of hearing and keeps her shades drawn, so she had no idea of all the commotion outside. She and Dustin and the dog were having a lovely visit. Meanwhile—"

"Sheely, have I ever told you that I hate long, convoluted stories, especially ones involving the Cormacks?"

"But—"

"Wow, look at that! Somebody actually got a hit in this game." Wade's attention was riveted to the TV screen, where a player was running to first base while the sparse crowd in the stands managed a few lackluster cheers. "It's a miracle."

"I get the hint. You'd rather watch a brain-numbing game than listen to my long, convoluted story."

"Your powers of perception are truly amazing, Sheely."

The waitress arrived with their nachos. Wade dug in. Dana merely stared at the plate, despite her earlier claim of hunger. Twisting her paper napkin with her fingers, she watched him eat.

"Sax, I—uh—have a little problem. . . . Well, I'm not sure if it's a problem or not. Would you mind if I ran it by you?"

His eyes never wavered from the ballgame. "If you feel you must."

"When Quint came back to the office shortly after two this afternoon I—didn't mention Sarah's call. I didn't tell him that Rachel has Brady. He still doesn't know." She worriedly chewed on her lower lip. "Do you think I should've said something to him?"

"Do I think you should've mentioned that his nanny dumped his kid on his worst enemy and then took off for the shore? That's a no-brainer, Sheely."

"You're no help at all, Saxon!"

He leaned back in his chair and fixed his gaze on her. "Let me make it easy for you, Sheely. If Sarah wasn't your little sister, would you have seen fit to mention it?"

"It's not like Rachel would hurt Brady or anything," argued Dana. "In fact, Sarah raved about how smart and understanding and kind Rachel was at the fire today. She said it really helped having a sane presence among the crazed Cormacks."

"I agree that the Cormacks are crazed. Quint seems to be the only one who isn't, but learning that Rachel—who always acts like a certified headcase around him herself— has his kid might activate a previously undetected lunatic gene. I predict trouble ahead, Sheely."

"Oh, shut up." Dana snatched the plate and pulled it closer to her. "And stop hogging all the nachos."

They sat in silence for a while, one that differed greatly from their usual companionable silences.

Dana was irritated that Wade had said exactly what she hadn't wanted to hear—that she should have told Quint his little Brady was with Rachel Saxon. Even more annoying, he'd cited the precise reason why she hadn't said a word—because Sarah was her sister who loved and needed her job as Brady Cormack's nanny. And dumping your toddler charge on your employer's enemy and then taking off for an afternoon at the shore was not stellar nanny behavior.

Dana had a sickening feeling that Quint was going to be very angry, just like Wade predicted. She glared at him. *Some friend!* Instead of trying to alleviate her anxiety, he'd deliberately made it worse!

Wade pretended to be watching the game on the oversize TV screen, but he kept casting furtive glances at his friend. Dana Sheely was one of his best friends. *Or so he'd believed,* amended that cynical lawyer's voice inside his head. As one of *her* best friends, he'd had no reservations discussing every aspect of the Pedersen case with her last year, yet she hadn't bothered to mention that John Pedersen had become a new client of Cormack and Son.

He didn't doubt for a moment that the Pedersens and their Car Shoppe were as good as gone as Saxon Associates' clients. Seeking pension advice from Cormack's firm would be the initial excuse; the notice that they were pulling the rest of their legal business from Saxon was the next inevitable step.

The vanquished Pedersen was eager to join forces with the victorious Cormack. It made sense in an alpha dog sort of way. Didn't everybody love a winner?

But Rachel wasn't going to see it that way. He was beginning to understand Rachel's consuming aversion to Quinton Cormack, Wade decided fiercely. He was getting damn sick of hearing that name himself.

And he heard it a lot these days, especially when in the company of any Sheely. Wade chugged his beer with all the finesse of a fraternity pledge determined to win a drinking contest. Hell, Cormack might as well be related to the Sheelys; he had certainly become an integral fixture in their lives. Dana was his paralegal, Sarah was his nanny, Shawn took care of his lawn, and Mr. and Mrs. Sheely—Bob and

Mary Jean—revered the man who so gainfully employed so many of their offspring.

Wade scowled. It was stupid, immature, and territorial, but he was jealous of Quinton Cormack's intrusion into the Sheely family. He considered the Sheelys *his* surrogate family. He'd discovered them years ago, back in high school, through his friendship with Tim, when they had both joined the town's soccer team league. Neither cared much for the game, but they'd become immediate, lasting buddies.

Wade, the only son of bankers Hobart and Kathryn, whose house was quiet as a tomb and as orderly and well run as a bank, had been stunned by the constant activity and noise level at the Sheely home. *They had ten kids!* Everything about the family astonished him, fascinated him, and drew him in. He liked the hectic spirit of life in an impossibly large family, the sibling warfare and loyalty, the never-a-dull-moment madness.

Tim, for his part, relished the privacy and quietude found in the Saxon home. He considered not having to share a bedroom to be earthly nirvana, he marveled that one could actually put an item down and still find it in place minutes, even hours or days later.

As students, the two boys had been as different as their families. Wade coasted through Lakeview Academy, putting forth as little effort as possible. He was accepted at Carbury College—like they had a choice about admitting him, with his uncle Whit a tenured professor there!—and graduated after four fun-filled but academically undistinguished years, then went on to an unrenowned law school for three more years of student socializing. He'd passed the bar exam on his first try and then signed on with the family firm. As with Carbury College, his connections were everything. Aunt Eve and Rachel had no choice about taking him as a junior partner.

Tim, on the other hand, that hardworking, super-achieving star of St. Philomena's, graduated first in his class and then headed to the Naval Academy, where he finished at the top of his class. Right after graduation, Tim married Lisa, a bright pretty naval cadet, who completed her service requirements and was now a full-time mom to their two small children.

Wade kept in contact with Tim, remaining friends over the years despite their disparate lifestyles. Tim was currently stationed at the U.S. Naval Submarine Base in New London, Connecticut, and Wade had visited him there. Naturally, Tim was a superlative officer, husband, and father.

Not wanting to lose touch with the Sheely family, Wade's friendship had gradually encompassed the other Sheely siblings, especially Dana. As adults, their personalities just clicked; for the past two years they'd been particularly good pals. There were times when Wade considered Dana more fun to be with than Tim ever had been, although he felt guilty for thinking that.

Now, sitting here in Riggin's, watching a dull Astros vs. Expos game, and reminiscing, Wade found himself longing for his old friend. Fun and laughs aside, he knew he could trust Tim completely. He slid another glance across the table. Until tonight, he probably would've said the same about Dana Sheely. But now, it seemed, her first priority was Quinton Cormack.

He tried to stem the spark of anger from flaring into full blaze. He should be cool, he shouldn't let it bother him. There was business and there was friendship, and it was ill-advised to confuse them, Wade reminded himself. *She* obviously had no difficulty keeping the two areas separate.

"How much longer are you going to sit there and sulk, Saxon?" Dana's voice shattered his frowning reverie. "Because it's getting boring, and if you're going to keep it up, I'm going home."

"I'm not sulking. And I'm sorry if you're bored, Sheely." Wade rallied with an evil grin. "It must be tough for you to hang out with ordinary mortals when you're accustomed to the sparkling wit and lively conversation provided by your actuary boyfriend Rich Vicker." Earnest, ever-serious Rich Vicker served as an endless source of entertainment to Wade. Making jokes about the guy was a surefire way to cheer himself up.

As Dana well knew. "Don't drag Rich into this," she issued a halfhearted warning.

"The thrills must be never-ending when he spouts those mortality table statistics." Wade was just getting started. "I bet the sound of his voice droning those numbers can inspire you to orgiastic heights, huh, Sheely?"

"Rich is very nice, very polite, and it's unkind of you to make fun of him," chided Dana. "After all, Saxon Associates uses him as an expert witness in cases, too."

"How long have you been dating Vicker, Sheely? A decade—or does it only seem that long? How do you stand it? I can barely make it through lunch with the guy without practically falling into a coma. And speaking of comas, have you been to bed with him yet?"

"As if I'd tell you!" Dana's cheeks flushed a soft pink. She hadn't come close to going to bed with Rich Vicker in the six months they'd been dating. Actually, it was only when Wade teased her about it that she gave sex with Rich any thought at all. Which probably meant something but she didn't care to ponder what.

She felt her lips curve into a smile. Wade's teasing was annoying but being one of ten kids, she knew how to take it and how to dish it out. And anything was better than his bout of sullen pouting.

"Who's your latest flame, Saxon? It's been—what?— two weeks since you dumped the debutante in Haddonfield, along with the mall chick from Deptford. You must have a new target in your sites."

"She's a *former* debutante, and it's been over three months since Olivia and I *mutually* decided to end our relationship, Sheely. Oh, and Carolyn manages a Limited Express at the Deptford mall and hardly qualifies as mall chick. We also had a mutual parting of the ways about the same time Olivia and I split."

"Mutual? That's not what I heard, Saxon. Word has it

that both Olivia and Carolyn were ready to pick out china patterns and you tucked tail and ran.''

"Can you blame me, Sheely? Think about it—china patterns! Does it get any worse than that?''

"Lots worse. There's not only china patterns, there are flatware and sheets and kitchen equipment. And then you have to register your choices in stores and look pleased when well-meaning friends give you that stuff as wedding gifts.''

"God!" Wade shuddered. "Stop terrorizing me, Sheely.''

"You'll be twenty-nine on Christmas Day, Saxon. Coming smack up against the big three-oh, just the age for a premature midlife crisis.'' Dana gave him a sweetly nasty smile. "My mom already sees it coming. She predicts it won't be long before you decide to take that long walk down the aisle with Miss Right. Just the other day Mom was saying how 'Wade would love to have a family of his own, like ours.' ''

"I love your mother dearly, Sheely, but she's slightly off her rocker. Having ten kids will do that to you, I guess. Or maybe that's how you end up with ten kids in the first place. No offense,'' he added hastily.

"None taken. I certainly don't intend to have ten kids, neither do my sisters and brothers. And I happen to disagree with Mom on the possibility of you settling down soon. I don't see it happening till deep into the next millennium.''

"You know me so well.''

"Well enough to know that, for you, three months between women is virtually unheard of. What gives, Saxon?''

"I don't know.'' He shrugged and stared moodily into his empty mug. "Lately, I just haven't felt like putting a lot of effort into dating.''

"Since when have you put *any* effort into dating? Your idea of a big night is renting a video and doing it on the couch. If she's really special, you might throw in a pizza first.''

Wade gaped at her, dumbfounded.

"No, I haven't been interviewing your dates, Saxon. Tim told me," she confessed gleefully. "He knows you best of all, and I pumped him for information the last time he was home for a visit. It's payback time for your relentless Rich Vicker remarks, Sax."

"Tim knew me when," Wade retorted. "He doesn't have a clue as to how I conduct my affairs as an adult."

"You're trying to claim that you've become suave?" Dana laughed at the notion. "When was the last time you took a date to the theater or to the symphony in Philadelphia, Saxon? For that matter, when was the last time you took a date to a restaurant that requires a tie? Or even to a first-run movie?"

"If a chick wants to do that stuff, she shouldn't be dating me," Wade growled.

"Hmm, maybe your breakups with the post-deb and nonmall chick really *were* mutual. The futility of owning china must've finally dawned on them as they ate pizza on a paper plate, one from your warehouse package of five hundred."

"You're enjoying this, aren't you?" Wade stared at her laughing face, her sparkling blue eyes. All the Sheelys had blue eyes, but hers were bigger and a deeper shade of blue than the rest. Truly striking eyes. "Portraying me as a cheap, sex-crazed Neanderthal?"

"Don't worry, I won't tell. Your next main squeeze can find out for herself. So who is she?"

"I have a date night tomorrow with Jennifer Payne," Wade admitted reluctantly. "She's—"

"I know who she is. Wow, Saxon! You're not only pushing thirty, you've started to rob the cradle. How stereotypical, how pathetic!"

"I'm not thirty and Jennifer Payne is not a kid. She—"

"Is only twenty-one years old, Saxon. She was in my sister Sarah's high-school class at St. Philomena's. She also happened to be my brother Shawn's date for his Senior Prom. We have the pictures in the family album if you'd care to check out her fifteen-year-old self."

"No thanks. But I am curious to know if Shawn got lucky and scored on prom night." Wade's leer was comically salacious.

"Nobody at St. Philomena's ever got lucky and scored, not during high school," Dana said flatly. "We were all too repressed."

"You're wrong there, Sheely. Tim and that girl he dated—what was her name, Bernadette something?—scored every weekend. Several times a night."

"Tim?" Dana nearly fell out of her chair. "My brother Tim? And—And Bernadette Colvin? You're kidding, of course." Her incredulity slowly began to fade. "It's just another one of your dumb jokes. Tim would've never—"

"I'm telling you, Tim did. As often as he could. We were best friends, remember? We used to go to the drugstore at the mall to buy condoms together. Tim kept his supply at my house, for obvious reasons."

Dana's jaw dropped again. "I—I just can't believe it." She looked shell-shocked.

"What's the big deal, Sheely?" Wade was exasperated. "Girls were throwing themselves at Tim all through high school, and he was a normal guy with the regular amount of hormones. Did you actually think Tim was a virgin when he and Lisa got married? Did you want him to be? C'mon, the guy's in the navy!"

"Do Mary Jo and Tricia know about this?" Stunned, Dana named the two sisters closest in age to her and Tim. Mary Jo was twenty-seven, Tricia, twenty-five, with Dana sandwiched between them.

"How should I know? Probably not, since you didn't. Tim isn't the sort of guy to regale his sisters with—uh—intimate details. Now will you stop looking at me that way, like a six-year-old who's just been told that the Easter Bunny doesn't exist."

Dana felt that way. "What about his marriage to Lisa? The two of them seem so perfect together, so happy. Is it just a facade? Is he—Does he—"

"Tim and Lisa are very happy together," Wade cut in

impatiently. "Why wouldn't they be? His earlier relationships with other women have made him even more appreciative of what they have together, Tim told me that himself. Jeez, Dana, don't tell me you think that a marriage is doomed unless the couple are both virgins on their wedding day!"

"I don't think that." She pushed back her chair and stood up, her thoughts hopelessly jumbled.

He'd called her "Dana," which he only used in front of her parents when he was in full Eddie Haskell mode. He thought she was hopelessly naive, a silly prude. Which, of course, she'd just proven herself to be. She'd given away more than that too, though he hadn't figured it out yet.

Her face flamed. She didn't want to be around him when he did. "I don't want any more beer. I'm going home."

Dana grabbed her purse and suit jacket and stalked out, leaving him to pay the check. She squinted against the bright sunlight, an almost-blinding contrast to Riggin's dim interior. And then she remembered that she didn't have her car. Wade had driven her here.

Abruptly, she turned around and marched back inside to the pay phone in the small vestibule. She was dialing Mary Jo's number when Wade came to stand beside her.

The answering machine picked up. "Hi," Mary Jo's voice chirped on the tape. "You have reached Mary Jo and Steve. Well, almost. We aren't here but please leave your name and number and we'll get back to you as soon as we can."

Dana hung up without leaving a message for her sister and brother-in-law.

"Guess they're not home from work yet," Wade observed. He lounged against the wall as she dialed Tricia's number. And listened to the voice on the answering machine announce that neither Tricia nor her three roommates were there.

"Going to try Shawn next? Good luck. He's impossible to get ahold of."

"I'm willing to try," Dana replied coolly. Shawn lived

at the Sheely home, as did she, but when she dialed, the number was busy. Of course. It was perpetually busy. The Sheelys had been one of the first families in Lakeview to install Call Waiting. Which didn't seem to be working.

Dana frowned at the receiver.

"Emily ignoring those persistent little clicks?" Wade asked. "She always does."

"I'm going to ask Mom to have another talk with Emily." Dana was disgusted. Fourteen-year-old Emily was the youngest and most talkative Sheely, and she actively resisted any technological attempts to interrupt her lengthy telephone conversations.

"Why don't I drive you home?" Wade suggested. "Unless you want to continue this exercise in futility? Because if you're dialing in birth order, Sarah is next on the list and we already know she's somewhere along the Jersey shore with Matt. Do you think they took Cormack's car or did they hand it over to Rachel, along with the baby?"

"There are times when I dislike you intensely, Saxon," Dana gritted through her teeth.

"I know. And this is one of them." He hooked his hand around the nape of her neck. "I'm sorry I shattered your illusions about your big brother. Let me make it up to you by driving you home."

She really had no other choice. Dana allowed him to steer her out of the bar to his car, trying to ignore the feel of his long, lean fingers on her neck. But heat crept along her nerve endings, sending a tiny shudder of awareness through her. Which she abruptly and firmly squelched.

After all, Wade touched her often, placing his hand on her shoulder or the small of her back to guide her in and out of places, reaching over to tuck a loose strand of hair behind her ear, laying the tips of his fingers on her forearm when he wanted to stress a particular point.

She was used to casual affection, Dana reminded herself. The Sheelys were one of those families who kissed hello and good-bye, who thought nothing of draping a loose arm around one another or linking hands or sitting close together on the always-crowded sofa to watch TV. No doubt Wade had picked up his habit of easy, informal touching from time spent with the Sheelys because the Saxons were not demonstrative.

Dana and Wade reached his car, and he glided his hand along the length of her back as he opened the door for her. Despite his cavalier attitude toward his dates, he had gentlemanly manners when he chose to exercise them.

Wade's dark green Mercedes—a special order from the Pedersen Car Shoppe—rolled smoothly out of the parking lot. Dana perused his collection of compact discs before selecting one that she had insisted he buy. Wade complained that the group was hopelessly commercial and derivative and didn't jibe with his sophisticated musical tastes; she knew he'd enjoyed the band's concert at the Spectrum when she had dragged him there last summer. Not that he would ever admit it.

He groaned as the familiar melody filled the car. "First, you cheap out on buying your round of beer and stick me for the entire cost of the nachos and now this. You're really gunning for me today, Sheely."

She was unrepentant. "You're a rich lawyer, Saxon. You can afford to pick up the entire tab from time to time. Oh, and if you plan on listening to music while you're in the car with Jennifer on your big date tomorrow, you'd better stop by Blockbuster and buy some of those dance-club mix CDs. Jennifer is really into that."

She knew how much he hated to dance and how he loathed dance-club mixes. His reaction was all she'd hoped for. He looked appalled. "Tell me you're joking, Sheely. Jennifer doesn't really—"

"Jennifer absolutely loves the dance-club scene. If you ask her where she wants to go tomorrow night, she'll say Club Koncrete, I guarantee it. You'll love Friday nights at Club Koncrete, Saxon," Dana taunted. "It's the place to be for the under twenty-five crowd. Sarah and Matt and Shawn are always talking about what a *radical* time they have there. You'll probably see them there, along with all the other kids their ages, dancing up a storm to the pulsing sounds of techno-pop.''

Wade gripped the steering wheel with such force that his fingers started to turn white. He and Sheely always kidded each other, but she was being particularly merciless tonight.

In fact, she was being downright cruel! Accusing him of being an aging swinger desperately seeking his lost youth. Cutting their evening together short. He'd planned to spend several more hours at Riggin's, maybe even buy dinner there, because he was tired of takeout food and nuking frozen meals in his microwave.

Wade glanced over at Dana, who was placidly listening to a song that always reminded him of her, and his slow burn grew hotter. He felt distrustful and ill-used. For as he reviewed her offenses of the day, her collusion with Quinton Cormack to pirate Pedersen from Saxon Associates returned sharply to the forefront of his mind.

He wondered how and when he should break that unwelcome news to Aunt Eve and Rachel. To say they were not going to be pleased was an understatement bordering on the absurd. He envisioned the approaching storm and longed to postpone it. Could he? Should he?

He had just turned the corner of the Sheelys' street when the loud, sharp blaring of a car horn startled him so much, he almost swerved onto the sidewalk.

"What the hell . . ."

"That was Brendan, in my car." Dana clutched her hand to her chest, her heartbeat thundering in her ears. They had come within inches of crashing into a telephone pole; she had eyeballed the wood grain. "He was just honking hello."

"Well, he almost got us killed," muttered Wade.

"No, your overreaction almost got us killed."

"Oh, sure, blame me! God forbid that one Sheely should ever speak against another one."

"You've got that right."

"Even if the Sheely in question happens to be in the wrong." Wade pulled his car in front of the Sheely house.

"As in the upcoming Sarah-Rachel-Cormack baby disaster," he added triumphantly.

He enjoyed the concern that flashed in her eyes. It was about time the Sheelys experienced the negative side of Quint Cormack! The Saxons certainly had—and with the Tilden will looming and Pedersen's departure, they were about to be Cormacked yet again.

On the front porch of the house, Katie Sheely sat on the wooden bench swing beside a skinny blond man with a scraggly goatee. The pair were engrossed in conversation, and Katie was gazing at the young man with rapt concentration; an expression Wade had never seen upon her face during office hours. He didn't think Katie was capable of playing close attention to anything or anyone; certainly she'd never displayed such ability at work. Yet there she sat, looking positively intelligent!

When he confided his observations to Dana, he expected her to share the humor. After all, she had laughed long and hard when he'd told her Saxon Associates was going to hire Katie as their new receptionist. She chuckled at the reports of Katie's continuing screwups, advising him that it wasn't as if he hadn't been warned, that employing the flighty Katie fell into the "no good deed goes unpunished" realm.

But there were no laughs or chuckles from her tonight. Not even the trace of a smile appeared. Dana's expression, already dark, turned thunderous.

"You might not have anything better to do tonight than to trash my family, but I don't have to stick around and listen." She opened the car door and sprang out. "Take your rotten mood and your premature midlife crisis and go home, Saxon!"

Wade took her insult square on the ego. "I am not having a premature midlife crisis." He attempted to sound cool and sardonic, but his voice shook with anger. "And if I'm in a rotten mood, it's because I've been with you, and you're in hormonal overdrive today. It must be that time of the month, huh, Sheely?"

He knew that was a cheap shot, he knew it would infuriate her, and it did. He was fully aware that women hated having their words and actions attributed to their monthly cycle, and Dana was no exception.

She slammed the car door shut and strode up the stone front walk to the house without looking back.

"Creep!" she called out as he zoomed away from the curb and down the street. "Smug, arrogant, sexist clod!" She felt like kicking something. Too bad Wade Saxon had taken himself out of her range.

"Hey, that's my boss you're insulting," Katie said cheerfully.

"Dude's got a helluva set of wheels," Katie's goateed friend opined.

"I never really appreciated until today how difficult working for the Saxons must be, Katie." Dana regarded her younger sister with newfound pity. "There is Rachel, a ticking time bomb of bad temper, and Wade, who is a shallow, egotistical, moody, cynical *pinhead*. Katie, you poor kid, you're definitely earning your money the hard way."

"It's not so bad." Katie smiled sunnily. "Wade and Rachel never yell at me, even if I screw up big-time. Sometimes I can tell I'm getting on their nerves, but they never say anything. Eve does though. When she's mad, you really know it, just like with Mom. I'm always glad when she's out of the office." She regarded Dana curiously. "What did Wade do that made you so mad, Dana?"

Dana glared at Wade's car, now merely a dark green dot in the distance. "What did he do? He—He just—He's—" Her face flushed as she lapsed into incoherence.

"Oh, wow!" Katie clasped her hands to her cheeks, her blue eyes round as saucers. "I think I know. It finally happened, didn't it? He finally made a move on you and—"

"Of course not!" exclaimed Dana. A pervasive tremor ran through her body at the very thought. "That's crazy! We're friends. L-Like brother and sister. You know that, Katie, everybody does."

"Everybody doesn't think so, Dana." Katie folded her arms in front of her chest and stared quizzically at her sister. "Tricia says you and Wade are lusting after each other and don't even know it yet."

Dana stood stock still. She couldn't move; she felt as if she'd been blindsided. *She and Wade lusting after each other?* No, never, not in a million years! And then, the sudden sharp memory of their little walk from Riggin's bar to Wade's car assailed her.

Dana struggled to keep her breathing in check as she remembered the feel of his hand around her nape, the brush of his fingers against her skin. Liquid heat surged through her. She pictured his mouth, focusing on an image of that full sensuous lower lip of his and for the first time ever, she wondered what it would be like to nibble on it. To taste him.

For the first time, she imagined the feel of his lips on hers. In her mind's eye she could see it happening, his head lowering to hers, his mouth moving closer and touching hers, gently, softly at first and then . . .

"That's the stupidest thing I've ever heard." Dana's voice rose to a breathless squeak, but she persevered. "The stupidest thing Tricia's ever said. In fact, it goes way beyond stupid, it's right up there in the pantheon of—of—" Her mind went blank.

"Uh, stupidity?" Katie's blond friend suggested helpfully.

"Yes!" snarled Dana.

"Oh." Katie shrugged. "So then what did he do?"

"What?" Dana stared at her, eyes glazed and uncomprehending.

"What did Wade do to make you so mad?" Katie pressed, a little impatiently.

"Nothing!" Dana flung open the front door. "He didn't do a thing. And I'm not mad!"

Katie and her friend exchanged glances. Their laughter followed Dana as she stomped into the house. It rang in her ears the whole way upstairs to her bedroom, which she used to share with Mary Jo and the traitorous Tricia. Now she had it all to herself.

The moment she closed the door behind her, she burst into tears.

5

Quint finished his dinner of fried eggs and bacon—his low cholesterol level was a physician's dream, eliminating any dietary restrictions—and stacked the dishes into the dishwasher. He glanced up at the kitchen clock, then at his watch, which confirmed the time on the clock.

It was a few minutes past seven, and the questions he'd managed to hold at bay broke through his wall of reasonable excuses. Where were Brady and Sarah? Why hadn't she called to inform him of their whereabouts, like she always did? Should he phone the Sheelys and ask if they were there?

Until now, he'd assured himself that they were. Sarah took Brady to her family's house for dinner several times a week and Quint used those days to work late, arriving home in time to put his son to bed.

The lack of the phone call today had nagged at him, but he hadn't permitted himself to dwell on it. He was a great believer in Occam's Razor, the scientific and philosophical rule which maintained that the simplest explanation was the most likely. Simple logic decreed that Sarah had taken Brady to the Sheelys, as usual.

However ... Quint purposefully steered his thoughts away from all those alarming *howevers*.

He'd never been prone to hysterical conjecture; that was Carla's province, she was the queen of it. Maybe that was why he'd been able to stifle his worrisome parental doubts

After the hours spent in Carla's company to-where hysterical conjecture ruled supreme—he wasn't about to succumb to more of the same.

But now it was past seven o'clock. Sarah never stayed with Brady at the Sheelys that late because his bedtime was seven-thirty, and a bath and bedtime story always preceded it. He could think of no simple logical explanation for their continued unexplained absence.

There were always those sickening exceptions to Occam's Razor, the gruesome stories that dominated the newscasts when the unthinkable actually did happen. One of those terrible exceptions had changed his life one night, the night his mother's and sister's lives had been ended.

Rigid and tense, he dialed the Sheelys' number. It was busy. Naturally. Quint heaved an exasperated sigh. Young Emily was ignoring Call Waiting again. He knew that Sarah circumvented Emily's own circumvention by calling the operator and claiming an emergency. On those grounds, the operator would break into the call, Sarah would lecture Emily and then deliver her message. Quint debated following suit.

He felt a cold chill run through him. This actually might be a dire emergency. Why hadn't the ever-dependable Sarah called? What if she and Brady weren't at the Sheelys? He knew that was the main reason he had delayed making the call to the Sheely home. Because he wasn't ready to cope with the possibility that the two weren't there, that nobody knew were they were.

The front doorbell sounded. Quint fought a fast growing fear. He knew from experience that state troopers made house calls if the news was bad enough.

He couldn't even hope it might be Sarah at the front door because she wouldn't ring the bell, she had a key. Anyway, she always used the kitchen door to enter the house because it was adjacent to the carport. He glanced through the window to see that the carport was still empty. The white Ford Taurus he'd bought for Sarah to drive Brady around in was nowhere in sight.

The bell rang again, and Quint decided to answer it, to put off making that call to the Sheelys. To gain a few moments respite before he had to face the unbearable . . .

He opened the door and found Rachel Saxon standing on the small cement porch. With Brady in her arms. Quint, rendered speechless by a breathtaking mix of relief and incredulity, could do nothing but stare mutely at the pair.

"Hi," Rachel said after a few silent moments. She sounded slightly breathless.

"Hi, Daddy." Brady's head was tucked into the curve of Rachel's shoulder, and he didn't lift it as he gave Quint a sleepy grin.

There was another moment or two of silence while the three of them watched each other.

"Hi," Quint finally managed a word. Was he hallucinating? *Rachel Saxon with Brady?* And this was a different Rachel Saxon than the one he was used to seeing.

She wore a pale yellow ribbed shirt that clung to her small breasts and a skirt of the same color in some gauzy material that swung loose and seductively around her legs. He could see their long, smooth outline beneath the material as she shifted her weight from one foot to the other, backlit by the setting sun. His eyes lowered to her slim feet, encased in sexy strappy sandals, her toenails painted a deep shade of pink.

He swallowed the saliva gathering in his mouth. God, he was practically drooling over her! He had found her attractive in her courtroom power suits and sensible shoes, but in these soft feminine clothes she was pretty much irresistible. And she was holding his son, who looked perfectly content in her arms.

Quint couldn't ever remember feeling so utterly confused. "Brady is with you," he said, in what had to be the winner in the Comment-Most-Deserving-The-Comeback-*Duh* Contest. If there were such a thing.

"You didn't know?" murmured Rachel.

At least she hadn't said Duh! "No, I didn't know where he was."

"Oh, I—I'm sorry." Rachel was nonplussed. Sarah hadn't told him? Was Quint going to consider baby-sitting to be baby-snatching, when done by her? They hadn't parted on the best of terms this morning. Actually, they'd never been close to being on anything other than bad terms.

Quint continued to stare, transfixed, as she cuddled Brady. The sight of his child in her arms seemed to be imprinting itself into every molecule of his being. Brady was safe and happy, and she was the most beautiful, appealing woman he'd ever seen, her expression tender, her wide hazel eyes soft with maternal warmth.

"Is Sarah back yet?" she asked at last.

"Sarah," he echoed. The name had a familiar ring.

"Sarah called Katie at the office to say she was stuck on the Garden State Parkway with a flat tire," said Rachel. "Matt was with her. Katie used Call Forwarding to connect her with me. Matt was changing the tire, and I told Sarah not to worry about the time. Brady and I were at my sister's house. We ended up eating dinner there."

She smiled at Brady, lifting one hand to smooth down his light, spiky hair. "You ate everything, didn't you, Brady? All your potatoes and chicken and carrots, and ice cream and cake."

"I eat it all up," Brady affirmed.

Quint wondered if what she was telling him was supposed to make sense. At least he'd recalled who Sarah and Matt and Katie were. That was a start.

"I pay with Snowy," Brady announced, snuggling closer to Rachel.

"I see," said Quint, who clearly didn't.

Rachel smiled, amusement momentarily displacing anxiety. She had never seen anyone look so befuddled. "I don't think you're following, Counselor."

"You're very perceptive," he said dryly.

"Snowy is my sister's little girl. She's three, and she and Brady played together today."

"And Snowy is short for what?" Quint was curious. It

struck him as a rather strange name. "Snowball? Snow-flake?"

"No, her given name is Snowy. My sister decided why not? After all, there are other names related to weather—Sunny, Skye, Rainie, Storm."

"Misty," added Quint. His dark eyes gleamed.

Rachel felt a queer little tingle of excitement flare through her, though she knew she should take offense at him for practically throwing down the gauntlet that was Misty Tilden. She cleared her throat. "About that will—"

"We pay Barbie, Daddy," Brady said importantly.

"What?" Quint's eyes widened. "Uh-oh."

Rachel couldn't help but laugh at his expression which was apprehension mixed with discomfiture. "Don't panic. Brady was very macho. He pulled the heads off every doll and then used the bodies as guns."

"Ah, so he is already reaping the rewards of his relationship with his uncles Austin and Dustin." Quint was sardonic. "I hope your niece wasn't too traumatized."

"Not a bit. Snowy was thrilled. Her parents are fervently antiweapon, and she hadn't realized how versatile Barbie can be."

"I think you'd better come in." Quint put his hand between her shoulder blades and gently but firmly propelled her forward, into the entrance hallway of the house. He reached for his son, but Brady tightened his small arms and legs around Rachel.

"That Mommy," Brady said.

Rachel blushed. Quint hadn't taken his eyes off her since she'd arrived with Brady, but now his gaze turned piercing and intense. She was acutely aware of the feel of his big, warm palm pressed against her back.

"Am I hearing correctly? Does Brady think you're his *mother?*" Quint growled.

"I don't think he thinks that," she murmured.

"That's what he called you. Mommy." Quint moved even closer to her.

Unlike this morning in his office, Rachel didn't try to

get away from him. He'd put his other hand on Brady's legs and she felt the warm strength of his fingers against her belly. She felt encircled by him, trapped. But she didn't attempt to escape.

Rachel offered herself an assortment of excuses why not: she had a baby in her arms and didn't want any sudden action to upset him, Quint wouldn't let her go anyway, it was childish to run.

Each one legitimate, yet paltry, she nervously admitted to herself. She also made herself face the true reason why she didn't move. Because she couldn't. She literally could not move. The physical sensations occurring in her body precluded any chance of flight. Her legs were trembling too much to walk; she felt sluggish, as if her blood had slowed to a turgid crawl through her veins. Maybe it had because her pulses were throbbing thickly, heavily, in her throat, in her chest, between her thighs . . .

"Explain, Rachel."

The deep sound of his voice made her shiver. The hard glint of something primal shone in his eyes. Not anger, but something far more dangerous.

Rachel gulped. "Some soccer moms were selling cookies at the mall, as a fund-raiser, and one of the women told Brady to ask Mommy if he could have a cookie."

She remembered Brady's thunderstruck expression as he followed the woman's gaze to Rachel. "Mommy?" he'd repeated uncertainly.

The woman had handed him a cookie, and Rachel watched comprehension dawn on the little boy's face. It occurred to her then that she hadn't given Brady her name or any clue as to her identity. Sarah had plopped him into her arms, and off they'd gone.

He must have been wondering who she was, and now the mystery was solved; Rachel easily interpreted his tod-dler logic. Spending the day with Snowy and Laurel had cemented the word in his mind. Snowy called the dark-haired woman who looked a lot like Rachel Mommy. Obviously, Rachel was one of those mommy people too.

"He's using it as a generic word," she suggested, stroking the little boy's head. "Like 'lady' or 'caregiver'."

"Lady doesn't have the same connotation as Mommy," Quint pointed out. "He's never called anyone else 'Mommy.' He's never once called Sarah 'Mommy,' and she is his *caregiver*." They were standing so close, she was practically in his arms. The heat of sexual arousal burned through him fast and hard. "And why were you and Brady at the mall hobnobbing with cookie-selling soccer moms?"

"Good question." She fought a crazy impulse to lean into him.

It was becoming difficult to maintain her normally straight, upright posture when her body wanted to relax. Against him. To let him support her with his strength. He could do it easily. Rachel felt her eyelids grow heavy, her neck felt weak. She wanted to lay her head on his chest and close her eyes.

"Yeah, I'm noted for my aggressive cross-examinations. And if you don't want me to treat you like a hostile witness, then stop stalling and answer me."

The authoritative demand in his tone sent a shiver through her. It seemed that the more submissive she was, the more domineering he became. A very telling response.

Rachel knew what she must do and tried to kindle a much needed spark of spunk. She had to take charge and stand up for herself. Which was directly at odds with this overwhelming need to cuddle against him and let him hold her.

"Down, Mommy," Brady demanded, suddenly beginning to stir in her arms.

Rachel was loath to relinquish her little charge, but knew she had no other choice. She bent to set him on his feet.

"It's time for your bath, Brady," said Quint.

Brady immediately stopped squirming and regained a stranglehold grip on Rachel. "Mommy do it!"

"Yes," agreed Quint. "She will."

He slid his arm around Rachel's waist in an ironclad hold. When she straightened, she was even closer to him, their bodies aligned and touching. Rachel had to remind herself to breathe.

"You're not leaving here until he's in bed and I have all the facts," Quint warned. "And maybe not even then." His voice was low and husky against her ear.

Rachel's heart thumped. The situation called for her to rip his throat out for daring to issue such a threat—or at least to make some sort of protest. Even a simple "No" would suffice.

Instead she remained silent, and she knew as well as anybody that silence could be interpreted as compliance. She was too amazed by her uncharacteristic subjection to be alarmed. Where was the snarling retort she normally would've given *anyone* who dared to order her around?

And Quint's command had been more than an order, it bordered on a threat.

Except she didn't feel threatened. Not by what he said or implied. Not when he hustled her up the stairs, holding her against him, their shoulders pressing, their hips brushing against each other. Not even when he failed to release her at the top of the landing, after she put the wriggling Brady down.

The little boy raced toward the bathroom, hollering, "Bath" at the top of his lungs.

"You're going to get soaked. Brady splashes around in the tub like a killer whale trying to bust out of Sea World," Quint warned, smiling down at her.

That smile obliterated the little that was left of her emotional equilibrium. He kept his arm locked firmly around her, gently, slowly kneading the hollow of her waist, and the thought of stopping him never crossed Rachel's mind. His fingers were long, and he stretched them so the tips reached the curve of her hip, the soft swell of her stomach, and it felt so good. So very, very good.

Rachel felt something that had been dormant within her all her life stirring, blossoming, unleashing tendrils of heat that streaked through her. She could almost feel her common sense abandon her as if melted by the fiery, deliciously erotic sensations surging through her.

She had never felt this way before, and she didn't know how to fight against it. She didn't even know if she wanted to.

Quint used his other hand to turn her toward him, bringing her fully against the long hard length of his body. She leaned her forehead against his chest, feeling helpless and weak as he smoothed his hands over her in slow, sexually explicit caresses. As if of their own volition, her arms slipped around his waist and she held him.

He lowered his head to nibble sensuously along the graceful, almost painfully sensitive curve of her neck. "Not now," he whispered, nipping her skin with his teeth, then soothing it with his tongue.

She shivered and clung to him more tightly, arching her neck to give him greater access.

"Later, baby," he said raspily, and reluctantly but firmly removed himself from her embrace.

Rachel, who'd never been drunk in her life, experienced intoxication of a purely sexual kind. She couldn't have walked a straight line; she was so shaky, she could barely walk at all. Her head spun, but the dizziness was pleasurable. Exceedingly so.

Quint kept his arms around her, half-walking, half-carrying her toward the bathroom.

She had never been handled in such a proprietary manner, but instead of aversion, she felt exhilarated. And unnerved. How could Quint Cormack, of all men, make her feel this way? Even more disturbing, she strongly suspected that *only* Quint Cormack could make her feel this way.

They arrived on the threshold of the bathroom. Brady was ambitiously removing his clothes. He'd managed to discard his sunsuit, socks, and shoes but was tugging at the adhesive tabs of his disposable diaper.

"Off," he insisted.

"What on earth are you wearing, Brady?" Quint released Rachel to kneel in front of his son. "There are pink bunnies on this diaper."

Rachel swayed and propped herself against the door-jamb. Freed from the overpowering sensual effects of Quint's touch, she found herself able to think again, though it was slow going. Her thoughts were muddled and fuzzy, and she had to concentrate to string them together in a coherent fashion.

"I didn't have any diapers for him, so I used ones that belonged to my niece." Her voice was thick and quavering, and Rachel winced at the sound of it. "Snowy is potty-trained but Laurel, my sister, still had a box of diapers on hand."

"Brady's diapers have trains or planes or firetrucks printed on them," Quint grumbled as he pulled the offending diaper from the child.

"Bunny," Brady exclaimed, pointing to one of the adorable pink figures.

"Never again," promised Quint. He reached over and turned on the taps. Water rushed to fill the big white bathtub. "Barbie dolls and pink bunnies," he muttered under his breath. "Brady is a boy, Rachel."

"He is only two years old." Rachel looked from the toddler's childish form to his father, that all-masculine hunk of strength and muscle. It was impossible to believe that sweet, lovable little Brady would grow into a man like his father.

Rachel swallowed hard. Then again, maybe he wouldn't. There weren't too many men like his father around, or if there were, she hadn't been aware of them.

Her eyes grew larger and rounder as she stared at Quinton Cormack. She took notice of the breadth of his chest and the hard bare muscles of his arms revealed by his navy T-shirt.

Her gaze compulsively lowered to study the jeans he was wearing and the way the well-worn denim conformed to his powerful thighs. To the straining bulge pressing against the metal-buttoned fly. He made no attempt to conceal his erection, not even when he caught her gaping directly at it.

He arched his dark brows at her, but instead of triggering her temper—her usual reaction to that particular gesture—it sparked an entirely different response. A sharp piercing stab deep in her abdomen that she felt again and again.

"I said later." Quint read the hunger in her eyes and smiled a seductive promise. "After we bathe Brady and put him to bed. Come here," he ordered, moving to make room for her alongside the tub.

Rachel froze. Memories of her behavior in the hall a few minutes ago swamped her. She had been clingy and dependent and now he fully expected her to jump to his command.

And take her to bed? That was what he meant by "later," wasn't it?

She quivered. He had called her "baby," a term as sexist and condescending as "sweetie" which she'd expressly forbidden him to use earlier today. Except hearing him call her "baby" didn't infuriate her *as it should*. It made her feel sexy and desirable. Rachel was horrified.

What next? she wondered. Was she on the verge of turning into one of those addle-brained women who fantasized to gooey romantic songs? Who cried whenever the man in her life spoke sharply to her or ignored her? Her sister Laurel was like that, a romantic daydreamer whose state of mind at any given moment was dependent upon the whims of the man she loved.

Laurel had completely bought into their mother's belief that life for a woman without a man was useless misery, that men are stronger and smarter, and women should always acknowledge a man's superiority in all areas. Even if it wasn't true!

Rachel had rebelled against that doctrine early on. By third grade she'd discovered that her aunt Eve believed that women were equal to men in every way, that it was quite possible for a woman who had a man to lead a miserable life while an unattached woman could be blissfully happy on her own.

Rachel eagerly signed on for Aunt Eve's particular brand of feminism. She aspired to her aunt's cool independence and sharp tongue, she tried to emulate Eve's aura of confidence. She would not be a fool over some man!

She had been successful in her goals. Until tonight, when Quint Cormack single-handedly shattered her illusions about herself. Rachel did not feel so cool and sharp and confident right now. And she had a sinking feeling that she could be a world-class fool over Quint Cormack.

"I have to go. I—oh!" Rachel's voice ended with a gasp as Quint's arm snaked out and he fastened his fingers around her ankle.

"You promised Brady you would give him a bath," Quint reminded her. With his free arm, he scooped up the little boy and deposited him into the half-filled tub.

Brady squealed with delight and began to splash. A flotilla of toys were bobbing up and down in the water.

"You have the situation well in hand," Rachel said tersely. "Let me go."

"No."

The flat, unnegotiable reply inflamed her. "You can't keep me here!"

"You don't think so?" he challenged. "Just watch me."

Quint turned his attention to his son, soaping him with one hand, talking to him, listening to the two-year-old chatter, all the while imprisoning her with his manacle of a hand around her ankle.

For a few minutes Rachel was too stunned to react, let alone rebel. Never before had anyone physically restrained her! It was outrageous, unbelievable. She tried to imagine what Aunt Eve would do in this situation.

Press charges? However, she would have to escape first.

Rachel gave her leg a tentative tug. Quint's grip tightened. The harder she pulled, the tighter his hand clamped. It was like one of those dreadful Chinese cylinder puzzles Wade had tormented her with when they were kids. Driven mindless with rage, she would invariably try to yank her finger out of the straw tube which would only make the sides tighten more. Wade would howl with laughter while she shrieked with frustration.

Quint Cormack would undoubtedly behave the same way were she to resort to yanking and furious yells. Rachel glared balefully at him. How could the man who was so lovingly and competently tending to his child hold her prisoner like this?

"I can kick you with my other foot, you know," she threatened triumphantly, when the idea finally struck. "My sandal might not be as forceful as, say, a jackboot, but I can still inflict some damage."

Quint remained undaunted. "If you try it, you'll hit the ground hard because I'll pull this leg out from under you." He squeezed her ankle as he gave her a smug smile.

"Mommy, bath!" squealed Brady. He held up a plastic tugboat. "Boat. Pay boat."

"He wants you to play with the boat with him," Quint translated.

"I know. He communicates very well, and I have no trouble understanding him. I spent the day with him, remember?" Even to herself, she sounded like a prissy scold. Rachel winced.

"Come here, Rachel."

She told herself that this time he sounded as if he were making a reasonable request, not ordering her around. She reminded herself that she'd made a promise to little Brady, and she was not the type to disappoint small children. With Quint's hand still shackled around her ankle, Rachel inched her way to the edge of the tub and knelt beside him.

Quint immediately released her. She felt his hand glide over her, from her ankle to the nape of her neck, before he removed it. Rachel tried to ignore the glowing warmth that surged through her. She pretended to be oblivious to Quint's presence as she leaned over the tub and grasped a bright orange toy boat. She bumped it against Brady's red, white, and blue tug.

"Crash!" Rachel and Brady chorused together.

She laughed. She'd learned from watching him play today that Brady considered toy collisions hilarious and exciting.

At his demand, she played boat crash with him over and over and over again.

Quint watched them. "I'm curious as to how Sarah and my car ended up on the Garden State Parkway," he remarked after a while.

"With Matt and a flat," added Rachel. "Sorry. I've read so many Dr. Seuss books to the children today, I'm starting to talk like one. Actually, I have no idea how and why Sarah was where she was."

"She was where she was and is where she is," offered Quint.

"Uh-oh." Rachel felt strangely giddy. "Seems like talking in nonsense verse can be catching."

"Seems like. Are you ever going to tell me how you ended up with Brady? I don't think the two are unrelated."

It wasn't easy to carry on a conversation with Brady demanding most of their attention but Rachel and Quint managed to exchange some relevent facts. He hadn't heard about Sarah's intervention with Austin and the BB gun, but she already knew that Dustin and the dog had been found safe and sound at a neighbor's. Sarah had relayed that particular good news over the phone, courtesy of Call Forwarding.

Quint told Rachel that Carla and the two boys were now staying with Carla's mother and that though the fire, smoke, and water had caused significant damage to the Cormack house, it wasn't a total loss. He mentioned that Frank Cormack still hadn't been located.

"Dad told Carla he was going into the office today, but he never showed up," Quint's tone was neutral enough but his hard, cold expression spoke volumes. "It's anybody's guess as to where he is or where he's been, but his usual haunts have to be considered. Maybe he's at one of the casinos in Atlantic City. Maybe he's with a new girlfriend. Maybe he's hitting the sleaze palaces on Admiral Wilson Boulevard."

"Poor Carla," Rachel said quietly.

"Poor Austin and Dustin. Having Frank Cormack for a father isn't easy. Nobody knows that better than I do." Quint grimaced. "And his marriage to Carla has lasted longer than any of his previous ones so his influence on those kids is bound to be more pronounced and more pernicious. Of course, it doesn't help that Carla is so—" He broke off. He turned his full attention back to Brady.

Rachel was uncertain what to say. She knew Frank Cormack's reputation as a lawyer was poor indeed. The local bar association considered him something of a joke.

She hadn't known much about his personal life other than the basic facts known to everyone else in Lakeview. That he had married the much younger Carla Polk. That he had been struck while crossing the street by a drunk driver fourteen months ago and suffered devastating injuries, that he hadn't been expected to live but somehow pulled through. His son Quinton had arrived from somewhere out West to keep Frank's legal practice afloat while he recuperated.

Rachel remembered that Frank Cormack's accident hadn't generated much sympathy; rather it had been regarded with black humor in the area's legal circles. News of Quint's arrival in Lakeview initially was met with scorn. It was said that Cormack's law practice was on life support, just like he was, and it would be kinder to pull the plug on both.

Aunt Eve said it was typical of the luckless Frank to be run over by a drunk who was driving without a license or insurance, and who died penniless of cirrhosis of the liver a few months later. Frank Cormack's family had no savings, no insurance or no income, and were further burdened by a pile of medical bills. Their future had looked extremely bleak until Quint began to turn things around.

Slowly, but steadily, he'd built the law practice in Lakeview, gaining new cases with every win. His string of successes accelerated the growth of the firm's client base, boosting the income of Cormack and Son to an unprece-

dented level. Now there was the Tilden will. Considering
the potential for appeals in that case, Quint's fee could easily run into the high six figures.

And he would have to share the profits with his father,
Carla and the boys. Rachel's eyes flew to Quint's face. For
the first time she fully appreciated that he was not only
supporting himself and his child, but also an entire second
family. Frank Cormack certainly made no contribution. He
couldn't even be found when his own house was on fire.

As if feeling her stare, Quint turned his head toward her.
Their eyes met and held. Her chest felt oddly constricted
and her skin began to tingle as he focused his gaze intently
on her. He seemed to be drawing her out of herself, exerting
a power that made her body tighten with sexual tension so
potent she was helpless against it.

Fortunately, a torrent of water from Brady's latest collision between a squeaky frog and his beloved tugboat,
splashed her cheek and immediately broke the spell she was
fast falling under. Rachel was grateful for the reprieve.
Shakily, she rose to her feet. "I really have to—"

"You're turning into a wrinkled purple prune, Brady,"
Quint announced. "Time to get out." He flipped open the
drain, and the water swiftly began to recede.

Brady noticed. And couldn't bear for the fun to end.
"No, no, no! Bath, bath," he wailed.

"Spoilsport," Rachel murmured. As one who also didn't
appreciate Quint's absolute authority, she sympathized with
the toddler's frustration.

"The water was getting cold, Rachel," Quint pointed
out.

"Brady didn't mind. He was enjoying himself."

He wasn't now. Brady stood in the few inches of water
that remained, crying his heart out as shivers racked his
naked little body.

"Oh, poor Brady, you didn't want to get out, did you?"
Reflexively, Rachel took the towel that Quint handed her
and wrapped it around the two-year-old. She picked him
up, talking to him all the while.

"His room is this way," Quint said, and she followed him down the short hallway carrying Brady in her arms.

By the time they reached Brady's room, wallpapered with zoo animals in primary colors—Rachel guessed Quint had deemed them suitably masculine—the little boy had stopped crying and was eager to show her his toys.

Brady insisted that Mommy, not Daddy, dry him and dress him in his pajamas, which he chose from a drawer. "Choo-choo train," he said, pointing at the blue engines printed on the cotton.

Rachel glanced at the other pajama sets. "More trains and boats and planes. Not a single pink bunny in sight," she said dryly.

"Certainly not," said Quint. He was standing aside, watching them.

Although Rachel was very much aware of his intensely focused gaze upon her, Brady's presence diluted its effect. It was almost impossible to be sensually blitzkrieged while a toddler babbled incessantly as he dragged books and toys into the middle of the room for her inspection. Rachel dutifully admired each and every item.

"I hate to break up the party but it's past seven-thirty, and Brady is usually zonked by this time," Quint finally announced.

Rachel glanced at her watch. It was nearly eight o'clock and Brady's little voice was beginning to sound hoarse with fatigue. "Brady, do you want me to read you a story or Daddy to read you a story before you go to sleep?" she asked.

She'd learned from her interactions with Snowy that offering a choice to youngsters in this age group often precluded a temper tantrum. Very young children didn't seem to realize that another, unmentioned option existed—to reject both choices offered and keep on with the current activity.

Predictably, Brady fell for her ploy. "Mommy read," he commanded.

"Okay. What book do you want?"

Brady immediately rummaged through the pile of books to find a well-used copy of that old classic *Goodnight Moon.* Rachel smiled. It had been Snowy's bedtime favorite, too.

Quint flicked on a lamp made of alphabet blocks and turned off the overhead light. Rachel settled in the rocking chair with Brady on her lap and began to read. The text was so familiar to her she could recite it by memory. While she read, Quint quietly put the toys and books away and cleared a space for Brady in his crib, lining up his assortment of stuffed animal against the bars.

At the end of the story, Rachel glanced up and met Quint's eyes. He gave a swift, silent nod and she lifted Brady into the crib. The baby glanced sleepily around, then reached for a stuffed brown raccoon. And promptly tossed it out of the crib.

Quint grinned. "Brady runs a very exclusive place. Only TV and video stars are allowed in. That raccoon is an irritating pest who keeps trying to break into the club."

Rachel looked at the remaining toys in the crib. Every one of them was either a *Sesame Street* or a Disney character. She smiled, instantly disarmed by Quint's amusing perspective.

Quint picked up the cast-aside toy and placed it on the child-sized table in the corner. "Sarah and I keep trying to slip the raccoon in, to see if it'll get by him. So far, poor old Reject Raccoon gets the heave-ho every single time."

Rachel chuckled. "I guess not even little kids are immune to the power of celebrity. Night-night, Brady," she leaned down to kiss him. He smiled drowsily at her, already half-asleep.

Then it was Quint's turn to bend down and kiss his son good night.

" 'Night, Brady." Quint covered the child with a well-used pale blue blanket that looked as if it had been hauled many places for a very long time.

Rachel touched the satin edge of the blanket. Snowy had a beloved old blanket too, but hers was baby pink. A smile curved her lips. It appeared that pastel blue had somehow passed Quint's machismo test.

She watched the quiet moment between father and son, consumed by a melting tenderness. The emotional feelings evoked were as strong as the sexual ones Quint roused in her.

Before she had fully comprehended the enormous scope of their cojoined power, Quint had hooked his arm around her waist and walked her out of the room.

6

Quint pulled Brady's bedroom door closed behind them when they stepped into the hall. And before Rachel could move, think, or even breathe, she was pinned between Quint and the wall.

She raised her head and met his eyes, seeing the urgency and the passion that he made no attempt to conceal. His gaze held her captive as effectively as his body, which was hard and burgeoning with desire. He made no attempt to hide that either.

She must be getting conditioned to this, Rachel mused dazedly. Because instead of reacting with shock or outrage—certainly her expected response to such overt caveman tactics—she felt giddy with her own feminine power. Quint's arousal was directly related to his proximity to her; his lack of restraint evidenced a lack of control. Which was especially thrilling because she knew how controlled the man could be.

Not now, however. Not with her.

"There is something very familiar about this situation," she murmured huskily. "You've got me backed up against the wall again. Literally."

"And figuratively?"

"If you're referring to that phony Tilden will—"

"Which is very real." Quint's dark brown eyes were alight with amusement.

"Mmm-hmm. You can't even say that with a straight face, Quinton Cormack."

"Rachel, speaking as one attorney to another, at this particular moment I don't give a flying f—um—fig—about *anybody's* will."

"Coming from you, I think that's something of a compliment."

She raised her hands slowly. It wasn't until Quint caught her wrists and pinned them at shoulder height against the wall on either side of her that Rachel realized she hadn't intended to push him away. She'd been about to slide her arms around his neck.

That startling realization finally cleared her head. What was she thinking, to allow Quint to manhandle her this way? While joking about the fake Tilden will!

Her pride demanded a struggle. At the very least, a token one. She tried to pull her arms away but his steely grip didn't give even an inch. Having no luck there, she shifted her hips from side to side trying, not very successfully, to dislodge him. But her movements resulted in him settling more firmly between her thighs, which had parted during their little tussle. In addition, the motions of her body had only aroused him further. She could feel how much.

Quint groaned. Or maybe it was more of a moan. "You do it deliberately, don't you? You're determined to drive me crazy, you know exactly how to do it, and you won't quit until I've gone totally over the edge."

Rachel giggled, startling herself. She wasn't the giggly type, she never had been. But Quint's lamentations tickled her. He sounded so aggrieved!

She had to sternly remind herself that this was no laughing matter and that Quint had no cause for complaint. *She* was the one being pinned against the wall—and for the second time that day. *She* was the persecuted party here.

Although what she actually felt was as far from persecution as MTV was from PBS.

"You think it's funny, hmm?" Quint nuzzled her neck as he spoke, gently nipping and kissing between words. She felt him pull on her skin with his teeth, drawing it between his lips to suck.

Her breath burned against her throat, and she swallowed with difficulty. "N-No. It's not funny at all."

His erection pressed formidably against her and she rotated her hips in an erotic rhythm she hadn't even realized she knew. She was acutely aware of his strength—and fiercely turned on by it. The shackles of inhibitions and repression that she had maintained for years suddenly disintegrated, leaving her at the mercy of this breakout of desire and need. She didn't care about anything but this man and this moment.

Quint affectionately rubbed noses with her. "Aren't you going to tell me to stop?" he whispered.

Rachel gazed deeply into his eyes. She felt as if she were drowning in the dark depths. "No," she breathed the word. Her tongue felt thick in her mouth. Speaking required a concentrated effort.

"No?" His lips brushed hers lightly. "No, you don't want me to stop?" The tip of his tongue traced the shape of her lips, and she parted them in aching invitation. Which he did not take.

"Do you want me to keep going?" he murmured instead.

"So many questions!" Rachel moaned a protest. And the answers were all too obvious!

"Remember my obsession with accuracy and specificity?" His smile was warm and teasingly intimate and made her shiver with yearning.

His lips flirted with hers, tantalizing her with featherlight touches, but lifting out of reach whenever she raised her mouth for deeper, stronger contact. "I think you carry accuracy and specificity to ridiculous lengths," she complained.

"Don't whine, Rachel." He laughed softly.

"I was not whining!" Rachel was instantly indignant. "I have never whined in my entire life! I can't tell you how insulted I am that—"

"Shh, baby, I'm sorry. The last thing I want to do is

insult you." Grinning down at her, he freed her wrists. "I want to make you feel good, I don't want to make you mad at me."

He was teasing her, flirting with her, and Rachel felt the antagonism that should've restored her sanity and sent her on her way, dissolving like an ice-cream cone in the sun.

What made her so susceptible to his roguish brand of charm? Rachel wondered desperately. It didn't seem to matter that she found him irritating, even infuriating; mere moments later she would be completely disarmed by him.

"Does this feel good?" Quint carefully cupped her breasts with his hands.

Though he'd released her wrists, a dazed Rachel kept her arms flexed against the wall on either side of her. Instinctively, she pushed her breasts against his palms. He fondled the rounded softness, and she exhaled on a sigh. "Feeling good" seemed a pallid euphemism for this sensuous bliss.

Yet, it was not enough. Her nipples peaked and strained against her bra; they were taut and sensitive and needed soothing. She was close to begging him to touch her there when his thumbs finally caressed her, alternately making lazy circles and applying gentle pressure exactly where she wanted it, how she wanted it.

Rachel whimpered. He'd worked her into such a sensual frenzy that her whole body was shaking.

"Open your eyes, Rachel," Quint murmured against her ear. "Look at me."

Her eyelids opened slowly, and her limpid hazel eyes locked on his lips that were barely touching her own.

"Do you want me to kiss you?"

Rachel could not ever remember wanting to be kissed as badly as she did at this moment. She gave her head a faint nod.

"I didn't hear you," he whispered.

She expelled a tremulous breath. "Yes." The word was full of want and need, her voice soft with surrender.

He nibbled on her lower lip, then the upper one, and a tiny moan escaped from deep in her throat.

"Say my name, Rachel," he said hoarsely.

In an act of wanton boldness that would've scandalized her usual guarded, coolly reserved self, she slid her arms around his neck. "You talk too much, *Quint*."

"I should just shut up and kiss you?"

"Yes!"

His arms fully encircled her then, fitting her soft curves against the hard planes of his body, as his mouth closed fiercely over hers. She parted her lips on impact, and, when his tongue thrust inside, Rachel met it with her own to engage in an erotically intimate little duel.

Desire flooded her with an urgency she had never before experienced. Her skilled analytical, rational thought processes were incoherent and overwhelmed, but she didn't care. She didn't even notice.

Not when his wonderful hands so exquisitely caressed her breasts. Not when he was hard and thick between her legs, moving against her in a way that sent shock waves of pleasure jolting through her. Swollen and aching and wet, Rachel squirmed, wanting, needing so much more than he was giving her.

His hands lowered to clench her buttocks, his fingers squeezing hard. She rubbed against him provocatively, aware of the empty, achy void within her, experiencing a previously unknown craving to be filled. By him.

The barriers of their clothing were suddenly intolerable to her. Daring and desperate, Rachel tugged his shirt from the waistband of his jeans and slipped her hands under it, gliding her palms along his bare back. His skin was smooth and warm and slightly damp.

She felt as if she were losing herself in him, drowning in the scent and taste and feel of him. But instead of being threatened by his compelling virility, she felt empowered and euphoric.

I want him. Her whole body vibrated with the wild urgency of that admission. And jolted her back to her senses, like an electroshock altering errant brain waves. She tore her mouth from his and stared up at him.

Quint saw the glimmer of uncertainty in her eyes. And rebelled against it. "We both want this, Rachel," he asserted, with as much certitude as a lawyer arguing his case in front of the Supreme Court.

He dipped his mouth to resume his seduction of her neck, his moist little kisses already beginning to undermine her fledgling resolve. "And it feels wonderful, Rachel. It feels right."

She could hardly argue with that. Still, she tried to present a case for lucidity and restraint. "We shouldn't do this, Quint," she whispered weakly.

"Probably not, but we're going to anyway, aren't we?"

He claimed her mouth again, his body hard and tight, the blood fizzing hotly through his veins. He wanted her with a ferocious urgency that rocked him. She was so passionate, so responsive, a feminine sensual paradox who was both pliant and demanding.

He was already at the point where kissing wasn't enough and the clothing they were wearing was way too much. He wanted to carry her into his bedroom and undress her, to feel her bare skin under his hands, to touch her intimately. . . .

He raised his head slightly but kept his mouth so close to hers that she could feel his lips touch her own when he spoke, could feel his warm breath mingle with hers.

"I want to make love to you, Rachel. So much." His hands slipped under her cotton top, and he skimmed the smooth skin of her midriff with his fingertips. "Let me. Please."

Before she could reply, he added seductively, "Tell me that you want it, too. Let me hear you say it."

"You really do believe in validation every step of the way, don't you?" An unexpected surge of affection swept through her, further destabilizing her.

"Yes," said Quint.

He stared so intensely at her that she felt he was looking inside her, seeing her exposed and vulnerable, divining all the secret feelings that she'd always managed to keep hidden, even from herself.

"Yes," she repeated dazedly. Despite her considerable verbal skills in the courtroom, she was inexperienced and inarticulate in expressing need or desire. But Quint was watching her, and waiting.

"Say it, Rachel."

"I—I want—what you do," she managed to rasp.

Quint kissed her again, and Rachel responded with all the passion she'd kept locked deep within her for so long. Lost in a maelstrom of lust and longing, she couldn't remember why she'd ever tried to call a halt to things in the first place.

They were so intensely absorbed in each other that neither one heard the car pull into the carport, neither heard the kitchen door open and close or the footsteps on the stairs.

It wasn't until an awestruck voice exclaimed, "Wow! Don't you two ever come up for air?" that Rachel and Quint sprang apart, startled and shocked.

The descent from their private sensual universe to the real one, where a fascinated Sarah Sheely stood in the hall gaping at them, was swift and brutal.

Rachel gasped. Quint cursed. Both began to move slowly in opposite directions.

"Sorry to interrupt," Sarah said, though her tone was merrily unapologetic. "Don't worry, I'm not going to stick around and bug you. I'm on my way to my room and I'll put on the TV—and keep the sound up high." She gave a jovially conspiratorial thumbs-up and went on her way.

Silently, Quint and Rachel watched her open the door of the room next to Brady's and disappear inside.

"I have to go." Rachel's entire body was one flaming scarlet blush.

"Rachel, wait."

If he tried to talk her into staying, she would scream. Rachel walked away from him, quickly reaching the staircase and taking the steps two at a time to the ground floor.

But Quint moved even faster and easily caught up to her before she reached the front door. His hand closed around her upper arm.

Rachel prepared herself for a fight, she almost welcomed it. Frustration, embarrassment, and the powerful force of unslaked passion roared through her, seeking an outlet. A ferocious quarrel with Quint Cormack, *the cause of it all,* would serve nicely.

"I want to thank you for taking such good care of Brady today," Quint said quietly.

Rachel looked up at him, nonplussed and deflated. She knew at that moment he wasn't going to do or say anything to keep her with him tonight. Perversely, she was disappointed, though she knew she wouldn't have stayed.

He released her arm and she unconsciously rubbed the skin there. "If you want to see him again—" Quint paused, looking uncertain. "If you ever feel like visiting—" He took a deep breath and started over. "I just want you to know that you're welcome to visit Brady anytime, Rachel."

She nodded her head, not trusting herself to speak. She rushed to her car, blinking back the tears that were burning her eyes. Quint didn't follow her, but he remained standing in the open doorway. Rachel saw him watching her as she got into her car and drove away.

The pent-up emotions she hadn't been able to release through lovemaking or fighting surged through her with tidal-wave force. Crying might provide some relief, but Rachel had never wept over a man, and she certainly wasn't about to turn lachrymose now.

To distract herself, she turned on the radio and hit the button set for a station featuring an all-talk format. An irate voice came blaring over the airwaves, immediately commanding her attention. Tonight's topic had something to do with a strange plan to resurrect the long-dead dirigible industry, beginning in Camden with two huge hangars that would build a pair of dirigibles every eighteen months and employ fifty thousand people. Most callers blasted the plan as either an insane pipe dream or a ridiculous scam, but a few were hopeful, citing the cottage industries that could be centered around dirigibles, for example, T-shirts and souvenir items of all kinds.

As Rachel had hoped, listening to the show was an ideal diversion. A dirigible factory? The urge to cry was replaced by sheer incredulity as the debate raged on.

"Look what I have for you, Katie." Wade placed a giant-sized chocolate chip muffin on the top of Katie's desk.

"My favorite!" Katie exclaimed eagerly. "And from Brunner's Bakery, too, my most favorite place!"

Wade was aware of that. He'd made a special trip this morning, driving several miles out of his way, to the bakery in Haddonfield to buy this muffin. He knew the younger Sheely siblings were quite receptive to bribery. He and Tim had done enough of it over the years—to buy silence, to gain privacy, to get information.

Information was what he was currently seeking.

Katie swung around in her chair and began to pull the wrapper from the muffin. The phone rang, and she answered it, only to instantly disconnect the caller. "They can call back later," she said airily. "I want to eat this while it's still warm."

Wade winced. When the phone rang again, he answered it and dealt with the caller himself while Katie ate her muffin.

"Dana was really upset when I dropped her off yesterday," he said casually, tucking the message he'd written into the pocket of his suitcoat.

"Yeah, she sure was mad," Katie agreed, chomping into the muffin. "And then I had to go open my big mouth and now she's ticked off at Tricia and Tricia is ready to kill me."

"Tricia?" Wade stifled a groan. He wasn't in the mood to follow Katie on one of her pointless flights of ideas. "Did Dana tell you why she was so angry?" he asked bluntly, trying to keep her on track.

"You don't know either?"

It seemed his bakery bribe had been a wasted effort. Katie was as in the dark about Dana as he was. Wade sighed his frustration.

"Looked like you were pretty mad, too—the way you peeled out of there at a hundred miles an hour! Man!" Katie sounded impressed.

"I did not 'peel out' *or* speed," Wade said tightly. Her admiration of what could only be described as juvenile behavior irritated him. "You must have me confused with your hotshot brother Brendan, who was doing both in Dana's car."

"Sure." Katie snickered. "Next you'll be saying you weren't mad either."

Wade walked to the window and gazed out at the lush lawn and towering trees in Lakeview Park, bordering the small man-made lake that had given the town its name. "By the time I got home yesterday, I couldn't remember exactly why I was so furious."

The admission alarmed him as much as this current scene he was trapped in—having a heart-to-heart talk with Katie who was scanning the entertainment section of the newspaper, more interested in celebrity gossip than anything he might say.

And yet he couldn't seem to stop talking. "I called your house last night—I actually got through in the five seconds between Emily's phone calls, and Anthony told me that Dana wouldn't talk to me."

It was still bothering him. Sixteen-year-old Anthony Sheely, currently caught up in a dark, brooding, alienated-artist phase had sounded as if he were relishing the melodrama and his own part as messenger. "Dana says she doesn't want to speak to you," Anthony had announced in theatrically resonant tones. "She says you know why."

Could she actually be holding a grudge? He couldn't remember the last time they had parted in anger. They'd always kidded each other, true, but neither took offense. Certainly not lasting offense.

"Well, just don't ask me what Tricia said because then

both Dana and Tricia would gang up on me," warned Katie. "And you'd probably be mad, too. So consider my lips zipped!"

"I don't care what Tricia said." Exasperated, Wade willed himself to be patient. He hitched a leg onto the corner of her desk and treated her to a buddy-to-buddy smile. "Katie, how close is Dana to Quint Cormack?"

Katie licked chocolate off her fingers. "He's her boss."

Wade's smile turned into a grimace. This was bordering on hopeless. "I *know* he's her boss but is she—are they—" His voice trailed off. Trying to subtly pump Katie for information was not working, but he wasn't sure how blatant he should go.

The possibility of Dana being involved with her boss had occurred to him last night and steadily nagged at him since. True, she was dating Rich Vicker, but he knew that relationship wasn't serious—maybe she was even using it in an attempt to make Cormack jealous?

Until last night, the idea of Dana having a clandestine affair with her boss—or anyone else—would've struck him as absurd. She was not secretive, especially not with him, her best pal Wade. But learning that she'd kept John Pedersen's appointments with the Cormack firm from him had altered his perceptions.

Dana was fully capable of keeping a secret from him. But why would she want to keep an affair with Cormack quiet?

As a longtime Sheely family satellite, the answer came to him immediately. If Dana and Cormack were having a fling, she would *never* want her parents to find out. Quint Cormack was divorced, and Bob and Mary Jean Sheely were as inflexible as the Pope himself on the issue of divorce.

Vaguely, then with growing clarity, Wade remembered the uproar a couple years back when Tricia Sheely had dated a divorced claims adjustor in the insurance agency where she worked.

"If you date someone who's divorced, it could lead to

marrying someone who's divorced, and that marriage could lead to excommunication,'' the older Sheelys had said. And shouted. While visiting Dana and the Sheelys during that period, he'd overheard her folks lecturing Tricia over the phone countless times.

Finally Tricia had stopped dating the guy, and only then was she back in her parents' good graces. No, a savvy offspring wouldn't want Ma and Pa Sheely to know anything at all about a relationship with a divorced person.

Did Dana think he would snitch to her parents if she confided in him? Wade felt hurt. Then he thought how much he loathed the idea of her with Quinton Cormack. Divorce had nothing to do with it, he assured himself; he simply hated that conniving, client-stealing weasel's guts. To his dismay, Wade realized that he was entirely capable of telling Bob and Mary Jean Sheely exactly what their darling daughter was up to. And with whom!

He watched Katie polish off the last crumbs of the muffin and daintily wipe her mouth. "Katie, would you know if Dana is—dating Quint Cormack?" he asked brusquely. He waited, stiff and tense, for her answer.

Which he couldn't quite interpret.

"Whoa, wait'll Tricia hears that!" Katie burst into laughter. "She won't be mad at me anymore, she—Oh hi, Rachel." The girl looked up and greeted a dour Rachel, who had entered the office and stood staring at them.

"Hey, Rach," murmured Wade unenthusiastically.

He recalled Dana telling him that his cousin had somehow ended up baby-sitting for Quint Cormack's child yesterday, but he decided not to mention it. Not with Rachel looking grimmer than the Grim Reaper on a pickup mission.

"Aren't you, like, roasting to death in that?" Katie asked, eyeing Rachel's dove gray turtleneck jersey that she wore under her navy pin-striped suit jacket. Katie was in a sleeveless chambray blouse and a demin miniskirt, in deference to the presummer heat.

"Rachel never sweats," Wade drawled. "She could

wear that outfit in a sauna, and she still wouldn't perspire.''

Rachel tugged the high cotton neck of her jersey even higher. "It's supposed to get cooler today," she arguedly weakly.

"Yeah, the temperature is supposed to plummet the whole way down to seventy-five," taunted Wade. "Brrr. Time to bring out the long-johns."

"There is no time for anyone to stand around and socialize!" Eve Saxon marched into the office like a five-star general reviewing a less-than-acceptable line of troops. "This is an office, not a chat room! Is it too much to expect the workday to begin with work? Is that a concept any of you can grasp?"

Katie jumped to attention. Wade and Rachel exchanged apprehensive glances. A day that began with a terse, tense Aunt Eve boded ill for everyone.

And Eve did look and sound terse and tense this morning, which was unusual. Eve Saxon almost always maintained her composure, saving her rare displays of emotion for the courtroom where they were calculated to have the intended effect on a judge or jury.

Her anxiety building, Rachel tried to guess what had caused her aunt to "blow her cool" as Katie would say. Something must be very wrong indeed.

After all, Aunt Eve had remained calm when Rachel lost the Pedersen case, although the verdict had galled her. And five months ago, though it hadn't pleased her, Eve had graciously endured the unwelcome fiftieth birthday bash her brothers and their wives had insisted upon hosting for her. Eve could easily pass for forty, even her late thirties. And she had, until that birthday party, indisputably revealed her age to all.

Rachel covertly studied her aunt, whose skin was smooth and unlined, her makeup artfully applied. An amber-colored rinse had gradually lightened her once-dark hair to conceal and blend with whatever gray had dared to appear. Her hair was cut in a short, chic style that flattered her classic features.

Rachel knew her aunt worked out in a gym at least four days a week, often more, and her body was firm and slim and shapely. The beautiful raspberry-colored suit she wore this morning accentuated her figure to designer perfection. Rachel admired the color and the fit of the suit. She would never dare wear raspberry or anything figure-enhancing for fear of appearing to be a nonserious bimbo, but Aunt Eve had the stately polish, and the age, to carry it off.

Rachel wanted to compliment Eve on her suit, which she hadn't seen before, but the icy glitter in the older woman's eye warned her that their aunt–niece roles had been supplanted by their partner–associate status.

And from the way Eve's eyes flicked over the trio in front of her, none of them passed muster. "Is there coffee in the conference room?" demanded Eve.

Katie nodded her head.

"Who made it?" Eve snapped. "You?"

"N-No, ma'am. Margaret did," Katie replied, naming one of the two Saxon Associate secretaries.

"Good. Rachel, Wade, come into the conference room with me right now. Katie"—Eve turned back to the girl—"We are not to be interrupted. Especially, not by you. Do you understand?"

"I won't come near you," Katie promised fervently.

The three Saxons entered the formal, finely appointed conference room at the end of the small corridor. Eve closed the door behind them and fairly raced to the coffee-pot, which stood on the antique cherrywood credenza. "God, this better not be decaf," she muttered.

"You know that Margaret is a traditionalist," Wade said lightly. "If it's not high-test, powered with caffeine, it's not worth making or drinking."

"I'm in full agreement with her today." Eve poured herself a cup and took a bracing swallow.

"Aunt Eve, maybe I'm going out on a limb here, but you're not your usual congenial self this morning." Wade flashed his winning, boyish smile, the one he'd perfected over the years, the one that never failed to charm its recipient.

It failed this morning. Eve glared at him. "A brilliant observation. How perceptive you are, Wade. If you applied such talents to your career, we might actually have a chance of winning a case around here. Let me amend that to include keeping our clients, too. Because the way things are going now, we might as well stand aside and watch our clients and our chances to win a case fly out the door while—"

"Aunt Eve, what's happened?" Rachel cut in, more than a little alarmed by her aunt's uncharacteristic tirade. She had seen Eve exasperated or irritated with Wade, but she'd never ripped into him like this.

"I was getting to that, but you interrupted me!" Eve turned her wrath on her niece. "Am I going to be allowed to finish, or do you intend to break in with more useless questions?"

"I apologize, I won't interrupt again," Rachel murmured, sliding into a chair.

Her aunt continued her diatribe and Rachel's spirits, already low after a confused, nearly sleepless night, sunk to a depth that made the pits seem like high altitude. Bad enough that she'd staggered into the bathroom this morning after the blast from her alarm clock made her feel as if she'd been shot in the head. Worse was to follow. She'd glanced in the mirror while brushing her teeth and nearly swallowed her toothbrush whole because on her neck . . .

Rachel blushed and drew her neck deeper into her shirt. On her neck was a sizable purple bruise, a bite mark, impossible not to notice, impossible to hide unless one resorted to a turtleneck jersey that was totally inappropriate for today's warm weather. She knew what the mark was, of course. She remembered the exact moment Quint Cormack had given it to her. A shiver went through her, and she could almost feel his teeth on her skin, sensually biting and sucking.

The erotic memory faded quickly in the harsh light of

day. She was humiliated, she looked like she'd had a run-in with Dracula last night. At the advanced age of twenty-eight she had her very first . . . Rachel cringed. She had never even said the word "hickey" aloud, and now she was sporting one.

Her first impulse was to march into Quint's office and show him the damage he'd inflicted. The prospect held a certain appeal, and the thought of seeing Quint made her jittery and giddy with anticipation. So jittery and giddy it scared her. She was acting like an infatuated schoolgirl! Of course she wouldn't go to Quint's office this morning; she would go to her own.

Which she did, arriving just in time to hear Wade ask Katie Sheely if her sister Dana was dating Quint Cormack. The mark of his passion on her neck had actually begun to throb like a painful wound as Rachel pictured Quint and Dana Sheely together. Kissing and touching the way—

"Have you heard a single word I've said, Rachel?" Eve's voice cut through her mournful reverie.

Rachel didn't bother to lie, she knew the truth was written on her blank face. Eve looked like she wanted to dismember both her niece and nephew, and while Rachel didn't really blame her, she couldn't help but wish her aunt had chosen any other morning but this one to regret taking her brothers' children into her highly successful practice. Her *previously* highly successful practice.

"With all due respect, Aunt Eve, you can't blame Rachel and me for Quint Cormack's arrival in Lakeview," Wade dared to interject.

"I can't blame you?" Eve's hazel eyes flashed fury. "Why is that, because you two refuse to accept any responsibility for Cormack's success? Well, you should! Instead of assuming he was an imbecile, as incompetent as his father, you two should have been watching him—and I don't mean watching him accumulate clients and win cases! You two should have been building your own practices, like he's been doing. Instead, you simply sat back and waited for the right kind of clients to come to you!"

"Aunt Eve, are you saying that Rachel and I should have befriended that lap dancer Misty while she was married to Town Senior like Quint Cormack obviously did?" Wade exploded.

Unlike Rachel, he had been listening to his aunt while she ranted on about her phone call last night from Townsend Tilden Junior. The Tildens wanted to meet with Misty's attorney immediately to discuss an out-of-court settlement. They had decided paying the little slut a few grand would be worth being spared the aggravation of a court fight over a bogus will—though they fully expected to win, should there be one. Just as they fully expected Misty to jump at their offer for some quick cash.

But when Eve had called Quinton Cormack at his home last night, he'd informed her that he would not discuss the case with her, that she could call him in the morning at his office and set up an appointment for some time next week. By that act of insolence, he'd made it clear that he was not going to cooperate, and Eve knew how enraged the Tildens would be if this dreadful matter was not quickly and conveniently resolved.

"What I am trying to tell you is that our position with the Tildens has become extremely tentative in a very short time." Eve made an attempt to calm down, though her flushed face and trembling hands didn't attest to much success.

"As you both know, Tilden Industries has their own legal department. Town hinted broadly that he would consider turning the family's personal business—*which Saxon Associates have always handled!*—over to the company's lawyers if probating this will turns into the kind of protracted mess we know Quinton Cormack is capable of creating!" Eve gave the table a quick dramatic pound with her fist.

Rachel flinched and touched the spot on her neck, concealed by the thick cotton. Was that what Quint had been doing last night when he kissed her and touched her and come within a hairbreadth of getting her into bed? Creating a mess? Messing with her mind by making her feel things she'd never felt before, hunger for something she'd never known?

Wade gulped down his cup of coffee, though it was so hot he feared his esophagus was singed. He thought of Dana's secret pension rendezous with John Pedersen and what it ultimately meant for Saxon Associates. One look at Aunt Eve's wild-eyed expression and Rachel's pained one, and he knew he didn't have the heart or the nerve to break that news to them. Not at this dismal moment in time.

He slumped in his seat, wishing he could discuss this latest disturbing development with his best friend. But she might be sleeping with the enemy, which made her his enemy, too. The thought was so unbearable he felt his stomach lurch and turn queasy.

"You look like two of the saddest sacks I've ever seen!" Eve's attempt at calm was over; she was revving up for another round of rage. "Where is your fighting spirit? Are you just going to give up and give in? If so, then this is not the place for you, it's certainly not the profession for you! Wade, why don't you resign and go join your parents in that nice quiet bank? Rachel, why don't you quit and get married like your sister, to a paternalistic man who will make sure you don't use any of your brain cells to think for yourself? Just stop wasting my time and my office space!"

Eve stormed from the conference room, slamming the door behind her.

Rachel and Wade lifted their heads and their eyes connected.

"Work in a bank? Ouch!" Wade's lips curved into a wry half smile. "Ole Aunt Eve sure knows where to stick the knife. There is nothing that bores me more than banking."

"That crack she made about Laurel's husband was entirely uncalled for." Rachel felt her anger knot in a ball in her chest. "I admit I had my doubts about Gerald myself in the beginning, but he's been a good husband to Laurel and a wonderful father to Snowy.''

''Aunt Eve's still incensed that Professor Gerald Lynton is way closer to her own age than to Laurel's.'' Wade guffawed. ''He's forty-three, Laurel's twenty-three, Aunt Eve is fifty. You do the math.''

Rachel's lips twitched. ''I think you're actually trying to cheer me up in your own weird way. These really are desperate times!''

Wade instantly sobered. ''Rach, you have no idea how desperate.''

7

"Your Honor, there is no need to send deputies to the Doll House Gentleman's Club. The club is closed," Quint reported to Judge Leonard C. Jackson.

"According to testimony, it was open for business last Tuesday," countered the judge.

"Yes, Your Honor. But it closed Wednesday and remains closed," said Quint.

His client, portly, oily Eddie Aiken stood beside him, nodding his head vigorously. Doing his best to appear like the law-abiding businessman Quint had portrayed him to be. Never mind that his business was the sleazy Doll House strip club which had been embroiled in an unending zoning fight with the township of Oak Shade since before Quint's arrival in Lakeview.

Aiken had been one of Quint's first clients in New Jersey. When Quint won an appeal to overturn a lower court's ruling and have the Doll House reopened, Aiken sung his praises and referred his friends. Aiken had some strange friends, but they paid their legal fees up front and in cash, and Quint had been in no position to turn away any cases. Not with a child to support and a worthless, irresponsible jerk of a father with a young wife and kids whose financial welfare he had turned over to Quint.

"Your client reopened that place in defiance of an injuction issued by this court last fall," growled Judge Jackson.

"Yes, Your Honor. And he has voluntarily closed it in deference to your ruling. Which, I respectfully add, we have appealed."

Quint didn't blame the judge for heaving an exasperated sigh. The nude dancers' gyrations might have ceased but the legal maneuvers continued, and would for months. Maybe years. Quint glanced across the small courtroom and met the eyes of the opposing counsel, Judith Bernard, the attorney for the township.

She looked bored. "We request that Your Honor schedule a hearing on civil contempt charges against the Doll House." Ms. Bernard pronounced the name with disdain. "Mr. Aiken has proven time and again that he has no intention of obeying the injunction to close the club while the zoning hearings are going on. And his attorney is adept at using judicial gambits to prolong this matter into—"

Quint objected. And then, somewhat to his surprise, the judge refused to schedule a contempt of court hearing.

"The club is currently closed," Judge Jackson pointed out. "And the Oak Shade police will check for future violations. Arrests will be made on-site if the club defies this court and reopens. Consider yourself forewarned, Mr. Aiken."

"Yes sir, Your Honor!" Aiken exclaimed. The case was dismissed, and Aiken grabbed Quint's hand and pumped it enthusiastically. "No contempt hearing! Way to go, Quint. So, what's next?"

"I've already refiled to appeal the latest injunction to Superior Court, but it'll take a while to get a hearing date," Quint explained. "Meanwhile, it would be helpful to the case if you keep the place closed till then, Eddie."

Aiken didn't bother to reply. At least, he hadn't made any false promises; Quint gave him credit for that. The Doll House would probably be open again for business this weekend. The only question was, would the police bother to check?

Probably not, guessed Quint. The Doll House employed some brutish bouncers who kept the clientele in line. There had never been any trouble there, which was not the case for many Oak Shade nightspots. The small police force had their hands full with too many other rowdy bars to spend time where there was no fighting, shootings, or selling alcohol to minors. In the past, the police didn't take action against the club until a sizable number of complaints were lodged by those citizens opposed to the Doll House's existence. Odds were, there would be no raids for a while.

Aiken knew it and gleefully raced from the courtroom. Quint gathered his papers together, placed them in his briefcase, and exited, joining Judith Bernard outside the courtroom.

"I saw you touch Aiken's hand. You'd better wash up with antibacterial soap," she advised.

"I half expected him to give the judge the Boy Scout salute during his 'Yes sir, Your Honor' spiel." Quint frowned. "How come cases—and clients—like these are always the money trains, Judi?"

"And why did we hop on board?" Judith grimaced and shook her head. "Well, for me, it's two kids in college and tuition bills coming in regularly. For you, it's your baby and the other little Cormacks."

"Aiken was so thrilled that there was no contempt hearing. Doesn't he realize that you and I get paid no matter what happens?" Quint didn't even try to combat the wave of cynicism rolling through him. "That we don't care what happens?"

"Speak for yourself. Places like the Doll House make me nauseated," said Judith. "I'd be thrilled to see that trashy dump closed permanently, although you're certainly right about the string of court dates. Win or lose, the more of them there are, the more we are paid for our—services."

"And you wouldn't mind too much if the Doll House is history *after* Bill Junior and Monica have graduated from Princeton?" Quint's eyes gleamed.

"Maybe not too much—but you never heard me say that."

"Never." They strolled side by side to the entrance.

"Listen, Judi, I just want to thank you again for last night," Quint said quietly. "If it would've been up to me, I'd've left Frank to sleep it off in jail, but Carla was hysterical. For you to go to Night Court and arrange his bail was—"

"Believe me, I agree with you," Judith interrupted him. "Frank has no incentive to change unless he hits rock bottom and with Carla harassing you to keep bailing him out— literally—well, the lesson just doesn't get learned."

"Frank will never learn, Judi," Quint said bitterly. "All the marriages, all the kids, and he is still carrying on like a bratty teenager who's never met a responsibility he hasn't ducked."

"He has a good son in you, Quint. I hate to think what would become of Frank and Carla's two little boys if you weren't there to provide some stability and support. Have you talked to either Carla or Frank this morning? Have you decided what—"

"Quinton Cormack." Eve Saxon's stentorian tones suddenly sounded through the courthouse corridors. She approached the two attorneys, her stride brisk, her expression thunderous.

"She looks capable of slitting throats," Judith whispered, startled. "Yours, in particular, Quint."

"If she does, offer to represent her, Judi. Gotta keep those kids of yours in their preppy plaids, y'know."

Eve joined them, acknowledging Judith with a brisk hello and a tight-lipped smile. She didn't bother with such forced pleasantries when she turned to Quint. "I want it understood right now that I will not be subjected to your mind games, Cormack."

"I might understand, if I knew what you are talking about." Quint hoped he didn't sound too glib, though the temptation was there. He really didn't want to offend Rachel's aunt, despite the provocation.

"I don't care to discuss this in front of a witness," snapped Eve. "You know very well what I mean." She glanced at her watch. "I have to be in court. Consider yourself forewarned!" She stalked off.

"Didn't the judge say that to Aiken?" Quint said dryly. "Something of a low-impact threat, I'm afraid."

"I've never seen Eve Saxon so unglued." Judith stared thoughtfully. "I guess it would be unprofessional of me to ask what's going on?"

"Let's just say that one of my clients—who would never get in the door of Saxon Associates—is at odds with Ms. Saxon's most revered clients."

"Revered clients—the Tildens!" Judith guessed at once. "My God, Quint, tell me that you aren't representing the Child Widow in a challenge to Town Senior's will!"

"I am Misty Tilden's attorney," Quint admitted. "And we aren't going to challenge the will because the late Mr. Tilden drew up a new will, quite favorable to his devoted young wife."

"A new Tilden will! What fun!" Judith was amused. "But I can only imagine how much the Tildens hate it, and that means the Saxons are not happy either. Thus, the mind-games charge."

"Which isn't true, Judi. I'm simply representing my client, not deliberately jerking the Saxons around. I don't want to feud with either the Tildens or the Saxons."

Especially not Rachel. Quint thought of Rachel and the sweet way she'd treated Brady. He felt a slow flush of color creep from his neck to his cheekbones. She had been sweet with him, too. So sweetly responsive, so sweetly passionate in his arms.

He was getting hard just thinking about her! He'd spent the night in that uncomfortable condition, his desire for Rachel even overcoming the downer news that had followed her departure.

First, there was the histrionic phone call from Carla telling him that Frank was in jail in Trenton, picked up for DWI. He'd wanted Frank to stay there—it wasn't as if his father had never spent a night or two drunk in a cell before—but Carla had been adamant. She wanted her husband home, she *needed* him. She'd been screaming, and Quint could hear his little brothers bawling in the background.

"Please get Daddy out of jail, Quint," Dustin had sobbed into the phone, while Quint seethed at Carla for using her sons to manipulate him. Because it worked.

Those poor kids! What a horrible day they'd had—their house on fire, moving into their grandmother's cramped house, their mother's hysteria, and now this—their old man arrested. Reluctantly, he'd called his friend and colleague Judith Bernard, whose office was in nearby Haddonfield.

While he'd stood in his basement office, debating whether or not to pour himself a stiff shot of Irish whiskey, the phone had rung again, and this time it had been Eve Saxon. Demanding that he agree immediately to a laughable out-of-court settlement for Misty Tilden. Quint had assessed the situation at once—the Tildens were aggressively pulling the strings of their attorney-puppet, and a panicky Eve Saxon was dancing to their command.

He might've worked up some sympathy for her predicament—he would rather be retained by Misty than the arrogant, self-important Tilden clan any day—but Eve's superior attitude irked him. She'd made no effort to conceal her utter contempt for both him and Misty. Clearly, she had relegated them both to the human refuse heap, and then been indignant and astonished when he refused to continue talking with her.

By the looks of Miss Eve Saxon this morning—she did project a certain cutthroat aura—she had been stoking her fury all night long.

Quint wondered if she'd told Rachel about the call and his refusal to cave to the Tildens' stupid and totally unrealistic demands. He wondered what Rachel was thinking right now. Was she regretting their hot little interlude and vowing never to go near him again? Would she include Brady in her ban?

The little boy had been chattering about "Mommy" this morning as he ate his cereal while watching his favorite Bananas in Pajamas video. Sarah had given Quint a most eloquent glance but hadn't said a word. Sarah had promised him last night that she wouldn't mention what she'd seen in the hall to anyone, and apparently she extended her promise to include even him.

"Well, you've obviously come up with a strategy," Judith's voice drew him back to the present. "I can almost see those wheels turning in your head."

"Yeah, just call me RoboLawyer."

"I assume there will be an out-of-court settlement, but what a spectacle it would be to see you and Little Orphan Misty go up against the Tildens and Eve Saxon in court."

"If the case goes to court, I'll win it, Judi."

"I don't doubt that. The Pedersen case springs to mind. You seem to have a talent for taking down Lakeview icons."

"Ah, Pedersen's not such a bad guy when you get to know him," Quint murmured, feeling awkward.

John Pedersen wanted to switch law firms, from Saxon to Cormack, and until last night Quint had been thrilled by the prospect. Until last night, he hadn't had to gauge the effect of that particular news upon Rachel Saxon. It did not take a great analytic mind to know how badly she would take Pedersen's defection.

"Not a bad guy?" Judith laughed. "You won a huge settlement for your client by convincing a jury that John Pedersen was Hitler incarnate running a car dealership."

"It was nothing personal." Quint shrugged uncomfortably. He could hardly bad-mouth his new client with another attorney. "All in a day's work, Judi, you know that."

Judith made no comment, but he guessed she figured that something was up. They said their good-byes and went their separate ways.

"Dana, I am so sorry to call you at the office," Rich Vicker apologized over the phone. "But I had to get in touch with you about tonight, and I can never reach you at home. The line always seems to be busy."

"That would be my little sister Emily." Dana heard the distant rumbling of a commuter train and braced herself for the noise and vibrations.

"I won't keep you, I wouldn't want to get you into trouble with your boss." Rich was not joking. Taking personal calls at work was no laughing matter to him.

"I appreciate that, Rich." Inside her head, a smart-alecky voice was interjecting comments about everything Rich said, including his deadly earnest tone of voice. The sarcastic little voice sounded a lot like Wade Saxon's. Dana's lips tightened. Just because he was in her head did *not* mean she was lusting after him, no matter what Tricia might say.

"So when Tony and Walt from my office suggested we join them and their wives and try the new Bangladeshi restaurant that's opened in Cherry Hill, I told them that we would," Rich said just as the train arrived to shake the entire building. "I hope that's okay with you, Dana. If there is somewhere else you'd rather go tonight—"

"No, that's fine, Rich," Dana assured him. Trying out a new restaurant sounded age-appropriate and mature, unlike the pitifully juvenile evening Wade Saxon would be spending with his young date. "I've never had Bangladeshi cuisine."

"I think we're in for another gastronomical adventure."

"Yes, we are," agreed Dana.

Thankfully, her parents stocked their medicine cabinet with every antacid currently on the market. Her last gastronomic adventure with Rich had been to a newly opened restaurant featuring native dishes from a country called Tajikistan. Dana had raided her parents' supply of digestive aids immediately after dining there.

"I'll pick you up at seven," said Rich, and Dana knew that he would be there at seven sharp. Not a minute before or a minute after.

"You can set your clock by Rich Vicker," her father had said more than once to Wade when they were sitting around the kitchen table having dessert and coffee. He and Wade would share a manly chuckle while her mother extolled the advantages of timeliness. But Mom always looked like she was suppressing a grin.

For a horrifying second or two, Dana wondered if her

parents knew about Tricia's ridiculous theory about her and Wade.

Impossible, she decided. Her folks made it clear in many ways that they still considered Wade more Tim's friend than Dana's.

"Mrs. Polk is here to see you, Quint," announced Helen, Cormack and Son's receptionist/secretary.

Quint and Dana, who were working together on a brief in a case involving the collision of two rented jet skis, looked at each other and grimaced slightly.

"Carla's mother?" Dana asked.

"Don't reach for your earplugs just yet," Quint said drolly. Carla's mother could shriek as loud and as long as her daughter and frequently did. "This is yet another Polk relation, a cousin from north Jersey. They needed a lawyer, and the Polks recommended me."

"Not Frank?"

"They made it clear they didn't want Frank. I think this is a personal injury suit. Maybe you'll want to sit in?"

"Definitely." Dana smiled. "When you deliver an absolute do-it-or-die order, you always phrase it as a question."

"You're a quick study, Dana. Kind of impudent but insightful, nonetheless."

Quint rose and left his office to greet his new client. His previous legal dealings with other Polks didn't leave him eager for more, but he couldn't say no to a quasi relative. And he'd generally had good outcomes in the Polk cases he'd handled. So far he'd gotten Carla's sister's bad-check charges reduced to a summary offense and a fine, had disorderly conduct charges against her older brother dropped, and convinced the district attorney's office to agree to ADR for a younger Polk cousin accused of petty larceny.

Though his area of expertise was civil litigation, his experience in criminal law had been via the Lakeview Polks, who'd provided on-the-job training.

So Marcia Polk was a surprise. Soft-spoken, almost to

the point of being inaudible, she told Quint and Dana about her husband's accident. Last month, on the first Sunday in April, Ken Polk, an airline mechanic and avid outdoorsman, was fishing in a rowboat on a lake owned by North Jersey Power for some of its hydroelectric business ventures.

"Was fishing permitted or was your husband trespassing?" Quint asked.

"It was permitted and always has been." Marcia's voice was little more than a whisper. "Everybody swims and fishes and boats on the lake."

"Which means the company is liable," Quint said to Dana, who nodded her agreeal.

"Not according to them." Marcia's eyes filled with tears. "They said they won't even help pay our medical bills. Ken is—Ken can't—" She paused and breathed deeply, struggling for control.

"Tell us what happened to Ken, Marcia," Quint said gently.

"We'd had a lot of rain the week that Ken and Tyler went fishing, and the level of the lake was up, higher than normal, though neither Ken and Tyler paid much mind," Marcia related the story as if by rote. "They didn't notice that the water level brought them closer to the high-tension wires that crossed the lake. When Ken stood up to cast his fishing rod—it was made out of some kind of metal, composite metal—"

Marcia Polk reached into her purse, pulled out a small packet of tissues, and wiped the silent tears streaming down her cheeks. Quint and Dana exchanged glances.

"Did your husband's fishing pole touch the high-tension wire, Mrs. Polk?" asked Dana.

Marcia nodded her head. "Ken almost died. His fishing rod touched the wire and he was electrocuted. He's still in the hospital and will be for months. For the first two weeks, the doctors didn't expect him to live. He was so badly burned the doctors couldn't save his hands and feet; they had to amputate them to save his life."

Quint drew a sharp intake of breath. "And your son witnessed the accident?"

"Thank God Tyler was there! He rowed the boat back to shore and called 911 on our car phone. He'd learned CPR in school and when he—he couldn't find a pulse, he gave Ken CPR. The paramedics say that Tyler saved Ken's life," she added, her eyes welling up again.

Dana's did, too. "You must be very proud of your son, Mrs. Polk."

"Yes," murmured Marcia. "And Ken and I aren't looking to cash in on this accident. We have to adjust and go on with our lives, we all feel lucky that Ken isn't dead. But—But Jack, Ken's cousin, said we should talk to you because—well, because we're having trouble with the insurance company. They think North Jersey Power should pay—"

"Which they should," Quint interjected, and Dana nodded vigorously. "And they will."

Marcia swallowed hard. "But North Jersey Power says it's Ken's own fault he was injured because he should have noticed the position of the high-tension wires in relation to the water level. They say he was negligent and so they aren't responsible."

"The standard party line," Quint muttered. "Please go on, Mrs. Polk."

"Our health insurance doesn't cover all the hospital bills, and the doctors say Ken won't be able to work again. They're right, of course. How can he be a mechanic, how can he work on airplanes, with no hands or feet?"

Dana flinched. Quint stood up and crossed the office to take Marcia Polk's hands in his own. "I want to represent your husband in this case. I guarantee we will win a settlement that will eliminate your financial worries and allow you and your husband and family to live comfortably."

Marcia looked relieved, then troubled. "We don't want to be greedy," she said worriedly. "We aren't looking to—to stick it to anybody. I—I mean, I know that things happen and—"

"I understand," Quint cut in. "Now I want you to promise me that you will not even think about hospital bills or insurance companies or the North Jersey Power Company. That is going to be my job. I want you to focus your time and attention and energy solely on your husband and family, and on yourself, Mrs. Polk. You're under tremendous stress, and you have to take care of yourself so you can be strong for your family."

Marcia began to cry. She stood up and hugged Quint, who held her, patting her back gently. "I've been so scared," she sobbed. "And to have to worry about money while Ken is so badly hurt has been—"

"A nightmare," Quint finished for her. "Consider the financial part of that nightmare over. Dana and I will begin working on this case right away. From now on, don't talk to any representative from anywhere, refer them all to me."

Quint and Dana walked Marcia Polk to her car and waved good-bye as she drove away.

"How could North Jersey Power be so heartless?" Dana marveled. "Telling a man with those kind of injuries, 'tough luck, it's your own fault'?"

"Imagine how that would sound to a jury! The company's tactlessness, much less their stupidity, is mind-boggling."

"Marcia Polk is a nice, quiet woman, and when she said the family doesn't want to be greedy and isn't looking to stick it to anybody, those corporate jackals immediately decided they'd stick it to her." Dana was indignant. "I'm so glad she's got us on her side, Quint. Think this will ever get to trial?"

"Nobody could be that stupid. North Jersey Power will settle out of court, though we'll probably have to play some hardball."

"Don't they realize they could get killed on the punitive damages alone?" exclaimed Dana.

"If they don't, they will after we've talked to them. Dana, can you drive up to the hospital this weekend and get copies of Ken Polk's medical records? Meet Ken and reassure Marcia, talk to the doctors and nurses. I'd do it myself, but Sarah is off this weekend and I don't want to ask Carla to baby-sit for Brady.''

"I'd be glad to, Quint. I had nothing to do this weekend anyway, and I want to help the Polks.''

"And maybe stick it to the corporate jackals?'' Quint parried lightly.

"Maybe a little of that, too.''

"Where are you two headed tonight?'' Quint asked Matt and Sarah as the couple clasped hands and sauntered to the kitchen door. Sarah had every Tuesday and Friday nights off, as well as every other weekend, leaving Quint in full charge of his son.

This evening, Sarah had abandoned her practical nanny clothes for an extremely short skirt, midriff-baring shirt, lots of earrings—were there five or six per ear?—and plenty of makeup. The effect was startling. She'd gone into her room a half hour ago looking young for her twenty-one years. Now she looked thirty-five, give or take a year.

Quint shifted little Brady in his arms and felt relieved he didn't have a daughter.

"We're doing our usual Friday night thing,'' Matt replied amiably. "Going out to eat and then meeting some friends at Club Koncrete. It's out on Route 70. That place really rocks.''

A portion of Route 70 ran through Oak Shade, Quint recalled. He hoped the rocking Club Koncrete wasn't anywhere near the Doll House. "Just be careful,'' he felt obliged to warn the pair.

"We will,'' Sarah assured him. "Are you and Brady going to McDonald's tonight?''

"McDonald's!'' Brady repeated excitedly.

"To him, it's gourmet fare served with toys he covets from TV commercials, plus a playground,'' drawled Quint.

"Hey, it doesn't get any better than that, huh, Brady?'' Matt grinned at the toddler. "Quint, is it okay if we take the Taurus? Is your car back from the dealership and running okay?''

''Yeah, it's fine. You two take the Taurus and keep it all weekend.'' Quint was impressed that Matt had asked to use the ''nanny'' car instead of assuming, and that he had remembered about the bothersome recall and expressed interest.

Matt was a good guy, he thought, not for the first time. Thoughtful, dependable. Not like himself at twenty-one, a self-centered, pleasure-seeking hell-raiser. His kid brothers flashed to mind and he tried to envision them at twenty-one. If only Austin and Dustin could grow up Matt-like. He thought about young Tyler Polk, who had saved his father's life by keeping a cool head and doing exactly what needed to be done.

How did parents raise sons that didn't screw up, not even as teens? Quint looked at Brady in his arms, and the answers to that question grew even more urgent.

Lost in thought, he followed Sarah and Matt to the carport to see them off. Sarah leaned over to kiss Brady. ''Bye-bye, Brady Bunch. Have fun with Daddy.''

''Bye, Sarah. Bye, Matt.'' Brady looked sad.

''Brady, why don't you and Daddy ask *Mommy* to go to McDonald's with you tonight?'' Sarah's blue eyes were alight with mischief.

''Mommy!'' A joyous smile wreathed Brady's little face. ''Mommy go!''

Quint felt himself turn a revealing, embarrassing color of crimson. ''That was low, Sarah.''

''Call her, Quint,'' Sarah advised. ''All she can say is no.''

''She can say plenty more than that,'' muttered Quint, thinking of Pedersen and the Tildens.

''Go for it, Quint.'' Matt gave him a bolstering pat on the back. ''I was nervous the first time I called Sarah, but I made myself do it. What if I'd just sat back and didn't make that call, huh? Think about it.''

God, they were giving him a pep talk! Quint was aghast.

Did they see him as callow as a middle-school kid trying to work up the nerve to call a girl for the first time in his life or an aged retiree who'd been without female companionship for decades? At the moment, he felt like a bit of both.

And now Brady had Mommy on his one-track mind. "Mommy, Mommy," he repeated, then demanded.

Sarah and Matt departed. "Call her," she leaned out the window to shout as they pulled away. "Brady's the perfect excuse."

Quint carried Brady into the house. He was going to do it, he realized. He was going to use his child to get next to a woman. He'd never before considered doing anything so manipulative, and the fact that Sarah had been the one to plant the idea in his head did not absolve him. He was guilty on all counts.

Appalled by his own actions even as he proceeded, he called directory assistance and got Rachel's phone number. That it wasn't unlisted seemed prescient, and he immediately dialed it. He put Brady on the phone whenever he heard Rachel's voice over the line.

"Say 'Hi, Mommy,' " Quint coached. He was a conniving, underhanded snake, and he braced himself to hear Rachel say so.

"Hi, Mommy!" Brady exclaimed.

"Brady!" To Quint's infinite relief, she sounded pleased to hear his son's voice. "Hi, Brady."

"Hi, Mommy," Brady repeated. Losing interest in the telephone, he spotted his toy truck across the room and began to struggle to get down.

Quint set the child on his feet and took over the conversation. "Hello, Rachel." There was a momentary silence. "You didn't really believe that Brady called you up on his own, did you?" He gave a slight laugh. "The kid is smart, but he's only two."

"It's not beyond the realm of possibility," Rachel said softly. "My niece knows how to speed-dial me."

"Smart little Snowy. Not to lessen her accomplishment, but your number must be programmed into their phone, Rachel."

Rachel knew the moment he said Snowy's name, thus proving he'd been listening and actually remembered their conversation last night, that she was going to accept whatever invitation he issued in Brady's name.

"Brady wants you to go to McDonald's for dinner with us." Quint cleared his throat. "I realize that isn't exactly a—"

"Tell Brady I'll have dinner with him." Rachel didn't let herself take the time to reconsider. She felt as if she were stepping off some metaphorical cliff. But she'd been so miserable all day, plagued between flashbacks of last night's passionate embrace and the haunting doubts set up by Wade's own suspicions. *"Katie, would you know if Dana is dating Quint Cormack?"*

"We'll be right over—if you'll give me directions to your place?" There was a smile in Quint's voice that had a profound effect on every one of her senses. Rachel shivered.

And gave him directions to her apartment.

8

―――――

"You take this for immediate, short-term relief." Bob
Sheely handed Dana two white tablets she was supposed to chew. "And this for slower-acting, extended hours
of relief." He gave her a small pill to take with water and
watched her consume the medication. "Bangladeshi restaurant, hmm?"

"The food is spicy. Very, very spicy." Dana turned to
her father. "Thanks, Dad."

"I guess Rich doesn't like places that serve things like
roast chicken or spaghetti," he mused.

"He likes gastronomical adventures, Dad."

"Must have a helluva digestive track," Bob Sheely said
thoughtfully. "He's one lucky guy. You can set your watch
by him, too."

Dana groaned aloud. "I think I'll go to my room and
read for a while, Dad."

The doorbell rang and moments later, they heard Mary
Jean Sheely exclaim in delight, "Wade! You must have
ESP. We got a letter today from Tim and Lisa and they
sent along the latest pictures of the children. I know you'll
want to see them."

"Yes, definitely, I'd love to see them," said Wade.

Dana sneered. *He probably thought he sounded charming, not smarmy. Ha!*

And then, Wade's voice again, "Is Dana here?"

She caught her father's arm. "Dad, trap him with the

133

pictures while I sneak upstairs," she whispered urgently.

"You don't want to see him?" Her father looked surprised.

"No, I—I'm sick of him, Dad. He's a pest. If he wants to hang out with a Sheely, it can be Tricia. Or Katie or Emily or one of the boys. Anybody else but me."

She heard her parents proudly regaling him with the latest photos of their grandchildren as she crept up the stairs and took refuge in her room. She turned on her CD player and reached for her book, *Bergin on Personal Injury Litigation,* a classic in its field.

She could still hear the faint sound of voices, so she turned the volume higher and determinedly studied the chapter on the trials of burn cases.

Her powers of concentration had always been first-rate and she was so engrossed in the theory of derivative liability that she jumped when a knock sounded on her door. Before she could call either "Come in" or "Go away" to whichever sibling was out there, the door opened.

And it wasn't a Sheely, but Wade Saxon who stepped into her room.

She gasped and sat up, dropping the book to the floor. "What are you—"

"I'm a *pest?*" Wade was indignant. "I should hang out with Emily or Anthony or Brendan?"

Dana blushed. "I can't believe Dad told you that," she muttered grimly.

"I can't believe you said it. I don't understand why." He crossed the room and sat down on the edge of her bed. "What's going on with you, Sheely?"

Dana immediately scooted over to the other side of the bed and tucked her legs under her. She was wearing a pair of plaid boxers and one of her oldest T-shirts with a faded Carbury College logo on the front. A long-ago reject of Wade's.

She'd scrubbed off all her makeup, pulled her hair back into a short ponytail, and knew she looked Emily's age—except Emily invariably tried to glam herself up to look older. Then she remembered that she didn't give a damn what she looked like around Wade—or she shouldn't. She hadn't until yesterday, but hearing that comment of Tricia's had upended her entire world, and she still hadn't figured what to do about it.

"Get out of my room, Saxon." To Dana's relief, she sounded normal. Grouchy, but normal. "Mom and Dad—"

"Sent me up to see you. Your mother is stunned that you consider me a pest and your dad just looked confused. So, are you going to tell me why you've suddenly decided that I make you sick?"

Dana frowned. Her father had quoted her a bit too accurately, the traitor! One small positive note was that if her parents had sent him up to her bedroom, they definitely hadn't heard Tricia's supposition about lust.

Her parents did not permit bedroom visits by the opposite sex to bedrooms, no matter what the hour, a rule high-schoolers Brendan, Anthony, and Emily were forever howling about. They claimed they wanted to listen to music with mixed groups of friends in their rooms after school, that this was perfectly innocent and allowed by every parent in the United States with the unreasonable exception of the Sheelys. The response remained a firm "No!"

"I thought you knew all the answers to everything, Saxon." Dana scowled at him. "So you'd better leave while you're still alive 'cause I might kill you in a PMS frenzy and even get acquitted. A hormonal defense actually works with some juries."

"Okay, I apologize for the PMS jokes," Wade gritted through his teeth. "Now, can we just forget it and move on?"

"Fine. Whatever. Now go home. I have some reading to do. Dammit, where's my book?"

Wade picked up the book from the floor and leafed through it. "Personal injury suit, hmm?"

She nodded. "I'm driving up to Sagertown in north Jersey tomorrow and visiting our new client in the hospital."

"Cormack is such a slave driver he makes you work on weekends?" Wade's teasing grin invited one from her, which Dana was on the verge of giving. Until his face abruptly turned cold. "Is *he* driving up there with you to visit your client?"

"Aren't you carrying professional rivalry a bit too far?" Dana shot back. "I know John Pedersen's decision to use Cormack and Son for his new pension plan bothers you— and maybe rightly so—but there is no reason for you to expect every personal injury suit in New Jersey to be taken to Saxon Associates."

"Like I give a damn about Cormack and Son's new personal injury suit!"

"You would, if you knew how big this one is going to be!"

"What were you saying about professional rivalry, Sheely? Seems to me that you're the one afflicted with a walloping case of it."

"I have to admit, it did kind of sound that way." Dana smiled reluctantly. "It's just that Quint and I really like our client, it's a truly worthwhile case, and how often does that happen?"

"I'm sure that according to the acclaimed Quinton Cormack, every case he takes is truly worthwhile. I bet he'll manage to convince you that Misty the Lap Dancer deserves every penny of the Tilden fortune."

"*Former* lap dancer, and she isn't getting every penny of the Tilden fortune, just what Town Senior willed her. Don't waste your sympathy on the Tildens, Saxon. Each one of them has their own trust fund and a big fat salary from Tilden Industries, even if they don't work for the company."

"You've done your homework on the Tildens." Wade frowned thoughtfully. "Which means that Cormack has, too."

"Believe it, Saxon."

"Rachel thinks this new will Misty's come up with is bogus. She and Aunt Eve are both certain that Cormack is bluffing, that it's all a ploy to get the Tildens to agree to an out-of-court settlement to avoid tying up the—''

"Saxon, why would Quint draw up a bogus will?" Dana interrupted incredulously. "That happens to be fraud and it's illegal. We paralegals learned that early on, but maybe you missed the class on deceptive practices and the consequences thereof in law school?"

"I was there for the class, Sheely. But maybe your boss wasn't."

"Quint plays by the rules, and he's not about to jeopardize his career for Misty Tilden or anybody else." Dana regarded him with a mixture of concern and impatience. "The will is valid, Wade. I *know* it is, because Quint included me in on it every step of the way. He wanted me to learn how to draw up an ironclad will, and that it is. You'd better convince Rachel and your aunt, or they're going to end up looking like idiots in court."

"You called me Wade." He appeared thunderstruck.

Her cheeks pinked. "I had to get your attention somehow. I'm trying to make a very crucial point about the legitimacy of that will. Have you finally gotten it?"

"God!" Wade leaned back against the headboard and stretched his legs along the length of the bed. "Do you know how much I didn't want to hear that, Sheely? As if this entire day hasn't been bad enough, now I get you swearing that Misty has a bona fide case. Please be honest, are you trying to psych me out like Quint's doing to Rachel and Aunt Eve?"

"I wouldn't try to psych you out, Saxon," Dana said quietly. "Our friendship predates my job, remember?"

"Yeah, it does." Impulsively, he reached over and caught her hand in his. "And I appreciate the warning, Sheel. It didn't seem very likely to me that Cormack would come up with a faux will, but Rachel and Aunt Eve are so adamant about it, I just went along."

Dana carefully removed her hand from his and got off the bed, walking to stand by the window at the other end of the room. She folded her arms in front of her chest,

acutely aware of her lack of a bra. Her eyes swept over
Wade lying on her bed in his striped sport shirt that emphasized his muscular arms and khaki trousers that accentuated his narrow hips, his flat belly, and long legs.

Suddenly, she felt as if her whole body was on fire, her
skin burning with heat, rivers of flames licking deep within
her. Beneath her shirt, she felt her nipples harden into taut
beads that poked against the worn cotton. The stimulation
was almost painfully intense. She closed her eyes and
turned her back to him, wanting to cry out a protest.

No, it couldn't be true!

But she knew it was. She was lusting for Wade Saxon,
fully aware of what she was feeling, unable to deny it.

"Hey, Sheely, listen to this."

She could tell by the nonchalant tone of his voice that
he did not feel the same way she did. When she turned her
head slightly to steal a peek at him, she could see for herself
that he didn't. He was staring at the ceiling, his arms pil-
lowing his head, blathering on about his cousin and his aunt
and that wretched Tilden will.

No, he was completely unaware that she was aroused and
aching for him to touch her. For one brief moment, she
wondered what he would do if she were to climb on top of
him and kiss him senseless. It was a satisfying bit of fantasy, but she knew it would stay a fantasy.

Furious tears pricked her eyes. If Tricia was correct and
Wade really was subliminally lusting for her, he remained
completely oblivious to it. And being introspectively challenged, he always would. Dana visualized her future, endlessly playing her customary role of sister-pal, listening to
him alternately rave and complain about the current women
in his life, while she suffered with this syrupy melting
warmth that made her yearn to touch him, to feel him
touching her . . .

The current women in his life. Dana suddenly remembered his date tonight with Jennifer Payne. "What are you
doing here, Saxon?" she demanded, turning on him like a
virago. "Where's Jennifer? Why aren't you—"

"Sheely, have mercy!" He held up his hand, as if to physically ward off her words. "I told you I've had a thoroughly abominable day, and now you throw Jennifer 'let's-go-to-Club-Koncrete-and-dance-to-the-radical-music' Payne at me?"

"You went to Club Koncrete?" The notion was diverting.

"Go ahead, rub it in. You warned me, I should've listened to you and broken the date. Idiot that I am, I didn't."

"The date didn't go well?" Dana didn't even try not to sound delighted.

"That smile of yours is chilling and cruel, Sheely. No, the date didn't go well! From the moment Jennifer hopped into the car, she insisted that Club Koncrete was the only place to be on a Friday night. Then she checked out my CDs and wasn't quite so perky. I think she started asking herself how she'd ever ended up in a car with a guy who listened to Tony Bennett."

"Poor Jennifer."

"Sheely, your sympathy is misplaced. I'm the victim here. I had to suffer through the longest hour of my life in techno-hell. The alleged music they play there is made on computers and electronic gadgets instead of—God forbid—conventional musical intruments. All these blue-and-white lights kept flashing—you've heard of 'blinded by the light'? Well, that place could cause permanent retinal damage. I think there's a potential *gold mine* of a personal injury suit just waiting to happen there."

"Did you dance?"

He leaped off the bed and crossed the room in just a few aggressive strides. "Now you've gone too far, Sheely."

She laughed, dodging him by adeptly sidestepping him, and the more she laughed and kept slipping out of his reach, the stronger his competitive instincts grew until he couldn't have simply given up and ceded her victory.

"You're doing some pretty tricky dance steps now, Saxon." Dana teased, still moving, still laughing. "Too bad Jennifer isn't here to appreciate your moves."

"Laugh while you dare, Sheely. Because—" He seized both her wrists and held them fast, bringing an end to her strategic retreat. "Because—"

He forgot to continue. He was suddenly struck by the provocative proximity of their bodies. His eyes sought hers and instantly, the lighthearted atmosphere in the room changed, turning heavy and thick with tension. Too late, Wade realized that not only his competitive instincts had been roused.

Feeling half-dazed, he studied her face, the white porcelain smoothness of her complexion, the subtle, classically lovely features. Especially her mouth. Somehow, he'd never noticed how beautifully shaped and temptingly sensual her lips were.

His eyes collided with hers again, and he waited for her to look away. To his surprise, she held his gaze. He spied apprehension there that mirrored his own, but he also saw something else reflected in the steady blue warmth of her eyes. Affection, curiosity, and . . . excitement.

Unresolved sexual tension vibrated fiercely between them. Neither moved or even tried to.

"Is that what this is all about?" he whispered, awed.

"I—don't know what you're trying to say, Saxon." She could guess but didn't dare. Not if there was a chance she could be wrong.

"Have you ever wondered what it would be like . . . between us?"

That note of wonder was still in his voice, and Dana smiled slightly. It was so obvious that he hadn't considered the possibility at all, until just a moment ago. Of course, she wasn't exactly eligible for any prizes in self-awareness herself. Until Katie had quoted the Tricia Doctrine yesterday, she'd been as clueless as Wade.

And she was still too uncertain of him to offer much encouragement. "I might be a little curious," she hedged.

"A little curious," he echoed. It seemed safe enough to admit, though he was experienced enough to know that this little game they were playing—if that's what it was—was as far from safe as he'd ever been.

"One kiss?" he asked silkily. "Just one, to see what it might be like?"

She didn't know what to say, if her answer should be yes or no. Her lips parted, but before she could speak she saw the way he was staring at her mouth, in utter fascination, and she couldn't say a single word. Instead, she gave her head a brief half nod.

Finally, slowly, they closed the small gap between them and their lips touched lightly in a chaste, almost experimental gesture. Wade heard his heartbeat thundering in his ears as he pulled back a little and stared down at her.

She was so small. He wondered vaguely why he'd never noticed how petite she was, barely five-three to his own six-foot height. She was delicate and small-boned and exceedingly feminine, and the realization floored him. His eyes drifted compulsively over her.

Her legs were shapely from all the exercise she did, much of it with him. Running, biking, swimming, rollerblading, skiing—both water and snow. Dana didn't wimp out like most women he knew; he expected no less from Tim's sister. And though he'd certainly seen her bare legs before—too many times to count—the heat that frissoned through him now was powerful and new.

He saw the outlines of her little nipples against his old T-shirt and the sight struck him as highly erotic—his shirt covering her breasts yet revealing her arousal to him. He wanted to touch her there and wondered if he dared. He didn't know what to do, how far to push whatever it was that was going on between them. Dana stood still in his hold, closer than they'd ever been, yet gave him no clues, neither pushing him away nor taking the lead.

Daringly, he leaned down and kissed her again exactly as before, but he felt the sensuality inherent in her response. A spasm of hot pleasure surged through him.

Dana felt the tremor that racked his body and quivered. Hot color burned her cheeks, and she lowered her face. But when Wade used a single finger to tilt her head back, making her meet his gaze, she made no effort to stop him or to look or move away.

"What are we doing, Sheely?" Wade murmured huskily.

The sound of his raspy, sexy voice was an aphrodisiac in itself, which Dana did not need because she already was more aroused than she'd ever been in her life. That might have scared her, if either fear or caution had been able to filter through the thick cloud of desire engulfing her.

But nothing could; it was too strong, too vigorous and intense. "I don't know. But whatever it is, we're doing it," she mumbled.

Her answer, such as it was, struck Wade as perfectly sound. "Yeah," he agreed.

He put his arms around her, tentatively at first, and then, as the warmth of her curvy softness penetrated through to the very fiber of his being, his embrace tightened. He held her firmly against him, the feel of her going to his head like a shot of hundred-proof whiskey.

"Kiss me," he whispered, brushing his lips against hers. He felt her mouth open to him, and her acquiescence sent him reeling. Clasping her neck with one hand, he deepened the kiss.

Dana's arms closed tightly around him and she sank against him. A tiny moan escaped from her throat as she kissed him back with exhilarating fervor. The kiss went on and on, and a sensual storm gathered force within her. She throbbed, she ached, she wanted . . .

Suddenly, he moved away from her. Dana felt oddly disoriented, as if trapped between wakefulness and a dream. She opened her eyes, and then her stomach lurched when she saw Wade at her door. Locking it.

She shivered and goose bumps covered her skin. A microsecond later, Wade was back, reaching for her again.

"Wade, we can't." Never had she sounded so unconvincing, especially to herself. The words she spoke did not match her encouraging tone or the way she was clinging to him.

Wade noticed. He smoothed his palms over her arms. "Can't we, Dana?"

"You called me Dana." When he said it, she found herself actually liking her name and not envying Tricia and Sarah theirs.

"I had to get your attention somehow. I'm trying to make a very crucial point." He borrowed her earlier statement, his hazel eyes warm. "And you called me Wade twice tonight," he reminded her. "Believe me, you have *my* complete attention." His breath was warm against her neck. "I want to kiss you again. Dana."

He wanted much more than that, he admitted to himself. Now that he knew how kissing her felt—wonderful, beyond any expectations—there were other questions that needed answering. He posed them in his mind. Did she like to be stroked and teased, deep and slow? Or did she like it hard and fast? Did she scream or sigh softly when she climaxed? Wade groaned with pleasure, contemplating the possibilities.

He slid his hands over her back to her waist. Over her hips. He kissed the fine line of her jaw while his hands slowly, inexorably glided beneath the hem of her T-shirt. He caressed her satiny skin and smiled as she exhaled sharply.

"Saxon, don't," she whispered, though her fingers were gripping his shoulders rather than putting a stop to his explorations.

"Don't do this?" He pushed her shirt up as his hands continued their journey. They closed over her bare breasts and Dana whimpered.

Wade stared down into her wide eyes. She looked—scared? He frowned, not liking the idea that she could possibly fear him.

"I would never hurt you, Dana," he said hoarsely. "Don't be afraid."

But she was, she was absolutely terrified. This was *Wade*, her fevered brain reminded her, one of her best friends, one of Tim's best friends, who'd been a part of her life for so long she could hardly remember a time when he wasn't. Wade, who had made it unmistakably clear many times that he was years and years away from even minimal commitment. Wade, who ruled out dating one woman exclusively to ensure his freedom, who wouldn't consider any relationship serious or long-term.

While she could not cope with physical intimacy in any other context. As a twenty-six-year-old virgin, a veritable throwback to another era, Dana knew very well that casual sex would never work for her. And if Wade were to find out she was a virgin . . .

She recoiled at the thought. He would either mock her mercilessly or pity her or be so shocked he might require therapy to deal with the revelation. Whatever, their friendship would be irrevocably ruined. Neither would be comfortable with each other again.

And she didn't want to lose his friendship. She liked him too much, she would miss him too much.

While Dana's muddled mind grappled with one worst-case scenario after another, Wade took it upon himself to alleviate her fears and doubt. His mouth closed over hers in a kiss that robbed her of breath and scattered every frantic thought in her head.

His hands tangled in her hair, which had slipped looose from the cloth scrunchie, and his tongue moved hotly in her mouth. He felt her body soften and weaken against his in elemental feminine submission, and the effect was powerfully erotic.

And though he had wanted this, had initiated it, the reality amazed him. All of a sudden, she wasn't simply his good pal or his old friend's cute, funny sister. She was Dana, a sexy, sultry woman whose kiss was affecting him as none before. It struck him that he'd never wanted anyone as much as he wanted her right here, right now, that the feelings raging through him were so much more potent than mere sexual desire. There was something else, something extra, that he didn't understand but definitely felt. Something sublime that went beyond the lusty urge to mate. . . .

When he finally, reluctantly, had to lift his lips from hers, and they both gulped in much-needed breaths of air, he stared down at her, studying her as if seeing her for the first time.

"You're so beautiful," he heard himself say through the ringing in his ears. He arched her against him. "Feel how much I want you." His body was shaking uncontrollably with need, with anticipation. "Dana, I want you so much."

He couldn't wait another second. Impulsively, he scooped her up in his arms and carried her to her bed. He laid her down on it, settling himself heavily on top of her.

"Saxon," she breathed.

She knew there was something else she meant to say but coherent thought eluded her once again. She felt helpless and fantastic at the same time, a paradox she would've found incomprehensible until this very moment.

His hard body pressed into hers and she twisted sinuously against him, wrapping her arms around him. Her knees flexed, enabling him to fit himself to her, their position intimate, only the barrier of their clothing separating them from physical union. The material of his trousers felt rough yet sensuously exciting against her bare thighs, and she clasped him firmly. He was hard and thick and full, exerting a constant subtle pressure on the most private vulnerable part of her. Tantalizing sensations roiled through her, driving her higher, making her feel wild, unleashing needs she'd never known she had.

He pushed up her T-shirt and his mouth fastened over one cherry red nipple. Dana groaned and clutched his head to her, threading her fingers through the springy thickness of his hair. His tongue flicked to graze the sensitive little tip as he suckled her, sending exquisite jolts of pleasure directly to her center. She squirmed against him, encouraging him, silently pleading for more.

"These clothes," she ground out an incoherent complaint. Their offending presence seemed devised to torture her, cruelly prohibiting the skin-to-skin contact her body craved.

With shaking hands, she yanked Wade's shirt free from his slacks and thrust her hands underneath, to glide along the warm smooth skin of his back. Touching him this way was a potent stimulant, empowering her to do more. She felt his muscles flex under her fingers, inhaled his tangy male scent, and her head spun giddily. She was drowning in his masculinity, in his virility.

Incited, she made the boldest sexual move of her life and slid one hand around to his front to sample the fine wiry texture of the hair just beneath the waistband of his boxers. She extended her fingers farther, and the tips of her nails lightly grazed something pulsing and smooth. Instinctively, in a virginal reflex, she jerked her hand back.

A savage shudder went through him. He caught her wrist, intending to wrap her fingers around him, his actions guided by an overwhelming hunger. It was purely by accident that he happened to look at her face.

What he saw made him drop her hand and roll away from her. And denounce himself. She looked like a nervous little girl. And no wonder! After pressuring her into their first kiss—and promising just one kiss—he had practically jumped her right here in her room! God, Tim would kill him for treating Dana like an easy lay—after first condemning him as a sleazy, unprincipled user.

But it wasn't like that! Wade silently protested in his own defense, but to his dismay he couldn't justify his actions to himself, couldn't forgive himself for what he wanted to do with, for, and to Dana Sheely.

"This is crazy, Sheely." Before he could talk himself out of it, Wade swung his legs off the bed and planted his feet firmly on the floor. He rested his elbows on his knees, gripping his head with his hands. "I can't do it."

He reviewed the situation again. And once again emerged in the unwanted role of louse. A treacherous, lecherous one. He'd been about to strip the clothes off his best friend's sister—who also happened to be his own best friend—and have sex with her, right here in her own bed!

Under the very roof where the trusting Bob and Mary Jean Sheely sat watching TV.

He had betrayed them, just as he'd betrayed Dana and Tim and the entire Sheely family!

"I feel like a rat," Wade gritted through his teeth. "No, lower than that. What's lower than a rat?"

Dana lay flat on her back, desperately trying to process everything that had gone on between them. The wild desire, the irresistible impulses to kiss him, to touch him, the fiery passion that flared and still heated her body—and finally, awfully, his abrupt withdrawal.

She closed her eyes against the pain that gripped her. He'd had second thoughts, he'd decided that he didn't want her, after all. And if she wanted to maintain even a semblance of their former friendship and salvage her pride, she was going to have to assure him that it was all right. That she really didn't mind being rejected by him, that it was just fine for him to go on his way and leave her here like this.

"What's a lower life form than a rat?" Her voice shook a little but she rallied. "Or what is more disgusting than a rat? Specify, please, because as Quint would say, 'Specific is terrific.' "

Growing up in a big family in a not-so-big house, one developed certain skills in order to maintain some personal privacy. Through the years, the ability to hide her feelings and hold back emotionally had saved her from being teased and challenged, lectured and interrogated. That talent held her in good stead now. She would never let Wade see how his rejection had devastated her.

"Hmm, let's see," Dana continued lightly, "since a rat is a mammal, a snake would be lower. A lamprey eel is even farther down the evolutionary chart and way more repulsive."

"Sheely—"

"How low do you want to go—the insect world? If you want disgusting, a roach is definitely worse than a rat, at least in my estimation. But why stop there when we also have the wonderful world of retroviruses? Is that what you are, Saxon? A disease-causing retrovirus?''

Wade laughed slightly. ''I feel like I'm back in zoology class.''

''If memory serves, you didn't do very well back in zoology class.'' She sat up and moved off the bed, her movements deliberately slow and casual. ''Tim said you barely passed it with a 'D' because you never studied for a single test. I think he secretly admired your nerve.''

''No, he didn't. Tim thought I was nuts to blow off my grades, he was always trying to talk me into taking things more seriously.'' Wade felt the force of his words like a physical blow, leaving him winded.

He'd ignored Tim's sincere admonitions down through the years and look where his capricious and irresponsible behavior had finally led. He had tried to seduce Tim's own sister right in the Sheely home!

No doubt about it, he was even lower than a disease-causing retrovirus.

Dana stood in front of the mirror mounted over the long chest of drawers and methodically eliminated all traces of their passionate kisses. She brushed her hair, patted on powder, and put on lip gloss.

When she met her eyes in the mirror, they looked blank and lifeless, reflecting her inner shutdown too well. Dana quickly looked away, darting a glance at Wade, who remained seated on the bed.

Berating himself. ''Sheely, I know what I did here tonight was all wrong and I hate myself for—for—''

''Saxon, indulging in an orgy of self-loathing after kissing someone is not very flattering to the person you just kissed. I know male angst is supposed to be a turn-on for some women but for future reference, I doubt that even the most soulful woman is going to want to listen to this stuff.''

''Sheely, can't you be serious for one minute?'' Wade stood up, angst turning to exasperation. ''How am supposed to apologize when you keep trying to make jokes? Bad jokes, at that!''

"No apology required, Saxon."

She turned to face him, satisfied that her mask was coolly in place. Her appearance gave away nothing, she looked untouched and unruffled, and if her heart was sinking inside, not a trace of her pain was externally visible. Dana wondered if perhaps she ought to look into joining the community theater group. Her acting skills were unexpectedly superb.

"I had a little too much to drink tonight," she said blithely, continuing her performance, "and all the noise and lights at Club Koncrete caused your brain temporarily to short-circuit. So we were both kind of out of it and we were both a little curious. So we kissed. So what?"

Wade gaped at her. She sounded so blasé. And hardened! As if their kisses and caresses hadn't meant a thing to her, as if she hadn't set his blood afire, tantalizing him with the anticipation of something promising and profound, something he had never experienced before.

"*So what?*" he spit out the words. He stood there, feeling shaken and febrile and wildly infuriated but doing his best to play it cool. "You're saying you got hammered in a Bangladeshi restaurant and that's why you kissed me?"

"Yes, that's what I'm saying."

"Oh, yeah, sure, everybody knows how Bangladeshi vodka—or was it their world-famous bourbon—really packs a punch and—"

"It wasn't vodka or bourbon," she interrupted coolly. "It was some brew I'd never heard of before. Some native specialty, uh, like that Greek stuff, ouzo."

"Ouzo from Bangladesh?"

"Their version is called something else, of course."

She was lying through her teeth, so blatantly she expected him to call her on it. The restaurant didn't even serve liquor. It was one of those bring-your-own-bottle places and the patrons she'd seen dining there hadn't, probably because no one was sure of which wine to drink with what dishes.

But Wade kept staring at her in the most peculiar way and didn't challenge her assertion.

He was feeling most peculiar. Like he wanted to throttle her—after he'd thrown her down on the bed and made love to her for a few hours—and then of course, the throttling would be moot.

However, he didn't move to touch her. She had made it plain that he meant nothing to her. He was simply a fellow participant in an experiment she found easy to dismiss.

So we kissed. So what? Her words rang in his head. It sounded like something he would say to a woman who had completely misinterpreted his advances, confusing sexual drive with something else. He gazed broodingly at Dana, who had retreated to the window again and stood obscured in the shadows. A palpable sadness washed over him in waves, and he couldn't shake it off.

"I—hope this won't interfere with our friendship, Da—Sheely."

"Of course not," she assured him breezily, then tacked on the killer appendage, "Why would it?"

Wade scowled. Why, indeed.

"Dana, the phone's for you!" An irritated Emily pounded on the bedroom door and then jiggled the knob impatiently. "The door's locked!" she announced crossly.

Dana's eyes met Wade's in a moment of mutual discomfort, and he moved quickly to unlock the door.

Emily flung it open and marched inside, followed by a coterie of five or six girls her age whose hairstyles and clothes were all startlingly similar to each other.

"Here." Emily handed Dana the portable phone. "We were talking to Josh and the operator cut in and said it was an emergency." Emily was not pleased and her clones made their own exclamations of disapproval. "This is, like, so embarrassing because if Josh asks what the emergency is, what am I supposed to say?"

"Maybe it really is an emergency," suggested Wade, "and none of Josh's business."

Emily acknowledged his presence with a long-suffering

sigh. "Just don't talk long, Dana. We have to call Josh back."

"Josh's friends are all over at his house," one of the other girls said, as if to underscore the importance of getting the phone back immediately. "We have to talk."

"You're into phone sex at your age?" Wade feigned shock.

"You are so gross!" Emily accused and flounced out, her tribe at her heels.

"Hello?" Dana was not surprised to hear her brother Shawn's voice over the line. Nor was she expecting a genuine emergency.

"Dana, you lent me your car tonight," Shawn reminded her, not that she'd forgotten. "Well, could I keep it till morning? And if I don't make it home by breakfast and Mom and Dad ask where I am—" "Just a minute," Dana cut in, still painfully aware of Wade's presence. She saw the ideal opportunity to get him out of her room without further humiliation. He was watching her and she returned his gaze impassively.

"This is a personal call, Wade. I'd like some privacy, please."

Wade felt as if he'd been dealt another body blow. The cool dismissal in her voice, the indifference in her beautiful blue eyes affected him viscerally. She wanted to be rid of him to talk *privately* to her caller! And he was certain who that personal call was from.

Quinton Cormack, of course. She would never send him away to talk privately to Rich Vicker or one of her girlfriends or another Sheely. Only a call from Cormack—her secret lover?—would get him the boot.

Dana turned her back and lowered her voice as Wade left her room.

"I'm back," she said to Shawn. "What am I supposed to tell Mom and Dad since you don't have any intention of being back by breakfast?"

"Say I'm at Greg's. Don't worry, it's cool with him."

"I'll need my car by ten o'clock tomorrow morning, Shawn. I have to drive to—"

"You'll have it, Dana, I promise. Thanks, you're the best."

"Shawn, wherever you are, whatever you're doing." Dana gulped. "Please remember to be careful!"

"Oh, hey, always!" he promised exuberantly. "You know we Sheelys play by the rules."

Did they? Dana wondered achingly. And what were the rules anyway? She thought about the debacle with Wade tonight, and if there was a rule to be followed in that situation, it would be never to mix sex and friendship.

A rule she and Wade had conveniently discarded on foolish impulse. She relived that pivotal moment when they'd gazed hungrily into each other's eyes. And crossed the line.

"*One kiss?*" he'd asked in a tone so warm and smooth and sensual she would've had to be dead not to respond to it. "*Just one, to see what it might be like?*"

And then he'd kissed her and she'd completely lost her head. Dana quivered.

"Maybe we play by the rules, Shawn. Or at least try to. But not everybody else does. That's why I want you to promise that you'll—" She paused when she heard her brother murmur something to another person with him.

She guessed that, at this point, Shawn would promise her anything just to get off the phone so he could resume whatever he was doing. With whomever he was doing it with.

"Be careful, Shawn," she repeated softly.

9

*B*rady Cormack wasn't tired, and he had no intention of going to bed.

Sitting beside him on the sofa in the small family room, Quint watched his small son, who had been bathed and dressed in his dinosaur pajamas and was now sitting on Rachel's lap enjoying the adventures of Bananas in Pajamas on video for the fourth—or was it the fifth?—time.

Brady didn't passively stare at the screen; he expected interaction with whoever was watching with him. Rachel was good at it, answering the two-year-old's incessant questions and asking her own while the pair of walking, talking bananas tooled around in their striped pajamas.

Quint admired her fortitude. When he watched TV with Brady, sitting through repeated showings of whatever video the little boy was fixated on at the time, he often tried to escape by reading or making notes on a case, or even flipping through catalogs. Anything to ease the brain-numbing boredom of repetition. Brady invariably caught him drifting and would demand full attention, capturing his father's face between his small hands and turning it directly to him.

But Brady didn't have to resort to those desperation tactics with Rachel. She remained totally engaged, her concentration never wavering, and the child was reveling in her attention.

What red-blooded male of any age wouldn't? Quint thought drolly. Being held in Rachel's arms with her warm hazel eyes focused exclusively on you would make any male feel like the most important, fascinating guy in the world. At two, little Brady experienced Rachel's attentions as maternal interest. Quint wanted to experience her arms and her eyes and everything else she had to offer in a distinctly nonmaternal way.

Quint's gaze lasered in on her neck and the dark purple mark he'd put there last night. His lips twitched into a reminiscent smile. When he and Brady had arrived at her apartment earlier this evening, she'd been wearing loose-fitting pleated beige slacks and a long-sleeved navy turtleneck, despite the eighty-two degrees outside. . . .

While Brady made himself at home in her apartment, running around the living room, climbing onto her couch and jumping off, Quint plucked at the jersey's cuffs around her wrists.

"Junkies wear long sleeves in hot weather to cover the track marks," he observed.

Rachel was nonplussed. "Are you making conversation or insinuations?"

"I like to try to throw people off guard," he admitted. "You can get a lot of information that way."

"And a lot of unpredictable reactions, too," Rachel added ruefully. "I remember some of the comments you tossed out at John Pedersen when he was on the stand. And I'll never forget how my case went straight down the drain because his responses in front of that jury were an attorney's bad dream come true."

"I don't want to talk about Pedersen," muttered Quint. An understatement, to put it mildly. "Brady, get off the table." Brady had climbed onto the coffee table and stood there, looking around while contemplating his next move.

"No!" Brady exclaimed gleefully.

"His favorite comeback." Quint groaned.

"All two-year-olds love to say no. It's a sign that they're seeking a measure of independence. A completely normal developmental stage."

"Thank you, Dr. Ruth. Knowing that every other two-year-old in the world is antiauthoritarian does sort of help.''

''The specialist I was quoting was Dr. Brazelton, a pediatrician.'' Rachel regarded him archly. ''As you well know, Dr. Ruth is a sex therapist.''

''I thought she'd branched out. She was on one of those talk shows Sarah watches, and I swear they were discussing kids. Brady, get down right now.'' Quint started toward his son, who was cruising the length of the coffee table, nearly tripping over two thick books of photographic essays.

Brady held his ground as his father advanced. ''No.''

Just before Quint reached him, the little boy dived onto the sofa and crawled across it, straight to Rachel. ''Mommy, up!'' he demanded, giggling.

A smiling Rachel scooped him up. ''I think he outfoxed you, Daddy.'' She settled Brady more securely on her hip as he investigated her gold hoop earrings.

''Earring,'' he said, and Rachel nodded her approval. ''Good job, Brady. You remembered.''

''Oh, he knows earrings,'' Quint said dryly. ''Sarah must have a dozen of them, total. It seems like overkill, but what does an old coot like me know about style?''

''It could be worse. Think nose ring or eyebrow ring or—''

''Stop!'' Quint shuddered. ''It may be trendy, but body piercing makes me queasy.''

''Stop!'' mimicked Brady. His busy little fingers moved from Rachel's earrings to the high cotton neck of her jersey. He tugged at the material and unerringly found what she'd tried to hide. ''Boo-boo.'' Brady was sympathetic. ''Awww. No cry.''

Rachel knew she was blushing and the more she willed the blood to pool elsewhere, the hotter her cheeks grew. Quint immediately came to investigate Brady's discovery, and he towered over her, his fingers tracing the mark.

Rachel shivered under his touch. This was getting too intimate. His nearness was stirring up last night's memories, the ones she'd been trying all day to suppress. Not that she'd succeeded at suppression, or even come close.

Aside from intermittent anxiety attacks over the Tilden will after Aunt Eve's tirade this morning, her thoughts had been dominated by Quint Cormack.

Rachel swallowed. All day long, her thoughts had been perilously close to what some might call sexual fantasies. And now here he was, the star of those vivid daydreams, right here beside her. Touching her, making her skin heat and her pulses throb.

In sheer self-defense, her arms tightened around Brady and she artfully stepped away from Quint, out of his reach. "Let's eat dinner, Brady," she said with credible enthusiasm.

"Eat it all up!" Brady crowed.

"Before we go, why don't you change into something more comfortable, Rachel?" Quint's tone was an intriguing mixture of tease and challenge.

When she raised her face to meet his gaze, he flashed those impudent arched brows at her. "Since I've already seen my—handiwork—there's no need for camouflage any longer, is there?"

"Your hands had nothing to do with it," she retorted, and her blush deepened.

Though she hadn't intended to reveal his *handiwork,* now that the secret was out she decided his crime should not go unacknowledged. She'd had to suffer with winter clothes and odd stares all day, because of him.

"Maybe orally branding women is a habit of yours, but I am not enchanted, Quinton," Rachel said sternly. "I am too old for this kind of—"

"It's not a habit, and I don't blame you for not being enchanted." He was beside her again, lightly stroking her hair. "I'm sorry, Rachel. It won't happen again."

Her defenses were effectively breached. She felt breathless, unable to move.

"Where anyone can see," he added in a low growl. His lips brushed her temple.

Rachel whimpered.

"I'll take Brady while you change," Quint said smoothly, taking the baby from her arms.

In a daze, Rachel retreated to her bedroom and returned a few minutes later wearing an apricot-colored matte jersey dress. The cut was slim yet fluid and not clingy, the length several inches above her knee, shorter than she normally wore.

Quint wondered how she managed to make such a simple dress radiate a tantalizing mix of sex and class. Merely looking at her made him feel so physically charged he wouldn't have been surprised to find himself emitting voltage.

The T-shirt-style neck of her dress exposed the purple mark on her neck, and though she'd applied makeup, it still showed.

"I didn't mean to do this, Rachel, I don't blame you for being ticked off." Quint touched the small bruise again. "I probably shouldn't tell you this, but you have an uncanny effect on me. When we're together, my mind doesn't work the way it normally does."

Rachel felt warm and flattered, aroused and sexy—until her rational thought processes kicked back in. He was clever, she conceded; his wry little admission had affected her the way he'd wanted it to, at least for a moment or two. She eyed him with a mixture of admiration and resentment.

Quint Cormack knew exactly what to say and how to say it, keeping her so off-balance that she could easily be manipulated by him. He'd done it professionally to her in the unfortunate Pedersen trial and was now using his technique to affect her outside the courtroom, too.

Rachel rebelled. She would not play marionette to his puppeteer, her every action controlled at his direction. She picked up Brady, grabbed her handbag, and headed for the door.

"Then I can only hope that my *uncanny power* over you will affect your mind in the Tilden case, Quint. When you lose, feel free to blame me." Her tone and expression made it clear that she wasn't buying his irresistible-impulse defense.

Quint frowned. He was not handing her a line and felt vaguely insulted that she saw it that way. "The Tildens have nothing to do with us, Rachel. Or Pedersen either," he added hopefully.

"They will if we're adversaries in the courtroom again." They walked to his car, Brady in her arms.

"If the Tildens insist on contesting that will, Saxon Associates is going to be trounced in court, Rachel."

"You don't know that," Rachel countered, irked.

He sounded so matter-of-fact, as if reciting an established fact. George Washington was the first president of the United States, Independence Day is July Fourth, Saxon Associates will get trounced in court. By him!

"Honey, I do." Quint strapped Brady into his car seat in the back of the tan Mercury station wagon, the one he'd bought after trading in his carefree single-guy little red Corvette when Brady came to live with him.

He seated Rachel in the front seat beside him. "Tell your aunt Eve that the Tildens ought to offer to buy Misty out. I doubt that living permanently in Lakeview is a priority of hers, so if they want the old family mansion back, they can get it—plus the stuff inside that oversize museum—by paying her for it."

"If that's what you plan to tell Aunt Eve and the Tildens when you meet with them, they'll laugh in your face, Quint."

"Their mistake, Rachel. And a big one." Quint shrugged and started up the engine. "I know it's a cliché, but 'he who laughs last, laughs best' is right on the mark when it comes to this case."

"You must be a fabulous poker player, I don't think anyone could tell you're bluffing," marveled Rachel. "You've almost managed to make me nervous even though I know that will is—"

"Want out!" Brady demanded from the backseat.

Rachel glanced around to see him struggling against the

confines of his car seat. "We'll be there in a just a minute, Brady," she cajoled, and diverted him with a silly word game.

Quint had been grateful for the reprieve. They'd enjoyed dinner with Brady without further mention of the Tildens or the will. When Rachel agreed to Brady's demands that she come home and give him his bath, they stopped by her apartment first, so she could pick up her car.

"You're invited to spend the night at our house," Quint said, knowing she wouldn't agree. Hoping that she might. "I can drive you back to your place in the morning."

"I'll drive myself home after Brady is in bed, thank you very much," she drawled.

"Sarah is gone for the weekend. You can have her room." Quint grinned as he said it. If he convinced Rachel to spend the night with him, she would not be spending it in any other bed but his, and they both knew it.

And though sexual tension stretched and hummed between them, Rachel stuck to her plan, got her own car, and followed Quint and Brady home.

The video, mercifully, came to an end.

"Again!" Brady decreed.

"No more, Brady, time for bed," said Quint.

He saw the little boy shoot him a curious glance. His voice definitely lacked the paternal authority such a demand required, and Brady knew it.

"Again, Mommy," Brady pleaded, smiling from one adult to the other.

The little conniver knew that his dad wanted Rachel around and would bend the rules to keep her. Quint was both amused and surprised by the two-year-old's insight. Because the kid was absolutely, positively right. "Well, maybe one more time."

Rachel heaved a groan. "I'd like to peel those bananas and put them in a cream pie. Brady, let's watch something else. Winnie the Pooh? Looney Tunes? Barney?"

"Bananas," Brady said firmly.

The doorbell rang just as the opening credits rolled again.

Quint jumped to his feet. "Probably some neighborhood kids hawking their latest fund-raising products."

"I've never seen anybody so eager to buy from a door-to-door salesman," Rachel mocked. "We know an escape when we see one, don't we, Brady?"

"Why bananas run?" Brady asked, already engrossed in the program.

"Yeah, Mom, why are the bananas running?" Quint teased, as Rachel patiently explained the plot point to Brady yet again.

Laughing, Quint left the room but during his trek to the door, his mirth faded fast. The doorbell was ringing incessantly. Whoever was out there had a finger jammed on the bell and wouldn't let up.

He grimaced. The neighborhood kids never did that, but it was standard Carla behavior. Apprehension gripped him. What had his father done now, to send Carla over here in a frenzy? It could be something ridiculously trivial, it could be something horrendous and life-altering. With his father one never knew, and Carla reacted to everything in the same way. WIth hysteria, screams, and tears.

He cast a regretful glance back at the family room where he and Rachel and Brady had been spending a normal, pleasant evening together and knew it was all about to come to an abrupt end. His father had a near-genius knack for disrupting anything good.

But when Quint opened his front door, it wasn't Carla but Misty Tilden who stood on the cement stoop, a vision in chartreuse from her talonlike fingernails to her high-heeled slides.

"Quint, thank God, you're here!" Misty rushed inside, breathing hard, her enormous chest heaving.

"Misty, what—"

Misty proceeded to supply the answers before he could ask the questions. "Quint, *they* were in the house when I got back tonight." Misty grabbed his arm in a viselike hold. "They were trying to take stuff! I caught them red-handed with some jewelry and Townie's collection of gold coins and that old stamp album, too. When I told them to get out, they wouldn't. They cursed at me." She burst into noisy sobs. "It was horrible, Quint. They wouldn't leave. They said—"

"Misty, I assume you're talking about the Tildens and not some ordinary, run-of-the-mill burglars you caught in the act."

"I woulda rather caught ordinary burglars, they woulda treated me nicer." Misty sniffed. "The Tildens were so mean! Without Townie there to shut them up, they said the most hateful things. They were even worse than they were at the funeral and remember how nasty they were that day?"

Quint well remembered Townsend Tilden Senior's funeral and Misty in her short, tight black mourning dress and five-inch spike heels. Her widow's veil, which she'd rush-ordered from New York, resembled something Queen Victoria might've worn to her husband's royal funeral. Town Junior had looked as if he were going to have a stroke, right there in the middle of the church when Misty walked in and seated herself with the family in the first pew. Words had been exchanged between the widow and Town Senior's surviving relatives, forcing the minister himself to intervene before continuing the ceremony.

"I think reality is finally beginning to dawn on the Tildens. Town Senior is gone and you're still in the house. Which family members broke in, Misty?"

"That son of a bitch Town Junior and his prick son Town Three. And that witch Marguerite and her wimpy husband and snotty daughter Sloane and jerk son Tilden. I hate them, Quint, I hate them so much."

"You're certain you didn't give them permission to enter the house?"

"Permission? Are you nuts? I wasn't even there! I went out to dinner with—a—a friend and when I got home that crew of vampires was there. I shoulda expected them to show up at night 'cause that's the only time they can come out of their coffins."

"Do you know if any of them has a key to the house, Misty?"

"If they do, they stole it. I changed the locks the day Townie died, just like you told me to, Quint."

"Okay. We can definitely nail them on breaking and entering. Tell me more. Did you call the police, Misty?"

"Like the cops would ever be on my side!" Misty gave a harsh, bitter laugh. "You know they'd suck up to the Tildens like everybody else in this damn town. Everybody but you, Quint." She squeezed his arm and gazed up at him. And though she'd been sobbing, there were no tears on her face and her dark, heavy eye makeup remained intact. "Everybody but you and—and my new friend who is a real sweetie-pie."

"Are the Tildens still at the house?" Quint pressed. "Did they drive you out, Misty?"

"My friend drove me over here," Misty misinterpreted. "He's outside in the car waiting; he said he'd better not come in."

Quint didn't let himself wonder about who her new-friend-the-real-sweetie-pie was. Why summon a potential headache before its time?

"My friend wanted to call the cops and since I wouldn't, he said I should come tell you what happened right away."

"Your friend was right, Misty. And I am going to call the police and file a complaint which could lead to criminal charges. I definitely want a written record of this incident on file."

"The cops don't care about me. They'll just blow you off, Quint."

"No, Misty, they won't. Now, are the Tildens still at the house? And if not, what did they take with them when they left?"

"They're gone. My friend made them leave, and they didn't take nothin'." Misty smiled, her eyes shining. She looked almost girlish as she talked about her heroic friend.

"They were bad-mouthing me and threatening me and meanwhile, my friend had a brainstorm. He grabbed one of those guns from Townie's collection and said he'd shoot them all on the spot if they didn't get out.'' Misty was positively glowing now. ''Quint, he made them empty out their pockets! Tilly had some gold coins stuffed in his and that bitch Sloane had some of the jewelry in her purse!''

''Your friend held them at gunpoint?'' Quint did not share Misty's elation. This was a complication he did not want.

''Town Junior was so pissed!'' Misty exclaimed happily. ''He cursed a blue streak, sounded like my old boss at Fantasy's. He said that gun was used in the Civil War or something and that my friend wasn't allowed to touch it.''

''So it was an antique pistol that probably wasn't even loaded,'' Quint thought aloud, visualizing the police report in his mind.

''Nuh-uh. That jagoff Tilden Lloyd started blabbing about how the gun doesn't take bullets, only balls or something and while he was talking, I got a brainstorm of my own. I sneaked up to go get my own gun from my bedroom.'' She smiled triumphantly. ''It was loaded and I fired once, just to show them I could shoot. They put down the freakin' stuff and ran out of there fast!''

''You're the homeowner and you were defending your life and your property. You'd been threatened and actually found your possessions on their person. Do you have a permit to have that gun, Misty?''

He would've said a prayer if he thought that was the kind of thing one could pray for. But he didn't think it was, so he held his breath and hoped.

''Sure, Townie got me a permit,'' said Misty.

''Good.'' Quint allowed himself to exhale. ''Now, concentrate, Misty. Is there a chance that one of the Tildens might've managed to take something from the house, something they smuggled out without you or your friend seeing? Maybe a rare gold coin or a priceless stamp or something?''

''Robbery! Cool!'' Misty grinned. ''Sure, there's a chance they swiped a stamp or coin or two. I didn't check out the collections. I don't even know all the stuff in 'em.''

"Robbery would involve attempted or sustained violence. Without it, the crime is larceny. Hmm, those coin and stamp collections are worth a fortune. That escalates it to grand larceny. Okay, I'm going to call the police and—"

"Daddy!" Brady ran into the living room. "Come see Bananas."

Rachel had followed and stopped dead on the threshold of the living room, when she saw Misty Tilden standing beside Quint. Her eyes widened. She'd seen the woman at a distance and heard many tales about her but none of the Tildens' remarks had prepared her for Misty Tilden in the flesh.

She exposed plenty of it. The young widow wore an eye-popping chartreuse spandex minidress, her heels were impossibly high, more like stilts than shoes, and her makeup and hair color defied description. Rachel stared at her, transfixed.

Misty had noticed her too. "Who's that?" she asked loudly, as if she had every right to know.

"That Mommy," Brady said helpfully.

Misty's reaction amazed them all. "So you're back, huh?" she shrieked at Rachel, and started toward her. "You rotten bitch!"

Fortunately, her heels were so high and her dress so tight, she could only take tiny, mincing steps. Rachel positioned herself safely behind a high-backed armchair, knowing she could easily outrun the other woman, if need be.

Misty obviously decided the same thing, for she stopped in her tracks and settled for a verbal attack instead. "You have the goddammed nerve to come back here after you already dumped that baby? Do you get off on jerking people around or are you just set on trying to ruin the kid's life?"

Rachel was speechless. She remembered feeling this way in a college physics class, uncomprehending and impossibly confused, yet expected to understand and participate. It had been as hopeless then as it was now.

"So what happened, bitch?" Misty's face was contorted

with rage. "Did your boyfriend dump *you* over in Romania or wherever the hell you chased him to? So now you're back to grab some bucks from Quint and plan to use the kid to do it?"

Rachel met Quint's eyes. Either Misty was truly insane or she knew quite a bit about Quint's ex-wife—except what she looked like, of course—and was righteously infuriated by her past behavior.

Quint cleared his throat. "Misty, I don't want Brady to— uh—hear any of this."

Brady was tugging on his father's hand, ignoring the adult conversation. "C'mon, Daddy. See Bananas."

For once Quint was grateful for the toddler's one-track mind, firmly set on his beloved video.

"I'll put him to bed," Rachel said quickly, hurrying over to take Brady from Quint. She cut a wide path around Misty, half-expecting the other woman to spring at her like a wild jungle cat. Those chartreuse claws of her looked like they could slash through internal organs.

"Bitches like you oughta be shot," Misty called as Rachel fled the room with Brady. "They oughta rip out your ovaries so you can't have any more kids to—"

"Misty, this is only making things worse," Quint cut in, but Misty was not to be appeased.

"You gotta take a stand, Quint. She doesn't give a damn about that baby and she'll—"

The voices became indecipherable as Rachel reached the top of the stairs but she didn't slow her pace until she reached Brady's room. She closed the door, feeling safe in the quietude and cheerful colors of the nursery.

"Who that?" Brady asked as he ran to his shelves to rummage through one of the bright plastic baskets filled with toys.

"Cruella De Vil's tacky cousin," said Rachel, then felt a twinge of shame because one shouldn't prejudice a child in such a way. "A lady to see Daddy," she amended, though Brady seemed uninterested in either of her answers.

He found what he was looking for, a small banana doll

dressed in striped pajamas, a replica of the character in the video.

"Is he going to listen to your story with you?" Rachel asked, and Brady nodded his head. She found his ritual storybook and carried him over to the rocking chair. He clutched the toy banana while she read and rocked.

Brady was almost asleep by the end of the story, and she placed him carefully in his crib. He smiled up at her, looking as cherubic as a little angel, and Rachel felt her heart ache with tenderness for him. Then he stretched out his arm, grabbed the generic raccoon by its striped tail and tossed it out of the crib.

Rachel laughed as the toy hit the floor. "Reject Raccoon is foiled again. Even half-asleep, you can spot those gate-crashers, can't you, Brady?"

She wanted to tell Quint that Brady's eviction record still stood. But as she crept down the stairs she could hear Quint's and Misty's voices in the kitchen. It sounded as if they were talking on the telephone, and Rachel decided not to hang around. Why bother to correct her mistaken identity when her true identity—an attorney for the Tildens—would hardly inspire any overtures of friendship from the widow, either. Not that she wanted to be Misty Tilden's friend.

But Misty was Quint's friend. Her drop-in visit, her knowledge of Brady's mother was evidence that her relationship with Quint Cormack extended beyond the formal limits of attorney–client. Rachel felt jealousy spiral through her. Was Quint sleeping with Misty Tilden? The thought made her sick. And where did Dana Sheely fit into the equation?

Thoroughly dispirited, Rachel left the house. She felt as if she were trapped in a soap-opera plot, an unwilling part of a quadrangle—or was it a pentagram?—because there was also Carla Cormack to add to the roster. Rachel pictured Quint's pretty young stepmother, who'd clung to him like he was her rock during the fire.

There were already too many women in Quint Cormack's life, and possibly more she didn't know about. Perhaps enough to form a sorority all their own. Rachel, never one for large groups, made a resolute vow not to join.

She was surprised to see lights shining from her apartment windows as she walked from her parking space to the front door of the restored Victorian gingerbread house, which had been subdivided and remodeled into four apartments. Each apartment consisted of only three rooms—kitchen, living room, and bedroom plus bath—but the rooms were large with high ceilings and window seats and other interesting turn-of-the-century touches that distinguished them from the dull high-rise apartment buildings which abounded along the highways surrounding Lakeview.

Only two people had keys to her apartment, her aunt Eve and sister Laurel. Rachel glanced at the wide wooden staircase as she inserted her key in the lock and wished that she lived on the upper floor instead of at ground level. At least she would have an extra few moments to compose her thoughts, for she was certain that Aunt Eve was waiting for her inside, ready to plan their Tilden strategy.

And to indulge in some major Quint Cormack and Misty Tilden bashing?

Rachel swallowed hard. She remembered everything she'd ever said about Quint, but her antipathy to that demonic lawyer felt unconnected to the man she'd come to know over the past few days. She couldn't summon the requisite hostility, and she wondered if Aunt Eve would notice.

Nervously, Rachel pushed open the door. Maybe, just maybe, it might not be in her own best interest to disclose where she'd been tonight. Or with whom.

But Eve Saxon wasn't waiting inside for her with stacks of will-busting law texts.

Laurel sat curled up on the flowered chintz sofa, leafing through a yellowing-paged paperback. Rachel read the title from across the room. *Games Mother Never Taught You.* Upon Aunt Eve's suggestion, Rachel had read it years ago but couldn't imagine Laurel ever picking up a book about corporate gamesmanship for women. Then again, she couldn't imagine why Laurel was here on a Friday night without her husband and child.

"Laurel, what's happened?" Rachel was concerned. "Is something wrong?"

"You think there's something wrong because I'm out alone on a Friday night past nine o'clock?" Laurel tossed down the book and stood up. "Can't I even drop by to visit my own sister without everybody assuming that something happened?"

She looked sulky and defiant, without a trace of her usual people-pleasing smile. And she was wearing tight jeans— Laurel never wore jeans because her husband didn't like them—and one of those short clingy T-shirts that Katie Sheely favored. The kind that Aunt Eve had deemed unsuitable office attire but Katie wore anyway because she paid no attention to Eve's wardrobe advice. The kind that the always conservatively dressed Laurel *never* wore.

"Where are Gerald and Snowy, Laurel?"

"At home, of course. Where else would Gerald be on a Friday night?"

Rachel felt anxiety strike her solar plexus and radiate outward as her sister's face grew harder. Laurel Saxon Lynton smiled and flirted and wept, but this rebellious attitude of hers—which even included her clothing—was something new. Something worrisome.

She followed Laurel into the kitchen, watched her open the freezer portion of the refrigerator and stare at the contents inside.

"Everybody else in the world might have plans for Friday night but never Professor Gerald Lynton. Oh no, he wants to stay home on Fridays and have his dinner served to him on a tray so he can watch C-SPAN while he eats. That's his idea of kicking off the weekend—eating dinner in front of the TV set watching Congress doing nothing. Wow! Really wild, huh, Rach?"

"You two had a fight," Rachel surmised.

Laurel sneered. "Duh!"

Rachel studied her sister closely. Laurel was something of a drama queen. She and her husband used to fight a lot but in the past year, their quarrels seemed to have diminished in number and ferocity. Rachel had been frankly relieved. It seemed to her that Laurel and Gerald were heading toward a higher realm, a comfortable mature companionship.

Now it appeared the couple had relapsed and were back in the lowlands of fighting and tears. Except Laurel's eyes were dry, not even slightly red-rimmed. She had not been crying, an observation that filled Rachel with trepidation. Laurel always cried!

"You don't have any ice cream." Laurel closed the freezer and turned to Rachel to flash her adorable smile, the one that Wade often joked she should patent because it worked so well. He had a similar version of his own.

"I know what, Rachel. Let's go out for ice cream. Please!" Laurel caught her sister's hand. "We can go to Richman's in Cherry Hill and we'll get banana splits, like we used to. Oh let's, Rachel. It'll be fun!"

Was it destiny or a peculiar coincidence that bananas seemed to be play an integral part of this evening? First, Brady with his video, now Laurel with her demand to go to the ice-cream shop. Scarily enough, Laurel was acting a bit like Brady, clutching Rachel's hand, practically jumping up and down . . . ready to throw a tantrum if thwarted? All of that was perfectly normal for a two-year-old, but Laurel was a married woman, the mother of a three-year-old girl.

Rachel thought of her small niece and her heart clenched. "Laurel, I think you should go home and make up with Gerald right now. Does he know where you are? I didn't see your car outside. How did you get here?"

"Gerald wouldn't let me have the car keys, so I ran out of the house." Laurel pouted, all traces of adorable amiability gone. "I decided to walk over here, and who should be driving along Lake Avenue but Wade, so I hitched a ride with him. He was in a horrible mood—he just about bit my head off when I asked him why he was alone on a

Friday night—but he dropped me off here.''

"Did you tell Wade you'd had a fight with Gerald?''

"I told him what I told Gerald, that I was sick and tired of acting like I was forty instead of twenty-three. I want to have some fun, I want to have a life!''

"You have a life, Laurel. You're married and a mother; it's what you've always wanted.''

"You sound just like Wade!'' Laurel snapped. "Well, I'll tell you what I told him. It's not enough! I don't have any friends, I don't have anyone to talk to or do fun things with. Gerald expects me to hang around with those dull faculty wives and most of them have kids as old as me or even older! Well, I have nothing to—''

"What did Gerald say when you told him all this?'' Rachel made herself ask.

"Oh, the usual. He tried to tell me what to think and what to do and how to feel; he acted like he's the brilliant master and I'm the nitwit slave.''

Rachel was very nervous indeed. She remembered Aunt Eve predicting this outcome, *this very argument,* during Laurel's engagement to Gerald Lynton, the professor who taught the required freshman course Government and the Constitution at Carbury College. Eighteen-year-old Laurel had found the subject boring but the bachelor professor fascinating. She and Lynton carried on a secret romance for a year before gossip reached the administration, forcing the taboo relationship into the open.

Aunt Eve wanted to press sexual-harassment charges against Professor Lynton for violating teacher–student strictures, she wanted him fired from his faculty position, tenure be damned. Laurel wanted to get married and her mother, though expressing a few reservations about the couple's age difference, was eager to begin planning the wedding.

Rachel remembered Laurel's big elaborate wedding— she'd been a reluctant maid of honor—with mixed feelings. She couldn't forget Aunt Eve's prediction of disaster for the couple whom she descibed as ''criminally mismatched in age and in every other way.'' But Laurel had been a lovely happy bride, Gerald seemed very much in love with her, and their mother was genuinely thrilled. Professor Whit Saxon, as usual, had little to say. He believed daughters were the main province of their mother and rarely offered opinions or advice to either Rachel or Laurel.

Since Snowy's birth, Rachel's doubts about the couple's future had begun to fade, she'd even taken a liking to her sometimes pedantic brother-in-law. She was certain Gerald loved his wife and child, and that elemental fact was what really mattered, wasn't it?

But now, here was Laurel claiming that her husband was old and dull while she was young and wanted to have fun.

Rachel didn't know how to deal with this new strange version of Laurel, who talked about having "fun." Was fun a euphemism for something as simple as Laurel taking tap-dancing and aerobics classes at the community center, which she'd once signed up for, then quit because Gerald deemed it a waste of her time? Or did this rebel-Laurel equate fun with the ominous concept of sexual freedom?

Rachel gazed assessingly at her sister. A reality check was definitely in order. "Laurel, this alleged *fun* you think you want to have is vastly overrated. You've been involved with Gerald since you were eighteen, and you went with Brian Collender for four years before that. You've been protected from the sadistic dating hell that's been misnamed *fun.* You already have what every woman wants, Laurel. A husband who loves you, an adorable child who—"

"Every woman doesn't want that, Rachel. *You* don't," countered Laurel. "Aunt Eve sure doesn't. And I can finally see why. Both of you do important, interesting things, you have exciting lives. You take trips and buy cool cars and don't have to ask anybody's permission to go where you want or get what you want. You don't have anybody hovering over you telling you what to do and say and wear."

"Your life isn't like that, Laurel," Rachel argued weakly because her sister's marriage was a lot like that. Gerald was the dominant partner; his word was final, no matter what.

Aunt Eve had said from the start it would be that way. But it was what Laurel had claimed she wanted more than anything else in the world.

"Yes, it is and we all know it!" Laurel's voice rose, and she spoke with a force and an intensity that was totally out of character for her. "I'm miserable, Rachel! It's been building and building inside me. I haven't said a word to anybody, but this past year I realized that marrying Gerald was a big mistake!"

"Oh, Laurel, no!" Rachel gasped her dismay.

Which incited Laurel even more. "It's true, and I can't take it anymore! I want what you have, Rachel. I want a life like yours and Aunt Eve's. It's not too late for me to start over, is it? I'm only twenty-three, I can go back to school and—"

The telephone began to ring and Laurel paused in midsentence. "Aren't you going to get that?" she asked when Rachel remained immobile, not bothering to take the three necessary steps to pick up the receiver.

Rachel shook her head, and the answering machine automatically clicked on at the sixth ring.

"Rachel, this is Quint. Pick up, I know you're there," Quint's voice came over the line. "Misty is gone, and we need to talk."

10

"Misty?" Laurel's eyes widened with interest. "Does he mean Misty Tilden? Is—Is that Quinton Cormack, the lawyer?" she added incredulously.

Even Laurel, who had always been uninterested in the goings-on at Saxon Associates, knew about the good-vs-evil Pedersen case and who had been on which side.

"Quint Cormack and Misty Tilden can wait, Laurel," Rachel murmured. "Right now it's more important for you and me to—"

"I'm not going to hang up, Rachel." Quint's disembodied voice sounded amused. "You might as well bite the bullet and pick up."

Laurel made a move toward the receiver but Rachel blocked her way. "No, don't, Laurel."

"I want to thank you for putting Brady to bed and getting him out of the cross fire," Quint continued, seemingly perfectly at ease with his one-sided conversation. "He's sleeping peacefully, thanks to you. Rachel, please pick up."

"*Brady?*" Laurel gaped at Rachel, agog. "Little Brady who was with you at my house? He belongs to *Quinton Cormack,* the lawyer?"

"Didn't I mention that?" Rachel looked sheepish.

"You know you didn't! You let me believe his parents were law-school friends of yours. But forget about that for now, Rachel. He wants to talk about Town Senior's trashy widow, doesn't he? That's got to be really important!"

Laurel pushed Rachel aside and grabbed the telephone receiver from its cradle. "Hi, this is Laurel, Rachel's little sister. Hold on a sec, she's right here."

Laurel shoved the phone into Rachel's hand. "Talk to him, Rach."

She strode into the living room and Rachel heard the television set switched on. Was Laurel matchmaking—old instincts died hard—or had her newfound interest in having a career inspired her to promote Rachel's?

Rachel gripped the phone and faced the inevitable. "Hello, Quint."

"You sound upset. With me or with your sister?"

His perception annoyed Rachel. She hadn't thought she'd given anything away with her noncommittal hello. "Why would I be upset with Laurel?"

"I've found that adults who refer to themselves as *little* have a knack for upsetting those around them. So why is Little Sister at your place at this hour? Is Snowy there, too, or was she left at home?"

Quint's insight unsettled her, irritated her, too. "Can't my own sister visit me on a Friday night by herself without something being wrong?" Rachel was startled to hear herself using Laurel's own argument. Unfortunately, it seemed as unconvincing coming from her as it had from Laurel.

A fact the ever-intuitive Quint instantly divined. "You sound a lot like I do after listening to Carla's litany of complaints. Am I on the right track here, Rachel?"

Rachel leaned back against the wall and closed her eyes. He'd caught her at a weak moment, she conceded, and he understood without her having to explain. "Yes."

"Has she reached hysteria and tears yet?"

"Not yet." Rachel peered into the living room, where Laurel was staring at the TV screen, her expression mutinous. "But it wouldn't take much. One more mention of Gerald would probably do it," she added, her voice low and tense.

"Then may I recommmend not mentioning him?"

"Thanks for the advice. Are you going to bill me for your professional expertise?"

Quint chuckled. "For you, it's free. Rachel, about Misty—"

"Don't apologize for not introducing us, I don't have a death wish. If she was willing to rip out my ovaries because she thought I was Brady's mother, she'd probably go for my jugular vein if she knew I'm the Tildens' attorney."

"You don't know the half of it." Suddenly Quint sounded grim. "I need to talk to you, Rachel. I was hoping you could come back over here tonight so I could—uh— bring you up to speed on some developments in the Tilden case. We really can't do it over the phone."

Heat flared through her, making her body feel heavy in some places, tight in others. Her instantaneous sensual response thoroughly unnerved her. He was speaking professionally, but she was reacting to him on an entirely different level—even reading a double entendre into "We can't do it over the phone"!

Were there really developments in the Tilden case urgent enough for an impromptu Friday night meeting, or did he want her to come to him for reasons that had nothing to do with Misty Tilden?

All thoughts of the Tildens dispersed as Rachel imagined being alone with Quint in the dark quiet house. Sarah Sheely would not arrive to interrupt anything and Brady, that dogged little chaperone, would be asleep and unavailable to protect her from . . .

Rachel felt herself blushing. She needed protection from herself, from what she wanted to do with Quint.

And that was totally unacceptable.

"I can't," she said quickly, her voice betraying an embarrassing breathlessness. "Laurel's here, and if you want to—to discuss the Tildens, Aunt Eve should be present."

"All right. Don't say I didn't try, Rachel." Quint cleared his throat. "How do you intend to handle your sister?"

"What do you mean?" Rachel felt a ridiculous disappointment that he'd so easily dropped the idea of meeting tonight.

She immediately took herself to task for idiocy unbecoming a lawyer, a state Quint Cormack seemed to induce in her. She should hang up now and focus on the fact that this man was her professional archenemy.

But she didn't.

"Your goal is to get your sister to go home without lighting her fuse, isn't it? For that, you'll need a plan," explained Quint.

"It sounds like you're well versed in this area." Rachel massaged her left temple with her fingertips. A steady pounding throb was beginning, the first symptoms of what promised to be a killer tension headache. She remembered how capably Quint dealt with Carla and Misty and couldn't help but wish he were here to defuse Laurel.

"And it sounds like you're not. A practical word of advice?"

"Please."

"Don't try to give *her* advice, not while she's still volatile. Divert her instead."

"Maybe by—going out for ice cream?"

"That could work." Quint approved. "It's hard to sustain melodrama in a place that sells ice cream. Meanwhile, adopt a supportive role, not a controlling one. Tell Laurel that you understand she's stressed, that she needs to take some time for herself."

Rachel was doubtful. It seemed awfully simplistic, especially in light of Laurel's angry dissatisfaction. "And you think that'll work?"

"It's worth a try. That's what Carla's mother tells Sarah and me when she palms the boys off on us every other weekend, that Carla needs time for herself. You might have noticed Carla doesn't handle stress very well."

Too true; Rachel thought of Carla and the ambulance she'd taken hostage. "So Carla and her mother have arranged to get free baby-sitting every other weekend?"

"They know Sarah's schedule and drop Austin and Dustin off on the weekends she's working. Brady likes having them around and Sarah doesn't mind. Sheelys are used to a full house.''

"And what about you?"

"It's not about me, Rachel."

She understood what he wasn't saying. That he had willingly assumed responsibility for his young half brothers, that he was building a relationship with them and encouraging a bond between the boys and little Brady.

"Sometimes Carla gets so stressed that she needs a break from the boys when Sarah isn't working, like tomorrow," Quint said dryly. "So I'm taking Brady, Austin, and Dustin to some sort of medieval fair in Bucks County."

"Oh, a Renaissance Festival, I've heard of those. People dress in period costumes and there are activities and games from that era."

Quint heaved a groan. "I was afraid of that."

"It could be interesting. Living history, and all."

"Austin's teacher recommended it. Since I've moved here, I've come to realize that when a grade-school teacher heartily recommends some activity or place, it's going to be deadly for the adult who dutifully drags the kids there."

Rachel smiled. "I'm sure you'll all have a wonderful time."

"If you and Snowy want to join us, give me a call before eleven."

The invitation caught her off guard. And then it made sense. "You—think I should offer to keep Snowy all day tomorrow so Laurel can have some time to herself?"

"Go to the head of the class, Rachel. Your deductive skills are top-notch."

"I don't know if Laurel will agree. Her—uh—stress doesn't have anything to do with Snowy; she is a devoted mother and—"

"Odds are, she'll jump at the chance to take a break from the kid. She's probably well on the way to convincing herself that Snowy is old enough to be independent, that she doesn't want to be one of those smothering mothers who won't give her child plenty of personal space.''

"Independent? Personal space?'' His cynicism, so cool and matter-of-fact, riled Rachel. "Are you crazy? Snowy is only three!''

"Brady was not quite a year old when his mother spun that tale for me.''

Rachel's breath caught. "She said she was leaving him because a one-year-old child ought to be independent from his mother?''

"That's the politically correct version which does play better than the real one . . . she wanted to follow her boy-friend—who has no use for kids—around the world.''

Misty had said Brady's mother dumped him and also mentioned a boyfriend in Eastern Europe. The politically incorrect version of the little boy's absent mother certainly explained Quint's cynical attitude and Misty's hostility.

"All mothers aren't like that, Quint,'' Rachel said quietly.

"I know. But some are.''

Rachel swallowed. "I'm sorry, Quint.''

"You're sorry Brady's mother could justify leaving him because she found more interesting things to do than take care of him? Yeah, so am I, but her rationalization is a theme that's been promoted for years. It's a convenient out for those who want to believe it, Rachel.''

"It's nothing but self-serving narcissism.'' And then she remembered what he'd said earlier, about her sister. "Laurel isn't like that.''

"I hope not, for your niece's sake. Well, good luck, Rachel. And good night.''

Rachel didn't want him to hang up, she wanted to talk more about Brady's mother and Laurel's troublesome behavior. She wouldn't even mind discussing Misty Tilden, despite the absence of Aunt Eve. She felt like she could've talked for hours to Quint, but he was no longer on the line.

Rachel gulped down two Excedrin tablets, then squared her shoulders and walked into the living room. "Laurel,

let's go to Richman's." She pasted a big smile on her face.
Divert her, Quint had advised. "I'm not up for a banana
split, but I'd love some coffee ice cream."

"With hot fudge sauce!" Laurel exclaimed. She threw
her arms around Rachel. "I knew I could count on you,
Rach. I knew you'd understand."

Wade pulled his car into a space in the parking lot behind
the Lakeview Police Station. He saw his aunt's Porsche
parked there, along with a fleet of luxury cars that he knew
belonged to various Tildens.

Maybe he should pinch himself. Wasn't that the traditional way to discover if one were awake or dreaming?
Waking up in bed to contemplate this very strange dream
would make far more sense than actually being here at the
police station to represent his clients, the Tildens.

According to Aunt Eve's phone message, Lakeview's
wealthiest, most prominent family had been ordered by
Chief Nick Spagna to come down to the station this morning to discuss the criminal complaints that had been filed
against them.

Just for the hell of it, Wade pinched his arm hard.

Ouch! Well, he was definitely awake.

It was a sunny, balmy morning, and on the wide grassy
lawn in front of the police station Eve Saxon stood with
Town Tilden Junior and his son Town Three. Town Junior's sister Marguerite Tilden Lloyd and her husband were
also in attendance with their daughter Sloane, who'd been
in the class behind Wade's at Lakeview Academy, and son
Tilden, also an academy alumnus, three years younger than
his sister.

Every one of them looked infuriated, Wade noted, although perhaps that was too mild a term to describe their
wild eyes, contorted features, and purple-faced rage. Rabid
seemed more apt.

"Did you contact Rachel?" Eve asked her nephew, as
he joined the group.

Wade shook his head. "I finally ended up calling Laurel,

who said Rachel took Snowy for the day. They could be anywhere, at the zoo or—''

''All right,'' Eve cut in. ''We can manage without her, of course, I just wanted her here as a show of solidarity.''

''Did you talk to Cormack?'' Town Junior demanded.

He did not bother to specify which Cormack. Quinton had become *the* Cormack, the only one, redefining the name and rendering his inept father Frank to the ranks of irrelevancy.

''No,'' Eve replied. ''I got his voice mail at his office and his answering machine at his home. I even tried the Sheely girl, who works for him, but her parents claim she is unavailable.''

''She is unavailable, she's in north Jersey,'' Wade spoke up.

He didn't like his aunt's implication that Bob and Mary Jean Sheely were being less than honest concerning their daughter's whereabouts, although that didn't mean his anger at Dana had lessened one iota.

He was still furious with her for evicting him from her room, for acting like that passionate little scene between them counted for nothing. Worse, he'd spent a rotten, almost-sleepless night, so mad at her he could hardly stand to say her name yet hotter for her than he'd ever been for any woman in his life, a conflict guaranteed to derange even the sanest man.

So here he stood, deranged, defending Dana while wanting to curse her. ''That's probably where Cormack is, too. They're working on a personal injury suit up there.''

And that had damn well better be all they were doing up there or he'd go straight to Bob and Mary Jean, who would never tolerate a liaison between Dana and the divorced Quint, job or no job. Wade felt a glowing moment of righteousness.

''Well, I'd like to make *them* victims in their own personal injury suit.'' Young Tilden Lloyd was venomous. ''I'd love to see them suffer catastrophic personal injuries. I want to personally pulverize—''

"There is no call for that kind of talk," Wade interrupted sharply, earning him an astonished glance from his aunt.

He couldn't help it. Listening to that little twerp make threats was more than he could stomach on this already-wretched morning. And the thought of anyone daring to wish a catastrophic injury on Dana made him want to inflict one himself on the little jerk right here and now.

"Wade used to be very close to the Sheelys," Sloane said, eyeing him coldly. "If he still is, you'd better make your threats exclusively against Quinton Cormack, Tilly."

"There will be no threats made at all!" snapped Town Three. "I wouldn't put it past Cormack to have spies lurking—they're probably hiding in the trees or something—and then he'll sling more accusations at us. That barracuda will stop at nothing!"

Town Junior cast a furtive, uncertain glance into the leafy branches of one of the giant oaks. "Let's go inside and dispose of this—this nonsense once and for all!" He marched up the wide stone steps, the other Tildens following in his wake.

Eve and Wade lingered behind, taking the steps more slowly. "God, I can't believe this," Eve gritted through her teeth.

"That the Tildens broke into the old homestead last night or that Misty filed a complaint against them for doing it?" quizzed Wade.

"*Misty!*" Eve made it sound more like a scourge than a name. "It would never occur to that tramp to go near the police. This is pure Quinton Cormack, Wade, another one of his legal maneuvers, and as usual, anything but subtle. He's trying to get some leverage to eke a big out-of-court settlement for that bimbo, of which he will happily take his one-third contingency fee."

"Yeah, but Cormack's getting a lot of help from the Tildens themselves, Aunt Eve. If they hadn't broken into the house—"

"They did not break in!" Eve snapped. "This was their father's home, the place where Town Junior and Marguerite grew up. Town Senior welcomed his children and grand-children into that home. They did not break in!''

She repeated her assertion just as vehemently to Chief Nick Spagna as the entire group crowded into his office. The chief was in his early fifties, swarthy and fit with thick dark hair beginning to turn silver. He radiated a menacing intensity, reminding Wade of the actor Tommy Lee Jones in both looks and demeanor, starring in one of his on-the-edge-psycho roles.

He knew Spagna had retired after twenty years with the Newark Police Department, the last decade as a homicide detective, and moved to Lakeview three years ago to become the chief. Compared to the mean streets of Newark, his position in Lakeview must seem more like a vacation than a job.

Chief Spagna was not at all intimidated or impressed by the affluent prominent citizens gathered before him. His face impassive, he leaned back in his chair, glancing through the papers in front of him.

"In her statement, Mrs. Tilden says that she'd had the locks changed after the funeral of her husband and hadn't given out any keys," the chief read flatly. "She contends that she was not at home during the perps' illegal entry and—"

"We are not perps!" an enraged Town Three interrupted. "We had every right to be in that house, it's that trashy slut who doesn't belong there!"

"Cut the slurs," Chief Spagna warned. "Your names are the ones on this complaint, not hers." He pinned the Tildens with a stern stare.

Wade felt a sinking sensation. He guessed that it probably hadn't occurred to the Tildens or Aunt Eve—they would find it patently unbelievable—but he was one hundred percent certain that Chief Spagna's sympathies lay with Misty.

And for one very crucial reason—because her attorney was Quint Cormack.

Standing there in the chief's office, Wade clearly remembered a conversation he'd had with Dana last summer, not long after she'd been hired by Cormack. . . .

They'd been at a Phillies game and during a lull, she'd turned to him and said, "Chief Spagna's father died up in Newark without a will, and the checking and savings accounts are in his name only, so poor old Mrs. Spagna can't get access to their money to pay the bills." Dana's big blue eyes had shone with sympathy. "I heard about it from Tricia, who used to date Kelvin Anderson, you know him, that really cute blond cop, and I told Quint. He called the chief and offered to take care of everything right away, and pro bono, too. Isn't that nice of him?"

Wade recalled scoffing something like, "Doesn't seem as if Cormack's got much to do if he's volunteering himself to work for free. Don't expect to have your job at Cormack and Son too long, Sheely. That firm is doomed to fold."

It hadn't, of course. It had prospered beyond anybody's wildest dreams.

Wade felt himself begin to perspire. Suddenly, it felt like it was a million degrees in the chief's office. Now, too late, he comprehended Cormack's pro bono work for Chief Spagna had nothing to do with fiscal stupidity and everything to do with ingenious strategic planning.

When Quint Cormack filed a complaint on behalf of one of his clients, it would not be regarded lightly. Even if it were filed against the illustrious Tildens.

"Mr. Cormack and Mrs. Tilden called to report the incident last night and came to the station this morning to officially file the complaint." Chief Spagna's voice rose above the irate mutterings of the Tildens. "Following procedure, the department is now considering filing criminal charges."

"That's absurd, Spagna!" Eve lashed out. "You can't possibly be serious!"

"Ms. Saxon, the charges listed on this complaint *are* very serious, and that's how we're taking them," the chief cut her off.

Wade worried his aunt had made a tactical error by ad-

dressing the chief without his title—and in such a disparaging tone too. Had she come across as elitist and
patronizing? Not a good thing, especially since the elite
firm of Saxon Associates hadn't offered to help his poor
old widowed mother last year.

"Would you please read us the complaint, Chief
Spagna?" Wade asked politely. His attempt at damage con-
trol earned him collective glares from Aunt Eve and the
Tildens.

"Breaking and entering. Burglary, because common law
allows an illegal entry at night to be considered burglary,"
the chief explained.

"Since when?" howled Town Three. "From what fascist
regime did you and Cormack dredge up that bit of insanity?"

The other Tildens had similar views and didn't hesitate
to express them. Loudly.

"Criminal trespass. Grand larceny," the chief raised his
voice above the ensuing commotion.

That last accusation drew even more vociferous protests.
"We didn't take anything!" screamed Marguerite. "That
thieving harlot shot at us! How can you charge us with
grand larceny when we didn't get a damn thing?"

"You tried," the chief said flatly. "And Mrs. Tilden
believes that some rare coins and stamps might be missing."

"Kindly stop referring to that whore as Mrs. Tilden,"
ordered Town Junior. "The title of Mrs. Tilden belongs to
my late mother and no one else."

Wade knew that Town Junior had expressly forbidden
his two ex-wives to use the Tilden name after divorcing
him. And now there was Misty, his father's widow, who
showed no inclination of giving up Tilden to resume her
maiden name of Czenko. How that must grate!

"My clients did not take anything from the house," Eve
reiterated. "Furthermore, I demand to know what action is
being taken against that woman. She fired a gun at members
of Townsend Senior's own family! Since charges are being

hurled around here, I believe that Misty qualifies herself—for six counts of attempted homicide.''

"No. There will be no charges filed against Mrs. Tilden,'' the chief spoke in an eerily ominous monotone. ''The gun is registered to her and she was defending herself in her own home against intruders. Which brings us to the terroristic threats made against her.''

"You cannot consider charging my clients with making terroristic threats against a greedy little viper who manipulated their vulnerable father and grandfather, who stole their inheritance, and then shot at them!'' Now it was Eve who was almost screaming.

Wade placed his hand on his aunt's arm, attempting to calm her. She shook it off like a bothersome gnat that had landed on her.

"Quint also suggested the possibility of conspiracy charges.'' Chief Spagna stayed cool, in sharp contrast to the others' loss of control. ''Since there were six people who collaborated in the B and E and the threats and—''

"You needn't run down the list again, we heard you the first time!'' Eve interjected sharply. ''Conspiracy! I had no idea that Quinton Cormack was so creative. And what a nice setup he has here—he dreams up charges against the innocent citizens of this community and the Lakeview police are happy to oblige him. This entire complaint is a joke, Spagna, a very sick joke, and you know it as well as I do.''

"Ms. Saxon, I don't think you've been listening to what has been said.'' Spagna stood up in an unmistakable gesture of dismissal. ''This complaint is very real and very serious, and we are treating it as such. You clearly are not, and you are doing your clients a big disservice if you treat this matter as a joke. I want to warn you now that unless this complaint is withdrawn, the department will be obligated to take action. And that means filing criminal charges against the six names listed here.'' He glanced at his watch. ''I have a meeting here in my office in two minutes. All of you will have to leave immediately.''

Spagna was kicking them out of his office! There was a

momentary charged silence, of such nuclear intensity that
Wade pictured Aunt Eve and the Tildens collectively self-
destructing, leaving nothing behind but seven piles of va-
porized ash.

In the next instant, he worried they were going to rush
the chief like a pack of mad wolverines.

Getting his aunt and the Tildens out of that office before
any capital offenses could be committed took top priority.
Wade began to steer the group out, circling them like a dog
herding sheep and nudging them forward.

"If the complaint is withdrawn, there won't be any
charges filed?" Wade asked. It was basic first-year law-
school information, but he wanted his clients to hear it and
to remind Aunt Eve of that vital fact.

"That's pretty much how it goes," agreed the chief.

"One more question, if you don't mind, Chief Spagna?"
Wade turned back, after literally shoving Sloane and
brother Tilly through the door. He saw a glimmer of amusement in the officer's eyes, which was quickly suppressed.

"What is it, Mr. Saxon?"

"Were there any witnesses to last night's, um, break-
in?"

Town Junior and Marguerite took instant offense and
again insisted that they could not break into their own father's home, they had every right to come and go there as
they pleased.

Wade tried again. "I'd like to know if this—incident is
just Misty's word against our clients?"

He felt his aunt squeeze his arm. "Good point, Wade,"
she whispered. "This outrage has made me so crazy, I
never even thought to ask."

Wade saw the Tildens exchange glances among themselves. Not a good sign, not by their expressions.

"There was a witness present," said Chief Spagna.
"Shawn Sheely. He came in this morning with Quint and
Misty to corroborate the report."

*   *   *

"A Sheely!" Eve exclaimed as the group followed the circular sidewalk around the building to the parking lot in the back. "He's not a viable witness. A Sheely girl works in Cormack's office, and any one of them would say whatever he told them to say. That's collusion, pure and simple."

Wade lagged behind, still reeling with shock. *Shawn Sheely with Misty Tilden?*

Shawn with the town's most notorious widow, the nude lap dancer from the sleazy porn palace in Camden? Why, he could still picture little Shawn in his Cub Scout uniform! And now that boy was keeping company with *Misty Tilden?*

Wade ran his hand through his hair, making it stand on end, but he didn't care. He felt like pulling it out. He had to tell Dana what he'd just heard. He was certain she didn't know, even though Quint Cormack obviously did.

Just imagining her reaction made his throat tighten. The Sheelys tended to revere each other; despite petty arguments, their loyalty ran deep. Dana had been upset when she'd learned her sainted brother Tim had high-school sex. Safe sex. That was going to seem downright tame compared to the specter of Shawn with Misty, whose sordid past had to be beyond the comprehension of the wholesome Sheelys.

And if Bob and Mary Jean couldn't deal with Tricia dating a divorced but respectable, conventional insurance claims adjustor, learning who Shawn had taken up with would launch them right into orbit, alongside the Hubble telescope.

Sloane Tilden Lloyd slowed to match her pace to Wade's. "I suppose you're still friendly with the Sheely tribe?" Her tone was condescending and sarcastic, as if quizzing him about a particularly childish pasttime, and an asinine one to boot, like putting bubble gum in girls' hair.

"Yeah, still friendly after all these years."

He wasn't fooled by Sloane's show of disdain for the Sheelys. He well remembered her obsessive teenage crush on Tim. All through high school, Sloane had relentlessly pumped Wade for information about his best friend. Sloane wanted Tim Sheely—even though he was not a member of one of the town's moneyed families, even though he had no interest in her whatsoever.

As a Saxon, ever viewed as a Tilden minion, Wade had been pressured to use his influence with the Sheelys to arrange a date for Sloane with Tim. Understanding—though resenting—his position, Wade had really tried. At Sloane's command, he'd extended countless invitations to Tim to parties and dances with Sloane's crowd.

And Tim had always refused.

"Just go out with her once," Wade remembered almost begging his friend. "To get her off my back." He sometimes switched tactics, offering a sleazy lure instead. "You'll score, I guarantee it. Bring a whole box of rubbers because that girl is so hot for you, she'll do whatever you want."

"Sloane is a stuck-up snot and I don't want her," Tim replied. He steadfastly resisted Wade's every entreaty on Sloane's behalf.

Still, Sloane had persisted, probably unable to comprehend not getting what—or who—she wanted. She'd called Tim herself and invited him to escort her to a society-page headliner, a debutante cotillion in Philadelphia. Tim had politely declined but the prospect of him dressed in white tie and tails mixing it up with Main Line blue bloods at a debutante ball still had the power to make the rest of the Sheelys roll on the floor laughing.

Wade found himself grinning at the memory. Sometimes he found it hard to believe that Tim had withstood all Sloane's commands. A sharp contrast to the Saxons, who invariably jumped to any Tilden command.

There were so very few people who didn't.

Quint Cormack was one who didn't. The connection leaped to mind and Wade didn't like it. He did not want any similarities at all between his best friend and the Saxon nemesis, Quinton Cormack.

Yet there it was. Just like Tim, Quint stood up to the Tildens and told them no.

"Since Wade is so chummy with the Sheelys and one of the Sheely girls works for Quinton Cormack, why doesn't he use her to get the inside track on Cormack's next move?" Sloane was talking to Eve now, drawing Wade's attention back to her.

Everybody stopped walking and formed a circle around him. Wade felt as if he were suffocating.

He glared at Sloane. "We don't need an inside track, Cormack has been anything but secretive. His tactics are about as subtle as a car bomb, and his next move is just as obvious. Aunt Eve?" he deferred to her to make his point.

Eve heaved a sigh. "Cormack's next move will be to offer to drop the complaint if you agree to make Misty an offer she can't refuse."

"We'd already agreed to ignore that bogus will she claims to have and to give her some sort of settlement," Town Junior said impatiently. "Didn't you convey our message to Cormack clearly enough, Eve?"

"Cormack refused to talk to me over the phone," Eve admitted, two spots of color staining her cheeks. A sign of how very upset she was, Wade knew. "He wants to meet with us at his office next week."

"That is unacceptable, Eve," Marguerite said harshly. "We will not go to that man; he will come to us. We will meet *only* in your office and the settlement will be exclusively on our terms."

"I don't think we should make it a turf war," Wade objected. "Agreeing to meet in Cormack's office is a simple enough concession and might—"

"*You're* the one who's simple if you think we're making any concessions to Cormack and his raving slut of a client," Tilden Lloyd said peevishly.

Wade considered decking him. Tilden was slim and pale, and one good whack would knock him down. Perhaps sensing her nephew's loosely tethered control, Eve stepped directly in front of young Tilden.

"I'll set up a meeting with Cormack in my office for Monday," she said firmly, giving Wade the same warning look she used to flash when he'd been a kid bent on teasing his cousins to the screaming point.

"Do that," decreed Town Junior. He and Town Three stalked off, leaving the Saxons with Marguerite's family.

"Yes, Eve, do that," Marguerite seconded haughtily, and made her own grand exit. Her ever-silent husband and their son and daughter followed.

Wade looked at his aunt, who was staring at the departing Tildens, her face a mask of barely contained fury. Marguerite was supposed to be Aunt Eve's dear old school chum.

"Man, with friends like her . . ." he unconsciously blurted his thoughts aloud.

He felt an unexpected flash of sympathy for his aunt. Getting Cormacked was bruising, and Aunt Eve and Rachel seemed exceptionally unable to cope. And they hadn't even heard about Pedersen's defection. Wade took off his coat and loosened his tie. He felt as if he were choking on the fallout of that yet-to-be-dropped bomb. Meanwhile, there were the Tildens to endure.

"Do you know there was a time when Marguerite and I hoped that you and Sloane would get together and our families would be officially joined?" Eve grimaced. "When you two were younger, it was our fondest wish."

"Aunt Eve, I'd rather be burned at the stake."

"Well, to be perfectly honest, I'm glad you're not with her either. The girl is insufferable."

"All the Tildens are insufferable," grumbled Wade. "What a stroke of bad luck that we're stuck with them and Quint Cormack gets Misty!"

"I'll overlook that remark since we've had a trying morning." Eve gave him a leveling glance. "What do you make of Shawn Sheely being with Misty last night and corroborating her complaint? A stroke of evil genius on Quint Cormack's part?"

"No. Dana would never condone that." Wade was emphatic. "If Shawn's with Misty, he arranged it all on his own. It's not that hard to fathom, Aunt Eve. Misty is only a couple years older than Shawn and he—well, he's not at all like Tim. Shawn has always been restless, kind of a daredevil. He loved his stint in the marines, except when he thought things were getting too tame. Bosnia just wasn't the same for him after they signed that peace agreement. And now he's back here in Jersey and bored. He wants to start up a lawn-care business but the banks turned him down for a loan and he's frustrated and—"

"The flashy young widow has lots of capital to invest," Eve filled in the rest. "Considering her past, she would appeal to a restless young man with a taste for adventure. I do feel sorry for Bob and Mary Jean Sheely, though. They won't like this at all. Are you going to tell them?"

Wade recoiled in dread. "Do you think I should? I—uh—thought I'd mention it to Dana. She could tell her folks if she wanted to."

"You said that Dana is out of town. This type of gossip spreads fast as wildfire, Wade. I believe hearing it from you first would be easier for the Sheelys."

"Then I guess I'll go over there now," Wade said glumly. "I'd almost rather date Sloane than break this news to them."

"I know, but it should—" Eve halted in mid-sentence. "Isn't that Chief Spagna leaving the building?"

Wade followed her gaze. The chief was striding purposefully toward the squad car in front of the station. "Yeah, that's him."

"He said he had a meeting in his office in two minutes, and that's why we had to leave. Well, his meeting couldn't be over that fast." Eve was indignant.

"True. Looks like we were evicted. Blown off." Wade laughed slightly. "There aren't very many people who would dare do that to the Tildens and the Saxons. Quint Cormack is one, seems like Spagna is the other. You have to kind of admire the chief for that."

"I will not be treated so disrespectfully!" Eve turned on

her heel and started toward the squad car herself. ''Chief Spagna, I want to speak to you right now,'' she called out to him.

Wade flinched. She sounded alarmingly Tilden-like, and the chief had made his feelings about the Tildens clear when he'd kicked them all out of his office a few minutes ago.

But Spagna did stop and wait, his body language readable even at a distance. Chief Nick Spagna was not pleased.

Wade chased after his aunt and caught her by the arm, halting her. It was surprisingly easy for him to physically restrain her. Startled, he found himself viewing her from a different angle, an objective one, for the first time in his adult life.

Eve Saxon was slender and only of average height; she looked particularly fragile and feminine in her powder blue suit. Wade blinked, nonplussed. He'd always thought of his aunt as more powerful and invincible than an armored tank destroyer.

''Aunt Eve, be careful what you say to the chief,'' he hissed in her ear. ''Spagna was a detective in Newark, remember? They don't mess around up there. Disrespect *him* and you'll end up in a cell. Probably with something broken. Maybe your head.''

''Go to the Sheelys, Wade,'' Eve muttered, her eyes fixed on Nick Spagna. The chief met and returned her fierce glare. ''I am perfectly capable of taking care of myself.'' She jerked free and stalked off.

''And those were the last words she spoke before she disappeared forever,'' Wade said sardonically, as his aunt headed straight for the police chief.

He turned and resolutely walked to his car. He had never been the type to slow down and stare at traffic accidents or to watch disaster footage, and the ensuing Saxon–Spagna clash promised to be nothing less than a gruesome spectacle.

He envisioned a ghoulish scenario in which Chief Spagna would claim he'd shot Eve Saxon in the line of duty and then retain Quint Cormack, who would get him acquitted of all charges. The Tildens wouldn't care at all, of course. They would probably decide to take their legal business to the victorious Cormack, just like Pedersen.

And now he faced the bleak prospect of breaking the Sheelys' hearts. Feeling as welcome as a bell-ringing leper in a medieval town, a grim-faced Wade drove off to tell the family about Shawn's new friend.

11

"*I*'ve never been to anything like this. It's fun." Rachel was caught up in the lively atmosphere of the Renaissance Festival. "Isn't it?" she asked Quint, who walked alongside her.

The four children were a few feet ahead of Rachel and Quint, their heads bobbing back and forth, like spectators following the ball in a tennis match, as they took in the strange sights and sounds.

Festival personnel wearing period costumes and speaking a kind of pidgin Chaucerian English moved through the fairground, staging miniscenes with each other, acting as drunk or amorous or loquacious villagers.

"Fun," Quint repeated doubtfully. He watched a medieval-garbed nun scold a pair of drunken villagers, and the men's muddled responses drew laughs from the surrounding crowd.

"Well, I'll admit there is pageantry and a certain infectious air to the whole thing, but I'm reserving judgment about how much fun we're having. Those affected Middle English accents are awful beyond imagining and the costumes—"

"You seemed to be enjoying the cleavage of that buxom blond wench selling ale back there," Rachel observed dryly. "You couldn't tear your eyes away from Canterbury Tales Barbie."

Her own ice green ribbed cotton sweater and slim-fitting

wheat-colored jeans were a drastic contrast to her severe courtroom wardrobe, yet seemed downright demure in comparison to some of the festival players' provocative attire.

There was plenty of overflowing cleavage on display, thanks to the low-cut gowns and corsets that plumped up flesh more efficiently than the modern-day Wonderbra. Some of the men wore tights and tunics, but most had on baggy pants and shapeless shirts, presumably the practical unflattering garb of peasants of yore. Long, dark, hooded cloaks, elegant yet somewhat sinister, were sold at one of the booths, but more fairgoers than actors were wearing them.

"I wasn't staring, Rachel," Quint assured her, tongue-firmly-in-cheek. "I was simply wondering if they had silicone implants back in the Middle Ages."

"Sure. They had funnel cake, too. And deep-fried vegetables drowned in cheese sauce and frozen cappuccino."

They'd passed booths selling that anachronistic cuisine, along with pizza slices, soft drinks, hot dogs, and ice cream. From the long lines at each booth, it was clearly modern crowd-pleasing fare.

They walked past a small crowd gathered around a festival actress—another blonde with an amazing chest stuffed into a brocade corset—who had engaged a male attendee in a bawdy conversation. The woman didn't break character while the man stammered his replies and the onlookers laughed, enjoying the scene.

"Poor sap, you can tell he feels like a fool," said Quint, warily eyeing those around him. "This is too interactive for me."

The festival actors aggressively approached people to start a mock quarrel or pepper them with ribald questions and suggestions which other spectators—who weren't targets themselves—found hilarious.

"I think I'm in hell," Quint muttered a short while later when a young man dressed in raggedy village serf clothes demanded "a tuppence" to buy himself a cup of mead, a drink made of fermented honey.

"No," Quint said firmly, refusing to be drawn into further banter.

Remaining firmly in character, the actor then turned to Rachel, and asked, "Why doth milady consort with Lord Cheapside here? If he doth not give gramercy to one such as I, certes you will be treated no better."

Rachel smiled gamely and tried to think of an amusing comeback but before one came to mind, Quint caught her wrist and pulled her away. His dour expression did not encourage the actor to continue the repartee, so the young man turned to more willing participants.

"You looked ready to mangle the poor guy. It's just pretend, Quint, like being in a play. Where's your sense of humor?" Rachel reproved with a smirk.

"I don't find it funny to be forced into a stupid skit where the other guy knows the script and I don't. I hate being cast in the role of village idiot."

"Since when do you need a script to follow? You certainly have no problem speaking extemporaneously, at least not in the courtroom. Of course, in the Pedersen case, *I* was the one cast in the role of village idiot, which would've been more to your liking."

She said the words before they fully registered, and when they did, Rachel was astounded. *She'd actually joked about the calamitous Pedersen trial!* She wouldn't have thought it possible.

Quint slid his fingers over her wrist and linked them with hers. "The problem with that case wasn't you, Rachel, it was Pedersen and his tyrant complex that landed him in court in the first place. The man was indefensible. Even he will admit that now."

"You are as slick as an oil spill, Quinton Cormack," Rachel said tersely.

She debated whether or not to remove her hand from his, but ultimately, she didn't. The warmth of his palm and the strength of his fingers felt too good joined with hers.

"I hope you don't really believe that, Rachel." Quint's voice was low and deep.

Was he really being *slick* or was he sincere? Whichever, he was certainly convincing. She was beginning to accept his point of view, maybe even agree with it. The fact that she could make a joke about the worst defeat of her career portended . . . something.

Rachel didn't care to examine what.

She glanced up at Quint, whose rangy, athletic build was emphasized by the faded jeans and Philadephia Flyers shirt he was wearing. She was instantly assailed by intense sensual memories, of his lips on hers, his tongue in her mouth, his hands on her breasts. She felt her insides liquefy as she imagined his hands and his lips touching her in places that were suddenly throbbing and ultrasensitive.

It was lunacy, this physical effect he had on her. She should hate herself for it, but she couldn't seem to work up even a middling dander. Reflexively, Rachel touched one finger to the purple passion mark on her neck. It had faded only slightly, but she hadn't bothered trying to conceal it with makeup today.

"Did your sister comment on that last night?" Quint asked.

Rachel's hand swiftly fell to her side. She was mortified that he'd been watching her and fervently hoped he hadn't intuited what she'd been thinking. And wanting.

"She didn't notice," Rachel replied. It was true. While eating ice cream at Richman's last night, the conversation had centered exclusively on Laurel.

"You could've had your face painted blue and she wouldn't have noticed," Quint said knowledgeably. "Laurel is the star of her own show, and you're merely a member of the audience. Front or back row?"

Rachel thought of Laurel's long soliloquy on the trials and tribulations of being Laurel. "I think I was way up in the balcony, last row," she admitted ruefully.

"That's usually where I am in those one-player scenes."

Quint gave her hand a sympathetic squeeze and pulled her a little closer to him.

She didn't even consider moving away.

They reached a row of stalls where medieval arts and crafts demonstrations were being performed. There were also booths with festival souvenirs for sale. The children ran back and forth from one booth to another, thrilled with the merchandise.

"Ah, ye old tourist trap," Quint murmured. "A taste of the twentieth century interjected into the fourteenth."

Rachel hurried to take Brady and Snowy by their hands and guide them away from a rather risqué scene being enacted by yet another buxom young maiden and a lecherous young man who was practically drooling over the woman's ample bosom. The crowd watching the pair were chuckling, but the two toddlers didn't get the jokes, much to Rachel's relief.

"Quint, would you buy me a sword?" cried Austin, his dark eyes glowing with excitement.

They all watched the blacksmith who stood over a fire, shaping metal into knights' helmets and swords. The finished products were offered for sale in the stall next to the workshop and looked like genuine medieval wares.

"Arm you with a sword?" Quint was incredulous. "You're kidding, right? After your adventures with the BB gun?"

"Sarah still has it," Austin said sulkily. "She and Matt said they won't give it back till they're good and ready."

"I hope that will be about ten years from now," replied Quint. "I won't buy you a sword, Austin. Find something else."

"Sorn," attempted Brady, pointing at one of the long metal swords. "Want that."

It was definitely time for a change of scene, Rachel decided. "Let's look at the puppets." She pointed to another booth and herded the smaller children toward it. "Wouldn't it be fun to have a puppet? Look, there are green dragons and—"

"I want a puppet," Dustin said eagerly.

"Puppets are for babies like Brady and Snowy." Austin was scornful. "Hey, Quint, I see what I want. Over there. A whip!"

Long, authentic-looking whips were being sold at one of the booths. Quint and Rachel looked at each other.

"This is going to be a very long day," Quint said resignedly, as Austin tugged on his arm, pulling him toward the booth.

Rachel watched a glassblower for a few minutes before Brady and Snowy lost interest and moved on to a theater stall featuring a traditional Punch and Judy puppet show. The humor and the language was beyond the toddlers, who created their own game, making their new dragon puppets pretend to eat the grass, an activity they found far more entertaining than any historical reenactment.

Quint joined them later with Austin and Dustin, each boy clutching a knight action figure—a compromise on the whip, perhaps?—and a wooden Jacob's ladder toy.

"There are lots of games for kids over on the far side of the field," Quint reported, "and there's something called a Living Chess Game, too. Do you want to see it?"

"Cool!" exclaimed Austin, pausing to whomp his brother on the back. He took off with chubby Dustin running after him, hopelessly outpaced.

Rachel managed to jolly Brady and Snowy into coming along, though they would've been happy to stay put, absorbed in their play.

"They've been playing their puppets-eat-grass game for the past twenty minutes and still find it endlessly fascinating," she marveled.

"A game they could play in their own backyards. Glad we made the two-hour drive and paid those stiff attendance fees for them." Quint was sardonic.

"The Renaissance aspect of this fair is wasted on them, but they're enjoying themselves in their own way. Uh-oh." Rachel touched Quint's arm, directing his attention ahead and to the right.

Austin had just pushed his younger brother into the path of a colorfully clad juggler, who was gaily juggling five or six bright rubber balls. Dustin fell to the ground and knocked the juggler off-balance. The balls went flying in five or six different directions.

"I think I'm finally beginning to understand the whys and wherefores of the Children's Crusade," drawled Quint. "The medieval Austins were shipped off to terrorize distant lands, leaving the villages in peace."

"If only you would make politically incorrect remarks like that in court, you would be a far less formidable opponent." Rachel was only half-kidding. "But in the courtroom you never hit a false note, not even in jest."

"I think you've built up my courtroom prowess to mythical proportions, Rachel," Quint said dryly. "A word to the wise . . . Don't let me psych you out."

She tilted her head, inquisitive. "Wade said you're deliberately trying to psych me out in the Tilden case. He said it's part of your strategy."

Quint grinned. "Wade has more perception than I credited him with. I've always viewed him as Saxon Associates' weakest link, but I may have to rethink that premise."

"So you admit it? You were playing mind games with me?"

"Of course. A stock-in-trade technique, Rachel. You should know that."

At this point she was more curious than angry. She looked up at him, her eyes meeting his, her lips slightly parted. It took a moment for her to speak. "But why are you telling me now? Isn't giving away your tactics a mistake?"

"No, because it won't change anything." He put his arm around her waist and slipped his hand beneath the ribbed hem of her cotton sweater to lightly stroke her midriff.

The gentle kneading of his fingers on her bare skin was electrifying. Her nipples tingled in reaction.

"Anyway, I've gotten to know you better since I—uh—launched that missile by messenger," Quint confessed. His dark eyes gleamed. "And to like you. I try to make it a point to be honest with the people I know and like."

Was he being flippant? Or unremittingly frank? Rachel couldn't tell. She wasn't thinking clearly at all, not while being bombarded with sensory impulses unleashed by his lazy caresses.

His fingertips reached the edge of her bra and touched the lacy material before he slowly withdrew his hand from underneath her sweater. Rachel's throat was dry. The way he'd casually fondled her—in public!—conveyed a possessive intimacy she hadn't granted to him. Or had she?

She was struck by an odd feeling of déjà vu. The last time she'd felt so bewildered had been in the courtroom, during the Pedersen trial when her case was collapsing around her. Quint Cormack had been instrumental in that head-spinning event, too.

"Hey, lookit that!" shouted Austin, running back to join them. He pointed to a facsimile of wooden stocks, used to punish and humiliate lesser offenders in olden times.

A crowd had gathered around to view the mock trial being conducted.

"It's a kangaroo court," explained Quint. The kids were excited until he broke the news that no actual kangaroos would be a part of the proceedings.

Rachel listened to the byplay while struggling to regain her bearings. It was jarring to emerge from a sensual haze to the practical and prosaic world of children, though Quint seemed to do so with ease.

The "defendant" in the mock trial was a teenage boy with multiple earrings and a tattoo of a grinning snake on his arm. It was almost identical to the design on his black T-shirt.

"There don't seem to be any lawyers involved in the proceedings. Do you think we should go over and offer our services?" Quint lightly nudged Rachel with his elbow.

"As a team or opposing counsel? Because I don't want to represent that boy. I have a strong hunch he's going to end up in those stocks, no matter who says what." Rachel cast Quint a covert glance. "I see it as a kind of medieval parallel to the Pedersen case."

Quint laughed.

Rachel felt inordinately pleased. Though she normally presented an ultraserious demeanor regarding her career—Wade was the jokester of Saxon Associates—making Quint laugh delighted her.

Although it wouldn't do for her to develop a stand-up comedy routine based on the Pedersen loss, she cautioned herself.

"Looks like you're right about the outcome of the trial," Quint said as the teen was led to the stocks. "A fix from the start."

Not that the accused seemed to mind. When his head and hands were firmly locked in place in the stocks, the crowd cheered, and the boy laughed and made faces, plainly relishing all the attention.

"He doesn't seem to be taking his punishment very seriously, does he?" Quint traced his thumb over Rachel's palm.

She felt the familiar pleasant tingling start all over again, deep inside her. This time, she tried to pull her hand away, but he held on and drew a slow widening circle in her palm. Those seductive little tingles quickly turned into a fiery glow of heat.

Which she had no business feeling, Rachel admonished herself, not while she was responsible for four young children at a festival in Pennsylvania. Especially when her young charges were headed toward . . . A mud fight!

"Quint!" she cried, and hearing the note of alarm in her voice, he dragged his eyes away from her beautifully shaped mouth.

He followed her gaze to a mud puddle the size of Lake Erie, where some actors playing drunken serfs were staging a fierce argument. It was inevitable that one of them would reach down and scoop up a handful of mud to pelt at another.

"Oh, no!" Quint took off in a run and swept Snowy and

Brady off their feet, seconds before they could wade into the sea of mud. He was too late to rescue Dustin, whom Austin had given a hearty shove.

Dustin ended up in the middle of the serfs' fight and caught a mud ball right in the chest. "Hey!" The boy looked around, torn between tears and anger.

"Get 'em, Dust," hollered Austin and plunged into the mud himself, merrily throwing gobs of the stuff at anyone within pitching distance. His aim was exceptionally good.

"Austin's the pitcher on his Little League team," Quint said to Rachel. He held on tight to the squirming toddlers in his arms. "The coach says the kid is a natural talent."

"That figures," Rachel muttered. Young Austin Cormack also seemed to have a natural talent for finding targets, no matter what his choice of projectile. "Shouldn't we stop them or something?"

The mud war was in high gear. The actors seemed to be having fun and so were Austin and Dustin and the younger recruits, mostly preteen boys, who'd joined in. The majority of adults beat a hasty retreat from the melee and watched from out-of-mudball range.

Despite Rachel's halfhearted suggestion for intervention, she couldn't bring herself to go any nearer to the rowdy brawl. She did not want a mud bath, and now the actors were beginning to drag surrounding onlookers into the mire, despite their reluctance to go.

A gleeful Dustin rolled around in the muck claiming to be Babe, the pig from one of his favorite movies. Austin continued to pitch mudballs with the accuracy of a junior Fernando Valenzuela.

"I think I'll take Brady and Snowy to feed the ducks down by the pond," Rachel said, snatching both children from Quint's arms. "We'll meet up with you later, okay?"

"Have fun. I'll just stand here out of the line of fire."

"Looking for clients who want to sue for damages attributed to assault by mud?" Rachel couldn't resist needling him. "I hope you brought along your cards to pass out."

"That's in the same league as ambulance chasing, Rachel. Ouch! I think I'm insulted."

"No, you aren't. Because you have to admit that Cormack and Son have taken some rather unlikely cases," Rachel reminded him. "The Doll House and its slimy proprietor jumps immediately to mind."

"Saxon Associates definitely wouldn't put out the welcome mat for the likes of Eddie Aiken. Which doesn't mean I like doing business with the guy either, my self-righteous little crusader," Quint added dryly.

Rachel blushed. "I'm neither self-righteous nor a crusader, I just believe in upholding certain standards."

"Extremely high ones, Rachel."

"Well, yes. I suppose so. I'm—not going to apologize."

"I don't expect you to. Choosing only the classiest, wealthiest clients is nice work if you can get it. Cormack and Son has to go with the old saw 'a reasonable doubt for a reasonable price.' Out of sheer necessity, my clients haven't always been on Lakeview's 'A' list." Quint was unrepentant.

He put his hands on her shoulders and turned her toward the pond. "Now go feed the ducks while I stick around here pretending I don't know my mud-crazed little brothers, who are wreaking even more havoc than the paid performers."

Snowy and Brady were pulling on Rachel's hands and the trio headed toward the pond. Rachel glanced over her shoulder to catch another look at Quint, who was watching his younger half brothers play.

He was as laid-back about the boys' behavior as he was about his repulsive client Eddie Aiken, Rachel thought, torn between admiration and astonishment. Though she could never condone representing an Aiken, her instincts told her that Quint's response to his kid brothers was more realistic than hers.

Her initial impulse would've been to lecture the boys, the way the older Saxons always used to scold Wade for running around and making too much noise and generally

getting into mischief, unlike the perfectly behaved K
and Laurel.

Quint let his kid brothers race around like wild boys. Or
were boys that age just naturally wild and full of energy?
The ones at this festival seemed to be, behaving a lot like
Austin and Dustin.

As a child, Wade had acted that way, too, though he had
been continually reprimanded for it, mused Rachel. No
wonder he'd preferred spending all his time with the Sheely
family when he'd finally discovered them. Nobody expected things to be quiet and orderly in a house with ten
kids.

Thoughts of the Sheelys inevitably brought Dana to
mind. Quint had mentioned that she'd gone to north Jersey
today to work on a personal injury suit his firm was han-
dling. Rachel had listened with radarlike intensity as Quint
talked about his paralegal but hadn't detected anything
other than fondness and respect in his tone.

In the light of day, she felt none of the niggling jealousy
that had disturbed her last night. Maybe it was because *she*
was the woman with Quint at the festival, not Dana Sheely;
maybe it was the way he looked at her, his dark eyes intent
with interest and an almost-irresistible hunger.

Rachel, Snowy, and Brady arrived at the edge of the
pond, where she bought specially packaged duck food from
a nearby vendor. The children were wildly excited by the
ducks, who swam over in increasing numbers for the meal
being tossed their way.

While she watched them, Rachel's mind drifted back to
this morning's drive from Lakeview to the festival. During
the more peaceful periods, when the two older children
were entertaining the two younger ones with stupid jokes
and even sillier songs, Quint had discussed his latest personal-injury suit with her.

It was their first neutral, professional conversation, and
Rachel enjoyed it immensely. She admired the way Quint's
mind worked; his analytical skills were first-rate. When not
in the position of opposing counsel, she could appreciate

his ability to almost instantly separate minutiae from essentials. The way he was able to cut directly to the heart of complex legal issues would prevent missteps and time-wasting diversions, yet conversely, made him an expert at obfuscation. The cloud of confusion he so ably created could send the opposing counsel into a morass of missteps and time-wasting diversions. It had happened to her in the Pedersen trial.

But as they talked, Quint seemed to value her own ability to evaluate and prioritize, to respect her input on hypothetical issues. He didn't mind her questioning the theories he tossed out, and she let her own ideas flow. Both relished the give-and-take like the lawyers they were, but this time they weren't adversaries.

She'd learned in their conversation today that Quint was a graduate of Stanford Law School and had been on Law Review, which placed him at the top of his class. She hadn't known that, hadn't bothered to check his credentials either before or after the Pedersen case.

Her mistake, Rachel realized ruefully. And a major oversight it was. Last year when Frank Cormack's attorney son had moved to town from California, all the Saxons had assumed that Quinton had undoubtedly received his law degree from some minimally accredited school whose campus was the beach with a curriculum featuring surfboarding and New Age crystals.

The collective Saxon hubris had contributed mightily to their fateful loss, Rachel finally admitted. They had wholeheartedly believed the Pedersen case was unwinnable for anyone but Saxon Associates. Certainly, no relation to the inept Frank Cormack could possibly be knowledgeable in complex labor and civil-rights litigation, the two underpinnings of employment law. But Quint had proven to be.

Truth be told, he had mastered the fine points, ones Rachel hadn't even touched upon. The jury couldn't be faulted for finding in favor of Quint's client.

He was also no slouch in the tort law department either, into which the subject of personal-injury fell. After listen-

ing to Quint outline his detailed strategy for the Polk
sonal injury suit, Rachel knew that North Jersey Power was
sunk if they were stupid enough to take the case to court

And she began to believe that not even Aunt Eve could
have won the Pedersen case against Quint Cormack. He
was that thorough, that cunning, that talented an attorney.

The rain wasn't falling in drops, it was coming down in
sheets. Though the windshield wipers of Wade's car tried
valiantly to clear the glass, the force and volume of the rain
made visibility a near impossibility. Many cars had given
up the battle and pulled onto the shoulder of the road to
wait out the storm, but Wade wasn't ready to concede defeat. He steered his Mercedes through the deluge, sandwiched between two monster trucks in the right lane who
had also chosen to soldier on.

Strange how it could be sunny in New Jersey, cloudy in
New York, but once across the Connecticut state line, a
rainstorm of Noah's Ark proportions suddenly reigned.
Wade groaned at his own bad pun. Things were really bad
when he started talking aloud to himself—and managed to
sound like a nerd while doing it.

Of course, things really *were* bad, he reminded himself,
and went down the list. This morning's disastrous meeting
with the Tildens and his aunt at the police station. The
disturbing news about Shawn Sheely's association with
Misty Tilden. As for Aunt Eve's confrontation with Chief
Spagna . . . Wade winced. He couldn't let himself think
about how badly that must have gone.

Admitting that his aunt was right about the speed of gossip in Lakeview—it could beat sound and light—and that
he owed the Sheelys advance warning, he'd driven to their
house to break the news of the Shawn–Misty connection.
And encountered even more frustration.

The only Sheelys at home were Katie and Emily, and
neither was functioning at top form. Katie's goateed friend
was with her and she had little interest in anything else,
especially not her ancient boss Wade Saxon. Emily was

chattering away with several of her clones while passing the portable phone among them. The young teens welcomed Wade with all the enthusiasm of racketeers receiving an IRS agent whose specialty was money-laundering.

After ascertaining that their parents were out of town for a wedding and wouldn't be returning until close to midnight, Wade casually inquired about Dana's whereabouts. He knew she'd planned the trip to north Jersey and was greatly cheered to learn that she'd gone alone.

It was the first and only bright spot of the otherwise dismal day, though he didn't allow himself to dwell on why it felt as though a dark cloud had suddenly lifted.

"Dana called from Sagertown and said she's going to drive up to Connecticut and surprise Tim and Lisa," Katie told him, her blue eyes amorously following the bad imitation of Brad Pitt around the kitchen. "She won't be back till tomorrow night."

Suddenly Wade felt an irresistible, overwhelming need to visit his best friend. It had been far too long since he'd spent time with Tim, not since Christmas, and it would be good to see Lisa and the kids—his honorary godchildren!—too. Plus, he could really use Tim's input on the Shawn-and-Misty situation. Maybe Tim would volunteer to talk to the kid himself, and they could work out what to tell their folks, Sheely-to-Sheely.

Thus sparing Wade the unpleasant task of breaking the news himself. And if Aunt Eve should need bail money after her Spagna encounter, well, his parents were in town. She could contact them.

That cinched it for him. Connecticut offered a necessary respite from this very aggravating day.

But that dark cloud which had metaphorically lifted in Lakeview seemed to have literally descended over the state of Connecticut, and as his car waded along the turnpike, Wade was beginning to regret his impulsive trip.

Which took much longer than it should have. It was late in the afternoon, after a drenching harrowing journey, when he finally arrived in the tidy neighborhood near the naval base where Tim and Lisa Sheely lived with their children.

He felt as if he were navigating a boat rather than driving his car through the watery streets. The fast-falling over-abundance of rain was taking its toll on the overwhelmed storm drains; being at sea level left no room for runoff. Already, rivers of water gushed along the sides of the street, beginning to meet in the middle.

But none of that mattered to Wade as he pulled his car into the driveway right behind Dana's little brown Chevy. Instantly, his road fatigue evaporated, and he felt a buoyant surge of anticipation, which he tried to tell himself was due to this impromptu reunion with his best friend.

It almost worked . . . until he saw Dana sitting on an Ad-irondack chair on the front porch of the house. Wade stopped dead in his tracks, shocked by the combined forces of desire and pleasure that overtook him.

He forgot that they'd parted on less-than-amicable terms last night, that in fact, he was furious with her for relegating their unmistakable passion to a mere footnote in experi-mentation. That she had cold-bloodedly mistaken the un-mistakable was just one of the many grudges he held against her. Kicking him out of her house was right up there, along with causing him a miserable, sleepless night the likes of which he had never before experienced.

Insomnia had never been a problem for him. Until last night he'd always managed to sleep like a baby no matter what.

But right now, swept away by the sheer euphoria of see-ing her again, he forgave her everything.

Dana, who sat huddled in the chair which she'd dragged as close to the side of the house as she could to avoid the blasts of rainy wind, leaped to her feet as Wade raced from his car to the porch. *Wade, here?* She couldn't have been more amazed if a spaceship had landed on the lawn and a troop of little green men were advancing toward her.

"What are you doing here?" she demanded as he joined her on the porch.

Though Wade had made the dash from his car in record

speed, he'd still gotten rained upon, and as he brushed the droplets of water off him, Dana scurried to the opposite end of the porch to avoid getting splashed.

And to avoid being near him?

Wade scowled. Clearly, she hadn't experienced the same exultation he'd felt upon seeing her. But then, why should she? Last night meant nothing to her; she had been buzzed on some specialty liqueur from Bangladesh and feeling a little horny, so she'd decided to use him—and then, just as arbitrarily, to kick him out.

All the negativity which had vanished at his first sight of her returned in full force.

"I'm here to visit Tim," he replied belligerently. "My best friend. Any objections?"

"Why did you come today?" Her question sounded more like an accusation.

"Because I wanted to see Tim and Lisa and the kids." Wade was really frosted now. "Why did *you* come today?"

Their eyes met. And widened with dawning horror at the same moment.

"Did you come to talk to Tim about what happened yesterday?" they both chorused the same words at the same time.

"No!" they both issued the same denial.

Their gazes held. Dana took a deep breath and her lips parted. Wade gulped, dragging his eyes away from the sight of her slightly open mouth, tempted beyond reason to put his tongue or his fingers or some other part of himself in it, just so he could satisfy his raging need to be inside her in some way, in any way.

He sank into the chair she had just vacated and covered his lap with his dark blue windbreaker to conceal the incriminating evidence of his unwelcome lust. "Dana," he began shakily.

"Don't call me that," she snapped.

"Why not? It's your name, isn't it?"

"One that you've never used. Don't start now."

Dana turned away from him to stare at the unrelenting

rain that was battering the pretty spring flowers into the ground, making everything look dark and dreary and dismal.

Which exactly mirrored her mood.

After she'd cried herself to sleep last night—she, who'd never cried over a man in her life, whose last fit of inconsolable weeping had been years ago, and appropriately at the funeral of dear old Grandpa Sheely—Dana had awakened this morning and firmly resolved to put the unfortunate incident with Wade Saxon behind her and never to think about it again.

She had successfully kept her vow during today's sojourn in Sagertown while interviewing Ken and Marcia Polk, a plethora of doctors, and photocopying medical reports. Unfortunately, all the driving time alone in the car gave her way too much time to think. To brood. To ache with pain over Wade Saxon's utter and absolute rejection of her.

The prospect of returning to Lakeview and her bedroom, where the most hurtful and humiliating repudiation of her life had taken place, had been too awful to consider. She'd decided to drive farther north and pay a surprise visit to her brother and his family, and then phoned home with her plan. Katie promised to pass along the word to their parents.

Too bad she hadn't also called Tim and Lisa to share the news of her visit.

"They're not home," Dana said flatly, looking out at the rain. If it kept up, this street would be more like a canal than a road. Already the water was covering the paved surface and beginning to spill onto the slightly raised sidewalks.

"What?"

Dana darted a glance at Wade to find him staring at her so intently, so strangely, that she was instantly self-conscious. "Tim and Lisa aren't home," she clarified, and nervously smoothed the pleats of her gray skirt.

After the long hours at the Sagertown hospital, not to mention all the driving, she knew she must look like a rumpled frump. Which normally wouldn't have bothered her, not around Wade, who'd seen her sweaty from exercising and dirty from rollerblade falls and a windblown, salty mess at the shore.

Except she hadn't been one of his cast-off rejectees then, and now she was. Now it hurt that he looked at her and saw a woman he didn't want.

"They're not here?" Wade heaved a groan. "Are you sure?"

"I wouldn't be out on the porch in the rain unless I was sure they weren't here."

They listened to the rain, watched the water lapping the sidewalk. "Maybe they'll be back soon," Wade offered hopefully.

Dana promptly dashed that hope. "No, they're gone for the whole weekend. When no one answered the door here, I went to the neighbor's across the street because I know she has a key to take in the mail and feed the fish when Tim and Lisa are away. She told me they took the kids and went with two other families to spend the weekend in Mystic."

Wade brightened. "If she has the key—"

"She gave me the key in case I wanted to stay in the house tonight, but I hadn't decided if I wanted to or not." Dana removed the house key from the pocket of her gray suit jacket. "I just got here about ten minutes before you did, and I was still thinking what to do."

She fingered the key another second. "Now I've decided—I'm not going to stay. I'll drive home tonight."

"Don't be ridiculous. Look at the street, it's already a swamp, and the ones closer to the ocean will be even worse." Wade rose to his feet to deliver his argument, just like in court. "Driving back in this rain would be suicidal. It was bad enough getting here, and I heard on the radio that the storm is socked in over New York and New Jersey now."

"I've driven in the rain before, Wade," she said snottily. He didn't miss the contemptuous inflection she gave his name; "shitbird" could've been substituted and been perfectly in context. And the look she gave him was icy enough to freeze fire.

God, she hated him now! Wade balled his fingers into fists as fury and despair washed over him in alternative waves.

"Just what in the hell is going on with you, Dana?" he demanded, giving her name the same treatment she'd accorded his. "If you're having an affair with Cormack, and you—"

"An affair?" She was too astounded to mask her incredulity. "With Quint? Me?"

Wade's eyes narrowed. He knew her well enough to know if she were lying or completely baffled. Her response fell directly into the latter category. "So you're not."

Too late, Dana wished she'd grabbed his misapprehension and gone with it. But she knew it wouldn't work now. "No, I'm not. Not that it would be any of your business if I were," she added coldly. "Now, if you'll excuse me, I'll return this key to Mrs. Madison and—"

"You're not driving back to Lakeview tonight, Dana. It's almost six o'clock and the rain—"

"I know what time it is, I know it's raining, and you're not going to tell me what to do, Saxon!" Her temper flared to flashpoint. "If you're afraid to drive in a little rain, okay, take the key and you stay here tonight."

She tossed the key at him. He caught it, disappointing her. It would've been infinitely more satisfying to watch him groping on the ground for it, preferably on his hands and knees.

Dana started to leave the porch for her car, striding purposefully but not at breakneck speed. Her pumps with their three-inch heels—on assignment, she found the additional height a useful advantage—did not allow for the quick pace of sneakers.

She was stunned when Wade's hand snaked out to grasp her arm. She hadn't been expecting any interference from him or she would've made a run for it, high heels and all.

"Look, you've voiced your concern. Consider it duly noted," she said crossly. "So you're off the hook if I crash or drown on the drive home. You can honestly say you tried to warn me, but I refused to listen to Wise, Wonderful You. It'll play very well with my family."

She pulled her arm free and attempted to continue her exit.

When Wade caught her around the waist with both hands just as she was about to step off the porch, Dana realized that she'd made a major miscalculation.

"I gave you the key, what are you—"

"Shut up!" he roared.

Dana gaped at him. She'd never seen him so angry, and the spectacle flummoxed her. Wade Saxon didn't get enraged—he got testy or irritable or annoyed but never wildly, emotionally furious like the Sheelys.

She and Tim and Mary Jo and Tricia had occasionally discussed Wade's temperament and decided he didn't have it in him to blow up the way the Sheelys sometimes did. They had their flaming Irish tempers while he possessed the cool, ironic detachment of a WASP. After all, his surname was Saxon, as Tim had pointed out. How much more White-Anglo-Protestant could you get?

Except Wade didn't seem at all cool or ironic or detached right now, he was as explosive as any Sheely had ever been. Dana gulped.

He lifted her off her feet and didn't set her down until he had placed her against the front door. When she tried to get away from him—which she did, quite frantically—he used his body to anchor her there while he shoved the key into the lock.

Pushing the door open, and her along with it, Wade and Dana stumbled inside the empty house.

12

---⚡---

Wade slammed the door so hard that Lisa's collection of lighthouse miniatures rattled on the shelves.

"Have you lost your mind?" Dana gasped, a little anxiously because right now it seemed like a very legitimate question.

"No! Although this must be what it feels like!"

Dana almost smiled. Almost. Then she reminded herself that this was not her good buddy Wade who made her laugh, but the arrogant creep who'd started to make love to her last night and then decided she didn't meet his amatory requirements. Now she could add physical bullying to the list of offenses she was compiling against him. No, he was not her friend now, and he wouldn't be, not ever again.

Wade watched the range of expressions cross her face. She'd nearly smiled at him, looking so much like herself that he missed her painfully though she was standing right there in front of him. Because the look of loathing was back on her face within moments, turning her warm blue eyes to stone.

"Why, Dana? I want to know why you're looking at me like you can't stand to be in the same room with me."

"Because I don't want to be in the same room with you, Saxon." Her voice was laced with sarcasm. "Especially not this room. I want to be in my car driving home and you're standing in my way. Naturally, I don't look very pleased."

215

Wade frowned. He was too angry to think clearly and she was exhibiting the equivocal arguing skills of an attorney, changing the focus slightly to readjust the debate to something else. Damn, she'd been around Cormack too long!

"That's not the issue," he insisted, trying to get their derailed argument back on track.

"It certainly is," retorted Dana. "*I* don't want to stay here, but I'm sure Tim and Lisa won't mind if you do." She started toward the door, which he immediately blocked by placing himself directly and immovably in front of it.

"Get out of my way," she ordered, sounding more forceful than she felt.

She took in the way his jeans and dark green cotton polo shirt hugged his trim, muscular body. Even with her additional inches of height, she had to look way up to meet his eyes. Dana knew she wasn't going anywhere unless he allowed it. He'd already proven that she was no match for his strength when he chose to exert it. Resentment flared through her, enhancing her anger like a rocket-stage booster.

"Answer my question!" Wade took a step toward her, then another, until they were practically standing toe-to-toe. He could feel the heat of her rage emanating in waves from her, and it banked the fires of his own fury.

Which was actually a good thing because she was so close he could smell the shampoo-clean scent of her hair. That, and the subtle spicy aroma of her perfume drew forth potent memories of lying on the bed with her last night, of holding her, kissing her.

He wanted to do that now and much, much more. Since he knew she wouldn't let him, he'd damn well better stay mad. It was as good a distancing device as any.

"What's going on, Dana?" he reiterated sharply.

Dana shook her head in disgust. "You know that book, *Men Are From Mars and Women Are From Venus?* Well, you're from Pluto."

"If anyone has a right to be ticked off about last night, it's me, Sheely."

Wade ignored her pop-psych reference, which he knew she had made to annoy him even more. She was fully aware of how much he hated the entire genre of so-called self-help books, which he never read and everybody else seemed to quote endlessly.

"Did I say Pluto? I meant Uranus." She used the pronunciation that always drew snickers in junior-high science classes.

He got her point. And set out to make his. "You kicked me out of your room and out of your house, you couldn't get rid of me fast enough last night. You acted like I was some kind of contagious spore."

Dana was incredulous. "You believe that I would want you around, that I *should* want you around after—after—" She couldn't finish. Bad enough he'd rejected her, she wasn't about to put it into words for him.

Which left plenty of room for misinterpretation.

Wade did exactly that. "After I kissed you?" he interjected. His eyes glittered. "Ahh no, I see where you're going with this and I'm not going to let you do it. You're not putting this all on me, Sheely. You wanted me to kiss you. You wanted me to—"

"Get out of my brother's house!" Was he daring to claim that his rejection of her was her own fault? She was aghast at his breathtaking insensitivity. "Give me the key and go!"

"And now you're trying to throw me out of my best friend's house because you won't accept responsibility for—"

"You're damn right I won't. First *you* tried to—to seduce me and then you—"

"I didn't have to seduce you, you were more than willing. Did you manage to conveniently forget that part, Sheely? You had your hand in my pants! Have you also forgotten that? Well, I sure haven't!"

Dana drew back her hand and slapped his face. Her palm

connected with his cheek with a resounding, satisfying crack.

Wade staggered backward a little, rubbing his stinging skin. "Some other guys would hit you back for that. Lucky for you I'm a gentleman, Sheely."

"Saxon, you are no gentleman." Dana ran across the room and picked up a poker from the fireplace set on the hearth. "So go ahead, try to hit me. It'll give me an excuse to brain you with this."

Wade sat down hard on the dark leather sofa. "You know I'd never hit you, but feel free to brain me with the poker, Sheely. Go on, fracture my skull! This day needs only that to go down as the worst in my life. Hey, better yet, whack my crotch with it. That oughta thrill a ball-busting babe like you."

Dana replaced the poker. "Since I'm a firm believer in nonviolence, I'll deprive myself of that particular joy."

She stood at the window and looked out at the teeming rain. Wouldn't it ever stop? Now the sidewalks were part of the expanding lake that used to be the road.

"I know you've convinced yourself that you hate me now, Sheely, but last night you didn't hate me or what we were doing." Wade's voice was flat and low. "Not while we were doing it."

Dana turned around to glare at him, folding her arms in front of her chest. "You know, the last time I hit anyone was about twenty years ago when my brother Shawn chopped off my Growin' Hair Crissy doll's ponytail while I was at school."

"Your point being?" Wade was exasperated. Maybe he was from Uranus, but she was from some other galaxy altogether.

"Slapping you was abnormal behavior for me," Dana said primly. "And no matter what you say, you're not going to goad me into doing it again."

"I don't want you to hit me again. Why would I try to goad you into doing it?"

"Then why are you—rubbing it in about last night?"

she blurted out. "Unless you're taking some kind of sadistic pleasure in—in—" To her dismay, she felt tears well in her eyes.

She tried to blink them away, but when one trickled from the corner of her right eye, she quickly turned her back to him again.

But it was too late. He'd already seen that tear and was on his feet in a flash. "My God, Dana." He stood behind her and after hesitating a second, placed his hands on her shoulders. "You're crying!"

"No, I'm not." She tried to shrug him off. The horror of having him see her in tears had caused them to instantly dissipate.

Instead, he tightened his fingers and began to knead lightly. "I don't know what's gone wrong but it's making me crazy, Sheely. I can't stand for you to hate me, I want things to go back to the way they used to be."

"All right, fine. Whatever you want." At this point, she would say anything to get away from him. She had betrayed way too much already, and only his stunning lack of insight prevented him from putting it all together. "As of right now, things are back to the way they were, okay?"

She ducked down and under his arm, heading to the front door. "I'll see you back in Lakeview, Saxon. 'Bye."

"Dana, wait!"

"I thought you said you wanted things just like they've always been. That means you won't try to stop me from leaving, Saxon." She tried to sound reasonable, but it took some effort because he had beaten her to the door and was leaning his shoulder against it. Something in his eyes made her very uneasy.

"Remember that ski trip to the Poconos when I left in the middle of a blizzard because I wanted to get home in plenty of time for Mary Jo's bridal shower? You didn't even try to talk me out of leaving then."

"That's because Rena Cheponis was there and I—oh, hell, Sheely, I should've talked you out of driving in that blizzard. I did worry, you know. I wanted you to make it back safely,'' he added lamely.

She smiled a little at that. "You can send those same good thoughts along with me today, Saxon."

But Wade was in the throes of vivid retroactive angst. That blizzard had been over two years ago but remembering how he'd blithely waved Dana off in the midst of it—his mind on voluptuous Rena Cheponis waiting in the ski lodge—made him feel like a thoughtless, heartless, self-centered jerk. He'd been that, and worse. What if something had happened to her driving in that storm?

What if something happened to her today? What if he were to lose her?

Thinking the unthinkable suddenly made everything re-markably clear. *Eureka, an epiphany!* He laughed quietly to himself. So that's what it felt like.

He was suddenly energized, spurred to action. "You're not going anywhere, Dana." He caught both her wrists and pulled her to him. "I said I wanted things between us to go back to the way they were, but that's not going to work."

Dana's heart jumped. "Another experiment like last night won't work either," she murmured shakily.

Wade kept both her wrists secured with one hand and curved the other around her hip, bringing her body close against his. He let her feel the full force of his erection as he nuzzled her neck, lightly nipping and kissing.

"This—is—not—an—experiment." He enunciated every word, his mouth against her ear. "Got that, Sheely?"

She didn't know if she wanted him to let her go or to hold her tighter. Her hands were trapped between them and she grasped the material of his shirt for better leverage, still undecided whether to push him away or pull him closer.

"Why are you doing this, Saxon? Because you're facing a boring evening up here alone in Connecticut? You didn't want me last night but now you—"

"Didn't want you last night?" He looked confused. His hands closed over hers, his knuckles brushing the tips of her nipples. Dana shivered. "Where did you come up with that? Didn't want you?" he echoed, and his voice rose.

"Does this feel like I don't want you?" He rubbed against her, hard and insistent. "I want you now just like I wanted you last night, Dana, but your parents were downstairs watching TV and Emily and her friends were just a couple doors down the hall. Hell, I think Anthony and a couple of his buddies were around too. It was practically a full house."

"You said 'I can't do this, it's crazy,' " Dana quoted him. Thinking of the pain those words of dismissal had caused her brought a lump to her throat.

He nodded his head. "That's what I said."

"You also said you felt like a rat because you didn't want me. You wouldn't even try to make yourself want—"

"Of all the stupid misconceptions, that one wins the prize! Dana, think! Think the way I did last night. We were in your bedroom with all those Sheelys right there in the house with us. What if we'd been caught? We had to stop!"

Viewed from that perspective, stopping made very good sense indeed. Dana wondered why she hadn't even considered it before. And immediately knew why. Because she was confused by her powerful feelings for Wade and insecure about her inexperience.

She tilted her head back and met his eyes. "I—I guess I thought you stopped for—other reasons," she dared to admit.

"Other reasons. The main one being that I didn't want you?" He narrowed his brow as he pondered that. "Is that why you acted so bitchy to me?"

"I wasn't bitchy, I was breezy," she defended herself.

He gave a snort. "And that's why you kicked me out when Cormack called?"

"Quint didn't call me, it was Shawn on the phone." She moistened her lips with the tip of her tongue and his gaze ardently followed every movement.

Shawn. Her brother's name sounded an alarm in Wade's head which he abruptly silenced. The only Sheely he was interested in right now was the one he was holding in his arms.

She thought he didn't want her. He was still floored by that revelation and the others that fell into place after hearing it. He'd felt more miserable than he had ever been in his life, and it had all been a stupid misunderstanding they could've cleared up in a two-minute conversation. Instead, he had suffered for nearly twenty-four endless hours.

He thought such profound haplessness only befell dim-bulb characters in TV shows written by hack screenwriters, but it had happened to Dana and himself. A humbling thought.

Wade stared down at her lovely face, drinking in the sight of her ivory complexion, that slight smattering of freckles on her nose, her luminous blue eyes. His gaze lingered on her sweet sensuous lips, and he knew he couldn't wait another moment to kiss her.

"I want you, Dana," he said huskily. He pulled her closer, closer. "I wanted you last night and I want you now. I want you." His mouth closed over hers.

She made a small, soft sound as she parted her lips for him and his tongue thrust into her mouth. It was as if the long, intervening hours between last night's kiss hadn't occurred. They picked up where they'd left off, their passion primed, their bodies soaring to full arousal.

Wade kissed her as if he were starved for her and she responded with equal hunger. The kiss grew more passionate, urgent and wild, until they were clutching each other fiercely, gasping for air.

He lifted his lips from hers. "Just to keep the record straight and prevent any further misunderstandings, the only reason I stopped kissing you now is because we both needed to breathe." He trailed hot little kisses along the curve of her neck, her jawline, on both her cheeks. "I didn't want to stop, but I had to or we'd've both passed out from oxygen deprivation."

"You're a laugh and a half, Saxon," Dana growled, squirming against him.

"And you're a little dope who jumps to the wrongest conclusions at the—"

"Wrongest isn't a word." She nipped at his lips, licking them, teasing him until he was groaning.

"Whatever you say, Sheely." Wade grasped her head with his hands and captured her mouth again, kissing her the way they both wanted, hot and hard and deep.

Dana trembled, moving her hands over him, greedy to touch him. She pulled his shirt from his jeans and ran her palms over the bare skin of his chest and his back. He sucked in his stomach as her thumb investigated the indentation of his navel.

"Nobody's here," Wade rasped. "I don't want to stop tonight, Dana."

A thrill streaked through her. It was going to happen right here, right now. Wade was going to make love to her and she wanted him to, desperately. She dismissed last night's apprehensions before they could surface. After suffering through what she'd thought had been his rejection and the loss of his friendship, the end of the bond between them, she could only welcome this unexpected second chance to be with him. To love him.

That gave her a moment's pause. Dana gazed up at his familiar handsome face and a sunburst of warmth glowed all through her. Tricia had recognized that she lusted for Wade but it had taken these past lonely, hopeless twenty-four hours for Dana to realize that her feelings went far beyond lust. And deeper than friendship.

She was consumed by a dynamic mingling of the two and she knew what it was. Love. She was in love with Wade Saxon. And now she was going to make love with him.

She smiled up at him. "Saxon, if you stop tonight, I really will brain you with that poker."

"Consider me adequately threatened."

He swept her up in his arms and carried her over to the wide leather sofa. Dana linked her arms around his neck and savored the unusual pleasure of being carried by him.

The gesture struck her as sexy and romantic, part of a fantasy.

She nuzzled the spot where his neck met his collarbone, inhaling the enticing male scent of soap and aftershave and a heady essence that was all his own.

He sat down beside her on the sofa, removing her jacket, then going to work on the buttons of her blouse. She'd barely blinked when he slipped that off too, dispensing with her bra along with it.

Dana was seized by a sudden paralyzing shyness. She had to force herself not to cover herself with her hands. "You're very fast."

Wade laughed wickedly. "So I've been told." He cupped her breasts, then lowered his head to take one taut nipple between his lips.

She felt a lightning-bolt response deep in her loins. Dana emitted a breathless moan and arched against his mouth. He teased and caressed her breasts until she cried out his name in a voice husky with need. She felt as if liquid fire was shooting through her body.

And then he turned his attention to the task of unzipping her skirt, which he did, pulling it off her and tossing it onto the chair which held the rest of her clothes.

"Panty hose," he grumbled, running his index finger under and along the waistband. "Very serviceable. But I hate them, and so does every other guy on the planet."

Dana blushed. Wade was in the process of pulling off her panty hose and taking her white cotton panties with them. This whole scene was getting a little too intimate for someone with her limited experience, but she intrepidly tried to keep up with the program.

"Sorry. If I'd known we were going to wind up here together, I would've worn my garter belt and stockings today." Dana made a mental note to buy those items as soon as possible.

And then it occurred to her that Wade was fully dressed while she—wasn't. Her heart began to beat so loudly she half expected it to burst out of her chest. She reached for his belt and unbuckled it. Then she unbuttoned his jeans and grasped the zipper. She wished he would help her, but he seemed to have been suddenly rendered immobile.

Dana glanced at him, her face flushed with an unnerving combination of embarrassment and need. Wade was staring at her.

He appeared oddly dazed. She remembered him looking that same way when he had climbed behind the wheel of his adored Mercedes for the first time. She'd been in the front seat beside him as he drove the car from the showroom. It was flattering to see that she'd had a similar effect upon him.

Beneath her fingers, underneath the denim and cotton boxers, she could feel his heat, his hardness. She had done this to him. Feminine power surged through her, renewing her confidence. Boldly, she flattened her hand against him, her fingers conforming to his shape.

Wade moaned.

"I could use a little help here, Saxon," Dana teased gently, tugging on the zipper which wouldn't budge over the considerable bulge.

She decided to postpone that task for now to continue her intimate exploration, tracing the length and breadth of him, feeling the thickness, the weight.

Wade's bout of passivity disappeared as quickly as it had come. Reactivated, he got rid of his clothing even faster than he'd divested her of hers.

He had intended to take it slow. She was so small and delicate, he didn't want to rush her or hurt her, he wanted their first time together to be perfect. Different from anything she had ever experienced.

Already, it was different for him. Sex with Dana was inextricably linked to the affection he felt for her. He knew her, knew all about her family. He understood what made her laugh, what made her angry or sad. They'd shared a myriad of experiences over the years.

But never one like this. In all the years he'd known and valued her as a friend, he had never dreamed that she could make him feel this way—or that anybody could. He didn't think it was possible to have such intense feelings, such rapturous pleasure.

He felt as if he were entering another dimension when they kissed, when her small hands closed around him.

His fingers glided through the intriguing auburn thatch between her legs and he felt her softness, felt her wet and ready for him. And then he couldn't think at all as his control abruptly snapped. He couldn't wait another second.

"Now?" he managed to pant the word.

She purred her assent, and he shifted on top of her, guiding himself into her.

Dana cried out, startling him, but then her hands were on his hips, locking him to her, urging him deeper. Her mouth was against his shoulder and she wet his skin with her lips and her tongue, kissing it, nibbling at him helplessly.

With shockingly unexpected speed, sharp waves of pleasure rocked him and he was unable to stop the wild sensual torrent from sweeping him away in its tide. . . .

The Living Chess Game at the Renaissance Festival included a board comprised of squares of spray-painted grass and two opposing teams of combatants, each assigned to a traditional chess position. Robin Hood and his Merry Men, with lovely blond Maid Marian as queen made up one team. The other team, predictably, was the wicked Sheriff of Nottingham and his assorted henchmen, but a wisecracking brunette served as their thoroughly unpredictable queen.

The captains of each team, Robin and the Sheriff, called the moves to their teammates and the human chess pieces complied with their orders. There was hand-to-hand combat to determine who was to be captured and plenty of ribald, raucous jokes.

Rachel watched and listened, amused. "I remember reading about Sherwood Forest as a kid, I've seen all the Robin Hood movies, from the old Errol Flynn one on TV to the Disney cartoon to the Kevin Costner film, but I have no recollection of Robin Hood's obsession with a wild wench who claims to be Maid Marian's evil twin named Maid Marissa.''

The Robin Hood and Maid Marissa characters in the Living Chess Game were having a fine time entertaining the crowd and each other with their lusty, suggestive gestures and remarks.

"Maybe it's because this Maid Marian gives a whole new meaning to the concept of vapid," suggested Quint. "She's the Living Stereotype, who inspires all those blonde jokes. Whose IQ barely equals room temperature."

Rachel studied the lovely Maid Marian who was smiling vacuously at the crowd. "Still, she does have her following, doesn't she?"

There were several groups of college-aged males who cheered and hollered any time Maid Marian shrugged her shoulders, which she did frequently, displaying her admittedly spectacular chest to best advantage.

"She kind of reminds me of one of your clients," Rachel observed. "I wonder if she can lap dance?"

"Behave, Rachel." Quint pinched her midriff and nipped at her earlobe. Rachel shivered, enjoying his sensual punishment.

She was sitting on the grass in the wide field with Quint behind her, surrounding her, his legs stretched out on either side of hers, her back leaning against his chest. He'd wrapped his arms around her waist and seemed more intent on smelling her hair or nibbling on her neck or kissing the sensitive place just below her ear than watching the Living Chess Game being performed.

In sheer self-defense, Rachel tried to keep her attention focused on the actors but all too often, her efforts faltered and she found herself giving in to the silken arousal pumping through her veins. She would lean her head back in the hollow of Quint's shoulder and let the feelings take her, closing her eyes and savoring the exquisite fit of their bodies and his deft, subtle caresses.

Brady and Snowy lay on their bellies a few feet away,

playing an avid game with their dragon puppets. Occasionally, Rachel would tune in to their play, but the dialogue struck her as excruciatingly repetitive.

"Num, num, grass is good," Snowy made her dragon talk in a deep guttural voice and pulled at the grass with her puppet's mouth.

Brady watched her with the rapt admiration of one being treated to a performance by a Shakespearean player. He slavishly imitated her in word and deed.

Both toddlers laughed long and often, captivated by their own wit and totally oblivious to the Living Chess Game and everything else around them.

Austin and Dustin had discovered the dunking stool on the other side of the pond, which proved to be an excellent antidote to their mud brawl. They were dripping wet, but not muddy anymore.

As with the stocks, the dunking stool was an olden-day punishment for minor scrapes and offenses. In the festival version, the offender was strapped to a seat on something resembling a seesaw and plopped into the pond for a thorough dousing. Dustin and Austin loved it and kept the kangaroo court busy by running up to the "judge" and confessing to some crime in the not quite Olde English they'd picked up.

The adult spectators displayed noticeable relief every time the boys were dunked because most didn't share their enthusiasm for getting soaked. Rachel saw several completely unwilling nonvolunteers forced onto the dunking stool by strong-armed court members and marveled that the festival wasn't rife with lawsuits.

The storm came up quickly. The sky grew cloudy and then dark. Rain began to fall in fat cold droplets onto the crowd, who until then hadn't paid much attention to the quick change of weather.

"Uh-oh. We'd better get out of here." Quint glanced up at the sky as a few drops landed on his face. "Fast." He rose to his feet in one swift movement, grasping Rachel and taking her up with him.

She secretly thrilled to his strength. He'd lifted her as easily as she picked up Snowy or Brady.

Seconds after Quint spoke those prophetic words, rain poured from the sky as if a billion showerheads had been simultaneously turned on. People began to dash from the fairgrounds, but the rain fell too hard and too fast to outrun. Very soon, Quint, Rachel, Snowy, and Brady were as drenched as Austin and Dustin, who'd spent the better part of the last hour in the pond.

The group scrambled into Quint's car, the two youngest ones sobbing inconsolably because they didn't want to go home and they didn't like being all wet either. It was a hopeless predicament, and all Snowy and Brady could do to express their displeasure was cry. Luckily, they both fell asleep in their car seats within ten minutes of leaving the fairgrounds.

Because of traffic and the storm, the drive back to Lakeview took considerably longer than the usual two hours. Austin and Dustin kept themselves entertained in the far backseat with their GameBoy games while the smaller children slept. Rachel dozed off herself, which surprised her. She had never relaxed enough around anyone to fall asleep in their presence but she'd done just that with Quint behind the wheel, beside her.

She didn't awaken until the car stopped in the Polks' driveway. She felt groggy, almost stuporous. The car heater was set on high, blasting heat to counter any chill from their wet clothes, but causing a heavy soporific effect. Rachel wondered how Quint had managed to stay awake and alert during the drive. She could hardly keep her eyes open.

As he took his young half brothers into their grandmother's house, she turned off the heat and rolled down her window. The cool air had revived her by the time Quint returned to the car.

"We'll go to your apartment and you can pack an overnight bag," he said, steering the car along the rain-soaked streets. "Then we'll drop Snowy off at her house." He glanced back at the little girl still sleeping soundly in her car seat. "And go home."

He was so matter-of-fact, nonchalant even, that it took Rachel a few moments to work out the planned scenario. But when she did, she knew she couldn't acquiesce. "Quint, I'm not spending the night with you."

"Why not? You want to, we both want it, Rachel." He sounded so reasonable that arguing with him seemed almost churlish.

A most effective technique. Win the argument without even having it. Rachel was impressed. However, "It's too soon, Quint. We both know that."

"No, I don't know that. I'm dead certain we should be together, Rachel, and if you'll be honest with yourself, you'll admit it, too."

Rachel sucked in her cheeks. "Wasn't there a time when you were dead certain that you belonged with Brady's mother? You remember her—the woman who Misty said is currently chasing a man around Romania or somewhere."

"That would be Bulgaria. And no, I never felt that I belonged with Sharolyn. And vice versa, I might add."

"Should I ask the obvious question or do you just want to go ahead and answer it?" Rachel asked wryly.

"I guess you mean, why did Sharolyn and I get married?"

"I guess I do," she agreed.

"Without romanticizing the situation—because there was nothing romantic about my relationship with Sharolyn—we both had too much to drink at a party one night, we got careless, and I knocked her up. It was our third date, which would've been our last because neither of us was very taken with the other. We had nothing in common, not even much sexual attraction. Goes to show the power of vodka, hmm?"

Rachel winced. Was she supposed to agree? It didn't seem like the time to mention that she'd never been drunk in her life, so she could not honestly attest to vodka's

power. But it must be mighty to make a careful and cal-
culating attorney like Quint careless.

"Sharolyn got pregnant that night?" Rachel quickly suppressed the image of a sexually out-of-control Quint with
the woman who was Brady's mother. It was oddly painful.

"Yes. Sharolyn came to me a couple weeks later with
the positive results of a home pregnancy test."

Rachel bit her lower lip. "And so you got married."

He nodded. "And our marriage was just as lousy as we
both knew it was going to be. We split up the week after
the baby was born. Brady lived with her and I had visitation
rights until she hooked up with the adventuresome travel
guide. Child care paled in comparison to the lure of Eastern
Europe. After all, who wants to change diapers when you
can sunbathe in Albania along the Adriatic coast? And no,
I'm not being sarcastic, Rachel, that's a direct quote from
Sharolyn herself."

Rachel stole a glance at Brady, so adorable and loving,
who was the product of that decidedly unromantic—not to
mention unloving—union. "That's not a nice story, Quint.
I hope you'll soften the edges when it's time to explain
things to Brady. He deserves better."

"He deserves the truth. I don't believe in lying to kids
by spinning them a bunch of candy-coated fantasies. That's
the way my father operates, and it makes it too easy to
develop a talent for self-deception. From there you progress
to being able to rationalize anything, to doing whatever you
want because you feel like doing it and to hell with everybody else. You have no problem with taking what you want
because you feel you deserve it. Believe me, I know what
I'm talking about, I've been there."

She regarded him curiously. "But you're not there now.
You wouldn't be in Lakeview, putting up with your father
and Carla and looking after your little brothers, if you were.
You wouldn't be a good father to Brady, and you are."

"Thank you for that. I had some hard lessons to learn,
and it took me a painfully long time to learn them." He
pulled alongside the curb of her apartment building, just

behind her own sporty little car. "Of course, shock therapy can work wonders, too," he added drolly.

"Shock therapy meaning your marriage to Sharolyn? And her—um—defection to Bulgaria?"

"You are a quick study, Rachel. You swap metaphors with the greatest of ease."

"What were the other hard lessons?" She wanted to know everything.

"I'm tired of talking about myself. I think we've heard enough of The Life and Times of Quinton Cormack. You are infinitely more interesting, Rachel."

He reached over and put his hand on her thigh, just above her knee, and began to draw concentric circles with his fingers. Each circle moved his hand higher along her thigh, and her legs parted reflexively, allowing him access. "Stay with me tonight, Rachel. Please."

She put her hand over his, stilling its progress. "If you count the last two evenings we spent together, then this could be considered our third date, Quint. Something of a daunting parallel, don't you think?"

He linked his fingers with hers. "That's a low blow, Rachel. I confide in you and you use it against me."

"I'm not using it against you, I'm just pointing out that you—seem to have a tendency to take things faster than I do. Fortunately, neither of us has been drinking tonight."

"Because it would be too easy for you to say yes to me, Rachel?" He lifted her hand to his mouth and pressed his lips against her palm.

She thought about denying it. And couldn't. "Yes," she admitted achingly. "But I'm not going to, Quint."

"I want to make you say yes." He nibbled on her fingers and she quivered. "I can, you know."

"But you won't because you aren't that kind of man, Quint," she pointed out, her voice soft and earnest. "You aren't able to rationalize everything, and you don't do whatever you want, just because you feel like it. You don't simply take what you want because you feel you deserve it."

"Aaargh! Hoist by my own petard." He shook his head ruefully. "Even worse, I'm starting to talk like a piece from the Living Chess Game."

He pulled her over to him and kissed her, a slow deep kiss that lasted a long, long time. They were both breathing hard when he finally lifted his lips from hers. He kept his arms around her, holding her against his chest, unwilling to release her.

Rachel lay against him, listening to the thudding beat of his heart. It seemed to be pounding in rhythm with her own. She gazed up at him with limpid hazel eyes, her lips moist and swollen from their kiss.

"Have I changed your mind?" he asked huskily.

"You weren't trying to." She reached up to stroke his cheek. "That was a good-night kiss and we both know it."

Quint grimaced. "When did you become so convinced of this alleged nobility of mine? Not too long ago you thought I had all the integrity and sensitivity of Pol Pot."

"I've gotten to know you better since then." She smiled up at him. "And to like you." She moved out of his arms and grasped the door handle. "I'd better get Snowy home now, Quint."

"If you insist." He sighed his resignation. "I'll move her car seat to your car. Have the door open."

Instead of bristling at his take-charge attitude, Rachel found herself grinning. "Sir, yes sir!" she imitated a new marine recruit addressing the drill instructor.

Quint performed Snowy's transfer with such speed and dexterity that the little girl opened her eyes only once before closing them again. When her car seat was safely buckled into the back of Rachel's car, he came around to the driver's side, where Rachel was already behind the wheel.

"I'll follow you there."

"Oh, Quint, you don't have to. It's not far and—"

"I'll follow you," he repeated firmly.

"I won't be leaving their house right away," she warned. "I'll stay and talk to Laurel and Gerald for a while."

He rolled his eyes. "Then I won't wait around for you,

I'll take Brady home. But if you should change your mind about coming over later—''

"Quint, I won't.''

He ignored that. "You know where I live, and I'll be home for the rest of the night. You don't have to call first, just come.''

"I—I can't, Quint.'' Each refusal required extra effort.

She knew she had to get away from him before it became easier to comply than to keep saying no. "Good night, Quint. And thanks for everything today. Snowy and I had a lovely time.''

"I bet you've been spouting that polite little speech since high school.'' Quint was sardonic. "It's right out of the *Dating Tips to Teens* handbook: the girl should always thank the boy for a *lovely* time. Even when it wasn't so lovely.''

"And how do you know so much about the subject?'' Rachel hoped she sounded blasé, but it was rather deflating to realize that he was correct.

She really had been spouting that same polite little speech since the beginning of her dating career—which seemed to stretch back to another eon yet managed to remain depressingly the same after all these years.

Except for her nondates with Quint. That was different, *he* was different. And she was certainly different when she was with him.

"My sister played by the same book,'' said Quint. "During her teens, that is. Then she outgrew it.''

Rachel was so surprised to learn he had a sister that she decided his subtle insult was vague enough to dismiss. "This is the first time you've mentioned a sister. Is she here in New Jersey, too?''

And where does did she fit into the Cormack scheme of things? Rachel left that question unspoken.

Quint shrugged, his expression suddenly enigmatic. "The rain is starting to come down harder again. Good night, Rachel. And thank *you* for a *lovely* time.''

13

Wade Saxon seldom fell prey to doubts and self-recriminations, but tonight he felt as if he'd been hit with a full lifetime's share of them. He sat next to Tim Sheely on the leather sofa—where he'd made love to Dana for the first time just a few hours ago—and tried to concentrate on the conversation going on around him. But it was hopeless. He kept drifting into the unhappy territory of guilt and uncertainty.

Performance anxiety. He'd heard the term but always dismissed it as nothing to do with him, certainly not sexually. But his performance with Dana earlier tonight—a half dozen strokes into her sweet wet heat which hurdled him into shattering orgasm—was definitely the kind to fuel anxiety.

He'd never lost it like that before; he was the master of his own passion and therefore of the woman he was pleasuring. He enjoyed his own control as much as he liked watching his partner surrender hers. He was a sexual virtuoso, but with Dana, the maestro had dropped his baton. So to speak.

As for Dana, she hadn't minded at all. He trembled with vivid sensual recall, imagining himself deep inside her, her limbs locked around him, her blue eyes filled with warmth and affection. But not replete with sated passion.

Because he hadn't satisfied her and he knew it. Worse, she *didn't* know it.

She thought that the rushed act he had so ignominiously botched was sex as it was supposed to be. Wade took no comfort in the fact that she'd been a virgin, and therefore had no basis of comparison. Instead, that realization launched another wave of gloom.

Her introduction to sex by him—that he was her first lover had filled him with a totally unexpected possessive pride—should have been passionately earthshaking, at least a nine on the sexual Richter scale. Had he even rated a two?

If only they'd had time to do it again. If only, at the very least, there had been enough time for him to give her the satisfaction she deserved and he was eager to provide.

But Tim and Lisa's unanticipated arrival, just critical minutes after his frantic eruption, scarcely left them time to dress and clean up—the sofa definitely needed some work—before the couple trooped in with little Seth and baby Mackenzie.

Deciding against a rainy night in a Mystic motel room and concerned about reports of possible flooding, the Sheely family had returned to find Dana and Wade Saxon in their house. Both Tim and Lisa expressed delight over their unexpected company, and Dana immediately turned into a doting aunt, lavishing attention on her young niece and nephew.

Wade followed her around, he couldn't keep his eyes off her. Casual gestures she was completely unaware of making were seared into his very soul. Yet he was supposed to act like nothing had changed between them, that he was still her buddy, a sort of proxy for Tim.

Pretending to be friends who hadn't moved on to that next crucial level had been Dana's brilliant idea. While they'd been throwing on their clothes in a panicked frenzy, Tim's and Lisa's voices growing louder as they approached the house, Dana asked him to maintain the best-buddies charade. Wade had argued against it—he'd never concealed anything from Tim, and he didn't want to keep his newfound feelings for Dana a secret—but ultimately, she prevailed.

"Right now I can't deal with any questions or jokes or anything they might say if they knew. It's still all too new to me," she'd whispered, gripping his hand, those gorgeous eyes of hers pleading with him.

He'd caved instantly. How could he refuse her anything? Especially after he had just deprived her of the physical pleasure he so desperately wanted to give her.

So here he was, pretending to be the same old Wade when he felt entirely different. Experiencing emotions that heretofore had been foreign to him, yet trying to appear unchanged. He probably couldn't have pulled it off, had not the Sheelys been wholly and grimly preoccupied with the news he'd brought them from Lakeview.

Reluctantly, but realizing the necessity, he had told Tim, Dana, and Lisa about Shawn's new friendship with Misty Tilden as recorded in the Lakeview police complaint. Lisa had the objectivity and distance of an in-law, but Tim and Dana, predictably, went ballistic. When they contemplated telling their parents, both looked ready to hurl either their dinners or any readily available object.

"I'll call Shawn tomorrow and talk to him, man to man," Tim decided. "No use dragging the folks into this when it might be not be anything to worry about."

"I'll talk to Shawn, too," Dana seconded. "And I'll tell Mary Jo and Tricia and Sarah what's going on. I know they'll all want to offer him some sisterly advice. Or make some threats," she added, unsmiling.

"And the collective Sheely message will be for Shawn to stay away from this Misty Tilden person?" Lisa looked troubled. "All that interference could backfire in a big way, you know. Ever hear of Romeo and Juliet?"

"Misty and her millions must seem like a fantasy-come-true, irresistible to a kid like Shawn," Wade pointed out.

Tim and Dana were not pleased with his comment and accused him of disparaging Shawn. *Their* brother would not be attracted to a lap-dancing sex goddess with an eight-figure inheritance simply because she was . . . well, a lap-dancing sex goddess with an eight-figure inheritance. No, Shawn Sheely was sensitive and altruistic and not moti-vated by the forces of sex and money.

Wade made the mistake of laughing. Well, they were kidding, weren't they?

Unfortunately not. That ardent Sheely blood loyalty of theirs had been fully activated, and Wade was relegated to outsider status. Lisa, who'd wisely managed to keep a straight face during the sibling accolades, was accorded neutrality.

Wade didn't have a chance to talk privately with Dana for the rest of the evening. He was put up on a futon in little Seth's room for the night and Dana bedded down on a mattress in baby Mackenzie's room. Because the master bedroom was located between the two children's rooms, and the uncarpeted hallway resounded with creaking floor-boards, she was as inaccessible as a princess in a castle surrounded by a beast-infested moat.

Everybody was cordial at breakfast the next morning. By tacit agreement, neither Shawn's nor Misty's name was mentioned at all. The sun was shining and the water had receded from the streets by noon when Dana and Wade departed for Lakeview. Separately, in their own cars.

It wasn't easy to keep his Mercedes restrained in the right lane behind Dana's plodding little Chevy. After all, a thor-oughbred racehorse wasn't made to trail a mule on the track, mused Wade. Nevertheless, he followed Dana the whole way from Connecticut to New Jersey and because she didn't veer from the right lane, neither did he. Not even when it seemed like every car in the state of New York had whizzed by them in the passing lane.

When she stopped at a turnpike rest stop for gas, so did he although he could've made it to North Carolina without stopping, thanks to his car's magnificent fuel capacity.

He filled the tank of her car at the self-service pump and bought two cans of soda, root beer for him and Orange Crush for her. It was their first real chance to talk, and if the location was not exactly a romantic site, at least they weren't surrounded by other Sheelys.

"About last night," he began, wishing he could think of a more original opener.

She blushed and immediately averted her eyes. "What happened, happened, Saxon. There's no need for postmortems."

Which had always been *his* morning-after attitude. Nothing turned him off faster than a woman who tried to manufacture a sense of intimacy out of a no-strings-attached act of pleasure. Dana knew exactly how he felt about that, of course, because he'd never been reticent about venting his morning-after irritation. Neither had she. She would call him an insensitive jerk and express pity for his misguided lovers, and often he would laughingly agree with her. Without a shred of remorse.

He was feeling remorseful now, for the all the things he'd said and left unsaid. As if caught in some kind of cosmic payback, he stood staring hungrily at Dana, wanting to feel close to her when she seemed set on establishing a disturbing distance.

She glanced at her watch. "We'd better go. I want to get home and call my sisters. We should come up with some kind of a plan before we confront Shawn."

Frustrated, Wade returned to his own car and tried to console himself with the fact that a food-and-fuel stop really wasn't the ideal place for the kind of conversation they needed to have.

He searched his mind for where the ideal place might be. Dana had been right on target when she'd accused him of being an unimaginative, unromantic date.

"When was the last time you took a date to the theater or to the symphony in Philadelphia, Saxon? For that matter, when was the last time you took a date to a restaurant that requires a tie? Or even to a first-run movie?" He remembered their conversation in Riggin's very well, though it seemed like it had taken place a lifetime ago.

Which in a way, it had. Back then, he had been carefree

and uninvolved with no intentions of changing. Now he was actually plotting where to take Dana Sheely on a serious, honest-to-God romantic date.

But he wasn't the only one caught in a bizarre cycle of change. The Tildens were facing criminal charges, his aunt Eve had been dangerously disrespectful to the chief of police, and Shawn Sheely was Misty Tilden's newest best friend. It was as if Lakeview had been transported to the Twilight Zone. Could things get any stranger than this?

Rachel had never been a proponent of drop-in visits, though she acknowledged they were occasionally necessary. This morning seemed to be one of those times. Her answering-machine tape played yesterday's numerous calls from Wade and Aunt Eve, alluding to the Tildens and a visit to the police station. There were no details, but Rachel's curiosity was definitely piqued.

She had tried to call both her cousin and her aunt, last night and this morning, but was unable to reach either one. Where could they be? Neither had mentioned any out-of-town weekend plans, but if they were in town, they weren't bothering to answer their phones.

Which was a distinct possibility. And if they didn't want to be bothered, she shouldn't intrude on them.

Rachel replayed the messages and tried to put together a likely scenario. *Meet the Tildens at the police station to discuss a criminal complaint?* Not even a psychic could make sense of that! Her curiosity expanded from merely piqued to all-consuming.

She decided she had no choice but to pay a visit to her aunt, though she knew Aunt Eve would not be pleased. Eve Saxon took advance precautions against drop-ins by grabbing her coat before she opened the door and then telling the uninvited guest that she was just getting ready to leave so there was no time to visit.

Rachel drove to her aunt's well-tended colonial-style brick house, half-expecting Eve to greet her at the door, holding her coat. But her knocks went unanswered, and the newspaper was still in the driveway where it had been tossed by the carrier earlier that morning. Clearly, Aunt Eve was not at home.

At Wade's apartment, she leaned steadily on the buzzer to rouse him, just in case he'd spent a hardy night carousing, before concluding that nobody could sleep through the infernal buzzing din. Wade wasn't home, and she still had no idea what had happened with the Tildens.

She wondered if Quint did. She suddenly remembered his call Friday night, claiming he wanted to discuss the Tilden case. But he hadn't mentioned anything about it yesterday, during the entire day they'd spent together. And neither had she, which seemed to portend something. Rachel didn't let herself think what.

She arrived at Quint's door, aware that her heart was beating a little too fast in anticipation. This visit fell into the professional realm, she reminded herself, and tried hard to focus on legalistic strategy instead of the thrill of seeing Quint again.

Quint opened the door holding Brady in his arms.

"Mom-mmee!" Brady squealed and launched himself at Rachel. She caught him and he wrapped his arms and legs around her like a little monkey.

"I know why Brady calls you Mommy." Suddenly Dustin was there, standing between her and Quint, stuffing a chocolate donut into his mouth. "It's 'cause he doesn't have a mother and you're Quint's girlfriend. My mom said so," he added importantly.

Rachel's eyes met Quint's, and she carried Brady inside.

"C'mon, Brady, it's our turn to be It." Dustin tugged on Brady's cotton overall–covered leg. "Austin is hiding and we have to find him. C'mon, count. One, two, three."

"One, two, free," Brady repeated, wiggling in Rachel's arms. "Down," he ordered, and she set him on his feet.

Dustin took his young uncle's hand and the pair scurried out of the room, trailing donut crumbs in their wake.

Rachel and Quint faced each other.

"Carla is stressed and needed another break?" Rachel surmised.

"Carla and her mother are both suffering from migraine headaches and need a quiet day of rest, thanks to Frank Cormack, who blew in at dawn, drunk and reeking of perfume—not his own," Quint said, his voice as impassive as his expression. "Carla's mother told him to leave and when he refused, she—uh—evicted him at gunpoint. Frank retaliated by throwing a rock through the front window and banging a garbage-can lid against the hood of Mrs. Polk's car. The police were called."

"And so were you?"

He nodded. "The police suggested that Frank be locked up to sleep it off in the Lakeview jail, and, for a change, Carla didn't balk. I think her mother would've clobbered *her* with the garbage-can lid if she had. The boys were dropped off here at nine A.M."

He seemed remote and dispirited, and Rachel forgot she'd come to grill him about the Tildens and those mysterious phone messages. She felt the urge to put her arms around him and recognized that the impulse was not a sexual one. She just wanted to hug him, which was unusual for her; she'd never been hug-prone except for Snowy and now, little Brady.

Rachel gazed at Quint, so strong and capable, the invincible man. His dark eyes were hard and cold, the way they'd been when he argued a contentious point in the Pedersen trial. He certainly was not vulnerable and cuddly-sweet like Snowy and Brady, yet somehow he was evoking the same emotional reponses within her that they did. Maybe it was because she could imagine how he'd felt this morning, seeing his father drunk, listening to Carla scream, worrying about the effect on his little brothers. . . .

Compassion flooded her. Poor Quint; he tried so hard, and the Cormacks' crises seemed never-ending.

She stopped analyzing and took action, closing the small gap between them and wrapping her arms around his waist. She pressed her face into the soft cotton of his shirt and closed her eyes. Instantly, Quint's arms enveloped her, and they stood together, leaning against each other. For those few quiet peaceful moments, Rachel felt closer to him than she'd ever been to anybody in her life.

The insight jarred her. Scared her, too. That she couldn't maintain her usual cool, aloof self around Quint gave him tremendous power over her. And they hadn't even made love yet. Rachel gulped. The *yet* made it seem all but inevitable.

"The kids and I will be leaving shortly for the Phillies game," Quint's voice sounded above her. She could feel his warm breath rustling her hair. "I thought we'd eat lunch along the way. Do you want to come with us?"

She drew back a little, to look up at him. Saw his arched brows and half smile. The hot gleam in his dark eyes. She could feel his body hardening against her, in response to their closeness. Rachel forgot to be scared. The issue of power seemed irrelevant.

"Do you have enough tickets?" she asked, shifting slightly to trap his right thigh between hers.

He retaliated by sliding his hands under her pale pink cotton sweater. "You don't follow baseball, do you?"

Rachel shivered as his fingertips kneaded along the delicate length of her spine. "What makes you think that?"

"A baseball game in May won't be sold out," explained Quint. "We can get the tickets we need at the gate."

He slipped his fingers around to the front clip of her bra and unfastened it. Rachel understood the gesture for what it was. A possessive claim. By not rebuking or pulling away from him, she had granted him that right. She understood that too, and remained in his arms.

"Ha, ha, you didn't find me!" Austin's voice bellowed from the kitchen. "I get to hide again and you're It again."

Rachel and Quint automatically drew apart. She reached under her shirt to fasten the clip, her cheeks burning. She knew Quint was watching her, his dark eyes hot and intense.

"Want to hide with me, Brady? That loser Dustin will never find us!" Austin chortled loudly.

"I'm not a loser, I'm telling Quint!" bawled Dustin. "Quinnnnt!" The seven-year-old arrived in the living room, his face contorted with fury.

"You're not a loser," Quint said before Dustin could voice his complaint.

"I'm tired of being It all the time." Dustin scowled. "Rachel, will you help me look for them? We can be a team." He slipped his chubby little hand in hers and tugged on it.

"Feel free to say no." Quint looked amused.

"I want to be on Dustin's team," Rachel assured the boy. She was as free to say no as Quint had been when he'd gotten that phone call at dawn from Carla. Her eyes met his in mutual understanding.

"We'll find them, Dustin," she said, following the boy out of the room. "And then it will be your turn to hide."

"And you won't help Austin find me 'cause you're on my team. Besides, Austin is the champion finder. He doesn't need any help," Dustin added, half-admiringly, half-resentfully.

Rachel smiled. There were times when the young brothers' relationship mirrored the one she and her cousin Wade had as children. Friendly enemies—or rivalrous friends.

Twenty minutes later, the group piled into the station wagon. Austin and Dustin pulled out their GameBoys and prompty went into a video-game trance.

"Where Snowy?" Brady asked plaintively. He stared at the empty space next to him, where her car seat had been during yesterday's trip to the festival.

"Snowy is at her house," Rachel explained. "Although I wish she was with us."

"We can swing by there and pick her up," offered Quint, steering the car out of the driveway.

Rachel knew he meant it. If she asked, he would include her niece in the outing.

"You're a born rescuer," she murmured.

"And does Snowy need rescuing?"

"Not today. Her father is taking her to spend the day with his parents. Laurel isn't going with them," she added.

"Uh-oh."

"Yes." A chill crept through her. "Last night Laurel and Gerald were in the middle of a terrible fight when I arrived with Snowy," she confided, unable to keep it to herself any longer. "Laurel was shrieking at the top of her lungs. I didn't want to leave Snowy there; I wanted to take her home with me."

Quint reached over and took her hand in his. He didn't have to say anything, words weren't necessary. She knew that he knew exactly how she felt.

"I'm worried about their marriage," Rachel blurted out. "Apparently, Laurel was gone all day yesterday and got home just before I brought Snowy back. She refused to say where she'd been but—she smelled of alcohol. Gerald accused her of being drunk, and maybe she was. I don't know what to say to her or how to talk to her. She is acting completely unlike herself."

"What a person does is exactly who they are, Rachel." Quint carried her hand to his thigh and placed it there, resting his own on top of it.

"But Laurel was acting like a spoiled, self-centered, nasty . . ." Rachel swallowed hard. "She isn't like that."

"She is bored and restless in her marriage, certainly a difficult situtation. But what a person chooses to do in difficult times shows their true character far more clearly than whatever is done in easy or so-called normal times."

"You sound like a fortune cookie!" Rachel jerked her hand away from him and tightly clenched her fingers in her lap.

"And you're getting mad at me instead of Laurel because you don't like what you've heard. That's a shoot-the-messenger reaction, Rachel."

Rachel thought about that. "I don't want Snowy to be hurt," she murmured at last. The prospect made her ache.

"I know. But all you can do is to be there for her, Rachel. Let her know that she can always count on you. You can't control either Laurel or her husband."

"You speak with such authority on the subject." Rachel smiled wryly. "Because you wrote the book on Coping with Dysfunctional Relatives?"

"Because I speak with authority on any subject, Rachel, warranted or not." He laughed. "A skill that comes in handy when I have to speak extemporaneously in court."

She gazed at him, remembering how very effective he was in the courtroom. "Quint, would you promise me something?"

"Maybe. What is it?"

"I was hoping for an outright promise. I guess I should've expected you would add some qualifying points," she said wistfully.

He didn't dispute it. "I guess you should've. I make very few outright promises, Rachel. And never without carefully thinking it over first."

He steered the car into the parking lot of a restaurant with a western motif, some kind of a steak house. The children cheered.

Rachel glanced nervously at Quint. "If Gerald and Laurel do get a divorce . . ." She trembled. *If?* She'd handled divorce cases where the couples weren't nearly as hostile and hateful toward one another as Laurel and Gerald had been last night.

"Quint, I want you to promise that you won't represent Gerald if he should ask you to. Because he'll sue for custody, I'm sure, and it would kill Laurel to lose Snowy."

"It would kill *you* for Laurel to lose custody of Snowy," Quint amended.

Austin and Dustin had unbuckled their seat belts and were busily extricating Brady from his car seat. Quint opened his door and started to get out of the car. Rachel caught his arm, halting him. "Please, Quint."

"Laurel certainly would be well represented by Saxon Associates," he pointed out.

Rachel was seized by panic. Saxon Associates hadn't handled a custody case that had gone to trial since she'd joined the firm. They had been successful in settling custody issues out of court, which was certainly better for the children involved and their parents, too, because a custody battle could be nastier and more complex than a murder trial.

Poor little Snowy. The thought of her high-spirited little niece being fought over like some kind of game trophy made Rachel feel sick. Quint would have no qualms about fighting for a father's right to full custody—after all, he was living proof that such arrangements could work well. Her stomach twisted queasily.

She watched Quint walk the three boys into the restaurant, then head back to the station wagon where she sat frozen in the front seat. He pulled open her door and held out his hand.

"The hostess is seating the kids. Come with me, Rachel."

She hesitated, staring at his proffered hand. "You know, right now I actually understand why Carla took that ambulance hostage. When you feel completely impotent in the face of an insurmountable problem, you have to do *something* to try to gain a little control."

"I hope you aren't planning to take my car hostage," drawled Quint.

"If I had the keys, I think I just might." But since she didn't, she put her hand in his and let him help her out of the car.

"What's the insurmountable problem, honey?" he asked, his tone indulgent.

She stared at him, askance. Didn't he know? Hadn't he been listening to her? "Wade and I would lose a custody fight in court to you, and I don't have much hope that Aunt Eve could beat you either, Quint." The words tumbled out in a rush. "She's a very good lawyer, but you're a better trial attorney than she is. So if Gerald sues for custody of Snowy, I want *you* to be the one representing Laurel."

Quint heaved a sigh. "Aren't you jumping the gun here, Rachel? They haven't even separated. Hopefully, they won't."

Rachel thought of what she'd heard and seen last night. "I'm not very optimistic, Quint. Do you want a retainer? That can be arranged."

"Suppose I demand a retainer other than cash, Rachel." He smiled wolfishly and hooked his arm around her waist, pulling her close to his side. "Could that be arranged? How far will you go to retain my indomitable courtroom prowess?"

"I can tell you aren't taking this seriously," Rachel reproved.

"I can't believe that you are. Hiring me to represent Laurel in a potential divorce when she has three lawyers in the family?" He laughed at the notion.

Rachel didn't. "I want to keep you from representing Gerald," she said flatly. "I'll do whatever has to be done. And stop looking at me that way! I know that look. It's the one you give Carla when you think she's being irrational."

"And you're not being just a tad irrational, Rachel?" He walked her into the restaurant and guided her to the table where Brady, Austin, and Dustin were already drawing on their place mats with the crayons provided.

Brady made several stripes and a wobbly circle. "That Mommy," he said proudly, pointing at his work.

"Yeah, we could tell." Austin snickered. "Looks just like her."

"It's wonderful, Brady," Rachel assured him, and Brady beamed. She took the seat beside his high chair and tied the plastic bib around his neck.

Quint watched her every move, and she tried not to feel self-conscious under his intense unwavering scrutiny.

They were halfway through their meal of barbecue, salad, and fries, when Quint leaned over and said quietly, "I promise I won't represent Laurel's husband in a divorce if he asks to hire me."

Her eyes widened. "Is that an unlimited promise? You won't take Gerald's case, no matter what?"

"I promise I won't, no matter what."

Relief surged through her. She felt she'd spared her small niece from a terrible disaster. Certainly her fledgling relationship with Quint had been saved; opposition regarding Snowy would've been the death knell. Looking at him across the table, she acknowledged how very much that would've hurt.

Rachel gave him a dazzling smile. "Thank you, Quint!"

He blinked. "Now you have to promise me something, Rachel."

Her smile dimmed a little. "I should've known this was coming. Okay, what's the catch?"

"There is no catch. I want you to promise that you'll always remember we aren't enemies, Rachel. We might be professional adversaries from time to time, but it does not extend to the personal level. Ever."

Attraction and affection and admiration joined forces, flowing through her in a powerful surge that reflected in her shining eyes. "That's an easy promise to make, Quint," she said in a husky, velvety tone that was light-years removed from her brusque professional adversary voice.

"It might not be so easy to keep," Quint warned, suddenly looking away. "But be aware that I intend to hold you to it, Rachel."

Rachel's first professional baseball game was a long one, extending beyond the usual nine innings to eleven. She would've been well satisfied with five. Brady lost interest early on, and she walked him around the stadium, stopping for snacks and looking at souvenirs, before he finally fell asleep in her lap. To her surprise, Austin and Dustin remained engaged by the action on the playing field. They seemed to know the players and animatedly discussed the game with Quint.

Rachel listened desultorily to their conversation. Strange to think that their mutual father, Frank Cormack, was probably still in the Lakeview jail, most certainly nursing a monstrous hangover. Quint was filling the paternal role for his young half brothers and doing it well.

She shifted the sleeping toddler in her arms, brushing a kiss on his soft blond hair. Little Brady didn't need a father-substitute, he was lucky enough to have a good father of his own, but the poor child had struck out in the mother department. The globe-trotting Sharolyn was as awful a parent as Frank Cormack, Rachel mused sadly. How could a mother leave her own baby? And then Laurel's impatient angry cry reverberated in Rachel's head. *"I want to have some fun, I want to have a life!"*

That didn't mean Laurel would abandon Snowy, did it? Rachel's eyes filled with tears, and she tightened her arms protectively around Brady. Moments later, Austin and Dustin tromped past her to hail the pretzel vendor. She felt Quint's arm slip around her shoulders.

"Are you all right?" he asked softly.

"I'm trying not to have an anxiety attack about Snowy's future," she confessed.

"Somebody has to worry about the kids, it's a vital family function." He smiled into her eyes. "We'll add Snowy to our merry band, Rachel. She already fits right in."

Rachel cuddled closer, loving him for his insight, his understanding, his quiet support. Brady stirred in her lap, and Austin and Dustin returned to their seats, clutching giant-sized pretzels. She was so glad to be a member of their merry band.

After dinner they returned Dustin and Austin to Carla— Frank was not on the premises—then bathed Brady and tucked him into bed.

"Dare I say it? Alone at last." Quint's eyes gleamed. "Come here." He caught Rachel's hand and pulled her onto his lap.

She went to him willingly and lifted her face for his kiss. He cupped her chin and brushed his lips over hers, softly, lightly. It was a preliminary kiss, brief and undemanding, but the gentle pressure of his lips and his warm breath against her mouth, sent desire rocketing through her.

He threaded his fingers through her hair as he slowly deepened their kiss. She felt his tongue in her mouth and she moaned a little and drew it in deeper. Her arms tightened around him, digging into the muscles of his back, and she twisted in his lap, parting her thighs slightly to welcome the throbbing burgeoning pressure of his arousal.

"I want you so much." His voice was deep and thick, all urgency and need.

She made a soft, soughing sound and snuggled closer, cradling his face between her hands. She kissed him fervently, her ardor matching his, giving him the assent he'd been waiting for.

Quint rose to his feet, lifting her in his arms.

"Are you really going to carry me up the stairs?" she asked dreamily, nuzzling his neck. She felt a wild urge to suckle the skin there and thought of the love bite on her own neck. Now she understood his primal craving for putting it there and debated whether or not she should indulge her own impulses. Picturing Quint Cormack wearing a turtleneck on a warm May day to conceal a hickey struck her as hilarious, and she grinned.

"Don't think I can do it?" Quint misinterpreted her source of amusement. He started toward the stairs. "You're a mere featherweight, milady."

"How gallant. Just like a medieval knight of yore." Her smiled widened. "But if you should happen to feel your back muscles giving out, never mind the chivalry, just put me down."

"Not a chance. I'm going to carry you to my bed where we—" He stopped in mid-sentence as the sound of the kitchen door slamming rocked the house.

Quint's eyes met Rachel's. "No." He groaned. "It can't be Sarah. Not now, not yet. She usually doesn't get back till around midnight on her Sundays off."

"Anybody here?" called Sarah.

Rachel squirmed, and Quint morosely set her on her feet.

They came face-to-face with Sarah in the living room.

"You're back early." Quint sounded accusing.

Sarah didn't seem to notice. "I had to get away. I just couldn't listen to Shawn for another minute. You should hear him, it's enough to make you gag! My sisters and Matt are still trying to talk some sense into him, but it's hopeless. I knew if I didn't leave, I'd end up doing something awful—like maybe running over Shawn with your car, Quint. Honestly, I'm upset enough to do it!"

"I'm glad you restrained yourself," Quint muttered. "The personal-injury suit would've been hellish, and I'm heartily sick of criminal charges, which have never interested me and still don't."

Rachel still felt weak and wobbly as her body tried to adjust to its abrupt sensual deprivation. She clutched the back of a chair for support and wished she was holding on to Quint instead. He dropped down onto the sofa and was staring at the carpet with fierce concentration, as if trying to memorize its weave.

"We threatened to tell Mom and Dad, and Shawn said he didn't care!" exclaimed Sarah.

"Maybe he's simply calling your bluff," Quint suggested.

Rachel gave him full marks for displaying interest in whatever Sheely family altercation had so aggravated Sarah. She herself couldn't even pretend to care.

"Maybe he is." Sarah manically paced back and forth. "We hate to rile the folks—we all remembered how upset Mom and Dad were when Tricia went out with that defrocked priest. But this—this is about ninety times worse! Even Tricia is shocked. Quint, what are we going to do?"

"I think I'd better go home," Rachel spoke up, and Sarah glanced at her, startled, as if only now aware of her presence. "I—have some things to do and you two obviously need to talk."

"Oh God, I just busted in here and messed things up for you two, didn't I?" Sarah was remorseful. "I'm so sorry! I can always—"

"I think you'd better stay and talk to Quint," Rachel said kindly. "It's all right, I—was just on my way home anyway."

"I'll walk you to your car." Quint followed her to the front door, and they walked outside to her car, still parked in front of his house.

Rachel remembered the original purpose for her visit today and the questions she'd never gotten around to asking him. Now, with an agitated Sarah Sheely waiting inside, the timing seemed all wrong. She would call Aunt Eve and Wade when she got home; surely they would be available now.

"You're very understanding," Quint said, tucking a loose strand of her hair behind her ear.

The tender intimacy of the gesture thrilled Rachel. She glowed with warmth, once again filled with that almost mystical feeling of closeness to him. And the humor of the situation suddenly tickled her.

"Look at it this way, Quint, a young man's life is at stake." She flashed a playful grin. "Unless Sarah calms down, she just might decide to hop in your car and run over her brother, after all."

Quint heaved an exaggerated groan.

"You're good at defusing family crises," Rachel continued. She opened her car door, leaning up to give him a quick kiss on the cheek before she slid behind the wheel. "I was glad to have you to listen to my woes about Laurel. Sarah needs you to do the same with Shawn."

Quint touched his cheek on the spot Rachel had brushed with her lips. "Rachel, the last thing I want to do right now is to listen to Sarah rant on about her brother."

"I know," she whispered.

He wanted to make love to her. Never had she felt so positive about her own allure. Quint had given it to her, this sexual confidence, this security. Her desire for him was as exciting as his for her. Rachel drove home in a heady haze of contentment mingled with exhilaration.

There were no new messages on her answering machine.

She tried to call her aunt and her cousin but both were still unable to be reached. Her frustration grew, and contacting them became an almost-compulsive challenge. She called every fifteen minutes, but neither Aunt Eve nor Wade answered their phones.

At ten, she decided to give up and take a bath. She'd just stepped out of the tub and wrapped herself in her thick white toweling robe when her doorbell sounded. Rachel's ears perked. It was either Aunt Eve or Wade, finally responding to all those messages she'd left them, she was certain.

She hurried to the door, taking her usual safety precaution of leaving on the chain to steal a peek at her visitor waiting in the vestibule.

Her heart did a triple somersault in her chest. Standing outside her door was Quint Cormack.

14

"**A**sk me in," Quint ordered, even as Rachel was fumbling with the chain.

She opened the door and he stepped inside her apartment. They faced each other wordlessly. Rachel was the first to break the silence between them.

"I—just got out of the bathtub." She felt an acute breathless shyness that metamorphosed into a pressing need to explain her robe, her humidified hair, her flushed damp skin.

"So I see." His hungry dark eyes drank in the sight of her.

Rachel blushed and reflexively tightened the terry tie of her robe.

"Thank you for not asking why I'm here," Quint growled. "We've moved too far beyond those games to start playing them now."

Rachel smiled wryly. "We're past that crucial third date, hmm? Time to—"

"I need to be with you," Quint said huskily. He saw her mouth tremble and part, and he traced the outline of her lips with his finger.

Rachel shivered. His touch was like electricity coursing through her. She felt the current flow to her every cell, as if sealing the connection between them.

"I need to be with you, too, Quint." Her voice ached with need. And love.

255

She was in love with him, Rachel conceded to herself. She knew it was too soon to say the words to Quint. Her hesitance had nothing to do with *Games People Play* or *The Rules* and everything to do with timing. She would tell Quint she loved him when the time was right for such an emotional declaration.

It wasn't now.

Right now the atmosphere was thick with sexual tension. With urgency and lust. Rachel was enthralled. Rampant sexual need glittered in Quint's eyes, and she knew her eyes reflected her own intense desire. It was intoxicating, knowing how much he wanted her, and returning his feelings in full measure. Right now there was no need for any words at all.

As if they'd been choreographed, they moved at the same moment, into each other's arms. Quint's mouth closed over hers in a passionate, possessive kiss. Rachel sighed deeply, her body softening in his arms as his body grew hard and taut, the primal male response to her enveloping feminine sensuality.

She clung to him as his tongue glided over hers, rubbing and stroking, and opened her mouth wider, inviting him deeper and deeper within. Her breasts surged and swelled and filled his hands.

They kissed and kissed, his thumbs moving lightly, deftly over her nipples that were sensitive and engorged and straining against the cotton barrier of her robe. Rachel twisted sinuously against him as sensual anticipation blazed. She wanted her breasts to be bare. She wanted to feel Quint's mouth on them, the pull of his lips, the flick of his tongue.

Liquid heat flooded her and she felt herself tumbling out of control. She gave a sharp little cry and arched into him, rocking her hips against him, further inflaming them both.

He slipped his hand into the folds of her robe and reached between her legs to cup her hot throbbing center. She moaned into his mouth and her fingers sought him, tracing the thick fascinating shape of him through the denim of his jeans.

And then the phone rang. And kept ringing.

"No!" Quint gasped as Rachel pushed away from him. "Ignore it. We've had too many interruptions already. We aren't going to have another one." He reached out to pull her back to him but she managed to sidestep him.

"What if it's Sarah calling about Brady?" Rachel's breath was shallow and rapid. "You told her where she could reach you, didn't you? What if Carla called about some new problem with your father? Or—Or it could even be Laurel."

She headed to the kitchen to answer her phone but before she could reach it, her answering machine automatically clicked on after six rings. Rachel stopped in her tracks and listened.

"Hey, Rach, this is Wade," her cousin's voice came over the line. "Just returning your ten thousand messages. I think you used up the whole tape," he joked. "Anyway, it looks like we're playing a game of telephone tag, so why don't we just call it quits for tonight? I'll see you in the office tomorrow."

Rachel looked up to see Quint staring at her. His breathing was ragged, his body was tense, hard and flushed with desire.

"We're unplugging the damn phone," he said, his voice low and raw. "The world will just have to get along without us for the next few hours."

He unplugged the phone, then swept her up in his arms to carry her into her bedroom and lay her down on the queen-size bed she had bought for herself two years ago. Her mother and sister had told her it a waste of her money. Why not simply use the old twin bed from her childhood room until she met Mr. Right, who would buy her a brand-new bed after she'd maneuvered him into exchanging wedding rings?

Rachel had not only bought the bed, she'd purchased an entire bedroom set and wallpapered to match her new sheets, quilt, and pillow shams. And now Quint was here, the first man to cross the threshold.

He looked big and masculine and jarringly out of place among the dainty violet, yellow, and green floral prints. The very feminine decor enhanced his virility and strength and sent a striking thrill of awareness through her.

"Think we can remember where we were a few minutes ago?" Quint stood beside the bed, staring down at her in a way that made her insides melt.

"We can try." Her smile was inviting, tempting.

Rachel rose to her knees on the bed and reached for him. A potent mixture of love and desire made her bold. She unbuckled his belt and unzipped his jeans while he shrugged off his shirt.

He quickly dispatched her robe to the floor, and she found herself kneeling naked in front of him. "I don't think we were quite this far a few minutes ago," she said in a high nervous voice. She felt almost virginal, she was definitely a sexual novice, having only done this once before.

Perhaps it was her lawyer's training in regards to the principle of Full Disclosure that made her admit her lack of experience to Quint. "Just thought I should warn you, instead of using it to ambush you."

"Let's make a pact." He smiled, brushing her hair back from her face. "We will never ambush each other in the bedroom. That's strictly a courtroom tactic."

"You're telling me. You used it to great effect during the Pedersen trial."

"If that's a compliment, thank you."

"It's a statement of fact to the lawyer who made dog food out of my case."

Quint laughed and moved even closer. "Sweetheart, I've told you time and again that your case *was* a dog."

The tips of her breasts brushed the wiry mat of hair on his chest. Rachel quivered. Every inch of her skin tingled and burned like sensuous wildfire. "Back then, who would've ever guessed that we'd end up like this?" Her voice was husky and thick.

"I wanted to, Rachel," Quint confessed. He freed himself of his jeans and his boxer shorts, then took her hand and wrapped it around the pulsing length of him.

"You did?" She stared, transfixed by the erotic sight of her fingers holding him.

"I know it's hard for you to believe because you wanted to behead me during that trial." He chuckled softly. "And it was pretty humbling, finding myself attracted to a woman who thought I had all the appeal of a serial killer. It took me quite a while to admit it to myself."

"I thought about you obsessively during that trial," Rachel murmured. "I've never been so aware of another person in my life. I thought it was hate." She shook her head ruefully. "I guess I had to think that."

"True." Quint laughed again."If you'd thought you were attracted to me while I was carving up your case, Lord only knows what you might've done."

"Maybe I'd've taken you hostage, counselor."

He caught her hand before she could tweak him in a vital area. "That could be construed as an ambush, Rachel," he reminded her.

"Then I'll switch tactics." She caressed him instead.

He sighed. "Much better."

His hands moved over her curves, leisurely touching her everywhere, lightly but not lingering, tantalizing but not claiming her. He kissed her the same way, his mouth taking hers in brief teasing little kisses. Kisses her lips clung to and returned.

Entranced, she explored him, running her fingers up and down and over him, kneading and caressing him, learning what particular touches made him groan with pleasure. Seducing herself as she seduced him.

Finally, unable to remain still any longer under her sensual explorations, he tumbled her down on the mattress and lay beside her. Closing her eyes, she held him, feeling his muscular body against hers.

His hands were warm and sensitive as he fondled her breasts, lifting the soft full curves, stroking her, brushing his fingertips around her nipples yet carefully avoiding the swollen tips. He was teasing her, enticing her, making her wait.

She pressed against his hands, seeking what she needed. Demanding what she craved . . . his fingers on the taut aching buds. ''Quint!'' she cried his name when he acceded to her wishes and rubbed his thumbs over her rosy nipples.

''Do you like that?'' he rasped. The slight stubble on his jaw scraped the sensitive valley between her breasts, the added stimulation taking her to a higher high.

''Yes,'' she groaned mindlessly. ''Oh yes, Quint.''

''Good. Just relax and let me make you feel good, Rachel. I want to make you feel good . . .''

And he did. He kissed her breasts, the way she'd been longing for him to do. The feel of his mouth on her nipples made her shudder with pleasure. She'd never dreamed anything could feel so wonderful . . . Until he trailed his lips along her the soft flesh of her belly while his hands continued to tantalize her breasts. Oh yes, that was just as good, perhaps even better?

While she was dizzily contemplating this erotic conundrum, he grasped her buttocks and pressed his mouth to her. Her body arched wildly, as if she'd been shocked. In a way she had, for the touch of his tongue on the most intimate private part of her was sensually electrifying, like nothing she'd ever experienced. Her mind spun into a zone of sheer hedonistic rapture.

Her hips began to move in helpless rhythm with his mouth; her breathing quickened and became choppy. She uttered a low moan of pleasure. And then another. The aching want overwhelmed her, a blood-rushing urgency made her crazy with tremulous need.

She gasped his name, cried it, as her body suddenly shattered in ecstasy. He held on, riding out the storm with her. When he felt her stop shivering, he moved up to take her in his arms.

''That was beautiful, you're beautiful,'' he said hoarsely. Rachel was too dazed to speak. When his mouth met hers, fiery, hot and hungry, she responded, though she was still lost in the sweet haze of sexual oblivion.

He rose above her, positioning himself to enter her. Her limbs felt limp and heavy and she lay open to him, a syrupy warmth suffusing her.

She watched him sheath himself with a condom from the box he'd brought with him, a bit awed by his dexterity. And by the sheer male size of him. She tensed.

Slowly, he thrust into her. Stretching her. Filling her. Rachel whimpered, overwhelmed. He was so big and this was all so new. She felt overmatched, overpowered. A sheen of perspiration dampened her brow.

But Quint whispered to her, complimenting her, encouraging her. Teasing her with sexy words that no one had ever spoken to her. She felt her body melting into a liquid silky heat as she began to adjust to his size and strength. She concentrated on the blend of sensations within her. Thick. Tight. Full.

Rachel decided that it wasn't so bad. In fact, she liked it. A streak of pure pleasure rippled through her. She loved it. Loved him, and sharing her body with him. Her eyes opened and she looked into his face, adoring him.

She slid her hands over his stomach, his hips, and he muttered something unintelligible. She felt a twinge of feminine pride. To have induced speechlessness in the usually prodigiously verbal Quint Cormack was no small feat, but she had done it.

Rachel shifted her hips and took him deeper. He set a slow, steady rhythm that she matched at first, until the excitement flaring inside her demanded a faster pace. She clenched her inner muscles and arched against him. He provided what she needed, moving harder and faster. They kissed, deeply, passionately, adding a loving intimacy to their urgency.

Rachel's control vanished, and she savored the wild abandon of their lovemaking. She gave herself to him completely, trusting him, reveling in the mindless bliss of pure physical pleasure. The sensations built and spun.

Together they soared to the heights and hung there for a timeless interlude of shared rapture. It seemed to last forever and it seemed to end all too soon.

Finally he collapsed against her, and they lay across the bed, spent, holding on to each other. Eventually, Quint shifted his weight off her but tucked her into his side, keeping her close. He pressed soft, hot little kisses on her throat and shoulder, her neck and hair.

Rachel held him, stroking her hands along the broad width of his back. She felt languid and lighter than air, bathed in the warm afterglow of sated passion.

Neither felt the need to speak. They were beyond words.

Seated at the table in the conference room Monday morning, an astonished Rachel listened to Aunt Eve tick off the list of complaints that had been lodged against the Tildens.

Breaking and entering. Criminal trespass. Burglary. Grand larceny. Terroristic threats. And if those weren't enough, an allegation of conspiracy loomed as a possible addendum. Criminal charges were pending, unless Misty agreed to drop the complaint.

Rachel tried to take it all in. "The police won't actually consider—"

"The police are most definitely considering pressing charges, Rachel," Eve interjected. "They have no choice, really. These complaints are extremely serious ones, and unless Misty Tilden withdraws—correction, unless *Quinton Cormack* withdraws them, arrest warrants will be issued."

"It's strictly Cormack's move to make because he is calling all the shots for his client," Wade said mournfully. "Everybody knows that, even the cops."

Eve closed her eyes, as if in prayer. "God, I could use a cigarette."

"You gave up smoking years ago, Aunt Eve," Rachel reminded her. "Here, have a mint." She pushed the candy dish in her aunt's direction. Eve groaned and shoved it away.

Rachel was floundering in a sea of confusion. Despite all

the time they'd spent together this weekend, despite their passion-filled night which had not ended until his departure shortly before six this morning, Quint hadn't mentioned a word of the Tilden crisis to her. The omission seemed deliberately deceptive but what worried her even more was her newfound ability to imagine—and condone?—his reply to her, should she ask him why.

He would insist that their professional and personal spheres were separate and did not intersect and instead of arguing the point, she would gaze into his dark eyes and forget everything but the need to be with him. To talk with him, to laugh and to argue with him. To have him inside her. He would know that, of course, especially after her total unqualified surrender last night. Rachel flinched.

"We need to meet with Quint Cormack to discuss dropping the complaint, but he won't see us," lamented Wade.

"Are you sure?" Rachel felt anxiety churning.

Eve nodded tersely. "The Tildens are scheduled to arrive here for a meeting at two o'clock and they think Cormack is going to be here. Unfortunately, he won't be. He adamantly refuses to come to our office and of course, the Tildens won't go to his. Town Junior has set it up as a power play, and Cormack knows it. I've called him several times this morning but he won't bend. In fact, his secretary said that he won't take any more calls from me today."

"Why should he?" Wade was glum. "He's holding all the aces, and all we've got is a lousy handful of deuces."

"We aren't even in the game." Eve grabbed a mint and practically inhaled it. "Cormack is toying with us by biding his time. He says he'll meet with us at his office next week but by then—"

"Charges might already be filed and arrest warrants issued," Wade finished. "The cops aren't going to wait forever. Of course, it won't be our problem by then because the Tildens are going to fire us today when they show up here and Cormack doesn't."

"Don't say that!" cried Rachel. "We can't lose the Tildens as clients! The Saxons have always represented the Tildens. It's a tradition!''

Three pairs of hazel eyes met in grim understanding. Representing the Tildens was a prestigious tradition. Tilden business was the bulwark of Saxon Associates' practice. What law firm could afford to lose their wealthiest, most important clients?

''Nick says our only hope is to get Misty to drop the complaint, and we can't get to her without going through Quinton Cormack.'' Eve shook her head wearily. ''The Tildens will blame us, of course, they'll blame us for everything. Somebody will have to take the fall and unfortunately, Saxon Associates is the most convenient scapegoat.''

''Who's Nick?'' asked Rachel.

Eve cleared her thoat. ''Chief Spagna. I've—discussed this matter at length with him privately.''

''I can't believe you had to talk to the police chief about possible criminal charges pending against the Tildens!'' Rachel clutched her head in her hands. ''It's surreal! Aunt Eve, how did you manage to endure that scene without going orbital? These charges are trumped up and everybody involved knows it. Just thinking about the—the blatant manipulation and the collusion and the total unfairness makes me want to scream.''

''Been there, done that, dear.'' Eve actually laughed.

Wade eyed his aunt keenly, impressed by her calm demeanor, a sharp contrast from her wild fury at the police station a couple days earlier. Was it possible that she hadn't exacerbated the situation by forever alienating the chief during their private talk? That was a positive sign—the only one they had going for them, as far as he could see.

''Wade, you're very friendly with the little Sheely girl who works for Cormack,'' Eve said. ''I know this is unorthodox, not to mention humiliating, but would you ask her to intercede on our behalf? Maybe she could convince her boss to meet with us today?''

''It won't work, Aunt Eve.''

"But it can't hurt to ask," Eve argued.

"I already did." Wade gave the candy dish a hard spin, and it rotated wildly until Rachel caught and halted it. He scowled. "I called Dana this morning. It was clear to me that Cormack told her not to get involved. He undoubtedly stressed Shawn's role in the situation, probably hyped it to the max. I'm sure Cormack warned her not to let herself be—be—used by me."

"How unfair and completely uncalled for!" Eve was indignant. "You've been close to the Sheelys for years."

"And I would *never* use Dana." Wade snatched the candy dish away from Rachel and sent it on another wild spin. "Of course, Cormack must've made it sound like I'm already trying to use her. Dana seemed so distant." He averted his eyes, afraid they would betray how very much that phone call had disturbed him.

Eve seemed to know. "Maybe you're reading too much into it," she suggested quietly. "Maybe she seemed preoccupied because she is so upset about her brother's involvement in this whole mess."

"She wasn't preoccupied, she was glacial."

The candy dish sailed off the table, spilling mints everywhere. The three Saxons sat still, lost in their own thoughts, oblivious to the flying mints.

Rachel stared, bemused by the sight of her cousin, disheartened and distressed in a way she'd never seen him. And Aunt Eve seemed to be taking the threat of the Tildens' defection with almost-Zen-like acceptance, totally at odds with her usually fierce fighting spirit.

Rachel was completely bewildered. She felt as if she'd missed a few vital clues and could make no sense with the ones she already had. "What does Shawn Sheely have to do with anything?"

Wade and Aunt Eve told her about Misty's companion, collaborator, and witness to the alleged Tilden crime spree. Rachel immediately made the connection to Sarah's distress last night. No wonder the girl had been upset!

"The Sheelys are so wholesome, so upstanding, and

Misty Tilden is—not.'' Rachel felt real sympathy. "I can't imagine one of them mixed up with her.''

"Neither can they, but according to Dana, Shawn claims they don't know the *real* Misty. He intends to continue seeing her—and says he hopes to be more than friends with her. Way more than friends. I—uh—saw Dana after she and her sisters tried to set Little Brother straight last night,'' Wade added, his voice trailing off.

He was aware that a flush was spreading from his neck to his face. There was additional information he had no intention of sharing with his aunt and cousin. Last night he'd hung around outside the apartment building where Mary Jo lived with her husband, the place where the Sheely sisters met to discuss the errant behavior of brother Shawn.

And when Dana had emerged, sobbing with sadness and frustration at Shawn's refusal to see things their way, he had driven her to his apartment so she could calm down before going home. She couldn't let her mom and dad see her so upset. In an earlier flurry of anxious phone calls, Tim and his sisters had agreed to spare their parents and younger siblings the news. At least for now.

Wade had offered Dana what comfort and words of advice he could. And he had ended up taking her to bed and giving her all the pleasure and fulfillment that he hadn't delivered in Connecticut. She had matched his hunger and need with her own passionate responses, leaving him dazed and replete with unparalleled sensual bliss.

After hours of mind-bending marvelous fusion, they had reluctantly parted—on the best possible terms, he had thought. But when he'd called Dana this morning to ask for help with Quint Cormack, she had replied with all the warmth of a recorded message reciting the latest weather forecast. Maybe even less.

Obviously, Cormack had warned her to beware of Saxons asking for favors and she had bought into her boss's poisonous suggestion that Wade was unscrupulous enough to use her to benefit Saxon Associates. The premise enraged him. Dana ought to know better! Certainly, she should

know *him* better than that; she should trust him. He wondered what he would do if she wouldn't trust him. If she
refused to see him. He closed his eyes, as if to shut out the
pain.

"What are we going to do?" Rachel's impassioned cry
jolted him back to awareness. She was burning with the
zeal that both he and Eve lacked today.

"There has to be something!" Rachel insisted. "We
can't just sit around and wait for the Tildens to arrive and
fire us!"

"I did consider filing a cross complaint on behalf of the
Tildens," Eve said. "Both Shawn and Misty held them at
gunpoint for a time that night. I wondered if it could be
considered reckless endangerment and maybe even unlaw-
ful restraint. It's a bit of a stretch but no more so than
Cormack's grand larceny and conspiracy concoctions. And
there seems to have been enough menacing words flung
about for a terroristic threats complaint of our own."

"That's brillant, Aunt Eve!" Rachel enthused. "We'll
go to the police station with the Tildens this afternoon."

"I already ran the plan by Nick and he says it won't
fly." Eve sighed softly. "He's right, of course. Since Misty
and Shawn filed first, a Johnny-come-lately counter complaint by the Tildens seems suspect. At best, it turns the
situation into a they said/they said stalement."

"We could live with that, couldn't we?" quizzed Rachel.

"Perhaps. If we weren't dealing with Quinton Cormack." Eve shrugged. "With him representing Misty,
we're forced to consider the worst-case scenario—that the
Tildens could be countercharged with harrassment. Nick
believes that Cormack would also include complaints of
slander and malicious mischief. It's daring, it's outlandish,
and only Quinton Cormack and Nick Spagna, who do not
view the Tildens as demigods, would go through with it.
But they will."

"If Cormack and Spagna are the only ones who don't
pay homage to the Tildens, what does that make us? The
town toadies?" Wade scowled.

Well, weren't they? He remembered all the times he'd felt like an ingratiating toady around various Tildens. The "truth hurts" cliché seemed painfully apt.

"*Nick* says it won't fly, *Nick* is right," Rachel repeated, troubled. "Are you sure we should be taking Chief Spagna's advice, Aunt Eve?"

"Yeah, according to Spagna, Cormack is Superman, Lawyer of Steel," Wade said derisively. "Kryptonite might stop him, but the feeble Saxons don't stand a chance against him. Chief Spagna is so pro-Cormack he might as well proclaim it on a bumper sticker on his squad car."

"You don't know what you're talking about, Wade." Eve rose to her feet. "Ask the little Sheely girl to come in here and pick up these mints," she added absently.

"Never mind, I'll do it." Sighing, Wade began to pick up the mints himself and throw them into the trash basket. "Katie would put them right back in the candy dish."

"Possibly to be consumed by the Tildens this afternoon." Aunt Eve seemed to be considering the idea.

Wade immediately transferred the mints back into the candy dish. "Seeing Sloane eat a mint that's been on the floor *and* in the trash might be petty revenge, but it works for me."

"We're in the midst of a serious crisis and you two are plotting revenge with mints?" Rachel was exasperated. She snatched the candy dish from Wade and dumped the mints back into the trash can with an air of finality. "We have to do something. We have to take action!"

"Okay, Rach. Why don't you go over to Cormack's office and ask him if he'll come here this afternoon and meet with us and the Tildens?" Wade challenged. "Is that enough action for you?"

He had used that same tone and smirk back when they were kids and he'd dared her to go on the Heart Attack, the triple-loop upside-down roller coaster on a boardwalk pier in Wildwood. Rachel had declined then, and she knew Wade fully expected her to refuse to go to Quint's office now.

But there were a few facts he was missing. Her face was flushed and hot, and her voice seemed to be echoing in her ears. "All right, I will," she heard herself say.

"While we appreciate your offer, I have to warn you in advance that it's useless, dear. Cormack will surely refuse." Aunt Eve patted Rachel's arm. "Don't go, Rachel. You were distraught over the Pedersen case, and I'm concerned about you putting yourself in Quinton Cormack's line of fire once again."

"Yeah, 'cause you'll get shot down like one of those ducks in a shooting gallery on the boardwalk," added Wade gloomily.

If they only knew! Rachel swallowed hard. "Nothing ventured, nothing gained. I'll go over there right now."

She paused as she headed down the plushly carpeted corridor. "And Wade, don't call Dana Sheely and warn her that I'm on my way over. Today I really would like to take advantage of—the element of surprise."

"Dana won't take a call from me anyway," Wade said darkly. "I talked to her once and then I was told she wouldn't accept any more calls from me."

"By their dragon receptionist-secretary," Eve surmised. "I was also told by Commandant Helen that no calls from Saxon Associates were to be put through."

"Shunned by Cormack and Son." Wade shook his head. "How the mighty have fallen and all that."

"We haven't fallen," Eve insisted. "This is merely a—professional setback."

"And the trouble in Northern Ireland is just a little spat among friends," mumbled Rachel.

The trio walked to the reception area, where young Katie Sheely was busily typing away on her computer keyboard.

"Katie, what are you working on?" Wade asked, after he'd recovered from the shock of seeing her so thoroughly engrossed in any kind of office function.

Katie didn't look away from the screen. "I'm in an *X-Files* chat room. You wouldn't believe how outrageous this one guy's theory is! I think he might be an alien clone himself.''

Eve opened her mouth as if to speak, then swiftly turned and headed back to her office without saying a word.

"Considering everything, Aunt Eve has shown remarkable restraint today," Wade murmured to Rachel. "I mean, contrast her attitude this morning to last week, when she was ready to take us apart, piece by piece. And you should've seen how infuriated she was in the police station Saturday morning! When she went over to talk to the chief after the Tilden meeting, I had visions of her being charged with felonious assault.''

"I'm worried. It's unlike Aunt Eve to be so—so mellow!" Rachel frowned.

It was confusing, this role reversal being played by her aunt and cousin. Instead of being laid-back by the threat to their firm, Wade was actually concerned, while Aunt Eve seemed to have adopted *'Que Será, Será'* as her official motto. Whatever will be, will be.

"Not mellow," countered Wade. "More like fatalistic. Whatever Spagna said to her really made an impression. Well, he is an intimidating guy.''

"Aunt Eve wouldn't be *intimidated* by any man, Wade."

"Then maybe he makes one helluva convincing argument. Remember, he was a homicide detective in Newark, so he's gotta know how to make others take him seriously. After dealing with murderers, Aunt Eve probably wasn't even a challenge for him.''

"You could be right. Maybe Chief Spagna shouldn't be underestimated.''

"Of course, we're good at that, Rach, at underestimating people," Wade said ruefully. "We sure did it with Quint Cormack, didn't we?''

She nodded slowly. "Yes, we did. But we shouldn't underestimate ourselves, either, Wade. Saxon Associates can't simply give in and give up!''

Rachel repeated it like a mantra during the drive to Quint's office. She practiced what she would say to him and how she would say it, professionally, politely, as one attorney to another. By the time she pulled into the parking lot—a train was roaring by, shaking her car so hard that her CD player skipped—she had worked herself into a state of throat-closing anxiety.

Sitting in her car, she tried to bolster her confidence by putting aside her rehearsed arguments to Attorney Quinton Cormack, legal opponent and relentless competitor, and focusing on the other Quint. Her lover.

Last night he had held her in his arms, he had filled her body, ferociously seeking pleasure for her as well as taking his own. They had touched and tasted every inch of each other's bodies, getting to know each other in the most intimate ways possible. The mark on her neck had faded but she had secret ones in places that made her blush just remembering. And she'd branded him, likewise.

She thought of their sexy whispered confidences, the soft words in the dark, the shattering intimacy that bound her to him in a bond she knew she could never experience with anyone else. It had to be the same for him. Last night, she would've bet her life on that certainty.

But now, as she walked into the grimly utilitarian offices of Cormack and Son, the twin devils of doubt and insecurity sprang back to life to plague her. Quint had mentioned the necessity of separating their professional careers from their personal lives several times; he'd stressed that the two were disparate and distinct.

Suppose the professional Quint refused to see her, in keeping with his Saxon boycott? Rachel's heart thundered in her chest. Despite Quint's warnings, those two separate spheres had converged for her, and she knew she would take his snub personally, as a rejection by her lover.

She wasn't ready to deal with the loss and the pain of that particular trauma. Would she ever be?

Helen, seated at her desk sorting through a stack of mail, no longer looked like a kindly grandmother, she appeared somewhat . . . well, commandant-ish.

Nervously, Rachel squared her shoulders and approached

the older woman's desk, a tremulous smile in place. "I'd like to see Quint, please."

"Miss Saxon." Helen stared at her curiously. "I know he isn't expecting you."

Rachel's smile grew brighter. She realized she was aping Laurel's irresistibly adorable smile and felt a twinge of shame. Which swiftly disappeared when Helen smiled back.

"I'll let him know you're here." Helen hit the intercom button. "Quint, you have a visitor. Rachel Saxon is here."

Two doors opened at the same time. Dana Sheely stood in the doorway of one, Quint in the other. Rachel saw them look at each other. Neither spoke as they watched her walk toward them. She realized that they both knew why she was here. The element of surprise had already been lost to Aunt Eve's and Wade's desperate barrage of phone calls this morning.

Dana retreated into her office and closed the door. Quint remained in the doorway until Rachel stood before him.

His expression was enigmatic, even his normally expressive dark eyes gave away nothing. Rachel couldn't tell if he was glad to see her or annoyed that she was here. She had no idea if he would honor or refuse her request to meet with the Tildens at Saxon Associates office.

Did he think she'd crossed the line by coming over here to ask him? At least, he had agreed to meet with her. She wished he would say something, but it was clear that he was waiting for her to speak first.

The last time she'd seen him, a few hours ago, she had been lying in bed, watching him get dressed to leave. She'd been satiated from making love, too drowsy to reach for the sheet to cover her nakedness. He had done that before he left, kissing her tenderly and tucking the sheet around her.

Now she was wearing her tailored gray silk suit and dark plum-colored blouse—conservative, serious clothing and colors to endorse her professionalism, not meant to entice or excite.

"Good morning, Quint." Her voice shook. Her clothing seemed to be serving its purpose. He didn't look at all enticed or excited.

Rachel felt the tremors rock her body, felt the weakness in her knees and the fluttering in her stomach, all the tangible signs of her awareness of him. Of her need for him. The sexual heat between them was fierce, but her feelings for him went so much deeper, to the elemental part of her.

She realized in that moment that he had become as essential to her as her heartbeat. It was a revealing yet depressing insight because she knew it wasn't reciprocal.

Quint had compartmentalized his feelings for her and openly admitted it. Lawyer in one place, lover in another. That was convenience, not elemental need.

And here they were, the legal eagle and the woman-in-love, who had both escaped from their respective compartments.

Rachel gulped. "I—guess you know why I'm here."

"Why don't you come into my office and tell me, so I won't have to guess?"

He placed his hand between her shoulder blades to usher her inside.

15

Quint locked the door behind them. Of course, he knew why she was here. The mighty Tildens were pulling strings, jerking around Saxon Associates like marionettes controlled by tyrannical puppeteers.

But their script was more ludicrous than the Punch and Judy show at the Renaissance Festival. Without consulting him, the Tildens and Saxons had decided he must be present for a meeting at the Saxon Associates office this afternoon. They hadn't bothered to inform him until this morning when Eve called, demanding his presence. Their arrogance—or was it idiocy?—took his breath away.

He had rejected the summons every time Eve Saxon phoned, finally directing Helen not to put any more of her calls through to him. Anticipating their next move, he'd instructed Dana to refuse when Wade tried to use their friendship to advance the Tilden-Saxon agenda.

"I know the guy's a good friend of yours, so feel free to make me the heavy," Quint told Dana shortly before Wade Saxon called her. "You can tell Saxon that I go psycho if somebody asks me for a favor, that my standard reply to any request is 'No.' Say whatever you want."

"Sorry, Wade," was what he'd heard Dana say, quite glacially, to Wade Saxon when he called with his predictable request. "I can't get involved. Anyway, I don't want to."

Which wasn't what Quint thought she would say when

he made his offer to get her off the hook with her dear old pal. Dana didn't seem to care if she angered Wade Saxon or not, which implied something about their friendship. Exactly what, Quint wasn't sure.

Even odder was the call he'd received this morning from Nick Spagna.

"Those Tildens are a real pain in the ass but Eve Saxon is one classy lady," Nick said in his rough-edged voice. "I think you should give her a break and go to that meeting today, Quint."

Quint had been so astonished that Nick knew about the meeting that he hadn't thought to ask how the chief had found out about it. And then the call was over, as was the chance to ask. He puzzled over it though. Chief Nick Spagna calling him to suggest a favor on behalf of Eve Saxon?

Dana didn't get it either, when he'd told her about the chief's strange call.

"Wade was worried Chief Spagna would end up arresting his aunt this weekend. He said she was as crazed as an animal-rights activist confronting someone wearing a Siberian tiger fur coat."

"So she started out crazed and ended up a classy lady?" Quint and Dana exchanged glances. "Hmmm."

It seemed inevitable that Rachel would make an attempt to get him to that infernal meeting. Which he had no intention of attending, no matter what, no matter who tried to coax, threaten, or weasel him into going. His mind was made up.

He prepared himself for Rachel's call, to tell her that he would not, under any circumstances, go to the meeting. He would remind her not to take his refusal personally, that their professional adversarial roles had nothing to do with Quint and Rachel, the couple.

And they were definitely a couple. He stared blindly at a client's will he'd been drawing up, and the printed words blurred as sensual images played before his mind's eye.

He saw his hands on her soft silken skin, saw her lips

parted and moist and swollen from his kisses. Desire surged through him, but he knew the need was emotional as much as physical. He didn't even try to kid himself that what was between them was strictly sexual.

Not after spending time with her and the children and watching her lovingly care for Brady and Snowy, not after observing her kindness toward his little brothers. She understood his obligations to them and to Carla and he appreciated that. He admired her own concern for her small niece and rebellious sister, her willingness to step in and try to help.

He enjoyed her company. She was bright and outspoken, and once she dropped her rather formidable guard, warm and funny. Last night, she had definitely lost it all with him. For him.

Would refusing to attend the meeting if she asked—*when* she asked—rebuild the barriers between them? He found that prospect unacceptable, yet knew that a no-show by him today might very well cost Saxon Associates the Tildens as clients.

Professionally, he shouldn't care, Quint reminded himself. The internal workings of a rival law firm might make for interesting gossip but really didn't matter to him. *Shouldn't* matter to him.

But it did, if it meant hurting Rachel. A frowning Quint recited his pledge to keep their professional and personal lives separate; he reminded himself it was absolutely necessary, like the separation of church and state was vital to the country.

He might've been able to pull it off if Rachel had subjected him to an obnoxious harangue by telephone or barged into his office imperiously demanding compliance with the Tildens.

But she hadn't called, she'd arrived quietly and when he saw her walking toward him, her eyes huge with uncertainty and fear, his firm resolve was suddenly as squishy as a plate of Jell-O.

He didn't want her to be afraid and unsure of him. That

was a professional plus in the courtroom but not what he wanted in an intimate relationship. Especially not after last night, when she had trusted him so completely, so openly.

A civil war raged inside him. Quint-the-cut-them-off-at-the-knees attorney on one side, and Quint-the-man on the other. Suddenly, the difference between profession and person wasn't so clear-cut. But he wasn't ready to call a truce.

Strive for professional distance, Quint silently asserted. *Keep it cool, impersonal.* He gave it his best shot. "We've been fielding calls all morning from our esteemed colleagues at Saxon Associates. I figured it was only a matter of time till you checked in."

Rachel saw her courtroom nemesis standing before her, the skilled smooth operator who delighted in making a fool of her. When she remembered the warm tone of her thoughtful, tender lover of last night, her eyes filled with tears. Mortified, she tried to blink them away. This coolly detached Quint might accuse her of trying to manipulate him with her tears.

"I can't do this; I shouldn't have come here," she said jerkily, pulling on the doorknob. She realized that the door was locked at the same moment Quint put his hand over hers, preventing her from springing the lock.

"Rachel, stop." He cupped her chin with his other hand and lifted her face to him.

She kept her eyes lowered, avoiding his. "I want to go, Quint. Coming to your office was a mistake."

"Look at me, Rachel."

As he spoke, she felt the almost-tangible pull of his dark eyes and looked up at him, although she was aware of the power of his gaze. It melted her will, her sense of self. She felt an almost-painful awareness that if he chose to take her right here and now, she would let him. A spark flared from her heart to the juncture of her thighs. She would even welcome it!

"You have to understand that I will not compromise my client's legitimate financial interests and judicial rights. I legally represent Misty Tilden and I am the executor of her late husband's estate." He stroked her cheek, her neck, with his big hand. "I have a legal and an ethical obligation to her, and I can't betray that, Rachel."

She nodded her head. "I know. I wouldn't expect you to."

Their fingers had become intertwined on top of the door-knob.

"And there is another reason why I intend to remain Misty Tilden's attorney and look out for her best interests, Rachel. A practical one, a monetary one. Being executor of Town Tilden Senior's estate will provide the firm with a high six-figure sum, and there are three children whose financial support is solely derived from the income of this firm."

"I know that, too, Quint," Rachel said quietly, thinking of Brady and Austin and Dustin. Carla, too. Even the loathsome Frank Cormack. They were *all* dependent on Quint.

"Good. Now that we're both clear on that"—Quint cleared his throat—"there is no reason why I won't cooperate when a colleague makes a reasonable request. I always try to spare my clients a court fight and if meeting with the Tildens today at the Saxon Associates office could result in a valid out-of-court settlement, I'll be there."

Rachel stared at him. "You will?"

He watched her teeth close over her lower lip and expelled a deep breath. He wished he were the one nibbling on that sweetly luscious lip. Arousal had gripped him hard and fast the moment he'd seen her in the hall. And now, simply looking at her, simply being near her had incited an erection that was becoming so potent he found it difficult to stay on his feet.

"Yes." He nearly groaned the word.

"But I didn't even ask you to be there." She was too stunned to be tactful. "You volunteered first."

A sardonic smile crossed his face. "It isn't polite to gloat, Rachel."

"I wasn't gloating."

She saw the physical effect her presence was having on

him and a responsive moistness flowed between her thighs. She took a deep breath and his scent filled her nostrils. He smelled like sex to her, masculine and virile. It was an aroma that should be bottled and sold, one that would be an instant hit, with no insanely pretentious cologne commercials needed.

"Quint, thank you." She raised her arms and linked them around his neck, fitting her body to his. "Thank you so much."

His arms surrounded her and his lips brushed her crown. "Is this the part where you reward me with sex?"

She leaned back a little and smiled up at him, her eyes bright. "This is the part where I say you didn't have to agree to that meeting to be rewarded with sex. You'd have gotten it even if you had said no."

His lips played with hers. "Now she tells me!" He traced the shape of her mouth and she opened to him, meeting his tongue with hers.

"After last night I should be satisfied for a long time," she whispered the words against his mouth. "I shouldn't want you this much, I shouldn't need you again so soon after . . ." She sighed and their breaths mingled. "But I want you even more, Quint. I need you so much it hurts."

"Ohhh, baby, I know." He groaned. Her words affected him as powerfully as the feel of her soft curvy body in his arms.

They kissed passionately, and mixed with the wild urgency that had driven them last night was a yielding tenderness.

"I want you, Rachel. Right here," he whispered. "Right now." His hand slipped under her skirt, sliding it up as he moved his palm higher along her thigh. "And I'm going to have you."

Rachel tried to catch her breath. She was not averse to his decision, in fact she was aflame with desire. But . . .

"Where? How?" Her eyes were glazed with passion but still able to focus on the hard flat surface of his ugly desk— that was covered by his computer equipment and stacks of paper. She'd seen office love scenes in movies and TV where the hero masterfully swept the desk clear of all paraphernalia for a lusty romp but in reality, there was no way Quint or anyone with a grain of sense would send a computer and all those legal files flying.

However, Quint's strategic talent was not limited to the courtroom. Even while she was contemplating the desk dilemma, he slowly walked her backward into the far corner of the office. Rachel found herself surrounded by walls on either side of her and Quint in front of her.

He leaned in close, his mouth covering hers as he slid his hands up her skirt again. Within moments, he'd taken off only what garments needed to be removed to allow him access to her. His entry was hard and fast but she was ready for him, all soft melting heat sheathing him. She propelled her hips to meet his thrusts, her body shuddering as the unbearable ache became an explosion of pleasure.

"Oh, Quint." Her voice was a barely audible whisper. She buried her face in his shoulder and clung to him as she convulsed around him. Her soft little cries of ecstasy were muffled by the starched cotton of his shirt.

Quint managed to hold off until the sensuous tremors racking her body subsided, then spasmed into completion himself. They stayed that way for a timeless interval, their bodies joined, their minds drifting in the dreamlike aftermath.

It wasn't until Helen's voice sounded over the intercom that Quint slowly, carefully withdrew from Rachel's body.

"Mr. Aiken is here for your appointment, Quint," Helen said crossly, her tone disapproving.

"That would be Eddie Aiken, Mr. Doll House himself." Quint groaned. "Helen makes no secret of her aversion to him."

Rachel opened her eyes and stared around the office, feeling disoriented. "Good for Helen," she mumbled. "The man is slime."

"Lucrative slime. His endless Doll House citations and appeals pay Carla's monthly mortgage payments." Quint handed Rachel a handkerchief, then proceeded to straighten his own clothing.

"Will you have dinner with me tonight, Rachel? Just the two of us, at a restaurant that doesn't feature toys and crayons."

"Are you asking me for a date?" she parried lightly.

She felt him watching her as she attempted to turn herself back into her former serious professional self. It seemed impossible when her body bore his sensual impact and imprint. How could her sober gray suit possibly mask his effect upon her? Rachel blushed.

"I'll ask Sarah to take Brady to the Sheelys for dinner tonight," Quint continued, his eyes following her every move. "And we'll have a quiet adult evening. I'll pick you up at your place at six-thirty."

Rachel glimpsed her kiss-swollen lips in the mirror of her compact as she tried to brush her tousled hair into its usual sleek bob. "That sleazehound Aiken is going to take one look at us and know exactly what we were doing in here." She knew she should probably be upset, but she had to stifle the urge to giggle.

"Aiken is only interested in what pertains to Aiken," Quint assured her. "Say yes to me for tonight, Rachel."

She raised her brows. "I thought you knew that yes is a given, especially after our—uh—quickie against the wall."

Her blush deepened. She was still unaccustomed to speaking frankly about sex, but she didn't want to be. She was tired of being straitjacketed by repression.

"A wallbanger means we wanted each other right there and then, Rachel. It doesn't mean that you want to spend the evening with me," he said quietly. "And it also doesn't mean that I'm going to give you and the Tildens the answers you want at the meeting this afternoon. Remember that."

Quint walked over to his desk and pushed the intercom button. "I'll see Mr. Aiken now, Helen."

His abrupt transformation startled Rachel. It was hard to believe the aloof attorney seated behind his desk was the same passionate man who had been inside her, a part of her, such a short time ago.

"Six-thirty, Rachel," Quint said as the door opened.

"Yes," she murmured.

Eddie Aiken entered the office and she lifted her head in Saxon disdain as she walked past him to leave.

"Great-looking babe," Aiken remarked, staring at the door Rachel had closed behind her. "Except she dresses like a Pilgrim. Looks like a snob, too. A client of yours?"

"No," Quint said brusquely. "Time's ticking, Eddie, and I charge by the hour, remember? Now, about your appeal . . ."

"This is an outrage!" Town Tilden Junior checked his watch again, which he'd been doing at thirty-second intervals since his arrival at the Saxon Associates ten minutes ago. "But I suppose we should've expected some sort of petty power play by that conniving, unprincipled shark."

Rachel sneaked a glimpse at her own watch. Two-twenty-five. She suspected that the Tildens' arrival, fifteen minutes past the appointed time, was supposed to have been their own power play. Unfortunately, they'd been bested by Quint who not only hadn't been kept waiting, but also kept the Tildens waiting for him these past ten minutes.

"This is an intolerable inconvenience," snapped Marguerite.

"Intolerable," echoed her son Tilden Lloyd.

"And it's too hot in here," Sloane added petulantly.

"Rachel, lower the air-conditioning a few more degrees," ordered Eve.

Rachel left the conference room—already a chilly sixty-six degrees—and walked to the thermostat in the corridor. She shoved the temperature back to sixty-five. If Quint didn't appear soon, he might find them all frozen stiff.

Not at all eager immediately to return to the furious Tildens, she strolled to the office reception area, where Katie sat at her desk, meticulously painting her fingernails a most disturbing color.

"Isn't it cool?" Katie noticed Rachel staring. "It's my newest shade, Curdled Blood."

"Different," murmured Rachel. "Distinctive."

"Yeah," Katie sighed happily. She caught sight of Rachel's plain, unpolished nails. "Hey, want me to do yours when I'm done mine?"

It was a measure of the desperation she was feeling that made her want to take Katie up on her offer, Rachel thought grimly. She would rather sit here and have Curdled Blood applied to her nails than return to face the collective wrath and indignation of the Tildens.

"Still waitin' for Quint, huh?" Katie asked.

"Still waiting," agreed Rachel. "I suppose I ought to go back to the Tildens now."

"Man, it sucks to be you." Katie was sympathetic.

"Katie, the moment Mr. Cormack arrives—"

"I know, bring him right to the conference room," Katie finished. "I sure hope it's soon 'cause it's getting awfully cold in here. What's up with those Tildens wanting to refrigerate us, anyway?"

Back in the conference room, the Tildens continued to rage. Aunt Eve, seated at the table with the six of them, made an occasional diffident remark. The eighth chair at the conference table—the one reserved for Quint Cormack—remained empty, establishing him as a looming presence, even in his absence.

Rachel and Wade stood beside the window. The table wasn't big enough to accommodate all three Saxons, so the two junior partners weren't seated.

"Are you sure Cormack agreed to come?" Wade whispered. "Could you possibly have mistaken sarcasm for genuine assent?"

"He said he would be here." Rachel was insistent. "And he wasn't being sarcastic."

"I have to hand it to the guy, when it comes to mind games, he is the world champion," Wade growled. "If he actually does show up—"

"*When* he does," corrected Rachel.

She thought of that torrid interlude in Quint's office earlier. He might play mind games with the Tildens but not with her, she assured herself. He would come to the meeting—but he fully intended to drive the Tildens to distraction first.

When the door opened and Quint strolled into the room a few minutes later, she felt vindication, triumph, and relief. And a dizzying rush of love. Her eyes feasted on him, her heartbeat racing as she watched him amble casually toward the empty chair.

Eve and the Tildens rose to their feet, as if they'd been ejected from their chairs by springs. Quint sat down in his.

"Please, sit down," Quint said, smiling that mocking, challenging smile that had made Rachel want to pummel him during the Pedersen trial.

Now she almost smiled herself. Quint was acting as if the others had risen as a sign of respect for him, though it had been a combination of fury and surprise that brought all seven to their feet. As he well knew.

"Do you realize that we've been waiting here since—" Eve began but Quint interrupted her.

"Sorry. I had a meeting run late." Quint shrugged, clearly unfazed by his tardiness. "You know how it is."

For the first time since entering the conference room, he glanced toward the window where Rachel and Wade stood. Rachel quickly averted her eyes. She didn't trust herself to meet Quint's dark-eyed gaze.

"Why are they exiled over there?" Quint asked.

"We aren't exiled," Wade hastened to explain. "There aren't enough chairs for all of us at the table so—"

"Then I insist that Miss Saxon take my chair." Quint rose to his feet. "I will not be seated while a lady is forced to stand."

Rachel knew exactly what he was doing—making the male Tildens look like boors for allowing her to stand while they claimed the seats. Everybody in the conference room knew it, but there was nothing anyone could do. His point had been made well. The Tilden men had lost this round in etiquette to Quint Cormack. Oh, he was a champion in mind games, all right!

But instead of fuming, Rachel felt proud of him. So much for keeping the professional separate from the personal!

"I'd rather stand, thank you," she said, but Quint would have none of that.

He insisted that she sit or he would leave the meeting. So she sat down and he stood, which gave him the advantage of towering over the Tildens, who seemed shrunken and powerless in their chairs.

Rachel watched Quint covertly as he prowled the room. She studied the curve of his mouth and remembered the feel of his lips on hers, she stared at his long fingers, the nails squared and immaculate and relived their intimate touch on her body. She wriggled restlessly in her chair and forced herself to concentrate on the decidedly unerotic goings-on around her.

"I take it you've read the last will and testament of Townsend Tilden Senior?" Quint directed his question to Eve, who nodded her head.

"Needless to say, we have a number of questions," Eve replied, her tone civil and professional.

Apparently too civil and professional for Town Junior. "That's putting it mildly! We all know that so-called will is a fake and a fraud, but we want to put that walking, talking nightmare named Misty out of our lives forever so we're prepared to give your client a generous sum. We believe ten thousand dollars, in cash, would be more than fair."

"I'm sorry to hear you're still spouting that same tedious misinformation, Town," Quint interjected. He heaved a sigh. "I'm heartily bored with it. First, I don't understand why any of you are surprised that a new will exists. Certainly, you Saxons know that a marriage automatically revokes any existing will. That means from the day Town Senior married Misty, whatever will was in place was automatically invalidated."

"But it doesn't mean the will you drew up is legal and valid," retorted Town III.

Quint rolled his eyes heavenward, as if summoning the Almighty for patience. "Eve, I trust you've done your research. Haven't you explained to your clients that this will most certainly is legal and valid? Or have you tried, but they refuse to listen to you?"

"The will is valid. And legal," Eve admitted. "Although my clients, understandably, are having a difficult time accepting this—uh—unfortunate turn."

All six Tildens began to screech at once. The cacophony gave Rachel an instant headache. She wondered if she dared to leave and slip into her office where a bottle of Excedrin was stored in her desk.

"Naturally, we intend to contest the will in court," Eve raised her voice above the din.

"A waste of time and money and you know it," said Quint. "If you studied this will, you've seen the no-contest clause, Eve."

"The *what*?" demanded Town Three. "There is no such thing, Cormack. You made that up!"

"A no-contest clause in a will means that anyone who challenges the will in court gets nothing," Quint said coolly. "Town Senior left each of you a token of his affection because he felt you were already well provided for with trust funds and your positions in Tilden Industries. So, in accordance to the terms of the no-contest clause, if any one of you contests this will, you will not inherit a thing. Since you are unfamiliar with the concept, I'd better warn you that the clause will automatically apply to any other will that you might try to substitute for the current one."

He saw the surprise in Rachel's eyes. So the no-contest clause had caught her off guard? Well, considering how busy she'd been with him lately—and that she'd believed the will a fake to begin with—it was no wonder that she hadn't familiarized herself with all its arcane details. Nor was his own client aware of the exact terms of the will. He'd deliberately kept certain facts from Misty at Town

Senior's request, as a precautionary measure.

"Wouldn't want my little Misty to give away our secrets to the wrong people," old Town had said, and Quint had agreed with him. Besides, trying to explain estate planning to Misty was as daunting as trying to explain the principles of Archimedes to her. One didn't.

"What are these tokens of affection that Grandfather mentioned in his new will?" Sloane asked, her eyes narrowing to focus intently on Quint.

Quint picked up a copy of the will and handed one to Eve. "Do you want to read the list or shall I?"

"I'll do it," Eve said briskly, reaching for her reading glasses. "According to this—document, Town Senior left his entire antique gun collection to Town Junior, along with the set of Hogarth prints that hung in his den and an original Frederic Remington bronze."

"Father knew how much I admired the Remington and those prints. And, of course, I have my own antique gun collection to which his will be a welcome addition," muttered Town Junior.

"Town Three is to receive his grandfather's coin and stamp collections," continued Eve.

"That seems rather appropriate." Town Three frowned thoughtfully. "As a kid, I spent hours with Grandfather, learning about those coins and those stamps. I've also maintained my own collections through the years."

"Marguerite inherits the two Fabergé eggs which Town Senior inherited from his father."

"Those are priceless treasures and I want to retrieve them immediately before that woman does something unspeakable to them." Marguerite rose to her feet, ready to go.

"Sit down, Marguerite," Town Junior commanded his sister. "You can't get anything until the matter of the will is settled."

"It's already been probated," Quint spoke up. "If you agree not to contest the will—which, I remind you, is ultimately contest-proof—Marguerite can collect her eggs, you can take your guns, Town Three can have his coins and stamps. Would it be overkill to add that should you decide to contest, all of those things are as good as Misty's?''

''It would definitely be overkill,'' grumbled Rachel. ''Like beating the issue to death and burying it ten feet under the ground.''

''I think I've just been called a repetitive bore.'' Quint grinned. ''Ouch.''

''I would like to continue . . .'' Eve frowned, and both Rachel and Quint ceased fire.

Eve resumed reading. ''Sloane is to have her grand-mother's antique dollhouse, fully furnished, including the doll family that resides there.'' She smiled at the bequest.

Sloane didn't. Her mouth curved into a sullen pout. ''The dollhouse? Didn't Grandfather notice that I'm not six years old? What about the jewelry?''

''I'm sure Misty gets it all,'' Wade guessed, a trifle too gleefully. His aunt shot him a reproving glare.

''And Tilden Lloyd is to be given ten thousand dollars,'' read Eve.

''That's all I get? A measly ten thousand dollars! Which will be taxed to almost nothing?'' Tilden Lloyd's voice rose to a squeak.

''Measly?'' Quint looked amused. ''Isn't it interesting that when my client was offered ten thousand dollars to get out of town it was considered to be a princely sum?''

''The things Grandfather left to everybody else are worth far more than ten thousand dollars,'' whined Tilden. ''Even that dollhouse could draw a tidy sum at auction. The fur-niture could be sold piece by piece.'' Suddenly, he pounded his fist on the table, adding a bit of theatrical flair. ''But it doesn't matter anyway, because we're holding out for everything! That ridiculous no-contest clause of yours is most certainly illegal, Cormack. We aren't gullible fools, you know. Tell him to quit bluffing, Eve.''

Eve gazed at the document in front of her. ''Well, ac-tually . . .''

"Perhaps Rachel will explain to all to you." Quint smiled at her. Not his intimate lover smile, not his wonderful Brady's daddy smile. His "gotcha!" attorney smirk.

She bristled. "It's not illegal to put a no-contest clause into a will," she admitted grudgingly.

"But we can always contest the no-contest clause in court," Wade put in.

" You could," agreed Quint. "But it would be a stupid, expensive waste of time for everybody."

"That seems to be your standard reply when anyone suggests taking you to court, Mr. Cormack," Eve said sharply. "You say not to bother because you'll surely win. As if it's inevitable."

"Because in this case it is," Quint assured her. "And you and Rachel and Wade know it. Or you should."

"Like we were saying earlier, Rachel, if mind games were an Olympic event, Quint Cormack would walk away with the gold medal." Wade smiled sardonically.

"This is not a game. Why don't we simply review the facts of this case?" Quint didn't lose his cool. "Are you Saxons ever going to point out to your clients that, in the unlikely possibility the new will is overturned—which it will never be, I assure you—the no-contest clause remains in force. And may I remind you that means anyone who might possibly inherit under the terms of an old will won't, not if they've challenged the new will with its unimpeached no-contest clause."

"Does anyone understand one word of the gobbledygook this—this charlatan is spewing?" howled Town Junior.

"He is telling us that unless we overturn the no-contest clause," began Town Three.

"Your chances are less than zero there," Quint offered helpfully. "I can cite at least a hundred-fifty years' worth of precedents that will make the clause completely enforceable."

Eve groaned.

"Furthermore, Misty and I will appeal any disallowance of the no-contest clause all the way to the Supreme Court if we have to," Quint assured them. "Not that we'll need to because the courts have been upholding those clauses since long before anyone in this room was born."

"Save the Law School for Dummies lesson, Cormack," said Wade. "Believe me, we all get your point."

"If that clause is upheld, anyone who has challenged the new will can't inherit anything, not even from the old will should it somehow be activated," Town Three said slowly. "God, Cormack, that's so perverse it's almost admirable!"

"Thank you." Quint smiled wryly. "But I can't take full credit. Actually, it was a joint effort between Town Senior and me. He was extremely knowledgeable about estate planning and inheritance laws and loopholes. So . . . any volunteers to contest the will?"

"If I were to volunteer and somehow win by getting the new will overturned," Sloane turned her chair and leaned back in it, crossing her legs to strike a provocative pose. "I would actually lose. I couldn't inherit anything, not even under the old will, because of that wretched no-contest clause that you claim would be upheld by the Supreme Court. So if we go to court, even if we win we lose. Have I got it right, Quint?"

"Absolutely, positively right, Sloane." Quint grinned.

Sloane preened.

Rachel seethed. Sloane was actually *flirting* with Quint. And he was certainly not discouraging the woman!

"We can contest anything we want!" Rachel jumped to her feet, unable to sit passively a moment longer. She stalked to the window to stand beside Wade.

Quint's eyes slid over her. "And what would be your grounds to contest, Rachel?"

Rachel knew he was deliberately inciting her, she remembered that particular tone and expression from the Pedersen trial. He'd maddened her then, but this time it was even worse because added to the spectacle was Sloane Tilden Lloyd slavering over Quint like a latent carnivore who'd just discovered the thrilling taste of meat.

Her jaw tightened. "Our grounds to contest would be fraudulence, undue influence by Misty—"

"You have to do better than that Rachel," Quint cut in. "I have notes and witnesses that effectively eliminates any trace of fraudulence. As for the undue influence by a spouse—that's a loser, sweetie. It is almost impossible to prove because a person is *assumed* to be influenced by a spouse, it's considered both legal and correct."

Rachel glared at him. "How about diminished mental capacity?" she snapped. "Sweetie!"

Wade snickered.

"You've seen the witnesses who signed the will, attesting to Mr. Tilden's mental acuity." Quint spoke calmly and slowly, as if he were attempting to explain subtraction to a group of not particularly bright second-graders. "Why would a priest, a minister, and a rabbi, all highly respected members in the community, perjure themselves?"

"Maybe you paid them off!" Rachel cried wildly. "Maybe we should check and see if those three congregations each received a large sum of money from Town Tilden Senior!"

"Ohhh, Rachel!" Eve shook her head.

"Actually, the idea does have some merit," said Marguerite's husband.

The Saxons stared at each other, momentarily riveted. It was the first time any of them could recall hearing the man speak up in a group.

"If you think we would summon the records of Lakeview Presbyterian Church, Temple Sinai, and St. Philomena's to accuse them of fraud, you're out of your tiny little mind," Town Three said severely.

Rachel wondered whose tiny little mind he was referring to—hers or Marguerite's husband.

"It would be extremely bad form," agreed Quint. "Although, you're certainly welcome to try. You'll find nothing amiss. There were no bribes and payoffs, only three decent, moral men willing to witness an aging husband's will to provide for his young and vulnerable wife after he was gone.''

"Oh, brother.'' Wade gritted through his teeth in an aside to Rachel. "First, we have to endure Sloane making goo-goo eyes and pulling up her skirt for Cormack and then he launches into that Heartbreak Hotel spiel. I've got to get out of here before I lose my lunch.''

"You can't desert Aunt Eve and me now,'' Rachel whispered. "It's dishonorable for the crew to abandon a sinking ship, remember?''

"Right now I'd rather be a rat deserting it,'' grumbled Wade, but he stayed put.

"Moving on, we would like to discuss that unfortunate misunderstanding at the Tilden mansion on Friday night, Quint,'' Eve spoke up, interrupting the Tildens in the middle of another fierce interfamily argument. "About the complaint that was filed—''

"The only *misunderstanding* was that odious, officious police report!'' cried Marguerite. "I took my children to my own father's house and—''

"That house belongs to Misty Tilden,'' Quint interrupted. He had been idly circling the room but stopped to stand in front of Wade and Rachel. "Are you familiar with the term 'tenancy by the entireties'?''

"Of course!'' Wade drew himself from his usual slouch to his full height. "That's one of the first things I learned in my Property Law class.''

Rachel felt a horrid feeling of foreboding. "Oh, damn!'' she whispered.

"Oh no!'' Eve said at the same time, but more loudly.

"What's going to happen now?'' shrieked Marguerite. "I know something will!''

"Are you about to pull another rabbit out of your magic hat, Quint?'' Sloane teased coyly. Her skirt hiked a few inches higher, exposing more of her firm, silk-encased thighs.

"All right, Cormack.'' Town Three heaved an exaggerated sigh. "We know it's going to be bad. Just give it to us straight.''

16

"Town Senior put the house in both names, his and Misty's." Quint dropped the bomb without blinking. "His death makes her the sole owner. It also means that the house and its contents are not included in the estate. Misty already owns it all outright, with the exception of the personal bequests made to each family member." He paused, waiting for the full effect of his words to impact.

This time the Tildens were oddly silent. They appeared dazed by the revelation, and an eerie stillness descended over the conference room.

"Which makes the breaking and entering and other complaints filed against you all the more serious," he said, hoping to get things stirring again. "You don't have the familial connection as an excuse. That wasn't your father or grandfather's residence you burglarized, it is Misty's home. It would be like the Nixon or the Johnson daughters breaking into the White House and claiming they were entitled to do so because their fathers once lived there."

"That's not even remotely funny, Cormack!" A livid Tilden Lloyd was the first to speak.

"I wasn't trying to entertain you, I was using an analogy to show you that the alleged right you've claimed to enter Misty's home is ridiculous," Quint shot back. He waited, adrenaline flowing, to take on the next Tilden but no one else spoke.

"Your actions were patently criminal," he added for good measure.

The silence dragged on. It seemed never-ending to Quint, who grew bored. "Correct me if I'm wrong, but I sense that you have more or less decided not to contest the will," he prompted at last.

Only Marguerite's usually dormant husband took it as a challenge. "I still think we should contest," he piped up.

"Yes, we should!" agreed Tilly. "Are my father and I the only ones here not fooled by Cormack's smoke-and-mirrors practice of law?"

The other Tildens looked at the pair with the unconcealed contempt they normally directed at Misty or Quint.

"*Divide and Conquer. That's the way to handle my family.*" Quint could hear old Town Senior's jovial voice echoing in his head. The patriarch seemed to have known his progeny well because the dividing lines were already being drawn within the family. Quint could easily discern them.

The namesake Towns and Marguerite had decided a court case was not in their best interests and wanted to inherit what had been left to them. Sloane was on the fence but would ultimately throw in with the more powerful members of the family. Which left only the two hapless male Lloyds as the dissident outsiders. Quint had a feeling that was their customary position.

"You claim that my father put the house jointly in his and Misty's names." Town Junior turned to Quint, making a token last stand. "Can you prove this?"

"Do I strike you as stupid?" Quint was irritated and didn't bother to disguise his impatience. "Of course I can prove it. It's a matter of public record and has been since Day One when the papers were filed. The information isn't secret. Anyone who bothered to check would know."

"I didn't bother to check, a definite oversight on my part because possibly, I could've talked my father into reconsidering." Town Junior leaned across the table and glowered at Eve. "But then, I shouldn't have had to check. My *personal attorney* should have had the foresight to keep watch over such matters. Isn't that why the Tildens have always retained Saxon Associates? Because we believed that we would be treated as the invaluable clients that we are?''

"Yes, Eve, why didn't you monitor our father's transactions more closely?" scolded Marguerite. "You should have discovered that the house was in joint name, that it wouldn't pass through the estate."

"For that matter, you should've known Grandfather had drawn up a new will," Town Three added sternly. "According to Cormack, that is Basic Law 101."

"You can be certain that if Quint Cormack had been our lawyer, we'd have been aware of all this long before Grandfather died," Sloane said, fluttering her lashes at Quint.

Rachel and Wade exchanged enraged glances.

"You can hardly blame Aunt Eve for—" Rachel began.

"We most certainly can blame our attorney for failing to safeguard our legal interests in my father's estate," Town Junior cut her off. "And since you are also one of Saxon Associates, one of our *illustrious* lawyers, you are to blame too, young lady."

"We should've known when she blew the Pedersen trial that we'd end up getting screwed, too," Tilden Lloyd said nastily.

"Watch your language, Tilly," his mother reprimanded him.

"But the boy does have a point, however crudely expressed," said Town Three. "We have been ill served by this firm. We deserve better."

"Of course. The Tildens deserve only the very best," Wade said acidly.

Rachel and Eve tensed, bracing for an outburst, but none of the Tildens seemed to have picked up on Wade's sarcasm.

"That is true." Even Marguerite seemed somewhat mollified.

"Eve, do you have anything to say in your defense?" Town Junior stood up. He didn't appear willing to spend much time listening, if she should happen to have something to say in her defense. Clearly, he'd already judged her actions as indefensible.

Eve knew it. "I am sorry that you feel dissatisfied with our representation," she said stiffly.

"That's *all* you have to say?" Tilly scowled at his mother's longtime friend. "You're sorry?"

"What do you want her to do, grovel at your feet?" Wade exploded. "Well, why should she? It's not her fault. Town Senior was the one who married Misty, he was the one who wanted her to have the house and the money, and he was the one who hired Cormack to draw up the new uncontestable will. Aunt Eve—and Saxon Associates—had nothing to do with any of Town's decisions. If you want to blame someone, blame him!"

"It's just like you to speak ill of a dead man, Wade," Sloane said haughtily. "Everybody knows that poor Grandfather was pathetically bewitched by that slut!"

"There was nothing pathetic about your grandfather." Quint used his stentorian courtroom tones which resonated throughout the room. "Town had no complaints about his wife, who was devoted to him. He died a very happy man," he added, smiling wryly.

"I guess if you've gotta go, at ninety-three, that's the way to go," Wade whispered to Rachel.

"Be quiet!" She hissed. "Things are bad enough without your cynical bad jokes."

"My cynical bad jokes are the only thing keeping me from charging across the room and mauling Cormack, Sloane, and Tilly." Wade grimaced. "In my Rambo fantasy, those three go first, then I take out everybody else. You and Aunt Eve excepted, of course."

"Plotting strategy?" Quint joined them at the window.

He tried to catch Rachel's eyes, but she purposefully avoided his gaze. She knew it annoyed him, knew that if they were alone he would take her head in his hands and make her look at him. Which made her all the more determined not to even glance in his direction.

"They don't know how to plot strategy." This from a caustic Town Three. "They've certainly proven that."

"Can we dispense with the aspersions and return to the very pressing matter of those complaints filed by Misty?" Eve made an heroic effort to conduct business.

The Tildens weren't interested.

"I mentioned that particular absurdity to our general counsel at the company and he suggested that we retain a criminal lawyer to handle it." Town Junior was walking toward the door as he spoke. "I have already spoken to a prominent one in Philadelphia. He assured me that charges will not be filed."

"Oh, he did, did he?" Quint drawled. "It seems to me that decision is up to Chief Spagna."

"Yes, the final decision rests with the chief," seconded Eve.

"Nevertheless, you surely understand why we don't trust Saxon Associates to deal competently with that—situation." Town Junior sneered.

"You mustn't take this personally, Eve." Marguerite joined her brother at the door. "After all, you don't specialize in—that particular field." She seemed unwilling to speak the word "criminal."

"I don't think this firm specializes in anything." Sloane flashed Wade a look of pure dislike, which he returned in full measure.

"Except maybe losing cases and clients," Tilly added acidly.

"So we should proceed to administer and distribute the estate according to the testamentary provisions?" Quint addressed Town Junior.

"Yes. I trust you will be present when we go to the house to claim what Father wanted us to have?" Town Junior demanded. "None of us cares to suffer through another excruciating meeting with that synthetic-bodied lunatic and her hotheaded amour."

"Give me a call and I'll arrange to meet you at the house

and for Misty to be elsewhere,'' Quint said briskly, not acknowledging the insults.

Town Junior turned to Eve. ''I regret that it must end this way but as of now, the Tilden family will no longer retain the services of Saxon Associates. Consider your-selves terminated.''

Town Three actually shook Quint's hand, though he was the only Tilden to do so. The family departed en masse, their complaints and insults filling the office suite until the office door slammed behind them.

For a few seconds, a stark silence reigned. Then Katie came racing into the conference room.

''The Tildens have left the building!'' she announced, giggling.

''Ah, Katie, I bet you've been rehearsing that.'' Quint smiled at the girl.

Katie beamed. ''Yeah.''

''Don't you have a phone call to make?'' Eve asked her. ''You certainly spend enough time on the phone making personal calls. Why don't you call your boyfriend right now?''

It was an unmistakable dismissal, but Katie didn't quite get it. ''I already talked to him three times today,'' she said earnestly. ''Anyway, he's in class right now.''

''Then go call someone else,'' Eve commanded. ''One of your sisters or brothers, your best friend. Any friend.''

''Okay,'' Katie agreed cheerfully, and bounced out of the conference room.

Quint found himself facing the three Saxons, who had lined up together on the opposite side of the table from him.

''I saw no reason to involve the little Sheely girl in this unpleasantness,'' Eve said tightly. ''But since she's un-doubtedly chattering away on the phone right now, I don't have to restrain myself.'' Her voice lowered and her teeth were clenched as she turned blazing hazel eyes on Quint. *''Get out of here before I call an exterminator!''*

Quint regarded the trio with sympathy, not seeming to

mind that he'd just been called an insect, albeit indirectly.

"I understand your anger. The Tildens are extremely unpleasant to deal with," he said in a placating tone that failed to placate any Saxon. It only served to further infuriate them.

"We had no trouble dealing with the Tildens until you arrived on the scene, Cormack!" snarled Wade.

"I don't believe that," Quint countered. "Sarah told me that Dana told her otherwise."

"What are you, Gossip Central?" Rachel found her voice. "Oh, just when I think you can't possibly get any worse, you manage to sink to a new low!"

"This is the thanks I get for coming to this insult masquerading as a meeting?" Quint arched his dark brows. "I'll keep that in mind the next time I'm tempted to do a favor for Saxon Associates."

"A favor? Is that what you think your presence here today was?" Eve was incredulous. "A favor to us?"

"Wasn't it?" Quint asked Rachel, but all three Saxons replied to the question in a forceful chorus.

"No!"

Quint shrugged. "Typical lawyers, hmm? Why agree on a point when you can argue over it?" He strode jauntily from the conference room.

"He actually thinks he did a good deed for us today." Eve was still mulling that over. "We've lost the Tildens as clients, and he seems to think we should thank him."

"So, what now, Aunt Eve?" Wade sank into a chair. "Do you think the Tildens will reconsider their decision to dump us?"

"Never." Eve sighed. "They surrendered unconditionally this afternoon and hold us responsible for it. Misty has prevailed, thanks to Quinton Cormack, who's proven himself to be both wily and relentless. The Tildens don't have the time or energy to take on Cormack and that will, and he knows it. He's made it clear that he'll counter any move that's made, he will not back down or go away, he'll only make things worse. They're not used to that."

"Let's face it, neither are we." Wade was blunt.

"No, we aren't, are we? We took our practice and our status for granted, we were passive when we should have been proactive, and we gave Quinton Cormack the priceless gift of underestimating him at every turn." Eve's voice grew thick. She cleared her throat and then glanced purposefully at her watch. "You'll have to excuse me, I have some calls to make."

"Are we really to blame, Aunt Eve?" Rachel asked, troubled. "I mean, about the property being transferred to joint names and the new will . . ." Her voice trailed off.

Eve paused on the threshold. "As Wade pointed out, Town Senior made his own decisions without consulting us. But we should have known there would be a new will. In hindsight, I should have visited the old man and tried to advise him or convince him to confide in me. I guess the same holds true for the change in the property title. It is a matter of public record. We would've known the house was in joint name and out of the estate, if we'd checked into it. I suppose a case could be made for some negligence on our part."

She turned, leaving the conference room and the two cousins together.

"We're lawyers, not spies!" Rachel protested.

"Well, Quint Cormack is both. Sloane got that part right, much as it galls me to admit it. I wonder if she waited around outside for him?" Wade's lips quirked into a malevolent smile.

"She's just the type who would," Rachel muttered fiercely.

"Wouldn't it be a kick if *those* two got together? Actually, they deserve each other, they'd win hands down as the couple from hell," Wade added, his tone heartfelt.

Sloane and Quint together? Rachel paled. The very idea won hands down as her own personal hell.

Doubts assailed her. She pictured Quint leaving this office brimming with the confidence of a conquering gladiator, unaffected by her insults, clearly not feeling worried or threatened or sorry that she was furious with him. Because he didn't care?

She thought about their whirlwind romance, if that's what it was. Maybe Quint was the whirlwind himself, impelled to move on from one quick fling to another. He had admitted to his impulsivity with the equally impetuous Sharolyn, resulting in little Brady. Suppose there were others, many others? Not children, but flings, women he'd used and swiftly cast off.

What did she really know about Quinton Cormack, except that he was a talented, insightful lawyer, a determined competitor who refused to lose? And didn't.

True, he was a devoted father and brother, she'd seen proof of that, but his past relationships with women suddenly loomed as mysterious, a cause for suspicion. He was kind to Carla, whom he considered family, and Misty, a valuable client, but wasn't it possible that he viewed those two more as vested interests than women?

Did she really know what Quint considered her or how he viewed her? Rachel wondered with painful uncertainty. He'd made it obvious that he wanted her sexually, and she'd jumped into bed with him with uncharacteristic haste. She'd felt things with him, for him, that she had never thought to experience. But what if—

"Well, well, it's déjà vu all over again." Wade's voice cut through her increasingly disturbing reverie. He had moved to the window and was staring outside. "Take a look at the gruesome twosome down there in the parking lot. Sloane is hanging all over Cormack, the way she used to do with Tim Sheely. Except Tim would shake her off like a dog with a flea."

Which implied that Quint was not shaking her off. Rachel dragged herself over to the window, though she really didn't want to see what was out there.

As she suspected, it was not a pretty sight. Nauseating was a more applicable description. Several stories below, Sloane Tilden Lloyd was sending Quint Cormack a plethora of "I'm available and willing" signals, listed in every women's magazine Rachel had ever read.

Sloane seemed to know them all. Touching his arm with her hand. Flirtatiously cocking her head to one side. Slithering ever closer, her face bright and animated.

Since Quint's back was to them, his responses could not be detected but the fact that he remained there was damning enough for Rachel. "I'd like to kill him!"

"Yeah, you always did have a penchant for public service," Wade murmured dryly.

He folded his arms in front of his chest and gazed at his cousin. "Hey, Rach, I've been meaning to ask you about Laurel. I drove her to your place on Friday night after she'd had a big fight with Gerald. Is everything okay with the two of them?"

Laurel. Snowy. Rachel flinched. "I don't know." Her voice quavered. She really should have called her sister yesterday, but she'd been too involved with the Cormacks all day and Quint *all night* and hadn't bothered. "Laurel isn't acting like herself at all."

Of course, Quint would dispute that statement with his "what you do is what you are" creed. Which meant that his actions—flirting with the brazen Sloane, taking what she was so obviously offering—labeled him as a backstabbing, opportunistic womanizer.

"Remember what Aunt Eve always said about Laurel marrying way too young and Gerald being way too old for her? Seems like she was right, hmm? I feel bad for Snowy if things get ugly." Wade looked sad. "She's such a cute little kid."

"All we can do is be there for Snowy. We can't control either Laurel or Gerald," murmured Rachel. When she realized she was quoting that snake Quinton Cormack, she lapsed into silence. He'd gotten into her head, as quickly and completely as he'd entered her body.

The flagrant admission galled her, terrified her, too. If she hadn't seized the world atlas, perched on its tall stand in the corner, and sent if flying across the room, Rachel knew she would've started to cry. Anger was certainly preferable to blubbering over a man.

The atlas hit the wall and landed askew, its pages open and bent.

"You don't mess around when you're mad, you trash the whole word!" Wade smiled his approval. "Think it would work for me?"

"Be my guest." Rachel invited and Wade picked up the ill-fated atlas.

Before he had a chance to take his turn heaving it, Eve poked her head into the conference room. "I'm leaving early this afternoon. In fact, I'm on my way out now. Carry on, you two." Her face was flushed, her eyes bright.

She appeared much happier than either her niece or nephew, and her buoyant stride as she left the office was not unlike the effervescent Katie's. Certainly, Eve Saxon didn't look like an attorney whose firm had just suffered the loss of a major, *major* client. A bewildered Wade shared his observations with Rachel.

Who had no reply at all. Rachel was mired in a morass of sadness, confusion, and fury. Not a good place to be. The beneficial effects of her atlas-tossing therapy had proven to be incredibly short-lived. She solemnly took the book from Wade, smoothed its pages, and returned it to its proper position.

Wade decided that since his legal career was heading south—he figured metaphorically it was somewhere close to the tip of Argentina about now—it was definitely time to concentrate on his personal life. Which meant getting it right with Dana Sheely and fixing whatever had gone wrong between the ecstasy and closeness of last night and her icy aloofness over the phone this morning.

What had gone wrong? If only he knew! The more he thought about it, his original hypothesis—that Dana had taken offense because he'd asked her to intercede with her boss in the Tilden fiasco—just didn't seem plausible. So now he was left without a single clue.

The real problem was, he had no experience in main-taining a smooth, ongoing relationship with a woman. Women came and went in his life, and he didn't care. Cer-tainly, he'd never wondered about their feelings and what role he might play in determining them. So he was essen-tially a novice, as virginal in the arena of love as Dana had been in sex.

Except she'd been an exceptionally fast learner who could excite and please him more than any of his experi-enced past lovers. He thought of last night with her, and a sharp rush of memoried pleasure tightened his body. He had to resort to reciting multiplication tables as he drove to the Sheely home to quell his all-too-evident arousal.

It was close to dinnertime at the Sheelys, and the smell of Mary Jean Sheely's delicious pot roast filled his nostrils as he hurried up the porch stairs. Sarah and Matt were sit-ting on the wooden bench swing on the porch, holding hands, while Brendan indulgently played a two-year-old's version of soccer with little Brady Cormack in the front yard.

"Cormack's kid is mooching another meal off your folks, huh?" Wade grumbled to Sarah. He knew the entire Sheely clan adored Sarah's little charge, but he did not share their enchantment with the Cormack spawn. Baby rats might be cute but, ultimately, they grew up to be rodents.

"Come on, Wade, just 'cause you don't like Quint, don't take it out on Brady." Sarah was stern.

"I guess Cormack is out celebrating his Tilden Will vic-tory tonight." Wade grimaced at the thought of the pro-found Saxon defeat. "Maybe with his busty, lusty protégé Misty?"

"Of course not! Quint is—" Sarah broke off, giving Wade a strange look. "Uh, busy tonight. But not with Misty."

"Misty is celebrating her victory with Shawn," Matt said glumly. "In ways I don't even want to imagine."

"Dinner won't be ready for a while, sit down and talk

to us, Wade," invited Sarah, sliding closer to Matt to make room for Wade on the swing.

Sheelys never minded crowding together to make room for one more. Wade sat down next to Sarah. "So you talked to Shawn about Misty again today, huh?"

"Wish we hadn't." Matt scowled. "I think the guy's obsessed with her. Is that possible, or does it only happen in horror movies?"

"Sometimes reality is stranger than fiction, and money aside, Misty's appeal must be awfully potent," Wade replied wryly. "It seems to span the decades, from ninetysomething Town Tilden Senior to our own twenty-something Shawn."

"Shh!" Sarah cautioned. "I hear Anthony coming."

The trio on the swing quickly switched to another topic, the upcoming Phillies-Pirates three-game series.

Anthony Sheely, dressed all in black, joined them on the porch. It was hard to be dark, brooding and alienated in the bustling Sheely clan, but Anthony worked hard to keep up his chosen image. "I just can't take it anymore," he announced dramatically.

"Join the club, kid," drawled Wade.

Matt was kinder. "What's wrong, Anth?"

"Megan Sperry is what's wrong." Anthony heaved a morose sigh. "I have to eat lunch with her and her friends at their table in the cafeteria instead of with my friends, I have to hang out after school with her instead of with my buds, and I'm supposed to call her every night, no matter what's on TV."

"So don't call her," Wade advised.

"If I don't, then she calls me! She's even figured out to use the emergency break-in excuse on Emily." Anthony groaned. "I hate having a girlfriend. It's like—like home-work! In fact, she likes us to do our homework together over the phone." He made a gagging sound.

Wade chuckled.

"You're too young to be involved with anyone, Anthony,'' a sagely Matt explained. ''Do the girl and yourself a favor and break up with her.''

''But do it nicely,'' warned Sarah. ''None of this 'I don't like you anymore' stuff like Brendan does. He's awful to girls, as bad as Wa—'' She caught herself and flushed guiltily, casting a covert glance at Wade.

''I know you mean me,'' Wade said. ''And I admit, I've had a bad track record with women in the past.''

''I'll say!'' Sarah heartily agreed. ''Tricia says your bad reputation with women is probably the biggest reason why—'' she broke off with a startled gasp. ''God, what's the matter with me today? I'm getting as blabby as Katie!''

''Definitely not a good thing.'' Matt affectionately rubbed her neck.

''What did Tricia say about me?'' Wade demanded. ''I thought we were friends.''

''You are,'' Sarah assured him. ''You're friends with all of us, you know that, Wade.''

''Especially Tim and Dana,'' added Anthony.

It was Wade's turn to feel a guilty flush spread slowly across his face. ''Uh, speaking of Dana, is she around?''

Not a bad segue, he congratulated himself. Cool. Subtle. He hadn't even had to mention her name first. Now he could amble into the house to see her—and hopefully, her mom would invite him to stay for dinner. The intoxicating aroma of pot roast was making his stomach growl with hunger.

''No, Dana left. She had a date with that guy—what's his name?'' Anthony searched his memory.

''Rich Vicker?'' Wade gritted through his teeth.

''Yeah, him,'' agreed Anthony.

Wade abruptly stood up, sending the swing wildly into motion. Matt and Sarah clamped their feet on the ground to halt it. ''Do you know where they went?''

''Somewhere to eat,'' Sarah told him. ''Daddy says Rich Vicker has a digestive system that ought to be studied by medical science. He can eat anything and has never even needed a Rolaid.''

Wade did not want to hear one word about Rich Vicker's attributes. Who cared about that jerk's superb digestive tract? His own stomach was now roiling with outrage, displacing the earlier hunger pangs. What in the hell did Dana think she was doing? Sleeping with one man while dating another!

"What restaurant?" he demanded.

Anthony gave him an indifferent how-should-I-know look. Matt and Sarah stared at him curiously.

"You could ask Daddy," Sarah suggested, her lips curving into a smile. "He probably knows."

"Bet money on it," joked Matt. "Mr. Sheely makes a point of grilling his daughters' dates—till they become fiancés. Then the inquisition eases up a little," he added, grinning.

Wade charged into the house, almost colliding with Emily who was walking through the hall clutching the portable phone, in the midst of an animated discusssion. He found Bob and Mary Jean Sheely in the kitchen. As usual, they greeted him warmly.

"We just heard the most wonderful news!" Mary Jean's face was aglow. "We're going to be grandparents again!"

Wade was momentarily diverted by the announcement. "Tim and Lisa are having *another* baby?"

"No, Mary Jo is pregnant!" exclaimed Mary Jean. "She broke into Emily's call to tell us. She bought one of those pregnancy test kits from the drugstore that confirmed it. We're just thrilled for her and Steve!"

It was at least another ten minutes before Wade could get a word in edgewise. Bob and Mary Jean wanted to talk about their secondborn, Mary Jo, who'd won a scholarship to nursing school, graduated to work in the neuro–intensive care unit where she'd met and married Steve, a successful neurosurgeon and genuinely nice guy who'd managed to stay single because he was both shy and determined not to wed until he'd repaid all his medical-school loans. He had just been pronounced debt-free when he met and fell hard for sweet, outgoing Mary Jo Sheely.

Wade remembered their wedding quite well. Bob and Mary Jean had been in a state of euphoria. He guessed that having a gainfully employed daughter who married a doctor—without debts!—was about as good as it got for any girl's parents. And now there was to be another member of the next generation of Sheelys.

Wade was happy for them . . . but had heard enough about darling Mary Jo. "I understand Dana is out with Vicker tonight," he cut in, just as Mary Jean mentioned Tim's name.

He knew that another ten minutes of accolades were likely to follow and as much as he valued his best friend, he just couldn't spare the time to listen. His first priority was Dana. "Do you know where they are?"

"At that new restaurant, the Library." Bob supplied the information. "It opened a couple weeks ago, I read about it in the paper. It's out on Route 70 and is trying to compete with the likes of Restaurant Row in Philadephia."

"The Library," repeated Wade. He would call the place on his car phone and find out its exact location on 70.

"It's supposed to specialize in French food," continued Bob. "And classic American, whatever that is. Of course, it won't matter to Rich Vicker, who could probably drink water straight from a jungle river and never even get a cramp. His stomach is a medical marvel and his intestines— well, *there's* something worth cloning!"

"Plenty of pharmaceutical companies would go out of business if everybody could digest like Rich Vicker." Mary Jean laughed. "And speaking of digestion, I hope you'll stay for dinner, Wade. I know how much you like pot roast."

"I like anything you cook," Wade said sincerely. "But I can't stay. I—er—have plans tonight." He started out of the kitchen.

"I hope your plans don't include going to the Library. And I don't mean the one that lends books, I'm talking about the one that serves food. Out on Route 70." Bob Sheely's voice stopped him cold.

Wade slowly turned around. "What—makes you think that?" he asked thickly.

"Stay here and have dinner with us, Wade," Mary Jean urged. "And then spend the evening. We don't get to see enough of you these days. We miss having you around."

"Dana always gets home early when she goes out with Rich." Bob was watching Wade closely. "You'll be here when she arrives and you can talk to her then. Take her out for a nice drive. Believe me, there's nothing to be gained by following her to the Library. Think about it, son. What would you do once you got there? Pretend the whole thing was a coincidence and get yourself a table? I mean, you could hardly pull up a chair and join Dana and Vicker, could you?"

"I don't know!" Wade threw up his hands in an admission of abject defeat. "Could I?"

"I'll tell you what I've always told my kids," Mary Jean Sheely said warmly. "Desperation is never attractive. And neither is a public display of jealousy."

"I feel like an idiot!" Wade groaned. "About as savvy with the opposite sex as Anthony or Brendan."

"You've never been in love before," Mary Jean consoled him. "Of course you're a little off-balance. If it helps at all, so is Dana."

His pride in tatters, Wade wanted to abandon it altogether and ask what she meant. That Dana was in love with him, too? Had she told her mother so? Or was Mary Jean simply being kind to shield his feelings?

But a contingent of young Sheelys, along with Matt carrying little Brady Cormack piled into the kitchen, all talking at once.

Wade told them he was staying for dinner and Sarah set a place for him at the table.

17

$\underline{\hspace{2cm}}$

"*I*nteresting decor," Dana remarked to Rich Vicker as she gazed around the interior of the Library.

The restaurant did bear a resemblance to a library. Tall shelves lined the walls, filled with books of all sizes and conditions, from ancient paperbacks costing a dime way back when to faux-leather hardbound classics. Wisely, the linen cloth-covered tables, each with a tapered candle glowing in the center, were a far cry from the bare, functional reading tables found in authentic libraries.

The lack of windows, caused by all those bookshelves stacked against every wall, gave the place an insulated-from-the-outside atmosphere. Which was necessary. A view of busy Route 70 with its continual stream of cars and trucks wouldn't have provided the ambience this ambitious new restaurant was striving to achieve.

As usual, Rich was thoroughly involved in studying the choices featured on the menu. It looked like a giant library card and was divided into categories with items numbered in faithful imitation of the Dewey Decimal System. Dana found it all too much of a sham and immediately chided herself for not being whimsical enough to appreciate it.

It had been that kind of a day today; she'd found herself irked by almost everything, no matter how inconsequential. She knew she needed a major attitude adjustment and tried to turn to the power of positive thinking.

For instance, the menu listed chicken with one of its

decimaled numbers. She ought to be grateful for the solid American fare offered among the rich French cuisine. Grilled lemon chicken would not require her to raid her father's stockpile of anti-indigestion aids tonight, and surely the mashed potatoes and coconut cake could do her no harm.

Her mood improved a little, but not much.

A narrow, winding circular staircase at the far end of the restaurant led to the second floor. Rich said some friends told him there were private booths up there, with thick curtains that could be closed for extra privacy. That struck Rich as excessively claustrophobic, surely an impediment to enjoying a good meal.

Dana dismissed the food angle and imagined what else could be done in such titillating privacy. Heat burned through her body. She probably would've shared Rich's bemusement herself, if she hadn't been so thoroughly corrupted by Wade Saxon over the weekend.

Her own innate honesty wouldn't let her get away with that pretext, not even to herself. Especially not to herself. She hadn't been corrupted by Wade, she'd been sexually awakened by him. And she'd wanted it, needed it. She wanted and needed him; she was deeply in love with him, not that she dared let him know it. Not even after last night, when he'd taken her to his bed and made love to her passionately, thrillingly for hours.

While Rich read the list of entrées aloud, Dana allowed the memory of last night, which she'd successfully suppressed all day, to surface. Prickles of excitement rose on her skin. She remembered what had followed their wildly urgent union, more lovemaking but of a different nature. Tender and exquisite loving that made her feel cherished and adored, the way she cherished and adored Wade.

She'd felt so close to him, at one with him. In addition to being her lover, he was her soul mate, the man she had been waiting for her entire life. Which was funny because she'd known Wade most of her life but hadn't recognized his true place in it.

Dana knew he still didn't recognize it. Nor would he want to. She'd been his friend and surrogate sister long enough to know his opinion of women who mistook great sex for love.

It wasn't very high.

Wade was appalled when a woman mistook the physical intimacy of sex for the bonds of true love. A "sexual acquaintance"—his term—did not constitute a lasting relationship. His dictum.

How many times had she heard him lament about those foolish women who tried to make no-strings-attached acts of pleasure into something more? Something lasting. Too many times to count, Dana reminded herself.

And this morning, when she woke up feeling wonderful—replete and glowing and madly in love—when she'd almost called Wade because she didn't think she could wait another second to hear the sound of his voice, she suddenly remembered that pathetic group of women who had probably awakened feeling much like she did after a magical evening making love with Wade Saxon.

And she heard his voice, but it was inside her head, venting his morning-after irritation with his former lovers. She remembered how she pitied them—while also thinking how foolish they'd been.

Well, not her. Not ever. She'd play it the way she knew Wade wanted it played. No demands, no expectations. Certainly no emotional ties or references to last night. No emotions at all.

So she'd been cool when he had called the office this morning. Quint had predicted Wade would try to enlist her aid in setting up a meeting, so she knew from the moment she picked up the phone not to be excited by the sound of his voice. That his call was strictly for professional purposes.

After Quint instructed Helen not to put through any more calls from Saxon Associates, Dana didn't bother to ask if Wade had tried to reach her again. And when Rich had invited her to dinner at the Library, she'd accepted at once, not even letting herself pretend that Wade might want to see her tonight.

Rich was discussing what particular dishes his friends had sampled when they'd been here last week, and Dana tried to appear interested. But her eyes kept drifting to the other diners at the tables around them, to the books on the shelves. She was close enough to read the titles and some sounded intriguing.

There was a whole series of very old books about twins. *The Cave Twins, The Spartan Twins, The Puritans Twins,* among others. Dana wished she could leaf through them. She'd never read much about cave people or Sparta or Puritans, and all three topics seemed far more interesting than her date.

Which wasn't fair to poor Rich, and Dana knew it. She tuned back into his conversation until, inevitably, her attention strayed again. This time to the circular staircase.

The steps were so narrow, most people going up moved slowly and gingerly. Dana noticed that only couples were ascending that staircase; groups of three or more were all seated downstairs. They were here for the food while those upstairs couples—were here for more.

Dana imagined them sliding into the private booths and yanking the privacy curtains closed. If she went up there with Wade . . .

The moment her imagination turned in that fateful direction, Dana abruptly shut it down. And refocused her full attention on her escort.

"I suppose I've never seen vegetarianism in quite that light, Rich." She attempted to respond to one of his comments on vegetarians, of whom he vehemently disapproved. "If animals weren't supposed to be eaten, God wouldn't have made them out of meat? It's certainly something to ponder."

She couldn't wait to share that particular insight with her dad. Dana hid a smile.

A well-dressed, good-looking couple crossed the restaurant to the base of the stairway. Dana's jaw dropped as she recognized at the pair, who were already beginning to climb upward.

She was too startled to keep silent. "Isn't that Eve Saxon and Chief Spagna?" she interrupted Rich in the middle of his detailed comparisons of bouillabaisse he had enjoyed. Since God made fish out of fish, they, too, were meant to be consumed, and why not in a savory stew?

Rich glanced at the stairway where the attractive brunette was mounting the skinny stairs. Her tough-looking, muscular companion was behind her, his hand proprietarily placed low on the small of her back. His fingers were long and extended to her bottom, which he was subtly caressing.

Dana and Rich exchanged wide-eyed glances.

"He was actually—actually—" Rich gulped.

"Feeling her up," Dana supplied, too amazed to be embarrassed.

Rich blushed. "The police chief! Imagine! And her, a lawyer, letting him do it! At their age, too! It's not as if they're wild teenagers."

As if wild teenagers were the only ones hormonal enough to indulge in sexual touches. Dana quivered. She knew better. But it was the unlikely pairing of Eve Saxon, Lakeview aristocracy, with the police chief—originally from one of Newark's old ethnic neighborhoods and not far removed from a career with that city's homicide division—that truly boggled her mind. A couple like that wouldn't have much in common.

Then again, the two certainly seemed—well, *familiar*—with each other. Obviously, they'd found some common ground. She remembered Quint puzzling over the phone call the chief had made this morning on behalf of Eve Saxon. Well, that mystery was solved.

Wait till she told Wade! He'd be as astonished as she was. Dana wondered when she could tell him, when she would see him again. Or if she would see him. Maybe he was lying low, dreading their next encounter, fearing that she would profess her undying love for him.

Dana smiled sardonically. He had no worries on that

score. She fully intended to out-Saxon Wade himself when it came to a no-strings-attached attitude. And, perhaps, she wouldn't divulge his aunt's surprising liaison, after all. She'd save that news for her boss, who would undoubtedly find a way to make good use of the information.

"So then Gerald told me he'd signed me up for tap-dancing and aerobics classes," Laurel muttered sullenly. "Like that's supposed to make everything all right."

"You wanted to take tap dancing and aerobics," Rachel reminded her sister.

Laurel had appeared at her door an hour before Quint was due to arrive for their dinner date but after the afternoon's office scene, Rachel *knew* he wasn't going to show up. Why would he? He'd won it all, the Saxons had insulted him, and Sloane's sexy parking lot antics promised him a far more enjoyable evening than he could expect to spend with Rachel the Saxon Shrew.

So when Laural barged inside and withdrew two cartons of ice cream from her grocery bag—Cherry Garcia for Laurel, vanilla for Rachel—Rachel welcomed her. After all, there was a chance that Laurel was bringing good news—she'd resolved her anger about her marriage—and the ice cream was a celebratory treat. A minute into the visit, Rachel tossed out that delusionary hope. Laurel was as hostile to her husband as ever, and the ice cream was her idea of either rebellion or consolation, possibly both.

Now the two sisters were sitting in Rachel's living room, each with her own pint of ice cream, eating out of the cartons with spoons. It was the sort of thing they'd never done as children, but Laurel had insisted, rummaging through the kitchen utensil drawers and shoving a carton and a spoon into Rachel's hands.

"I *used* to want to, but now it's too little, too late!" Laurel said dramatically. "Gerald's trying to make up for stealing my youth but—"

"Stealing your . . . Laurel, where did that come from?" Rachel cut in sharply. "It sounds like a—an outtake from a soap opera bloopers reel. And while we're on the subject of youth, let's be real. You wanted to be with Gerald, you insisted on it!''

"Mom couldn't wait for me to get married," Laurel retorted. "She'd given up on you, and she was desperate to plan a great big wedding and to have a grandchild."

"You're saying you married Gerald and had Snowy to please Mom?" Rachel was incredulous. And horrified. And furious.

"Yes!" Laurel said defiantly. "And I'm tired of living my life pleasing others! It's time to finally please myself!"

"The most incongruous part of this revisionist history of yours is that I can't remember a single time when you didn't do exactly what you wanted to do, Laurel."

Rachel stood up. The few bites she'd taken of the unwanted ice cream had given her teeth a bone-jarring chill, but that was nothing compared to the emotional chill Laurel's words sent to her heart.

"You must have *me* confused with *you*, Rachel!" Laurel jumped to her feet, too, her eyes glittering. "You live here in your very own apartment fixed up just the way you want, you have a great job and a cool car while I spend every minute of my life doing what Gerald wants, what Snowy wants, what Mom wants! And when I come to you for help, all you do is yell at me." Laurel heaved a noisy sob.

Her tears followed. Rachel watched for a few moments. She'd always been a little in awe of Laurel's crying prowess. Her younger sister's tears didn't trickle singly down her cheeks, they teemed, flowing as thick and fast as a waterfall.

But it was a performance she'd seen too many times before. Rachel sighed. "Laurel, what do you want me to do? What do you want me to say to you?"

Laurel's tears stopped. Instantly. She could turn them on and off like a faucet, Aunt Eve and Wade often scorned, which would compel Rachel to defend her sister.

"Well, I want to—" Laurel began but was interrupted by the sound of the doorbell. "Who's that? It better not be

Gerald trying to hunt me down!'' Rather eagerly, she stomped to the door and threw it open.

Quint Cormack stood there, dressed in his well-cut court-room blue suit and holding a long white box that had to contain long-stemmed roses and a gold-embossed box of designer chocolates.

His eyes swept over Laurel. ''Let me guess. You're Rachel's *little* sister. Snowy's mom.''

''I'm Laurel! I'm sick of being defined through other people. Rachel's sister, Snowy's mother, Gerald's wife. My mom's daughter. I'm myself, I'm *Laurel*. And who are you? What are you doing here?'' Laurel demanded resentfully, ignoring the obvious clues, the flowers and candy, his clean-shaven face and expensive suit.

Her legs wobbly, Rachel joined the two of them at the door. Though she hated herself for it, her heart was pounding and every nerve of her body felt as if she'd been struck with bolts of sensual lightning.

Quint's eyes met Rachel's. ''I can see that you haven't told Little Sister about our date.''

''You didn't mention you had a date tonight, Rachel,'' Laurel seconded, her tone accusing.

''Did you give her a chance to?'' Quint countered. ''My guess is that you haven't stopped talking about yourself long enough for Rachel to get in a word about herself or her plans. Which is par for the course, I'm sure.''

Laurel gasped. ''Rachel, who is this person?''

''Laurel, meet Quinton Cormack,'' Rachel said edgily, retreating farther into the room.

Quint followed, brushing by Laurel to enter the apartment. Laurel gaped at him, her expression mingled with horror and guilty fascination, as if he'd just revealed himself to be the Devil Incarnate and she couldn't look away.

Quint's eyes flicked over Rachel, taking in her loose-fitting khaki shorts and sleeveless chambray blouse. ''When I said a restaurant that didn't offer toys or crayons, you must have thought I meant Taco Bell,'' he said lightly. He glanced at his watch. ''Hurry up and change, Rachel. We have reservations at Wainwright's half an hour from now.''

He named one of the newest—and most—expensive restaurants in Philadelphia, located in a hotel in the center of the city.

''Rachel, you're dating Quinton Cormack?'' Laurel's head swung from one to the other.

''No,'' said Rachel, at the same time Quint said, ''Of course.''

''Well, which is it? Yes or no?'' Laurel retrieved her pint of ice cream and began to shovel heaping spoonfuls of it into her mouth.

Rachel stood, tense and still. She truly hadn't expected Quint to keep their date tonight, not after the contentious meeting in the office this afternoon. Not after watching him with Sloane Tilden Lloyd in the parking lot.

Righteous anger and indignation—stoked by her long talks with Wade this afternoon blasting the Cormacks, the Tildens, politicians, sports figures who left their loyal fans to pursue megamillions in other cities, and any other group they could think to slam—had kept her from concentrating on Quint's perfidy. Or on how awful she was going to feel when she finally acknowledged his absence from her life.

Laurel's arrival had continued to keep her diverted. Until now.

But with Quint standing in front of her, looking more virile and masculine and appealing than any man had a right to, Rachel was hit with a bursting dam of emotion. If she were Laurel, she would turn on the waterworks. Her eyes did fill with tears, but Rachel determinedly willed them away.

''Why don't you take your reservation and your flowers and candy and give them to Sloane?'' she heard herself say spitefully. She was immediately aghast at her blatant display of jealousy.

Which Quint mistook for a joke. He laughed heartily. ''Sure. And then I'll ask Town Junior, Town Three, and Tilly to join me in a foursome for a round of golf.''

''Isn't Sloane the one Wade has always hated so much?''

Laurel asked, delving deeper into the ice-cream carton.

"Who can blame him?" Quint laid the two boxes down on an end table. "That greedy little viper practically jumped me in the parking lot this afternoon and tried to talk me into pulling a fast one on Misty by substituting the dollhouse she inherited for the jewels Town left to my client."

Rachel's first impulse was to blurt that it didn't look like he'd been protesting Sloane's attentions in the parking lot all that much, but logic quickly prevailed. From her vantage point at the window, she'd seen only Quint's back. But if Sloane had been suggesting that he cheat his client, Rachel could well imagine what his expression had been. Knowing his loyalty to Misty and his own personal integrity, he would've considered Sloane's bid to be a dire insult.

"What did Sloane offer to give you?" Laurel asked, her eyes bright with curiosity. "She did offer you something to get you to go along with her, didn't she? I happen to know the way these kinds of women operate. I do watch TV, you know."

"Probably too much, and all the wrong shows," Quint said flatly. "But Sloane did offer something."

"I knew it!" Laurel giggled. "Money or sex?"

"Both. As if either would be an inducement for anything, let alone betraying my client!" Quint was indignant. "I told Ms. Lloyd exactly what I thought of her and her dishonesty and lack of ethics. I told her that Misty is rungs above her on the morality ladder."

"More than anything, Sloane would hate being compared unfavorably to Misty," Rachel said pensively. "You knew exactly where to plunge the verbal knife, Quint. You always do."

"If that's a compliment, thank you. If it's your own plunging verbal knife, pretend that I'm wounded. Anyway, it's safe to assume that Sloane won't speak to me again during this lifetime." Quint glanced at his watch. "I'm hungry. Let's get moving, Rachel."

Rachel's breath caught. "Laurel, would you put my ice

cream in the freezer, please? It's starting to melt."

"And put these roses in water," added Quint, thrusting the box into Laurel's hands.

"You just want me out of the room so you two can talk alone," Laurel complained.

"Good for you, Laurel. You picked up on that hint right away," Quint said drolly.

Both Rachel and Quint watched Laurel heave a martyred sigh and shuffle reluctantly from the room, the box of roses and ice-cream containers in hand.

"Time for me to say something astute, like 'it never rains, it pours,' hmm?" Quint moved so fast that his arms were around Rachel before she even had time to think of backing away from him.

"That's hardly astute. More like an overused, unoriginal cliché," she said shakily.

"Whatever." His lips brushed the top of Rachel's head and he inhaled the clean scent of her shampoo "You've had a bad day, baby. First, the nasty Tildens and then Li'l Sis shows up in a cranky mood." His hands moved over her, simultaneously comforting and arousing. "Time for me to make you feel better."

Rachel stared up at him. "I didn't think you were coming," she confessed, trying to appear blasé. The quaver in her voice betrayed her.

"Why not?" Quint appeared genuinely surprised.

"How can you even ask?" she asked rawly. "After the way we parted at the office today, all the insults and angry words! And you strolled out like you didn't care what I'd said." That hurt badly, that he could be so unaffected by her.

"Rachel, I didn't take anything you said personally. Your aunt and your cousin were practically foaming at the mouth with fury, and if you hadn't displayed a bit of anger yourself, they would've damn well wondered why. Anyway, who could blame you for getting mad at the way things turned out for Saxon Associates? I understand."

She stared up at him, amazed at the considerable gaps in

their perceptions of this afternoon's nightmare. At least, it had been a nightmare for her! Quint had discounted her slurs, dismissing them. Not taking them *personally*.

Which was what lawyers did in the courtroom all the time. Hurl invectives and outrage on behalf of their clients and afterward, congratulate or commiserate with their colleagues. Rachel knew the dynamics, she'd made use of them herself. But never with Quint Cormack.

It had alway been different with him, from the moment she'd first laid eyes on him. The Pedersen trial hadn't merely been a case to her, it had been some kind of mating dance with Quint, though she hadn't known that at the time.

"You might've managed to fool Eve and Wade but not me." Quint touched his lips to hers, and her knees suddenly went weak. "As far as denunciations go, yours were pretty paltry, sweetheart. You managed a generic barb or two but nothing remotely comparable to some of the ones you've leveled at me in the past. And I can tell a professional strike from a personal one."

Rachel tried to remember what she'd said—she hadn't thought her insults were a pale imitation of previous ones, she'd been sure she had offended him grievously, *personally*. But she was feeling dizzy from the sexual tension vibrating between them and couldn't properly focus. She didn't care anyway. Her anxieties and insecurities had been explained away.

Quint lightly caressed the skin of her cheek with this thumb, and she closed her eyes, allowing herself to enjoy the pleasure of his touch. He kissed her gently, delicately, and her mouth opened to him.

She slowly slid her arms around his neck in age-old sensual surrender. He deepened the kiss and she responded and returned his passion, stoking the flames, driving them both higher.

"I knew you two would get hot and heavy the minute I left the room." Laurel's petulant tones shattered the silence.

When Rachel made the obligatory responsible-big-sisterly attempt to move away from her lover, Quint kept her pressed tightly to him, his arms strong as iron bands.

"You were right on target there, Laurel." Quint was still breathing heavily and made no pretense of not resenting the interruption.

Rachel felt the vigorous, irresistible male strength of his body and wanted nothing more than to shed the already-tenuous threads of her self-control and let their desire take them.

But Laurel's presence was inhibiting.

Quint found it annoying. "It's time you went home, Laurel," he said pointedly. "You have a family, you have a small child to put to bed. Or do you intend to abandon your responsibilities as a mother and force your husband to try to fill the roles of both parents?"

Definitely the wrong thing to say to an already-agitated Laurel. She launched into the same tearfully angry monologue she'd given Rachel, centering on her own repressed needs and unjust enslavement.

"Let me summarize, to make sure I have your bill of particulars straight. You want to leave your husband, give him custody of your child, and go off to find adventure?" Quint was in full trial-attorney mode by the time Laurel finished her tirade.

"You just don't understand." Laurel dropped dramatically to the sofa, weeping still more tears. Quint's arms firmly encircled Rachel, preventing her from going to her sister's side.

"Oh, I understand very well, Laurel. You see, I've heard this same song before," he said roughly. "Have you considered the travel opportunities in Eastern Europe? I can give you a couple names to look up over there."

"Rachel, is that man crazy?" raged Laurel, once again abruptly tearless.

"No, I'm sane," Quint assured her. "And I am the father of a little boy whose mother decided she was tired of taking care of him. She literally handed him over to me, giving me full custody. Now I have complete power over whether or not she will ever see or talk to her child again, and I have no intention of letting her do either.''

Laurel recoiled with a sharp gasp.

''Don't make the mistake of thinking that if you walk out on your husband and daughter, you can simply waltz back into their lives whenever you please, Laurel.'' Quint drove his point home. ''Some actions are irreversible.''

''You're just trying to scare me! Gerald wouldn't keep me from visiting Snowy if I decide to—to—'' Laurel swallowed nervously and her eyes grew round as saucers. ''Tell him that can't happen to me and Snowy, Rachel. I have you and Wade and Aunt Eve to make sure it won't.''

''Rachel can't give you that kind of guarantee,'' Quint shot back. ''Not with Judith Bernard practicing over in Haddonfield. Judi is practically unbeatable in child-custody cases, and she favors representing fathers. Should Gerald retain her, Snowy is as good as lost to you.''

Laurel screamed. A piercing high-decibeled shriek that made humans wince with discomfort and probably would have made dogs howl in pain had any been in the vicinity.

Rachel gazed up at Quint's face. He was in full crusader mode, and though part of her wanted to soothe her younger sister, another part noted that Laurel was intently listening to Quint, in a way she rarely paid attention to anyone.

''I've met your daughter,'' Quint continued, following up his terrifying indictment and moving toward his closing argument . ''I'm fond of that little girl, I care what happens to her. If I find out she's being hurt by selfish and irresponsible conduct on your part, I'm going to call your husband and recommend Judi Bernard's services to him. Don't make the mistake of thinking that I'm bluffing, Laurel. Ask your sister—I never make idle threats, I just go ahead and take action.''

Laurel didn't bother to ask. She grabbed her purse and ran out the door to her car parked in front of the apartment building. Quint released Rachel long enough to reach over to close the door, which Laurel had left standing open in her haste to escape.

"A version of shock therapy?" Rachel asked softly.

Quint nodded. "I cranked up the voltage to excessive levels, but she seemed like the type who wouldn't respond to a light prod. Do you think she's headed home?"

"I hope so. Poor Laurel looked scared to death. She really does love Snowy, you know. She's been a good mother, she's taken very good care of her baby. I know she wouldn't want to lose her."

"I hope you're right, for Snowy's sake."

Rachel eyed him curiously. "Is Judith Bernard really that good? I don't know her very well, or her track record."

"She's good," Quint affirmed. "She kicked my ass all over the courtroom in the one custody case where I went up against her. I was new in the area at the time, I represented the mother, and after my resounding defeat, I heard from lawyers throughout the county that you can't expect to beat Judi in a custody trial."

"Well, if she beat you, she must be stupendous."

Quint smiled. "Thanks for your vote of confidence." He ran his hand along the length of her back. "Now, will you please get ready for our dinner date? I really am starving, Rachel."

She arched her brows provocatively. "Making mincemeat of the Tildens and Saxon Associates and terrorizing Laurel really gives you an appetite hmm?"

"I have a raving appetite for *you*, sweetheart, but consider yourself duly warned—unless I get some food to bolster my stamina, it's going to end up being a version of 'the spirit is willing but the flesh is weak' kind of thing."

Rachel considered herself duly warned. She hurried into her bedroom, pulled on a dress of clingy apricot silk and high-heeled sandals and was applying makeup when Quint came into the bathroom.

"You don't have to bother with that stuff. You look great without it."

"A starving man will say anything," Rachel said dryly. She took another few moments to brush her hair, then permitted him to hurry her outside to her car. Which he asked to drive.

"I've been wanting to get behind the wheel of this beauty," he confessed, eyeing her convertible appreciatively. "And to escape from the prosaic confines of the station wagon for just a little while. Anyway, we'll get there faster if I drive."

"Is that so?"

"Definitely. I rode with you before, honey, remember? Even on the way to a fire, you slow down and stop for yellow lights."

"And in the midst of a monsoon, you speed up and zoom right through them." But Rachel handed him her car keys and climbed in the passenger side while Quint took the wheel.

"Since you're so hungry, maybe we should stop at a supermarket along the way and buy you some raw meat to tide you over," she drawled as they sped toward Philadelphia, taking every yellow light.

"Think that's what it takes to satisfy my inner caveman's atavistic urges?"

"So you admit there is an inner caveman that dwells beneath that civilized exterior of yours?" Rachel grinned. "I figured as much."

"There is one that lurks within every male," Quint assured her. "Well, the Tildens might be the exception. Especially that insufferable little creep Tilly."

They crossed the Ben Franklin Bridge over the Delaware River into Pennsylvania and made it to Wainwright's, not quite ten minutes late for their reservation.

The atmosphere was that of an exclusive men's club, with dark red leather-upholstered booths, wainscotted walnut-paneled walls, and a coffered ceiling. The moldings were eight inches wide and three inches deep.

Rachel assessed her surroundings. "This reminds me of the Union League, the sort of place where robber barons congregated at the turn of the century and ran the country."

"An old-fashioned gentlemen's club where high-stakes

deals were made with a handshake," agreed Quint.

"Gentlemen's clubs do run the gamut," observed Rachel. "Compare this to a certain other kind of gentlemen's club called Fantasy's. Of course, the deals struck there probably aren't much like the ones made in places like this. And Fantasy's could never be called exclusive."

"Except in the worst possible interpretation of the word." Quint filled Rachel's glass with champagne from a bottle on ice in a bucket beside their table. "We passed Fantasy's on Admiral Wilson Boulevard on our way here."

"I noticed. Who could miss all those capital X's on the marquee—plus the promise of nude lap dancers. Do you suppose Misty serves as an inspiration to the girls currently working there? I wonder how many other aspiring millionaire widows are lap dancing at Fantasy's? If they all strike it rich like Misty, and she kindly recommends your legal services to them, you can be a—"

"Don't be a sore loser, Rachel. Town Senior, Misty, and I beat you and the others, fair and square."

"We'll have to agree to disagree on that." Rachel drained her glass, feeling a blaze of warmth spread through her muscles. A hazy mist began to slowly blanket her mind. "I should've eaten something first. This is going straight to my head."

She gave it a shake, as if to clear it but only succeeded in making the colors of the painting hanging on the wall in front of her—a detailed scene of a fox hunt—blur and whirl.

"Good." Quint smiled and refilled her glass. "That's my intention, of course. To get you drunk and have my wicked way with you."

Feeling daring, she kicked off her shoe and caressed his ankle with her toes. "You don't have to get me drunk to do that." She glided her foot under the hem of his trousers and teased his calf with her toes, delighting in the hot flare that darkened his eyes. "You didn't even have to spring for the expensive dinner."

"I could've had you for the price of a burrito at Taco Bell, huh?"

"You can have me anytime, anywhere." Her foot moved higher. "But you already know that."

It was the kind of remark her old self—the repressed and prim Rachel—never would have made. Or even thought of making. But falling in love with Quint, making love with him, had changed her in so many ways.

Quint took a long swallow from his own champagne glass. "Did I mention that I booked a room in the hotel tonight?" His hand was on her knee, sliding slowly under her skirt. "Brady is safely ensconced at home with Sarah, so all we have to do is take the elevator to the third floor after dinner."

Rachel shivered as a powerful surge of desire rocked her. She felt hot spirals of pleasure uncoil deep within her. If Quint hadn't made such a point of announcing his near-starvation status, she would've hauled him out of Wainwright's and into that elevator right then.

But the waiter arrived to recite the specials of the day, and Quint respectfully withdrew his hand from under her skirt to listen attentively.

Rachel smiled a secret smile. She would summon her patience and wait for dinner to be over. She and Quint had the whole night ahead of them.

18

Wade sat on the sofa in front of the TV set with Bob and Mary Jean Sheely, but he wasn't watching the hair-raising video footage of shark attacks on swimmers, The Discovery Channel's special presentation to kick off Sea Predators Week.

It was past ten o'clock and he didn't know where Dana was. Neither did her parents, who seemed spectacularly unconcerned whenever he brought up the subject. Which could only be during commercials because, unlike himself, Bob and Mary Jean were deeply engrossed in the shark program. When Wade interrupted with queries about Dana, they shushed him—as if he were Emily's age!—so he waited impatiently for the appropriate breaks.

"You said she always gets in early when she goes out with Vick Richer." Wade tried to make a joke of it. To seem casual and merry.

"Usually does," Bob affirmed. "Maybe they went somewhere else after dinner. To a movie or something."

"Shouldn't she have called to tell you?" Wade was no longer pretending to smile.

"Dana is twenty-six years old," Mary Jean reminded him. "And it's not even eleven o'clock."

The sharks came back on the screen, reclaiming the Sheelys' attention. Wade wandered out to the kitchen where Emily was fixing herself a snack, the phone attached to her ear. Surprisingly, she put it aside when she saw Wade.

"Shawn cut in on me a couple minutes ago." Emily was clearly irked by the intrusion. "He said to tell Mom and Dad that he's staying over at his friend Chad's house. He'll be by tomorrow. Would you tell Mom and Dad? I'm in the middle of an important call." She turned her back to Wade and resumed her phone conversation.

"Chad, huh?" Wade was fairly certain that Shawn was not staying with his friend Chad—if such a person actually existed. He envisioned Shawn at the cavernous Tilden mansion with Misty and stopped himself from imagining any further.

"I'm not passing along Shawn's alibi to your parents, Emily. Tell them yourself, if you want."

Emily made a shushing sound at him, just the way her parents had earlier. As far as Wade was concerned, it was the proverbial last straw. The one that broke the camel's back.

"I'm outta here," he announced to no one in particular, since Emily was whispering and giggling into the phone receiver, and Bob and Mary Jean sat, mesmerized by a California shark with a predilection for surfers in wet suits. Nobody else was around.

Wade got into his car—the one he loved and was so proud of—and wished it were something else entirely. Something less respectable, less establishment. He wanted something wild and dangerous to ride. Something rebellious. Like a vintage silver-and-black Harley-Davidson, the choice of tortured rebels in every film he'd ever seen that featured a tortured rebel.

He pictured himself tearing out onto the open highway— without a helmet so he could feel the wind against his head. Maybe it would blow away the torment festering in there.

He was furious, he wanted to rebel against everything, especially this intolerable, unbearable, completely miserable day. And who was to blame? Not Quint Cormack, even though the attorney seemed bent on single-handedly wrecking Saxon Associates. Not the Tildens, neither the supercilious Towns nor the dumb-like-a-fox Misty, not even snotty Sloane.

No, it was Dana Sheely, recently revealed to be the love of his life, who was responsible for casting him into this bleak hell. That was the worst part of all.

Wade reviewed the anguish he had suffered since the day began. Dana, avoiding his calls, as if he were a pest she was determined to avoid. Dana, choosing to spend the evening—all of it!—with that boring stiff Rich Vicker instead of with him.

How could she treat him this way, especially after last night? She had to know how he felt about her, that he was in love with her.

He drew in a sharp breath. Suppose that was the problem . . . Dana knew that he loved her but didn't reciprocate his feelings? Maybe she'd just wanted sex, not true love. But he wanted both. With her. He wanted to share his whole life with her, to marry her and have kids.

He'd officially belong with the Sheelys then. The image warmed him. It all seemed destined, from the moment he'd struck up his friendship with Tim all those years ago, to lead up to him loving Dana. To marrying her and joining the Sheely tribe.

A ghastly thought shattered his blissful vision. Suppose Dana didn't want that? She knew him well—maybe *too* well. He'd been bluntly, totally himself with her; she knew his faults better than anyone. Could he really blame her if she'd thought it over and decided, "*Wade Saxon? No thanks!*"

Wade felt a sudden visceral pain, as if his insides had been gripped in a vise and were now being twisted. He'd never experienced anything like it, emotional pain so sharp it was actually tangible.

Suddenly, those soggy romantic terms—heartache, heartbreak—made sense because his chest was actually hurting. Like his heart was aching or breaking inside. God, it was like living one of those country-western songs he'd always mocked because he just couldn't identify with the heartfelt lyrics. He felt them now.

Worse, he'd known the Sheelys long enough to realize that Dana's quandary would be a family affair, at least among the siblings. He pictured her, appalled by his love and his neediness, wondering what she should do, lamenting the loss of their friendship which they'd ruined by having sex. He could easily imagine the conversations as the Sheelys burned the telephone wires with this latest crisis.

Forget Shawn and Misty Tilden, that was yesterday's news. Today's story was Dana's dilemma and how to gently, kindly explain to that chump Wade Saxon that she didn't want him. That going to bed with him had been a huge mistake which she deeply regretted.

Wade could almost hear the individual Sheely responses. Tim would be ticked off that his friend had slept with his sister and have little sympathy for Wade's plight. Empathetic Mary Jo would suggest dealing kindly with poor Wade; the less merciful Tricia would advise taking the brutally frank "get lost, jerk" approach.

The more detailed his thoughts became, the worse he felt. Wade knew he couldn't go home to his apartment where loneliness and pain, combined with those bittersweet memories of making love to Dana last night, would constitute sheer torture.

Since he was feeling bad, he decided to do something bad. Something wild and stupid and out of character. He kept driving, while trying to think of something suitable— or unsuitable, as the case may be. And found himself on the portion of 70 that cut through Oak Shade.

This wasn't his usual route, and that alone seemed like the good—bad?—omen he needed. A number of dilapidated bars lined both sides of the highway but they all looked like shot-and-a-beer-type places where a television was perpetually tuned to some sports event, pinball machines were always in use, and threats, profanity, and fights were regular occurrences.

None of the places captured Wade's interest. None was bad enough, wild enough ... and then he saw it. A place called the Doll House. Which billed itself as a gentlemen's club, although no gentleman of taste and class would ever set foot in that place, except maybe on a dare or bet.

The Doll House boasted live entertainment. Dancing girls. It looked as sleazy as any of those places along Admiral Wilson Boulevard but its Oak Shade location spared patrons the longer trip into Camden. A humongous black Range Rover—an expensive import, didn't Pedersen sell those?—was in the litter-strewn parking lot along with a few rusting pickup trucks and other assorted crumbling vehicles. Everything about the place screamed seedy and downtrodden.

Wade decided it was perfect.

He looped around and pulled into the parking lot, next to the Range Rover, which looked brand-new. The sight of the two expensive vehicles almost brought a smile to his face. They both looked ridiculously out of place here.

Pushing open the door to the Doll House, he was greeted by a blast of music, the eighties tune "Centerfold." An obvious choice, perhaps, but Wade wasn't looking for subtlety.

He squinted his eyes, trying to adjust to the smoky darkness. Three girls, nude except for their truly string-width, flesh-colored G-strings, were dancing on top of the U-shaped bar in eye-poppingly high heels. Two of the girls swung around poles strategically arranged on either side of the U. They straddled the poles, rubbing up and down, their gyrations too crude to be erotic.

Instead of being aroused—supposedly the point of such a place?—Wade felt abruptly, utterly depressed. His earlier anger was gone, and he tried to summon it back because fury was better than this awful seeping depression that made him want to crawl out to his car and—

"Hey, Wade!" The sound of his name stunned him. Never in a million years would he have expected to run into someone he knew *here!*

"Yo, Saxon! Over here!"

At first Wade, stupefied by the sight of Shawn Sheely waving at him from one of the tables beyond the bar, was unable to make any response at all. He simply stood stock still, his arms at his sides, his jaw agape.

And then he noticed that Shawn wasn't alone at the table. Misty Tilden, wearing a strapless sundress that more than showcased her ultra-enlarged breasts, sat beside Shawn. Her platinum hair seemed as incandescently bright as a lightbulb.

At the same table sat a tubby, greasy man who might as well have been wearing a badge proclaiming "I am a sleazebag." Because he was clearly that and probably worse.

Wade gradually began to recover from the shock of seeing his surrogate kid brother in such squalid surroundings— with the town's most notorious widow. Years of loyalty to the Sheelys produced a sense of obligation and propelled him forward when Shawn waved at him again.

Wade stumbled through the noisy darkness, his eyes burning from the thick acrid clouds of smoke.

He debated on what course of action he should take. Sarah had mentioned that Shawn seemed obsessed with the Widow Tilden. Could an obsession be treated like a brain-washing? If so, perhaps he could lure Shawn into his car and kidnap him while the Sheelys hired a deprogrammer.

He'd already discarded that plan by the time he reached the table. Where would the Sheelys find a deprogrammer at this time of night? Or at any other time. It wasn't as if they were listed in the Yellow Pages. And how could he drive and kidnap Shawn at the same time? He did not make it a practice to keep restraining gear in his car.

"Eddie Aiken." The sleazoid leaped to his feet and offered Wade a sweaty hand to shake. "Any friend of Misty and Shawn is welcome here. Name your poison and Tiffany will bring it to you."

Wade was tempted to request strychnine. It was turning into that kind of a night. "A beer, whatever's on tap," he said instead.

"We're not exactly friends," Misty corrected as Wade took the fourth chair at the table. "You probably hate me like the other Saxons do."

"Wade doesn't hate you, sweetness. And he's not like the other Saxons, and not like the Tildens, either. Wade is cool!" Shawn proclaimed.

Wade was torn between laughing and gagging. But he kept his face poker-straight, not wanting to alienate Shawn. He knew a thing or two about psychological strategy despite his aversion to psychobabble.

"Thank you." Wade attempted what he hoped was a friendly smile. "But what I think is really cool is that Range Rover out in the parking lot. I understand those things can cover any terrain, too bad so much of South Jersey is paved. Is it yours, Mrs. Tilden?"

Misty nodded. "I bought it today from Mr. Pedersen. What a nice man!" she cooed. "Such a gentleman!"

"Misty wanted something to drive herself," Shawn explained. "She gets tired of always being chauffeured around in the limo."

"Perfectly understandable. By the way, congratulations on winning the War of the Will today," Wade said to Misty. "I'm sure Quint Cormack told you how the Tildens and their lawyers folded. Of course, we're their ex-lawyers now."

"Bummer for you, Sax," Shawn sympathized. Then he turned to Misty and smiled boyishly. "But it was great news for Misty. Now she won't have to go through any court-hassle stuff."

"Quint said we won it all." Misty beamed. "Shawnie and I are celebrating."

"Why here?" Wade asked. He couldn't help himself. "I mean, all that money and that great big house and everything else and you come *here?*"

"We went to Planet Hollywood in Atlantic City last night," said Misty, as if that explained it all.

"Who wouldn't want to celebrate here?" demanded Eddie Aiken. "This is a first class lounge. I got a great bartender, and just look at those girls!'' With a sweep of his arm, he indicated the bored-looking young women gyrating on top of the bar, as if on autopilot.

"I think it'll be more interesting when we replace the girls with men." Misty sipped the frozen pastel concoction in front of her. "That's my plan, to open a place for women to go where they can ogle dancing guys."

"Misty knows all kinds of stuff about what makes a dance club hot. A place of hers could be as big as Club Koncrete!" Shawn exclaimed, brimming with enthusiasm.

"Club Koncrete," echoed Wade. "An unparalleled experience."

"All you have to do is meet my asking price, and the Doll House is yours, lovely lady." Aiken tried to sound suave.

Wade stared from one to the other, his eyes finally fixing on Misty. "You want to buy this place from him and open a strip club featuring men?"

Misty nodded. "I've always wanted to run my own business, and I like the idea of a club for women. There are sure enough clubs for *gentlemen,* right? I got lots of ideas, too, like dressing the waitresses real classy and serving all kinds of fancy drinks while the boy toys slither around those poles in tiny little G-strings. It'll be a real Grrrls Night Out kind of place."

"I'll bet." Wade was beginning to enjoy himself, for the first time all day. "In fact, I like that name better than the Doll House. Grrrls Night Out. It has attitude, it says it all."

"I'm going to have my own business, too." Shawn's Sheely-blue eyes glowed. "Misty is going to loan me the money to set up my own greenhouse and lawn and landscaping business. The banks didn't want to give me a loan," he added banefully.

"Gee, I wonder why not?" mocked Aiken.

"I wanted to *give* Shawnie the money, but he insisted on a loan," said Misty.

"Interest-free?" probed Wade.

Misty and Shawn looked at each other, and Wade knew

they hadn't discussed the going interest rate on loans these days. Did they even know what interest was?

"Interest-free," the two chorused together, heads bobbing in unison.

"What do you think of Shawn's Garden Shop and Lawn Service as a name for my business, Sax?" Shawn wanted to know.

"Catchy. I can already see it painted on the outside of a fleet of vans. Have you discussed your plans with Quint yet, Mrs. Tilden?" Wade asked politely.

"Call me Misty," she invited. "No, I haven't told Quint. I'm sure he'll be excited for us."

"Oh, yes, he ought to be." Wade was gleeful.

Wait'll Cormack hears what they are planning! He could only imagine how the executor of the Tilden estate would react to the news of *two* such high-risk-prone ventures, given the extremely high percentage of failure for new small businesses. And neither Misty nor Shawn struck him as entrepreneurially gifted. Both would need to be, or their projects would eat up Tilden capital without providing any return.

"And the funny thing is, Quint Cormack is my lawyer, too," Aiken inserted himself into the conversation. "So the sale will be all in the family, kind of."

"That is a funny thing." Wade grinned broadly.

He wanted to laugh out loud. Cormack was stuck squarely in the middle of this mess! How could he talk two of his clients out of this insane sale if they both demanded it?

Wade lifted his mug of watered-down beer. "I'd like to propose a toast—to the future Grrrls Night Out and Shawn's Garden Shop and Lawn Service."

The others lifted their glasses containing their own particular drinks.

"Hear, hear," Aiken seconded the toast.

The four glasses clinked together.

"See, sweetness, I told you Wade was cool," Shawn said happily, squeezing Misty's hand.

* * *

Dana arrived home in the middle of the eleven o'clock broadcast of Action News.

"Of all the nights for you to stay out late with Rich Vicker, why did it have to be tonight?" her mother greeted her with a maternal lament. "Wade was waiting here since dinner for you. He finally left a little while ago, and he didn't look happy."

"Why would he wait for me?" Dana asked cautiously.

"Oh, honey, you don't have to pretend anymore. Wade isn't." Mary Jean crossed the room to give Dana a hug. "We know how you two feel about each other."

"Mom's been sniffing glue again." Dana attempted a feeble joke. What had Wade said to her parents? Or had they become delusional with no assistance from him?

"So how's the Library?" Bob Sheely tactfully steered the conversation in another direction.

"You could read *War and Peace* there while you're waiting for the food." Dana sighed. "That's why I'm so late. The service was beyond terrible. Each course took forever to arrive. Rich was displeased but not enough to pass on dessert, so that added an additional forty-five minutes. Then he took a wrong turn driving me home and ended up going south on 70 instead of north."

Frowning, she sat down on the sofa. "We ended up in Oak Shade and I saw the strangest thing."

"Don't go anywhere near those bars in Oak Shade," her mother warned. "Too many drunk drivers on the road out there, it's getting out of hand. Just the other day I heard Oak Shade worked out an agreement with the Lakeview Police Department to help patrol the area. Chief Spagna's heading the joint unit."

"Things will definitely improve with Nick Spagna in charge. The chief knows how to motivate young cops and how to intimidate drunken idiots," Bob Sheely said admiringly.

"Speaking of the chief, I saw him at the Library tonight with Eve Saxon, of all people. They must've passed on dessert because they left way before Rich and me."

Dana didn't add that she was certain the couple intended to have a different sort of dessert, not offered within the confines of the Library despite the private booths. The chief and the lawyer had been holding hands as they left the restaurant, Eve looking positively dreamy-eyed, Spagna appearing a little less menacing than usual.

"Nick would be good for Eve," Mary Jean decided, nodding her approval. "And vice versa. He is strong enough to stand up to her but can accept her own strength."

"Didn't you say the same thing about Erica and Dimitri on *All My Children?*" teased Dana.

"The weather's on," her father announced, bringing an end to the conversation. Both her parents quickly turned to watch the weather forecast.

Dana started to go upstairs to her room and ended up outside on the front porch. She hadn't told her parents what the strangest thing she'd seen in Oak Shade happened to be, but she couldn't put it from her mind.

While lost on Route 70, Rich had driven past a cheesy dive called the Doll House, and she'd seen a dark green Mercedes in the parking lot outside. It looked enough like Wade's car to actually be his car, but Wade would never venture into a dump like that.

Parked next to the Mercedes was a big black Range Rover like the one in Pedersen's Car Shoppe window. Rich had seen the cars, too, and remarked on the folly of parking such valuable vehicles in front of such a low-scale place. He quoted the statistical odds of car theft in relation to car models and locations.

A short while later, after Rich had turned around to head in the right direction, they passed the Doll House again. This time Dana saw the first three letters SAX of Wade's vanity plates on the green Mercedes. *It was Wade's car!* Stolen? That seemed more likely than Wade as a Doll House patron.

"It's supposed to be warm and sunny tomorrow," her

mother reported, standing in the doorway. "Are you coming inside, dear?"

"I think I'll sit out here and wait for Shawn," said Dana.

To keep her mind off Wade, she might as well concentrate on her brother. She decided to try a different approach with Shawn tonight. To be friendly and accessible instead of furious and condemning. Last night she and her sisters had deepened Shawn's loyalty toward Misty by forcing him to defend her while they attacked her. Just what Tim's Lisa had predicted would happen.

"Shawn is staying over at Chad's tonight. Dad and I are heading to bed now. Good night, hon."

" 'Night Mom." Dana sounded calm but she was not.

Shawn was not at his pal Chad's tonight; she would wager a whole year's salary on that, and she wasn't a gambling woman. He was with Misty Tilden and suddenly various images fit together like pieces of a jigsaw puzzle to clearly reveal the entire picture.

Wade actually was at the Doll House, and now Dana knew why—because Shawn and Misty Tilden were there. That black Range Rover parked next to Wade's car had to belong to Misty; she must have bought it right out of Pedersen's showroom window.

At the office today, Quint had mentioned that his star client was going to Pedersen's Car Shoppe to buy herself a set of wheels. Helen had speculated Misty would insist on a bubblegum pink Ferarri. "Something like Barbie drives," she'd added, uncharacteristically snide.

But if Misty had taken Shawn along on the car-shopping trip, he would direct her toward something like the Range Rover, because it was big and dark and hulking like the military vehicles he admired.

That Misty Tilden would go to the Doll House seemed unremarkable to Dana. A place like that probably felt like home to the former nude lap dancer. And somehow Wade had learned Shawn and Misty were there and gone to take his turn talking some sense into the younger Sheely brother.

Dana knew that no matter how Wade Saxon might currently feel toward her, he cared deeply for her family. He would do anything for her parents, for Tim. He'd want to help Shawn. So he had gone to the Doll House to try.

She didn't think any further than that. Acting on sheer impulse, she went back inside to grab her purse and car keys and drove straight to the Doll House.

When she pulled into the lot, the Mercedes and the Range Rover were still parked side by side, their undisturbed presence a challenge to Rich Vicker's car-theft statistics.

Her courage faltered when she reached the Doll House door. Now that she was here, she wasn't sure what she was going to say to either Wade or Shawn. Nor was she eager for any kind of a face-to-face confrontation with Misty, with whom she'd always dealt politely in Quint's office.

She could hear the music from within, a blaringly loud rendition of En Vogue's "Never Gonna Get It." Dana tried to tell herself it wasn't prophetic, but she couldn't shake the feeling that coming here had been an excruciatingly bad idea.

She stood there, paralyzed by indecision, unable to make herself enter the Doll House but unwilling to give up and go back home.

Later, Dana wondered how long she would have remained there and what she eventually would have done, if the decision hadn't been made for her by the arrival of an Oak Shade police car. Its siren was silenced, but the blue-and-red lights on top flashed ominously.

Though the urge to dash to her car and peel out of the lot was powerful, Dana didn't cede to it. The officers had already seen her. Better to take the initiative and approach them first.

She walked toward them as they advanced to the door, their guns drawn.

"My little brother is in there," she told the taller, meaner-looking one of the pair. The courage she'd failed to summon earlier was suddenly there. Or perhaps talking to policemen, even stern-faced ones, was preferable to entering a pit like the Doll House.

"I've been standing here, trying to work up the nerve to go in and get him but I couldn't do it," Dana forged ahead bravely.

"Is the kid underage?" the cop asked grimly.

Dana shook her head. "But he's a very impressionable twenty-three. He told our folks he's staying with a friend tonight, but not the one he's really with. And I'm sure he's in there with her."

"You're right to be concerned about your brother if he is in there," said the other officer. "This place isn't supposed to be open. Judge Jackson ordered it closed, but Sweaty Eddie doesn't like to obey court orders."

"Are you going to raid it?" Dana asked, wide-eyed. "Oh, please, let me take my brother home first."

"I'm sorry, we can't do that, miss," said the tall cop. "We're here to close down this place and we're taking everybody inside to the station."

"And arrest them?" Dana was horrified. *Shawn and Wade arrested!* "Are they going to be put in jail?"

"Sweaty Eddie, sure. And maybe the dancing girls because we heard they dance topless or less, and that's a zone violation. The others—depending on how it goes—maybe we'll just put a scare into them," confided the younger, shorter, more friendly cop. He seemed to be trying to reassure her.

Dana knew enough about the law to surmise they had no grounds to arrest the patrons of an illegally open bar. But she wasn't positive, and even if no charges were ever filed, getting hauled to the Oak Shade Police Station where a "scare" was to be deliberately induced struck her as bad enough.

"If people keep coming to this place, Aiken will keep defying the orders to close it," continued Officer Friendly. "As long as this place makes money, it's cheaper for him to stay open and pay the fines."

And his lawyer's bills, Dana thought but didn't say.

"But if the customers are taken to the police station and held there a while, even if no charges are brought against them, they just might decide it's not worth it to come back to this dump." She nodded her comprehension of the strategy, trying to stall the raid, although she knew it was hopeless.

"You come on down to the Oak Shade Police Station in a couple or three hours and possibly, we'll release your brother to you," the meaner-looking cop said. "Now take yourself out of here. This is no place for a nice kid like you."

Dana decided maybe he wasn't so mean, after all. She headed slowly to her car. She felt like a traitor, abandoning both Wade and Shawn without even sounding a warning. But already a plan was beginning to formulate, a plan requiring that she remain free to summon help.

Eve Saxon wouldn't want her beloved nephew to undergo a scare at the Oak Shade jail, would she? And as long as Eve was springing Wade, she might be talked into getting Shawn out, too. Misty, Dana decided, was on her own.

Dana pulled out onto Route 70 as the officers entered the Doll House. There was a convenience store just down the highway, where she could place a call to Eve. She wondered if Chief Spagna would be there, and a nervous shiver rippled through her. The chief didn't seem as if he suffered lawbreakers gladly, and if he and Eve were—*busy*—he would resent the interruption even more. Not that Wade or Shawn were lawbreakers but even so . . .

Dana pulled into the convenience store and headed straight for the phone booth before she could talk herself out of placing the call for help.

19

Rachel's eyelids kept fluttering shut. She would force them open, though each time required greater effort. She was lying with Quint, spoon-fashion, his arms around her, her bottom tucked into the cradle of his thighs in a king-size bed in their Philadelphia hotel room.

They'd just spent the past hour and a half experiencing the most profound and primal pleasure, and she wanted to savor this fantasic glowing aftermath. But her own body was fighting to lapse into an exhausted, sated sleep.

"Just let yourself go to sleep, Rachel." Quint had been observing her struggle to stay awake. He kissed the top of her head lovingly, indulgently.

"I don't want to go to sleep. Because when I wake up, it'll be morning and time to check out of here. We'll be back to dealing with the Tildens and Saxon Associates, back to Cormack and Son, and Laurel and Carla."

She much preferred this private fantasy they were living, the two of them naked and alone in their own sensual world.

"And Brady?" Quint asked carefully. There was a sudden air of alert edginess about him.

Rachel sat up. "I'm sorry you have to ask, Quint. But since you did—No, I don't consider Brady an intrusion or an obstacle."

"Sure he is." Quint chuckled, relaxing once again. "But at least he's a small one. The others are full-grown."

"I want to be with Brady, but I freely admit that I could use a vacation from the others."

"Same here." He pulled her back down to him. "There's no chance of that vacation anytime soon, but we can both be with Brady tomorrow. It's Sarah's night off. Come over after work, and the three of us will have dinner together. We can go to—"

"Why don't I cook dinner at your place?" Rachel suggested. "Brady seems to eat out a lot for a child his age. Maybe staying home for dinner will be a welcome change of pace for him."

"It'll be a welcome change of pace for me," stated Quint, kissing her lingeringly. "It's a deal. I'll grill us something but if you make macaroni and cheese, especially the kind from the box, Brady will be ecstatic. Mommy."

Rachel lay his arms, facing him. The room was dark but a shaft of moonlight shone through the gap in the curtains, providing some illumination. She traced her fingertips over the features of his face.

"I should have corrected him the first time he called me Mommy, but I liked hearing him say it too much," she confessed softly.

"I wish you really were his mother. Maybe if I had come to Lakeview a few years earlier and met you then, you would've been." Quint allowed himself a revisionist fantasy, a practice he rarely indulged. His arms tightened around her.

Rachel thought of little Brady and how much she wished things had happened that way. But that meant obliterating the existence of the woman who really had given birth to Quint's son and taken care of him for nearly a year before turning him over to his father. Had she meant her exit to be permanent? And if not, then what?

"When Sharolyn comes back and asks to see Brady—" she began.

"*If* she comes back and *if* she asks to see him," corrected Quint. "Both are unlikely."

"Are you really going to keep Sharolyn from ever contacting Brady or were you just saying that to shake up Laurel?'' Rachel felt Quint tense, and she snuggled closer, to soothe him. ''We can't just pretend she doesn't exist, Quint. It wouldn't be fair to Brady in the long run.''

''It isn't fair to Brady that she does exist, and that I was stupid enough to hook up with her in the first place,'' Quint growled.

''Which is something of a paradox,'' Rachel felt obliged to point out. ''If you'd never hooked up with Sharolyn, you wouldn't have Brady. Do you intend to keep her away from him forever, Quint? Can you, if she should want to see him?''

''God, Rachel, don't play devil's advocate now! The last thing I feel like doing is debating custody issues.''

''I don't want to debate either.'' She trailed her forefinger down his chest. ''But you know how lawyers are, we can't quit arguing till we've gotten in at least one token point.''

Quint groaned. ''Okay, get it over with.''

''It's just that Brady isn't always going to be a little boy. What happens when he becomes a teenager and—''

''I see where you're going with this,'' Quint cut in. ''Believe me, if anybody knows that little kids will tolerate parental mistakes a lot better than adolescents, it's me.''

''You were the epitome of the angry teen, hmm?'' Rachel brushed her lips across his throat. ''Who can blame you with Frank Cormack for a father?''

She drew back a little and met his eyes. ''I want to know everything about you and your life, but I don't want to aggravate you with a barrage of questions.''

''You've got me pegged, sweetie. A barrage of questions would definitely aggravate me.'' He took her hand and kissed her palm, teasing it with the tip of his tongue. ''But I might make an exception for you.''

''Thanks, *sweetie*.''

They smiled at each other.

''It doesn't sound quite so offensively sexist when you say it here,'' Rachel admitted.

"So you'll grant me permission to call you 'sweetie' in bed?"

"Permission granted."

"I'm deeply grateful," he said dryly. "And ready for question number one."

"It's funny but with some people, you don't even have to ask a single question, they pour out their entire past the first hour you spend with them." Rachel cuddled closer, thinking back on years of dating, listening to one life story after another. Feeling safe from that now. "But not you. I don't even know your sister's name or where she and your mother live."

Quint was quiet for so long, Rachel wondered if he'd fallen asleep. She hoped not, because she was wide-awake now and eager to talk.

"Quint?" she prompted in a low whisper, not wanting to wake him if he really was sleeping.

"The way you phrased it," Quint murmured his response. "So easily, so normal. I was thinking how much I've missed that, in reference to Mom and Colette."

An uneasy Rachel tried to remember exactly what she'd said. Something about where his mother and sister lived . . . Her heart caught in her throat and her eyes flew to his face. She knew it before he said it.

"My mother and Colette, my sister, don't live anywhere. They're both dead, Rachel."

"Oh God Quint, I'm so sorry." She hugged him hard. "What happened? And when?"

"They were in a freeway accident near Santa Monica five years ago. Colette's husband Daniel was driving, Colette was in the passenger seat and Mom in the back. A tractor-trailer rear-ended their car and threw it across four lanes of traffic. All three were killed, along with another driver and two passengers in other cars. The highway patrolman told me it was one of the worst accidents he'd ever seen."

"I don't know what to say except I'm so sorry, again." Rachel clung to him, as if to warm him with her own body heat for his voice and his words were chilling. "It must have been terrible, losing your whole family."

"That's exactly what happened. In one instant, my whole family was gone. Mom and Colette and Daniel, too. Colette was five months pregnant with their first baby." Quint felt Rachel draw a sharp, shocked breath, and her reaction pleased him in a perverse way. He liked people to be horrified and shocked by the scope of the tragedy; his family deserved nothing less.

"Oh, Quint," she murmured sadly. There were no words.

"I wasn't one of those people who are ennobled by loss. I'd been self-centered before, commitment-phobic but not owning up to it, running through women and relationships, deliberately charming and deceptive. You know the type." Quint grimaced wryly.

"Very well. But you don't fit that profile, Quint."

"I used to, and after the accident I was even worse. It wasn't until Sharolyn turned up at my office demanding money for an abortion when it finally hit me. Despite my mother's valiant attempts to raise me to be the right kind of man—like her older brother, my uncle Joe—I was no better than Frank Cormack, whom I'd despised all those years."

He sat up against the pillows, and she moved up, too, staying close, her arms around him.

"Once I got over the initial shock, it dawned on me that Sharolyn's *problem* was my child. I thought of Colette's baby that never had the chance to be born. I convinced Sharolyn to marry me and go through with the pregnancy. To do otherwise meant losing another member of my family, and I couldn't take that."

Quint smiled mirthlessly. "When I finally got around to calling my father to tell him I was married and going to be a father, he told me I was an idiot. I tried to explain the baby's connection to my mother and Colette, but he just didn't get it."

"Was Frank always so—" Rachel paused. There were

too many pejorative words to choose from. "So—"

"Yeah, always." Quint already knew them. "He walked out on my mother when I was four and Colette was two. We lived near Trenton then, and for the next eight years, he went through women and marriages and stumbled in and out of our lives. As a little kid, I was always thrilled when he remembered Colette and I existed. I enjoyed every minute of those visits with him. He was extravagant and fun, and he didn't act like any other adult we knew. He was almost a fantasy figure."

"More like a phantasm. But a child wouldn't be able to understand the difference."

"True. For every time Frank took us out, there were ten times he didn't show up when we were expecting him to. Finally my mother decided to take her older brother Joe up on his offer to help her move to California and put some distance between us and Frank. We left Jersey when I was twelve and Colette was ten and moved into the same town as Uncle Joe. He was a cop, a good one. A good man with the patience of a saint. He needed it because a year later I became one of those furious adolescents, acting out all the rage I'd swallowed when I was a kid trying to make excuses for Frank Cormack."

"But you managed to be a high achiever at the same time," Rachel said thoughtfully. "Stanford Law School, Law Review. You certainly beat your father at his own game professionally."

"I know. I guess I intended to. I wanted to be different from him and at least professionally, I was. I took pride in that difference until my marriage to Sharolyn ended up being even shorter than any of Frank's. That shocked me into facing some very unpleasant truths. I seemed to be following in the footsteps of the man I professed to loathe. Was I going to keep on marrying and having kids, over and over again?"

"How many times has your father been married?" Rachel was curious. "Does he have other children besides Austin and Dustin?"

"Frank's second marriage, three years after he divorced my mother produced twin boys and lasted nearly two years. I remember them as infants, they were identical with dark hair and dark eyes. They looked a lot like their mother Julie."

"Where are they now?"

"I don't know. When Frank and Julie divorced, the twins were a year old and she moved to Miami. Not long after, she met and married the son of Cuban refugees who owned a chain of appliance stores and were quite successful. Julie called my mother and told her that Frank had relinquished parental rights to the twins and that her new husband was going to adopt them. She'd decided never to tell the twins the truth about Frank, that everybody in the new family agreed it was best for the babies to believe they were their stepfather's real sons. Julie asked my mother to tell Colette and me never to contact the twins; we were part of their past which she intended to erase. Mom agreed to Julie's wishes and didn't maintain contact with them. I have no idea who or what or where the twins are today."

"It seems like a bad idea, trying to reinvent the past like that." Rachel frowned. "Imagine what a shock it would be for the twins to find out the truth after years of believing something else. There are books written about that trauma, talk shows devoted to it."

"I know. I've warned myself not to be surprised if someday they turn up on my doorstep, furious that they're not Cuban, and demanding to know all about the jerk who actually fathered them. For their sake, I hope the truth never comes out."

"Who was the next Mrs. Cormack?"

"Someone named Madeline. A real bitch. Even as a kid, I could tell. I'd liked Julie but I detested Madeline. She and Frank had a daughter Zara that Colette and I only saw twice as a baby because we moved to California not long after she was born. Frank visited us a few years later and said Madeline was long gone, that she'd moved to Texas with Zara. He didn't know where she was and didn't care, he was just glad he was out of the reach of child support."

"Back then, he was."

"Yeah, those federal laws made to mandate child support payments across state lines are the antidote for the Frank Cormacks of the world. Sometimes I think that's why he's stayed with Carla this long, because he knows he'd still have to pay for the kids, that he could be tracked down and his wages garnisheed. Maybe Frank's finally grasped the concept that he can't financially maintain multiple households."

"That, and the fact he's getting older and it would be harder to attract women," suggested Rachel.

"Age won't stop Frank. He still sees himself as irresistible, a prime specimen of manhood. Truth is, he never was, not with that raging personality disorder of his—which keeps getting worse."

"Poor Carla." It wasn't the first time Rachel had thought or said it. She knew it wouldn't be the last. "More than ever I admire your commitment to come to Lakeview after your father's accident, Quint. To help Carla with Austin and Dustin."

"I had a long talk with my uncle Joe after I got the news of Frank's accident. I thought about the way Joe had stuck by me, even when I was a hellion teen and a total embarrassment to him. He was always there for me, and I knew it. That's probably why I didn't completely screw up, why I did make it through college and law school. I saw a chance to repay Uncle Joe, to do for somebody else what he'd done for me."

"And by then, you were a father yourself. You were able to see Brady in Austin and Dustin, and you just had to help them."

"Stop, I don't recognize this paragon you've created," drawled Quint.

"A paragon *you've* created," she amended warmly. "Quint, you mentioned the possibility of the twins arriving, wanting to know about their background. Do you ever wonder if your half sister Zara will show up on your doorstep someday?''

"Hell, I'm half expecting her to."

Rachel's lips curved into a dry smile. "Let's just hope it's not the same day that the twins arrive. Your house isn't big enough to accommodate everybody."

They both laughed.

"So now you know the truth about the Cormacks, something of a white-trash saga. Nobody would blame you if you ran out of here screaming, Miss Saxon. Why would a high-class lady like you want to fraternize with the likes of me?"

"Your mother wasn't white trash and neither was Colette. You aren't, and neither is Brady or Austin or Dustin." Rachel gazed at him, her face radiant with warmth and pride and love. "I love you, Quint. I'm not going to leave you unless—" she gulped. "Unless you tell me to go."

"Never."

She liked the sound of that. Resolute and resolved. Without a trace of commitment phobia. "That's it, then." She strove for the same finality. "We're together."

He looked down into her shining hazel eyes and gently brushed a lock of tousled hair from her face before touching his lips to hers. "Just like that? No cautionary lectures that we're moving too fast?"

"Are we moving too fast, Quint?" A faint smile played at the corners of her mouth. "Do *you* want to run out of here screaming?"

"Not a chance, baby." His lips quirked into an answering smile. "I love you, Rachel."

Rachel reached up to touch his face, caressing his cheek with her fingertips. She'd wanted those words, needed them. And Quint had given them to her.

"This is almost too easy." She fairly sighed it.

"Easy? Are you kidding?" Quint gave an incredulous laugh. "Rachel, you've hated my guts for the past year. I would say that definitely qualifies as an obstacle on the road to true love."

"But we didn't know we were traveling on that particular road until very recently, did we?" Her eyes gleamed as she ran her hands over the breadth of his shoulders, his chest, and then down to his flat stomach.

"I guess not." Quint's breath caught. "Now we do and—" His mind splintered as Rachel's hand found him. Extending the already overextended metaphor wasn't possible. His gift for extemporaneous speech was overcome by a rush of sensual pleasure, so intense it bordered on pain.

He had to be inside her, a part of her.

His wild need matched her own. Rachel carefully guided him into her, with the expertise of a woman well versed in pleasing her lover. She could hardly remember the not-too-long-ago days when she'd been so inexperienced she hadn't even realized she was missing anything by not having Quint in her life. Or deep inside her body, just the way he was right now.

Dana sat in her car outside the Oak Shade Police Station, trying to interest herself in the magazine she'd purchased at the convenience store where she had placed her call for help to Eve Saxon. That had been well over an hour ago. She'd driven directly to the station and parked discreetly along the side of the building.

She had been here when the police car arrived, and the two officers she'd met at the Doll House emerged from it. A few minutes later a police van pulled up, and a steady stream of suspects filed out.

Dana flinched when she saw Wade and Shawn troop from the van, up the stairs and into the station, under the policemen's watchful eyes. Misty Tilden was there, too, clinging to Shawn. Clearly, this was the group from the Doll House raid and—with the exception of Wade and Shawn who looked startlingly clean-cut and out of place—a misbegotten group it was.

She felt her pulse rate soar. Even that very brief glimpse of Wade had a potent physical effect upon her. It was the first time she'd seen him today, and for a few moments

Dana let herself feel how very much she'd missed him. And how much she missed their former easy camaraderie.

Normally, he would have called her a number of times today to keep her updated on the latest Saxon-Cormack clash, to protest the outcome of the Tilden will. She'd have commiserated with him, too, though his loss was her boss's gain. Being on opposite sides of the legal fence didn't affect their relationship; they'd sailed through the Pedersen trial without a hitch.

SEX CHANGES EVERYTHING. Dana stared at the words printed in bold block letters on the magazine cover. In smaller, lighter type readers were advised to READ THIS BEFORE CROSSING THAT LINE FROM PLATONIC TO SEXUAL. She tossed the magazine into the backseat, too disheartened to attempt the article. Crossing that line seemed to have turned her and Wade into adversaries, and she didn't want to see it confirmed in print that their relationship was irredeemable.

She shifted restlessly. Still no sign of Eve, who hadn't sounded very happy to hear about her nephew's unfortunate plight. Still, she had agreed to come to the police station, and Dana was sure that she would.

Now she was beginning to have her doubts. Maybe Eve had just said that to get rid of her. Maybe she'd taken her phone off the hook immediately afterward and enjoyed a good laugh with her police-chief companion about how easily she'd blown off the naively trusting Dana Sheely.

Dana glanced at her watch. Eve Saxon's house was less than fifteen minutes away. She'd had plenty of time to get dressed and drive to the station, regardless of what she had been in the midst of doing at the time of the call.

Dana had no doubts as to what Eve was in the midst of doing—and with whom. There had been a telltale huskiness in the other woman's voice during their call, and she'd heard a man murmuring in the background. Chief Spagna, of course. Dana thought about the torrid looks the pair had exchanged during their walk through the Library.

It occurred to her that maybe the chief had talked Eve out of coming. A distinct possibility.

Dana glanced at her watch. If Eve didn't show up within the next ten minutes, she was calling Sarah at Quint Cormack's house. Their boss would hate being summoned to Oak Shade at this hour, but he would come once he learned Misty was involved. Quint would not allow his richest client to be detained and scared as an object lesson. And as long as he was down here, he could help free Shawn and Wade.

She had no sooner decided on her alternate plan when Eve Saxon's always recognizable Porsche glided to a stop in front of the police station. Dana was not at all surprised to see Chief Spagna get out on the driver's side to open the other door and gallantly assist Eve from the car.

The attorney wore an amber silk shirt and pants designed to flow loosely and sensuously over the gentle curves of her body. It was the kind of outfit that could be dressed up or down, except Eve Saxon never dressed down. Even now, in what she undoubtedly considered casual clothes, having been summoned out of bed late at night, she looked appropriately turned out for a White House reception. Chief Spagna, on the other hand, wearing gray sweats and a steely-eyed stare, looked ready to put some recalcitrant criminal in a choke hold.

Dana had been hurrying toward them. Now she hung back, feeling intimidated. Alas, Eve spotted her and motioned her over.

"Hi, Eve. Hello, Chief Spagna." Dana joined them on the stairs leading into the building.

"Waiting for the felons?" Eve asked dryly. She turned to the chief and lightly ran her fingertips along his forearm. "Nick, would you mind bringing the little Sheely girl up to current status?"

The chief looked like he might smile, but he restrained the impulse. His hand rested possessively on Eve's shoulder as he addressed Dana. "I put in a call to the station shortly after your call to Eve. The Doll House has remained open despite court orders to close down, but the cops wouldn't have bothered them—they're busy enough with drunk drivers and underage drinking at the bars—except they noticed two expensive imported cars parked in the lot. They figured there was probably some drug dealers in there and God-knows-what kind of deal going down.''

He paused. ''Then I find out one of the cars belongs to Evie's nephew.'' Left unsaid was the accompanying adjective ''fool'' or ''idiot'' or ''pain-in-the-butt,'' but his tone supplied it instead.

Dana smiled weakly. ''And the other one belongs to my brother's girlfriend, and he's with her tonight.''

She shuddered at the acknowledgment, but there it was. Misty was Shawn's new girlfriend, and she'd better get used to it. Unlike Tricia, Shawn would never buckle under pressure from their parents. If he and Misty decided to stick together, Lakeview's infamous young widow would be sitting at the Sheely dinner table at Thanksgiving, exchanging gifts at Christmas and dyeing eggs with them at Easter.

Dana swiftly put the future from her mind. Dealing with the present was arduous enough.

''I'm so grateful you two came. I hate to think of Wade and Shawn being held in there and maybe threatened with jail. Of course, I'm sure the police will treat them well and read them their rights and all,'' she added in a rush, not wanting to offend the chief by insulting his brother officers.

Eve merely arched her eyebrows. Chief Spagna sucked in his cheeks. They were a most formidable pair. Dana decided to be quiet for the rest of the time she was with them.

Ten minutes later, Wade, Shawn, Misty, and Dana trailed Eve and Nick Spagna out of the police station. The chief's phone call had resulted in the trio being separated from the others and taken to a private office, where they were lectured on the foolishness of patronizing an illegal operation such as the Doll House.

''They were looking to book everybody on drunk and disorderly charges,'' Wade told his aunt. ''Since the cus-

tomers were already drunk and started acting disorderly as
soon as the place was raided, they had grounds.''

"Eddie Aiken wasn't drunk," Misty interjected. "But
the way he was carrying on you'd think he was. He tried
to punch out that big cop!"

"Aiken has already been charged with assaulting a police
officer and resisting arrest," said the chief. "Additional
charges are pending."

"Aiken insisted on making his one call to his lawyer so
he called Quint's house." Shawn sniggered. "He got Sarah,
who told him that Quint wasn't home, and she wasn't going
to disturb him unless it was a matter of life or death. Getting picked up by the cops at the Doll House didn't count.
Aiken started screaming at her, but you know how stubborn
Sarah can be."

Shawn nudged Dana, who nodded knowingly. "Finally,
the cops took the phone away and threatened to charge him
with making terroristic threats 'cause he was saying all
kinds of rotten things to Sarah. I bet she was saying them
right back."

"I wonder where Quint is tonight?" Dana was curious.

"Who cares where he is!" Wade said sharply.

"I want to thank you for your help, Ms. Saxon," said
Misty. "If it hadn't been for you, I could've been stuck in
there for hours with those drunks and Aiken, on account of
my own attorney wasn't available. You didn't have to get
me out, especially after what happened today with the will
and all."

Eve shrugged. "Consider it my good deed for the day."

"Eve Saxon is a class act," Nick Spagna announced. "A
real lady with brains and a heart of gold." His arm was
around her waist and he hugged her to his side in a proprietary gesture that caused Wade's jaw to drop.

Wade continued to stare, bemused, as the couple got into
the Porsche, the chief behind the wheel, and drove off.
"Class, brains, a heart of gold, and a Porsche, maybe?"

"Cynic!" scolded Misty. "I think they're in love."

"Aunt Eve and Chief Spagna!" Wade shook his head.

"How? When? Was she only pretending to be mad on Saturday when she lit into him at the police station? And he sure didn't seem to like her either."

"It was probably just an act," Misty said knowledgeably. "After all, the Tildens wouldn't like it if their lawyer was having an affair with the police chief who's going to bring charges against them, so they had to hide their love. I know from personal experience that the Tildens have no heart when it comes to people being in love."

"But now they're free. They can be open about their love because the Tildens fired Saxon Associates," concluded Shawn.

"You two are turning this into a tortured melodrama," Wade complained. "But the facts don't fit. There was no reason for secrecy earlier because there were no complaints filed, not until the Tildens broke into your house, Misty."

"Well, I don't know." Misty was beginning to look bored. "Or care, really. If you're so curious, why don't you just ask her when she started seeing the chief?"

"Easier said than done. My aunt and I have never discussed our love lives with each other."

"Though you'd have plenty to discuss, should you ever choose to," Dana said blithely. "All right, everybody, here's the plan. I'll drive you three to the Doll House to get your cars and then I'm going home. It's late and I'm tired."

"Ahh, poor little Dana is tired." Wade caught her arm and slowed his pace, so they both lagged behind Shawn and Misty. "You shouldn't have stayed out so late with Vicker tonight."

"Oh yes, Mom and Dad mentioned you'd stopped by the house." Dana was cool.

"Stopped by?" he repeated. "That's what they told you?"

"I was trying to be tactful." She stopped walking and pulled her arm free from his grasp. "Actually, they told me you'd been hanging around since dinner waiting for me.

And that you finally left in a huff because I came home later than expected.''

"They said *that*?''

"Relax, Saxon, I was only kidding. Mom and Dad continue to revere you as Tim's proxy. Don't be so tense.'' She gave him a sisterly nudge, like the brotherly one Shawn had delivered to her a little earlier, and resumed her stroll to the car. "Although getting busted in a strip joint and then finding out that your aunt is having a hot affair with the police chief is a lot to handle in one night. Maybe you're entitled to be tense.''

"Dana, don't.'' He sounded tired and dispirited. "Please.'' He took both her hands in his, halting her. They faced each other.

"Don't what?'' she asked warily, keeping her gaze fixed on a point well beyond him. On Shawn and Misty, who were getting into the backseat of her car.

"Don't pretend that nothing has changed between us.'' His fingers tightened on hers, and she automatically looked up at him. He gazed into her beautiful blue eyes and felt a sharp ache in his chest that spread to his throat, almost choking him.

"A lot has changed, Dana.'' His voice was tight.

"For instance, you've taken to calling me Dana instead of Sheely. Which is a wise practical consideration because when the name Sheely is called, any number of us might answer. It's better to specify which one you mean.''

"Stop it, Dana.'' Wade swallowed thickly. "Look, I can't, okay? The banter, the smiles, the pretense. I just can't keep it up.'' He dropped her hands and started walking toward her car.

Trudging toward her car. He was definitely trudging, his shoulders stooped, like a prisoner in a forced gulag march. Dana stared, wanting to call his name, to run after him. But the same indecision that had plagued her at the Doll House door seized her again.

He had almost reached her car when she found her voice. "What banter?'' she called. "What smiles?''

Wade turned. She was watching him, her arms folded in front of her chest, looking defiant and defensive. And small and uncertain.

"You've hardly spoken to me today, you've come nowhere close to *banter*. And you haven't smiled once. So whatever pretense, you're talking about . . ." She shrugged. "I haven't seen evidence of it."

He was walking toward her. Still unsmiling, as was she. He stopped directly in front of her. "After this weekend, after last night, I thought you loved me."

Her eyes met his. "If you were expecting a vow of undying love from me after sex, you have nothing to fear, Wade."

"What if I don't fear it? What if it's what I want, Dana?" The words seemed to erupt from him, his voice low and hoarse. "It *is* what I want more than anything. I want you, Dana. Please let me have you."

She stared at him, tears filling her eyes. "Wade," she whispered.

He panicked at the sight of her tears. After his pathetic declaration, she would be feeling sorry for him if she'd already decided that all she wanted from him was friendship. Or not even that. He had to forestall such a dreaded assertion.

"I love you, Dana." His threw his pride away and spoke from his heart. He had nothing to lose by keeping silent, by playing it cool. His feelings for Dana were too important, too intense to be masked by pretense a second longer.

"I've loved you for a long time, as my friend and my confidante. But now I'm in love with you, too. I want you every way there is to want someone—to talk to, to hang around with, to have fun with. To make love with. I need every part of what you are to me, Dana. My friend, my confidante, my lover."

A slow smile lit her face. "How about the father of my children, too?" She flung herself into his arms, and he picked her up and swung her around.

"If that's a proposal, I accept," he said with a trace of

his usual Saxon confidence. He let her slide down the length of his body, turning the release into a long caress.

"*You* have to do the proposing," she argued when her feet hit the ground. She stood on tiptoe to rub her lips against his. "It's Sheely policy."

"Your mother did tell me the family's secret motto— Desperation Is Never Attractive." He didn't lift his mouth as he spoke, arousing her with his every word.

"Well, don't tell Mom this, but I'm desperately in love with you, Wade."

"Finally, she says it!" Wade laughed as sheer elation pumped through him.

He cradled her face between his hands and kissed her, long and hard. She responded with all the joy and love she felt for him.

A loud sharp series of honks from Dana's car horn finally made them reluctantly break apart. They looked over to see Misty hanging over the seat, hitting the horn and giggling. Shawn rolled down the back window and stuck his head out.

"Okay, break it up you two!" he called jovially. "Or I'll be forced to make a citizen's arrest for first degree PDA. That's public display of affection," he added, and Misty shrieked uproariously at his joke.

"Them!" Wade touched his forehead to Dana's, and groaned. "Talk about a reality check."

"Right now I'm feeling too happy to worry about anything, even them."

"Dana, before we rejoin the dynamic duo over there . . ." Wade took a deep breath. He didn't want to mess up the most crucial speech of his entire life to date. "Will you marry me?"

Her eyes were brimming again, but this time Wade knew they were tears of happiness. His own eyes were suspiciously moist.

"Oh yes, Wade!"

Wade wanted to kiss her again so badly, he was willing to brave Shawn's hoots and Misty's squeals and the infernal blasts of the horn. But Dana took his hand and headed toward the car, so he walked with his fiancée.

"We're engaged," he announced proudly, sliding behind the wheel. He and Dana had a long-standing unspoken pact that he would always drive, no matter whose car they were using. He waited for Shawn's gasp of astonishment.

"So you finally decided to reel him in, huh, Dana?" Shawn kidded, clearly not astonished at all by the momentous news.

"What?" Dana and Wade said together. They exchanged puzzled glances.

"Tricia said Dana's had you hooked for years, Sax. That it was only a matter of time till she decided to reel you in."

"Not more of Tricia's theories!" Dana exclaimed, annoyed. "Don't pay any attention to him, Wade. You and I both know that we—"

"Y'know, I think I agree with Tricia." Wade grinned as he started the car. "I have been hooked and I've been biding my time, just waiting for you to reel me in."

"That is so sweet." Misty began to weep noisily. "A true love story. It reminds me of me and Townie."

Dana handed her the box of tissues she kept in the glove compartment, but Misty was already recovering. "Of course, life goes on," the young widow said philosophically. "And true love is supposed to be even better the second time around."

20

As he drove down Route 70 toward the Doll House, Wade encouraged Misty and Shawn to tell Dana all about their plans for the proposed Grrls Night Out and Shawn's Garden Shop and Lawn Service.

"Won't Quint Cormack be surprised?" Wade's smile was decidedly wicked. Cormack was going to have his work cut out for him, dealing with those two money pits.

"Sorry to spoil your fun, Saxon, but Quint won't care." Dana leaned closer, lowering her voice. "He'll take his executor's fee from the estate and continue as Misty's lawyer but he'll never interfere with what she does with her money. Quint's said all along that he has no intention of being Misty's guardian; his family already has him fully booked for that role."

"You do know how to suck the pleasure out of a moment of petty vengeance, don't you?" Wade complained mildly.

Not that he really minded, not now. Dana's hand was on his thigh, her fingers kneading and stroking, and his body hummed with anticipation. Neither Misty Tilden nor Quint Cormack mattered at all.

The sudden screeching wail of sirens sounded in the night.

"Police, fire or, ambulance?" quizzed Shawn, launching a round of a Sheely family game. Whoever guessed correctly won.

"Fire," said Misty at once.

"Police. And they sound awfully close," Dana observed. "I wonder if the combined Lakeview and Oak Shade patrols are raiding the bars for underage drinkers?"

"Our new friend Chief Spagna probably called to set it in motion," drawled Wade. "Figuring as long as he's up and dressed at this hour, why not have another raid or two or three and fill up the cells in both jails?"

"If you ask me, they've done enough raiding tonight," said Misty. "Although I wouldn't mind if they raided the Tildens and filled the cells with them."

"It sounds like they're heading this way." Wade frowned. He was only going a few miles over the speed limit and he slowed down to a mile below, just in case. "Can't wait till we're off this road."

He'd no sooner finished saying the words when the headlights of a pickup truck, high beams and blinding, appeared seemingly out of nowhere, heading toward them. It was an exceptionally alarming spectacle because the highway was divided, and the car was traveling in the wrong direction against the one-way traffic.

The sirens grew louder. From their rear window, a phalanx of police cars, sirens wailing and lights flashing, appeared in sight.

"A zillion cops are behind us!" shrieked Misty.

"What's happening?" Dana cried in confusion. The noise and all the headlights, in front and in back of them, were almost disorienting.

Wade grimly assessed the situation. They were on a collision course with the wrong-way driver, who had picked up speed and was headed directly at them. Behind them, the police were closing in, obviously in pursuit of the pickup, yet forced to pursue him from the opposite direction.

He glanced to the left to see a string of police cars passing him in the middle and left lanes. In the right lane, the wild, wrong-way pickup truck seemed to be aiming for them.

He had three choices. Swerve into the left lane and crash into the speeding police cars. Stay where they were and hit the pickup truck head-on. Or pull off the road on the right, which meant skidding into the small crowded parking lots of Oak Shade's nuisance bars. There were no safe shoulders available; all the lots bordered directly on the highway.

Dana, Shawn and Misty were screaming as the pickup truck drew dangerously close. Wade made his decision and steered the car sharply to the right. They bounced from the smooth highway surface into the bumpy unpaved parking lot of a place that had the word Bar glowing in neon letters inside its grimy window. It was an old Burger Chef franchise which had gone through several incarnations as other fast-food restaurants before turning into the dilapidated no-name place it was now.

But the place did have a clientele, who'd haphazardly parked their vehicles all over the lot. Wade did some tricky maneuvering to avoid them but it was like driving through a maze. And just when he thought he'd successfully navigated it, an ancient Buick zoomed out. The driver hadn't bothered to follow that pesky rule of checking before backing out of a space.

Wade had slowed down considerably, braking since he'd pulled off 70, but the big blue Buick was moving too fast to miss. Wade struck it with enough force to deploy the two airbags in front. Instinctively, Dana put up her hands to cover her face as the airbag billowed around her.

None of the police cars pulled over to investigate the collision. They were racing north, looking for a place to turn around, while the renegade pickup truck continued his mad drive south, running several more cars off the road in the process.

For a moment, a shocked silence filled the car. The airbags deflated, and Shawn was the first to speak.

"Jesus, Mary, and Joseph," he breathed, something of a combined prayer and incantation.

"Is everybody all right?" Wade was already reaching for Dana. "Darling, are you hurt?"

"I'm okay," Dana said shakily. She looked at her hands which were covered with small scratches from the airbag. Wade had some of the same marks on his cheeks and his nose looked as if someone had socked him. "Oh, Wade!" Her breath caught on a sob.

They launched themselves into each other's arms and held on tight.

"We could've been killed!" Misty, infuriated, punctuated each word with an obscenity. "Those jerks never even looked, they pulled right out! We escaped that psycho on the highway, only to get creamed by some drunks in a parking lot!"

She seemed to take it as a personal insult. Cursing, she flung open the car door to confront the group of very underage boys who had gotten out of the Buick. They stood beside the two wrecked cars, looking young and stupid.

Shawn joined Misty, but didn't speak. He didn't need to.

Misty's rage was awesome to behold. Within moments, she had the teens terrified and tearful. "My lawyer is going to sue you so bad, you'll be taking the bus for the rest of your lives 'cause you'll never be able to afford a car," she promised. "And we'll sue this bar that served you and—"

"Hey, Misty, you might not have to buy the Doll House from Aiken, after all," Shawn interrupted, grinning hugely. "Quint will sue this place out of existence, and I bet you'll be able to practically get it for free."

Inside the car, still smoky from the airbags, Dana clung to Wade, who held her as if he would never let her go.

"Dana, let's not waste any more time, let's get married right away." As if in a dream, Wade watched his hand stroke her silky red hair. "If I've learned anything tonight, it's that anything can happen at any time, and I'm through just coasting along, biding my time. Wasting it."

"You want to make every moment count, huh?" Dana lifted her head to meet his eyes.

"Yes. And every moment I'm not your husband is

wasted time. Let's apply for our license tomorrow and get married over this weekend.''

"That sounds good to me.'' Dana sighed and sank back against him. Her heart was slowly beginning to resume its normal rhythm, though her limbs still felt like jelly. "But Mom will try to talk us into having a big wedding like Mary Jo and Steve, and Tim and Lisa had.''

"It'll take months to put together an extravaganza like that and we're not going to waste all that time living apart,'' vowed Wade with the firm resolve of a man on a mission. "I'll explain it to your folks and get Tim to back me up. I know he will.''

"On second thought, Mom and Dad will be so pleased we're getting married, they won't mind a quick private little wedding. Anyway, they still have Sarah and Matt's wedding to plan next year.''

"They have plenty more weddings to plan,'' agreed Wade. "I love you, Dana. This time next week, you'll be my wife.''

Dana smiled tremulously. "Oh, Wade, I love you so much. We were so lucky tonight.''

He nodded. "It's been very memorable, something to tell our grandchildren. Not only did we get engaged, we managed to avoid getting ourselves killed. Who could ask for more?''

"I hope that maniac gets off the highway before something terrible happens to somebody.'' Dana shuddered.

They both turned to look as the police cars raced along the other side of 70, sirens screaming. The pickup truck with its driver gone beserk had already disappeared into the night.

The ringing of the phone jarred both Quint and Rachel out of a deep sleep.

"Yeah?'' Quint barked into the receiver. "Damn!''

Rachel's eyes opened wider. She was becoming alert enough to feel anxiety, but Quint looked and sounded more irritated than worried. Which meant Brady was all right, and his little brothers, too. Rachel stayed calm.

"Sarah, I'm not going to call Carla tonight. This isn't her problem and it isn't mine. It's all Frank's and—what?" He sighed heavily. "Really? Well, at least that's good news. Yeah, I understand. Okay, the Lakeview Police Station. I'll be there."

Rachel was already sitting up. "Frank got arrested again?" She drew the obvious conclusion.

"And you thought we wouldn't have to deal with our full-grown obstacles and intrusions until morning. Ha! Optimist!" Scowling ferociously, Quint got out of bed. "I wouldn't have bothered with this one except Sarah is upset. It seems Frank hotwired a pickup truck and went on a wild ride down Route 70 and onto the Atlantic City Expressway. One of the cars he ran off the road along the way belonged to Dana Sheely. Your cousin Wade was driving, and after swerving to avoid Frank, they were hit by a carful of high-school drunks."

"Were they hurt?" cried Rachel.

"Sarah says no." Quint was already headed to the shower. Rachel followed him.

"In a strange twist, Misty Tilden was also with Dana and Wade," said Quint, turning on the taps. He pulled Rachel into the roomy shower stall with him.

She was visibly astonished. "How did she end up with Wade and Dana Sheely?"

"I didn't ask."

Their mutual shower was quick and functional, though Rachel found it incredibly sexy to be showering with Quint. Since she knew no one had been hurt in the accident, she let her imagination run rampant, visualizing future showers with her lover.

Who was currently contemplating his father's latest misadventure, she could tell. Quint's mouth was set grimly, his eyes burning with fury. Rachel wished she could spare him the legal headaches awaiting him, courtesy of the vile Frank Cormack.

"I can't forgive him for this, I can't overlook it," Quint

said fiercely as they drove back across the bridge. "My
mother and Colette—his own daughter—were killed by a
reckless driver. For Frank to pull a stunt like this is a direct
insult to their memory."

Rachel couldn't disagree.

By the time Quint and Rachel arrived at the Lakeview
Police Station, quite a crowd had gathered. There were officers from other municipalities mixed with the Lakeview
police. A sizable group of outraged citizens, victims of the
multitude of accidents spawned by the chase, had been
herded to one side of the station and were being addressed
by Chief Spagna himself.

Rachel was surprised to see her aunt Eve standing with
Wade, Dana, and Shawn Sheely and Misty Tilden. She
joined them while Quint went to speak with Chief Spagna.

Eve and Wade stared at her, bewildered. "What are you
doing here, Rach?" asked Wade.

Rachel remembered that her aunt and cousin knew nothing of her relationship with Quint. But Misty did. She
thought Rachel was Brady's mother who'd deserted him
and who ought to have her reproductive organs altered to
prevent further procreation. From the look on her face, the
widow looked like a prime candidate to do the job right
now.

"You know her?" Misty demanded, turning on Wade.

"She's my cousin Rachel. One of those Saxon Associates you and Quint mopped up the floor with today."

"Well, she's definitely a traitor to you guys because she
is so hot for Quint she's even using his baby to get to him.
Playing the role of mommy to that poor little kid who was
dumped by his real mother." Misty shot Rachel a scathing
glare, letting her know she was on to her and was not going
to be duped again.

"I'm not using Brady to get to Quint," Rachel countered. "I don't have to."

"Because you already got him?" Misty wanted to know.

"We have each other and we both love Brady," Rachel
corrected gently because she really didn't want to feud with

Quint's wealthiest client. Indisputable evidence of how much she loved Quint because there had been a time when she would've done or said anything to cause harm to the firm of Cormack and Son.

"Rachel and Quint Cormack?" Eve was clearly stunned. "Since when?"

"I might've been surprised earlier, but after finding out about Aunt Eve and Chief Spagna, I'm shock-proof," Wade murmured to Dana.

Quint joined the group, postponing a Saxon inquisition of Rachel. "Nick told me what happened tonight. Frank has really outdone himself this time. He's headed to jail for a long time. After stealing the pickup and traveling the wrong way on 70, he switched roads and almost made it to Atlantic City. Along the way, he sideswiped cars, both moving and parked ones, including police cars. He clipped a toll booth and ran drivers off the road, he eluded road-blocks and crashed through a chain-link fence."

"How did they finally catch up to him?" asked Shawn.

"He got boxed in at a cul-de-sac," Quint continued grimly. "According to Nick, twelve police cars blocked the only way out, but Frank wasn't finished yet. He got out of the truck and made a run for the woods. Since he was drunk, he wasn't too agile but he kept fighting until he was Maced. Then he finally became quiet and cooperative and claimed amnesia. Said the last thing he remembered was reading a bedtime story to his little boys and tucking them into bed."

"As if!" Misty exclaimed indignantly.

"Exactly," agreed Quint.

"What is he being charged with, Quint?" asked Rachel, moving to stand beside him. She slipped her arm around him. She could feel him wired with tension, his body rigid and taut. When she thought of how relaxed and happy they'd been a few hours earlier, her hatred of Frank Cormack grew stronger.

"The question is, what isn't he being charged with?" Quint shrugged and shook his head. "He passed through a number of municipalities so local police agencies dropped in and out of the chase as he charged through their districts. That means he's facing charges all through South Jersey. Nick said so far there have been thirty-six different traffic violations cited, including several with multiple counts. Then there are the criminal charges, twelve counts of aggravated assault, ten counts of simple assault, sixteen counts of reckless endangerment, criminal mischief, and criminal trespass. I won't go into the misdemeanor charges, but there are plenty of those, too. Reports of cars that were struck are still being called in to various police stations, and that entire group of people over there have come down to file their reports in person.''

"Nick says your father was returned to Lakeview and is in custody downstairs," said Eve. "Obviously, he needs a lawyer. Are you going to represent him?"

"No." Quint shook his head. "I'm through cleaning up after him, he's on his own. Frank is to be arraigned at a preliminary hearing tomorrow morning, and I told Nick he would need a public defender."

"Good!" exclaimed Misty. "Because Dana and I are going to sue and of course, you'll be our lawyer. I'd like to have that bar who served the kids and Dana wants a new car. Okay, Quint?"

Rachel watched Quint compose his features into a believable semblance of patience. But she knew him well enough to know it was only a facade. Quint Cormack was feeling anything but patient at this moment.

"Misty, we'll talk about a lawsuit later. Right now I have to see Carla. Nick said she's hysterical, no surprise there. He told her not to come down here and that I'd be by to explain things to her." Quint turned to Rachel. "Do you want me to drive you home on the way to Carla's or can you find a ride?"

Rachel knew he didn't mean to sound so dismissive, but his abrupt abrasive manner stung.

"I have a Range Rover with plenty of room, I'll give you a lift," offered Misty.

A preoccupied Quint merely nodded and left the station.

"His mind is on Carla and the boys, don't take it personally, Rachel," Dana tried to be kind.

"Frank Cormack is a human scourge," Eve put in. "Nick said he and Quint have had many talks about him and the problems he's caused. Nick advised him to cut Frank off, and it seems like Quint is finally taking his advice."

Eve seemed pleased by this, though Rachel couldn't understand why. She wondered if she might possibly be trapped in a weird dream, perhaps induced by a little too much champagne. A dream where strange and subtle alliances had shifted, and everybody knew the new coalitions except her.

Rachel piled into the Range Rover with Wade, the Sheelys, and Misty Tilden while her aunt stayed behind at the police station for reasons Rachel didn't know and nobody seemed inclined to explain.

Her cousin's seeming friendship with the young widow amazed her, and the Sheelys were clearly part of the crowd. The accident appeared to have been a bonding experience for the four, although how they'd all ended up in the same car traveling along Route 70 at this hour of the night remained a mystery to her.

Rachel didn't sleep at all for the rest of the night. She kept hoping Quint would call, but he didn't, and she couldn't call his house and risk waking Sarah and little Brady. It was actually a relief to get out of bed and get ready for work in the morning, and Rachel donned a dark green suit, not quite as severe as usual, and an ecru silk blouse with a high collar.

Before she left her apartment, she gave into temptation and called Quint's home. Sarah was awake and chipper, and Brady could be heard babbling in the background along with a swell of kiddie parade music.

"Quint left early to go up to north Jersey," Sarah reported. "He'll be back tonight because it's my night off.

Oh, hey, isn't it great about Dana and Wade? About time too, huh?''

Before Rachel had a chance to ask her for specifics, Sarah exclaimed, ''Uh-oh! Brady just dumped his whole glass of juice all over the sofa. I have to rescue the remote control before he drops it into the—Oh, no! Bye, Rachel.''

Rachel arrived at the office and was greated by a beaming Katie Sheely. ''Isn't it great about Dana and Wade? About time, too, huh?''

Rachel smiled. ''I think I just had this conversation.'' She heard voices in the conference room and went back to find her aunt and cousin chortling together over the newspaper.

''Two Sheelys have told me it's great about Dana and Wade. Do you plan to tell me what?''

Wade looked up. ''Dana and I are getting married this weekend. You're coming to the wedding, I hope. It'll just be family, and then we're all going out for lunch.''

''Just family is a pretty sizable group when it comes to the Sheelys,'' said Aunt Eve. ''We're very happy for you, Wade, but of course, you know that.''

''You and Nick better be there, Aunt Eve,'' said Wade, grinning. ''And you can bring Cormack if you must, Rach.''

''Such a gracious invitation, how could she refuse?'' Eve teased.

Rachel studied her aunt, whose spirits were almost girlishly buoyant. *Nick.* ''Aunt Eve, are you—uh—seeing the police chief?'' She half expected her aunt to admonish her for her foolish speculations.

Eve merely smiled enigmatically. ''I suppose you could say so.''

''Now there's a slippery answer, the kind that gives all of us lawyers a bad name. She's most definitely *seeing* the chief, Rach.'' Wade laughed. ''Here, read this.''

He thrust the New Jersey Metro section of the *Philadelphia Inquirier* into Rachel's hand. She saw the article immediately. PROMINENT LAKEVIEW FAMILY FACE CRIMINAL CHARGES.

"The police have reviewed the complaints against the Tildens and decided to file criminal charges." Rachel glanced up in surprise. "Well, they've already hired a criminal attorney, who will surely get the charges reduced to a few misdemeanors."

"Sure, the charges are just an annoyance to them, but having a story printed about the whole affair is nothing less than a catastrophic humiliation," Wade exclaimed triumphantly. "And read the way the story is written—Misty's age is never mentioned and neither is the fact that she was Town Senior's second wife. From that article, you'd think she is a poor old widow being preyed upon by her greedy, sociopathic offspring out to rob and terrorize her."

Rachel's eyes swept the article. "You're right. The Tildens must be chewing nails over this. Rusty ones."

"Guess whose cousin works the south Jersey beat at the paper?" Wade was gleeful.

Rachel looked at her aunt, whose smile fell unmistakably into the cat-who-swallowed-both-the-canary-and-the-cream category. And planned to keep on doing it. "Chief Spagna?"

"The chief didn't like the way the Tildens treated Aunt Eve, who is a real lady with brains and a heart of gold," added Wade.

Eve didn't deny it. She merely shrugged and finished her coffee. "Nick is the most interesting man I've ever met," she said, setting down her cup. "Meanwhile, we do have some clients left, so let's end the coffee break and get to work."

"Brains, a heart of gold and a slave-driver mentality," amended Wade, but Eve took it good-naturedly, as he'd intended. The three Saxons went to their respective offices, where they remained until midmorning when Katie delivered the mail.

Eve called Rachel and Wade into her office. She held an opened registered letter in her hand. "John Pedersen is informing us that as of today, he's pulling all his business, personal and the Car Shoppe, from Saxon Associates.''

Rachel chewed her lower lip. "Aunt Eve, it's all my fault. Pedersen has never forgiven me for losing his case. I am so sorry. Do you think it would help if I went to see him again? Did he mention what firm he intends to use?''

"He doesn't say," said Eve. "And don't even think about begging to represent him, Rachel. It's over.''

"Pedersen's new lawyer is Quint Cormack," Wade said quietly.

Rachel felt her heart plummet. She listened to Wade tell about Pedersen's defection, first seeking a new pension plan, then finally making the Saxon break. The fact wasn't lost on her that Quint hadn't bothered to mention a word about any of it. Wade knew what was brewing from Dana, who worked for Cormack and Son's firm, but Quint, *who was the firm,* had chosen to keep silent.

"Rachel, are you all right?" She looked up to find her aunt watching her.

"As well as can be expected, considering our practice is hemorrhaging clients," Rachel was sardonic. "Not to mention Quint Cormack's nasty habit of backstabbing which—''

"Rachel, you can't take this personally," Wade cut in. "It's strictly a professional choice. It's Pedersen's choice, and he chose Cormack. Which isn't really backstabbing— and keep in mind that defending Quint Cormack does not come naturally to me, Rach.''

"Wade is right, Rachel," agreed Eve, looking incredibly composed.

"You're saying we should just forget all about it?" Rachel's anger grew in proportion to the others' lack of it. "Maybe we should send Pedersen a bottle of wine, congratulating him on the move!''

"Rachel," Eve began.

"Don't take it personally! Separate the personal from the professional! I've been hearing a lot about that lately," Rachel raged. "But, you know, I don't think it's possible.

How about Chief Spagna, Aunt Eve? If he wasn't seeing you, do you think he would've bothered to turn Misty's complaints into criminal charges? Would he have phoned his cousin at the paper, and if the reporter wasn't a relative, would the article have been published at all? That strikes me as extremely personal, and it's all mixed up with the professional.''

"You have a valid point, Rachel," Wade conceded. "But—" He shrugged. "So what?"

"So what?" Rachel repeated. She was flummoxed. What kind of a response was that? And how was she supposed to repond to such a banality?

"Sometimes, the personal and the professional aspects of our lives do intertwine, dear," Aunt Eve said in the faux-patient tone she often used when talking with Laurel. "But I have to agree with Wade. If it's not an unethical or illegal conflict of interest, then, well, so what?"

"With a philosophy like that, no wonder Saxon Associates is going down the drain!" Rachel stormed back into her own office, glumly aware that her own failure in the Pedersen case had cost them that particular client.

And if her aunt and cousin didn't seem to mind the loss, well, she minded enough for all three of them.

It was raining when Rachel left the office late that afternoon—hadn't she heard it was supposed to be sunny all day?—and with no umbrella, she was soaked to the skin when she arrived home.

She changed quickly into jeans and a melon-colored T-shirt and had just finished blowing her hair dry when she heard pounding on the door. The kind of nonstop knocking that made her instantly think of Laurel. Since her car was parked right in front of the building, she couldn't pretend not to be home. Groaning inwardly, Rachel opened the door.

"Hi, Mommy, hi, hi!" Brady sang as Quint dropped the little boy into Rachel's arms.

"Just in case you had any ideas of not showing up for

dinner tonight, Brady and I came by to get you," Quint drawled.

Brady was wriggling in her arms, and Rachel looked over his head to meet Quint's eyes. He raised his dark brows, challenging her to refuse to go.

"Dana said you might be mad at me for not calling to tell you I'd gone up to Sagertown on a case today," he said. "Sarah told her you'd called the house this morning. Dana also said that Wade told her you were steamed over Pedersen taking his business to me."

"Dana is a veritable fount of information, isn't she?"

"The Sheelys are well connected. And if you've got a connection to one of them, you're plugged in to the entire network." He closed his hand around her upper arm. "Let's go home and have dinner, Rachel. Brady is hungry."

"That is really low, Cormack. Using a small child—a hungry small child—to—to—"

"You should know I'll do whatever it takes, Rachel. And I'm not up to fighting about Pedersen or anything else. Not after last night."

"And now you drag in your father, who is so horrible that anyone with a heart can't help but feel sorry for you being stuck with him. Another unfair ploy."

"Let's face it, Rachel, I've stacked the deck. Next, I'll play the Carla card. Think of me last night, listening to two solid hours of her screaming."

Rachel winced, but still didn't fold. "Don't forget to mention poor little Dustin and Austin."

"Who we're picking up, by the way. They're having dinner with us and watching a video before we take them back home."

"Because Carla and her mother need some more peace and quiet?"

"Because Carla and her mother are going shopping to redecorate the house that burned down. The insurance check is in the mail. Come on, let's go."

"Austin, Dustin, Mommy, eat it all up. Mommy and

Brady, Daddy eat chicken,'' Brady cut in. The little boy was delighted to see her. He talked incessantly, occasionally reaching up to stroke her cheek.

Rachel conceded defeat. She followed Quint to his car, carrying Brady in her arms. Actually, she was glad Quint was taking his little brothers tonight. The news of their father's latest exploits—and their mother's reaction— would be tough for both kids to handle. She liked that they had Quint to depend on, Quint's house as a refuge.

And she knew that Quint would never begrudge the time and effort spent in providing a refuge for Snowy, should she need one. Rachel worried that her little niece was going to need her as much as Quint's brothers needed him, but she was secure in the knowledge that Quint would help Snowy, too.

Not that she was going to admit to any of this now. Not while Quint's noticeable lack of penitence over Pedersen was still grating on her. He might not have hijacked Pedersen, but the defection was the next closest thing, and he'd not offered even a token apology.

"This discussion is by no means over, Quint,'' she warned him, as they drove off.

"I was under no illusion that it was, Rachel,'' he countered calmly.

By the time they'd returned the especially active and fractious Austin and Dustin to their mother, and put Brady to bed, Rachel's internal monologue about the Pedersen injustice had substituted as a discussion with Quint. She was tired of thinking about Pedersen, she'd wasted too many of her brain cells on that employee-harrassing car salesman already. Quint was welcome to keep the cad as a client!

He poured each of them a glass of wine and sat down with her on the sofa. She noticed how tired he looked, dark circles under his eyes, and she lightly ran her finger along one, frowning.

"You have to go to bed early tonight. You're exhausted.''

He smiled. "Only if you'll go with me, Rachel.'' He slid

his hand slid along the length of her inner thigh.

Rachel captured his hand and held it still in her own. She'd forgiven him for Pedersen, but there were still a few other matters to be dealt with. "You know, Dana was right, you could've called to let me know you were going to north Jersey today."

"I should've, but I left before six. I thought you would be asleep. And I would've called you later this afternoon but by then, I knew you were mad. After my chat with North Jersey Power, I wasn't up to a fight with you."

"Your chat with North Jersey Power was—less than cordial?"

"A lot less. Lucky for me, I was still energized by my rage over Frank's latest escapades, so when I went in to meet with the execs and they tried to stonewall me, I went nuclear—like one of their plants. By the time our meeting was over, they were convinced they're dealing with a madman. In that same mood, I visited with the insurance people."

"And terrorized them?" guessed Rachel.

"Pretty much. I see a seven-figure settlement in the works for Ken and Marcia Polk. It seems that nobody wants to go to trial."

"No wonder! You are a formidable opponent." Rachel smiled slowly. "I can certainly attest to that."

"I don't want to be your opponent in any way, Rachel." He kissed her temple and gazed into her eyes. "Can't we combine our resources? Cormack and Son is actually just one Cormack. Despite the name, my father hasn't been a partner in the firm since I came to Lakeview. The first thing I did when I arrived in town was to buy out his equity interest. I've been paying him a salary because he has no ownership in the practice."

"Which means when Frank is sued—which he certainly will be after last night—your firm can't be touched."

"No. Or his house. The second thing I did was to put the deed to that house in Carla's name only. It can't be seized to pay for Frank's blunders."

Rachel played with his long fingers. "Retitling houses for women seems to be a specialty of yours."

"One of them. Now about the law firm . . . I'd like to add a name to Cormack. Your name."

"You mean, like Saxon and Cormack? Or Cormack and Saxon?" Rachel shook her head. "I can't do that to Aunt Eve and Wade, Quint."

"I was thinking more like Cormack and Cormack. A husband-and-wife team. And I wouldn't mind being associates with the Saxons, if they don't mind."

She stared at him. "Are you—"

"Asking you to marry me? Yes." He lifted her onto his lap. "Say yes, Rachel, and don't list a hundred reasons why we should wait. I don't want to wait, I don't need to. I love you, and I always will."

"I have no intention of trying to talk you into waiting. I said 'yes' to everything the first time I went to bed with you," Rachel confessed. "Although I probably didn't realize it then."

"I knew I wanted to marry you even before we went to bed," Quint claimed. "The night you showed up on my doorstep with Brady in your arms."

"That competitive spirit of ours is truly phenomenal." Rachel laughed. "But how about this? I knew I wanted to marry you when—when—" She paused, searching for a suitable incident for this revisionist courtship.

"When the verdict was handed down in the Pedersen trial?" suggested Quint. "I saw the fire in your eyes in the courtroom that day. I thought it was homicidal fury but perhaps—it was love?"

"Yes." Rachel agreed. "It was love."

"You just hadn't realized it then." Quint kissed her, ending the friendly argument.

Dear Reader,

If you've just finished this Avon romance title and are looking for more of the best in romantic fiction, then be on the watch for these upcoming romance titles—available at your favorite bookstore!

Affaire de Coeur says Genell Dellin is " . . . one of the best writers of ethnic romances starring Native Americans." And her latest, AFTER THE THUNDER, is Native American romance filled with sensuality and emotion. When a young Shaman falls for a scandalous young woman he must decide if he will fulfill the needs of the spirit—or the body.

For lovers of Scotland settings, don't miss the luscious A ROSE IN SCOTLAND by Joan Overfield. When a desperate young woman marries the handsome, brooding Laird of Lochhaven, she expects nothing more than a marriage of convenience. But what begins as duty turns into something much more.

Maureen McKade's A DIME NOVEL HERO is a must-read for those who like their heroes tough and their settings western. This tender romance about a woman who writes dime novels, her adopted son and the man she's turned into an unwilling hero—and who is unknowingly the boy's father—is sure to touch your heart.

Contemporary romance fans are sure to love SIMPLY IRRESISTIBLE by debut author Rachel Gibson. A sassy charm school graduate is on the run—from her own wedding. She's rescued by a sexy guest but never dreams that, nine months later, she'll have a little bundle of joy—proof of their whirlwind romance. And when he barges back into her life, complications ensue—and romance is rekindled.

Remember, look to Avon Books for the very best in romance!

Sincerely,
Lucia Macro
Avon Books

AEL 1197